The Banner of David

J P DAY

GOMER

First Published—1992

ISBN 0 86383 754 9

© J. P. Day

This volume is published with the support of the Welsh Arts Council

Printed in Wales by:
J. D. Lewis & Sons Ltd., Gomer Press, Llandysul

To my parents

Genealogies

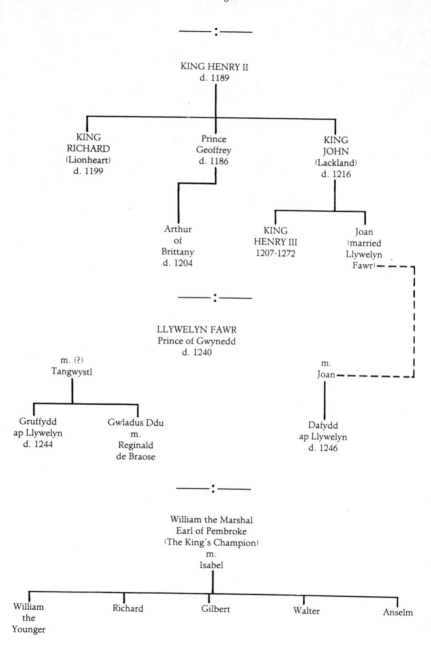

—— : ——

KING HENRY II
d. 1189

KING
RICHARD
(Lionheart)
d. 1199

Prince
Geoffrey
d. 1186

KING
JOHN
(Lackland)
d. 1216

Arthur
of
Brittany
d. 1204

KING
HENRY III
1207-1272

Joan
(married
Llywelyn
Fawr)

—— : ——

LLYWELYN FAWR
Prince of Gwynedd
d. 1240

m. (?)
Tangwystl

m.
Joan

Gruffydd
ap Llywelyn
d. 1244

Gwladus Ddu
m.
Reginald
de Braose

Dafydd
ap Llywelyn
d. 1246

—— : ——

William the Marshal
Earl of Pembroke
(The King's Champion)
m.
Isabel

William
the
Younger

Richard

Gilbert

Walter

Anselm

Gerald of Wales
The Welsh Connection

——— : ———

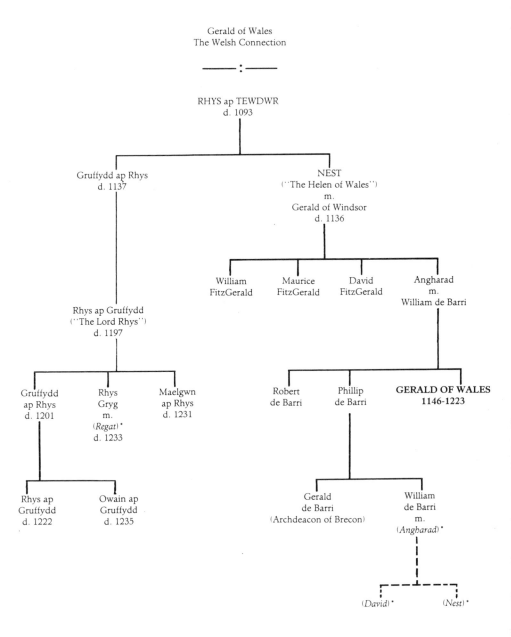

RHYS ap TEWDWR
d. 1093

Gruffydd ap Rhys
d. 1137

NEST
("The Helen of Wales")
m.
Gerald of Windsor
d. 1136

William
FitzGerald

Maurice
FitzGerald

David
FitzGerald

Angharad
m.
William de Barri

Rhys ap Gruffydd
("The Lord Rhys")
d. 1197

Gruffydd
ap Rhys
d. 1201

Rhys
Gryg
m.
(Regat) *
d. 1233

Maelgwn
ap Rhys
d. 1231

Robert
de Barri

Phillip
de Barri

GERALD OF WALES
1146-1223

Rhys ap
Gruffydd
d. 1222

Owain ap
Gruffydd
d. 1235

Gerald
de Barri
(Archdeacon of Brecon)

William
de Barri
m.
(Angharad) *

(David) *

(Nest) *

* *For the purpose of this narrative the characters of Regat (wife of Rhys Gryg), and of Angharad, David and Nest (the family of William de Barri), are fictitious.*

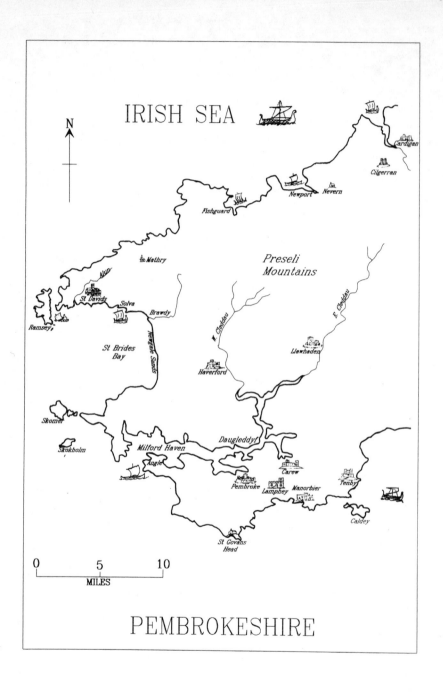

IRISH SEA

N

Cardigan

Cilgerran

Newport Nevern

Fishguard

Mathry

Preseli
Mountains

Alun

St Davids
Solva
Brawdy

W. Cleddau

E. Cleddau

Ramsey

St Brides
Bay

Newgale Sands

Llawhaden

Haverford

Skomer

Skokholm

Milford Haven

Daugleddyf

Angle

Carew

Pembroke Lamphey Manorbier

Tenby

Caldey

St Govans
Head

0   5   10
MILES

PEMBROKESHIRE

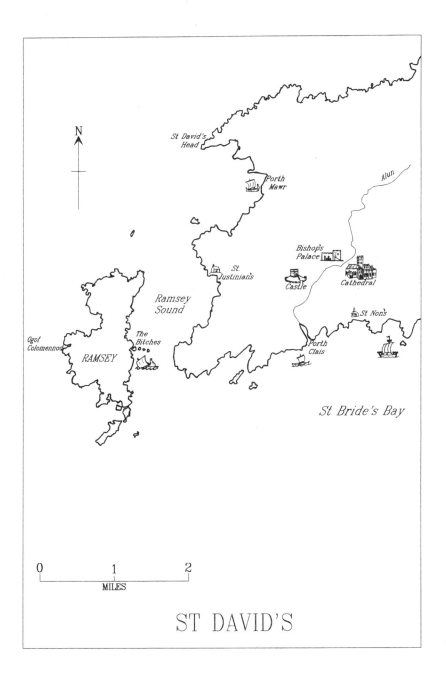

N

St David's
Head

Porth
Mawr

Alun

Bishop's
Palace

St.
Justinian's

Castle

Cathedral

Ramsey
Sound

St Non's

Ogof
Colomennod

The
Bitches

Porth
Clais

RAMSEY

St Bride's Bay

0   1   2

MILES

ST DAVID'S

So long as Wales shall stand
by the writings of the Chroniclers
and by songs of the Bards,
so shall Gerald's noble deeds be praised

Llywelyn ap Iorwerth, Prince of Gwynedd

I

C1]e Castle of St Davi8's

20 JUNE, 1215

'. . . and I tell this history yet again, not to weep over its ashes but
to state my case, for I believe it to be unanswerable. Only by
acknowledging the independence of the Welsh Church can
Canterbury hope to gain our willing allegiance.'

The old Archdeacon finished the reading of his letter and
smoothed down the parchment. He tilted his candle to melt a
pool of red wax beneath his signature, and pressed into the
hardening surface the great seal of the Bishop of St David's.

The seal was not rightly the Archdeacon's to use, yet it might
have been. It should have been. His eyes, pale and grey, rested
upon the seal, and upon his own signature. *Giraldus Cambrensis.*
Gerald of Wales.

The candle flickered. A cowled figure stood in the open doorway
of the Bishop's chamber, two leather-bound books clutched in his
arms as if his very soul depended upon their welfare. The man
hesitated, until the Archdeacon's nod bade him enter. He set
down the books upon the table and stepped back to await
judgement.

Gerald examined the penmanship, the illumination, the quality
of the binding. 'Very good. Yes, very good. Who made the copy?'

Brother Hugh attempted a smile. The expression sat uneasily
upon his ever sombre face, but praise from Gerald of Wales was
praise indeed. He gave a modest cough. 'Much of the work is
mine, my lord Archdeacon.'

'Then you may be the first to offer your opinion of my book.'
Gerald spoke his Norman French with no accent save that of the
University of Paris. He leaned forward in the Bishop's carved
chair, cradling his chin in the bony fingers of one hand. Had he

1

stood, he would have towered above the young monk. Once, his great height had been imposing, had drawn the attention of the masses to the orator's fine words, yet now it seemed angular and unwieldy beneath his archdeacon's robes. He was over sixty years old, yet he awaited the praise of his new book with all the excitement of a novice.

Brother Hugh fought for the appropriate phrase. He harboured some hope of advancement to Dean, and was uncomfortably aware that much might depend upon what he was about to say. It was not that the Archdeacon's work was poorly written. It was not that he disagreed with the Archdeacon's intent. The problem was a minor one, but it troubled Brother Hugh greatly. He stared at the tooled leather bindings of the Archdeacon's books, at the half-written manuscripts littering the table, at the raven wheeling in the cloudless evening sky beyond the window. He looked everywhere but at the clear, expectant gaze of Gerald of Wales..

'Well, Brother Hugh? Has the eloquence of my argument robbed you of speech? We must pray that it has the same effect upon Archbishop Stephen Langton!'

'Yes...er, no. No, Archdeacon.' Brother Hugh had been choosing his words with care, but Gerald's question had quite driven them from his mind. 'Your book is...finely worded.'

'It is not the fine trappings that concern us, but the truths that lie within.'

'That...' Brother Hugh stammered, aghast at his own boldness. 'That is the one thing I might venture to question.'

'You doubt the veracity of my work?'

'Not of your work, my lord. Only of your *sources*.' Hugh took an involuntary step backwards, for the Archdeacon seemed to be on the point of rising from his chair.

'What of my sources?'

'You said that St David's once had an archbishop...'

'It has had twenty-five archbishops! And Saint David himself was the first, appointed by Almighty God, answerable only to the Pope.'

'I know the story well enough, Archdeacon.'

'Twenty-five archbishops, Brother Hugh! And then the Pope took away the pallium and compelled the Church of Wales to bow and scrape to the Archbishop of Canterbury.'

2

I

The Castle of St David's

The dust was long settled upon this ancient dispute, yet Gerald of Wales could still view it as a personal insult. His one ambition, his sole obsession, was to elevate the bishopric of St David's to metropolitan status, thus gaining an Archbishop in Wales equal to the English Archbishop of Canterbury and making the Welsh church independent of English rule. Gerald considered himself the ideal candidate for this position, yet despite the support of powerful friends in both England and Wales he had never realised his ambition. In the end he had vowed to let the matter rest, yet his new book, *The Rights and Privileges of St David's*, was more strongly devoted to his cause than any of his previous works.

'Surely, Archdeacon. . .surely there is no real proof that St David's ever was an archbishopric?'

'Proof, Brother Hugh? When did a man of God ever demand proof!'

Brother Hugh hid a smile behind his hand. He knew his old tutor well enough to sense the irony behind his outrage, and realised that there was no point in trying to suggest a change in the manuscript. Nor, indeed, would he truly have wished to do so.

'Here.' Gerald rolled the parchment and rose to place it in Brother Hugh's hands. 'You are to deliver this letter with my book, in person, to His Grace the Archbishop of Canterbury.'

Brother Hugh gasped. The personal messenger from Gerald of Wales to the Archbishop of Canterbury. This was an honour indeed! 'I will prepare at once, my lord Archdeacon. Er. . .should I journey by land, or by sea?'

'By sea, I think. Yes, most certainly by sea. I have no faith in these rumours of peace. In my experience, they come to nothing.'

Brother Hugh bowed his head to the Archdeacon. It was prudent to show great respect for Gerald's experience. He gathered his courage before daring to broach the next subject. 'Before I depart, Archdeacon, may I ask if you have word from the new Bishop?'

'No.' Gerald was sharp with his answer, for he knew that Brother Hugh's reasons for asking were selfish ones. Hugh had been clerk to the late Bishop Geoffrey, and would doubtless hope to continue in the same privileged position. . .unless something better were offered. 'I have had no word. And remember, Brother

3

Hugh, that Abbot Iorwerth of Talley is not Bishop of St David's *yet*.'

'But he will be, my lord, by this hour tomorrow.'

'Much can happen in a day, Brother Hugh. Winchester was chosen for his consecration because it lies midway between St David's and Canterbury. It was a foolish choice in my opinion, but on this matter my counsel was not sought. The city may yet fall to the traitors among the English, God forbid. Abbot Iorwerth might be set upon by cutthroats in the Marches. Or what if our revered Archbishop Langton were to come to grief on his journey from Canterbury?'

'All England would mourn.'

'All *England* would mourn, perhaps. But there are men in Wales who would rejoice.'

With increasing discomfort, Brother Hugh fidgeted with the crucifix at his neck. He knew well enough what Gerald wanted to hear. 'You should have been Bishop of St David's, Archdeacon! You had the right to expect...'

Gerald held up his hand. 'I am too old, Brother Hugh. In the past I was too Welsh, now I am too old.'

'But Iorwerth of Talley is a Welshman.'

'Is he? He may be Welsh by birth and by name, but he is lost to his noble ancestry. He refuses to speak his native tongue. Even in the presence of the Welsh princes he demands an interpreter, though he understands them well enough. No, the King and Canterbury will have nothing to fear from their new Bishop.'

Gerald sighed, and gestured towards the door. 'Go now, Brother. And God be with you.'

Brother Hugh bowed to the Archdeacon. As he picked up the book, Gerald's hand caught his sleeve. 'No, Brother Hugh. Take *your* copy to the Archbishop, not mine.'

II

Gerald of Wales stood at the narrow window of the Bishop's chamber, high in the old wooden castle of St David's. His gaze wandered along the valley of the River Alun towards the great square tower that rose from the Sacred Hollow, and he remembered the drawing of the plans for the new cathedral on the orders of Bishop de Leia, thirty-six years before. He remembered the forest of scaffolding, the unremitting toil of the masons, the endless clamour of their tools. He remembered the long lines of tumbrils from the quarries of nearby Caer-fai, and how, despite the best efforts of the Norman architects, the muted purples and greens of the sandstone even yet imparted to the place the unique essence of Wales.

This new cathedral was a fine and beautiful building to be sure, but above all Gerald remembered the old Welsh church that had been torn down to make way for it. . .

A sharp knock at the door interrupted the Archdeacon's reverie. He let them wait a moment, whoever they were. A raven circled above the valley in the twilight. Gerald smiled. He liked ravens.

'Come in!'

The captain of the guard of St David's castle stood in the doorway. Among the Welsh, thought Gerald, Captain Nevern was as conspicuous as. . . as a gull among ravens. Nevern was a fifth-generation memory of the Viking raiders who had brought terror to the Welsh coast. His voice was as Welsh as the northerly village whose name he had taken, but his hair was fair and his eyes blue as the fjords of his ancestor's homeland.

'My lord Archdeacon, the son of the Earl Marshal is here. Squire Anselm.'

Gerald frowned. Anselm was the youngest son of William, Earl of Pembroke, Marshal of the King's armies. If he bore a message from his father, it could only mean disruption of the smooth running of the Church and yet more work for the Archdeacon. 'Oh, very well, send him in.'

'He is not *here*, my lord,' Nevern corrected himself. 'I meant to say that he is here in the castle. He asked to see you, but I suggested that he wait in the bailey.'

'Why?'

'He is in no fit state to. . .'

'What? Has he been robbed?'

Nevern cleared his throat. 'He reeks of the dungeon, Archdeacon. His clothing. . .'

5

'What has happened? You should have brought him here at once! I can abide the stench of a dungeon. I've been in one myself. It was on my return from Rome, after I had conferred with Pope Innocent. I met him twice, you know. No sooner had I crossed the Alps, an arduous journey indeed, than I was seized by . . .'

'Your Grace?'

Both men glanced to the doorway, Gerald irritated by the interruption, Nevern much relieved, for the old Archdeacon seldom neglected the opportunity to relate the well-known adventures of his own chequered history.

Squire Anselm stood ill at ease before the Archdeacon. He had neither the commanding presence nor the muscular build of his illustrious father, but now Gerald could only stare in astonishment at the stinking rags which covered him. A tattered tunic reached barely to his knees, his feet were unshod and bleeding. His face, beneath a tangle of unkempt hair, bore an expression of utter misery.

'Your Grace, I apologise for appearing before you in these rags, but I must tell you . . .'

'A moment, if you please. You are mistaken in addressing me as Bishop.'

'I beg your pardon . . . my lord. I naturally thought . . .'

'His Grace Bishop Geoffrey died six months ago. I am merely assuming the responsibilities of his office until his successor arrives.'

'I meant no offence.'

'A natural mistake.' Gerald cleared his throat. The stench from the squire's clothing was indeed overpowering. 'Captain Nevern, would you find our guest some more suitable attire?'

The captain bowed and made his hurried exit, leaving the Archdeacon to stare, intrigued, at the son of the Earl of Pembroke. 'I have seen many pilgrims who drape themselves in rags to make their penance at the shrine of Saint David, my son, but . . .'

'I am not here on pilgrimage, my lord. My father expects me in Pembroke . . .' The squire choked into silence. Anger, or fear, or despair, held his tongue.

'Have you been shipwrecked?'

'No, my lord.'

6

'Then what troubles you? I hope you are not afraid of me!'

'No, my lord, not of you.'

'Ah. Your father then! I heard he had been summoned to England to support King John against the barons. I did not realise he was returned so soon to Pembroke.'

Anselm made no reply. It was clear that, for whatever reason, he was terrified of meeting his father again.

The Earl Marshal was not a cruel man, but neither did he suffer fools gladly. What crime or dire mistake could Anselm have committed to instil in him such fear? Prompted more by curiosity than concern for the wretched squire, Gerald was determined to uncover the truth. 'I am not without influence, Anselm. Tell me what troubles you, then perhaps I can help you. But if you will not trust me...'

Anselm hesitated. In his childhood he had heard many a tale of Giraldus Cambrensis. Gerald of Wales was a figure almost of legend, and Anselm had, in truth, been somewhat surprised to see him still alive. Now he saw across the cluttered expanse of the table the gaunt, lined face of an old man, his eyebrows bushy, his thinning hair straying beyond the confines of his tonsure, and yet his eyes were clear and brimming with an eager curiosity. Was he to be trusted, this old priest, this chronicler past his prime, this archdeacon who had ever yearned for the mitre?

'Well, my son?'

'Two weeks ago I was with my father in England, at the court of King John. One morning, the Earl Marshal called me to him and told me that he had doubts as to the safety of... of certain hostages held in the King's prison at Corfe Castle. He charged me to escort them to Pembroke.'

'Doubts for their safety, you say? What hostages? Their safety from whom?'

The squire shifted his feet among the rushes that bestrew the floor.

'Come now. How can I help you if I do not know the whole truth?'

'King John, my lord... my father says his moods grow worse by the day. When the rage comes upon him no man is safe! The King spends much time at Corfe, my lord, and the hostages were in

7

grave danger from him. Every time he heard reports of the Welsh raids upon his land, their lives were in greater peril. . .'

'So these hostages are Welsh?' Realization dawned in the Archdeacon's eyes. 'Is Llywelyn's son among them?'

'He was the reason my father sent me to Corfe. He fears for the boy's life, and bade me bring him to a safer captivity in Pembroke.'

Gerald seized upon this revelation. Llywelyn ap Iorwerth was Lord of Gwynedd, the most powerful of all the native Welsh princes. Under his leadership the Welsh had grown in power and unity, until King John of England could ignore the threat no longer and had sent his armies to seize land and hostages. Since that time, four years before, nothing had been heard of Llywelyn's son. 'So the boy still lives!'

'Yes, my lord. I journeyed with my father's warrant to Corfe, and the hostages were brought before me. There was Llywelyn's son, with a score of others who spat and swore at us in their filthy heathen tongue. One of my men was able to interpret, and I told them they were to come with me to Pembroke, and that I desired their parole to attempt neither violence nor escape. Llywelyn's son told me to. . .'

'To what?'

The squire reddened. 'I cannot repeat it, my lord, but I can tell you that only my oath to my father prevented me from felling the wretch where he stood.'

'How did you reply?'

'I told him that he and the other Welsh hostages would be released, on condition that they came with me first to Pembroke.'

'But that was not the truth, Squire Anselm.'

'I had to tell them something, my lord! My father could spare me only six men from his escort, and the castellan of Corfe would give me no more. I own that the hostages were unarmed and not in good health after their confinement, but there were too many of them. . .' Anselm stood uncomfortably before the Archdeacon's gaze, his inexperience laid bare. 'Llywelyn's son would give his agreement only on condition that they left none behind.'

'I hardly find that surprising, Anselm.'

'But they had no intention of honouring their parole! I chartered a galley from Wareham, and we sailed for Pembroke as soon as the wind blew fair. That was a miserable voyage! All the time the Welshmen spoke amongst themselves, but never whilst my interpreter was near. Yet I knew well enough the treachery in their voices, and I heard them mention *Dewi Sant*, time and again. I should have realised then what they planned.'

'I still know nothing of how you came to be in St David's in this plight.'

'Last night they overpowered us. They robbed us of our weapons and even of our clothes. I had to beg to be given these stinking rags!'

'And yet. . . and yet, they did not harm you.'

'No, they lacked the courage for that. The galley put into an inlet, not a mile from here. Porth Clais, I heard the captain say. They did not even drop anchor! The Welshmen just pushed us overboard into the shallows and the ship headed out to sea again.'

'So you lost your charges. . .'

'The Earl Marshal will never forgive me.'

The fear in the squire's voice was genuine enough, but for the moment Gerald's sympathies were entirely with the Welsh hostages. '. . . and Llywelyn's son is on his way home to Gwynedd! This may change things, Squire Anselm, you do realise that? Young. . . I forget his name. . . is an enterprising lad, it seems. Takes after his father. My advice to you, my son, is to prepare your story well. Tell your father that the valour of the Welsh was too great for you and your small escort. In such a circumstance, to praise your enemies can only reflect well upon yourself.'

'He will have me flogged.'

Gerald nodded. He thought this was very likely indeed, and well deserved, yet he gave the squire a reassuring smile as Nevern reappeared in the doorway. 'The captain will give you some better clothing, Squire Anselm, and will find you a place to sleep. I will speak with you again in the morning.'

'I am much in your debt, my lord.'

Gerald returned to the window as the voices receded down the stairway. What was it that Anselm had said? The Welshmen had been talking of Dewi Sant, and Anselm assumed they had plotted

9

to set their captors ashore at St David's. Anselm was no scholar, nor did he bear any love for the language of his enemies, but surely he should have known better than that. The Welsh name for the city of St David's was *Tyddewi*.

Gerald's eyes rested upon the cathedral as they had a thousand times before. If the hostages had used the name Dewi Sant, then they had not been referring to St David's. They had been speaking of Saint David himself.

III

It was no great distance from the castle to the Sacred Hollow. Each morning at dawn, Gerald of Wales would leave his cell beneath the Bishop's chamber, walk along the river bank, and cross the stone bridge to make his devotions in the Cathedral of St David's.

This was no ordinary morning. This was the morning of the twenty-first day of June, the day of the consecration in Winchester of the new Bishop of St David's, and Gerald knelt longer than was usual before the great stone altar. Here should have rested the bones of Saint David, but the precious relics had been lost to the Vikings more than a century before. Gerald could pray only to the memory of the Saint, but he prayed with fervour. His plea was simple. He wished for the safe and speedy delivery of his book to the Archbishop of Canterbury. . . and that His Grace might think well upon its contents. *The Rights and Privileges of St David's* was the great vessel into which he had poured every cunning argument, every eloquent turn of phrase, every scrap of evidence acquired during his long struggle to be appointed head of a free Welsh Church.

For thirty years Gerald had toiled toward this aim, and yet he had not achieved even the first step in his ambition. He knew, now, that he never would become Bishop of St David's. Twice he had been elected by the Cathedral Chapter, and twice their wishes had been denied by the authority of Canterbury. He had declined appointments elsewhere, he had turned down lesser bishoprics. He had even refused the unprecedented gift of two

10

bishoprics at once, always with the conviction that the next year would witness the fulfilment of his one desire.

Time was running out. Gerald knew in his heart that he could never realise his great vision, but he had not abandoned hope. If he himself could not succeed, then another must take up the challenge. The tragedy of it was that no man in the contemporary Church had the courage or the single-minded ambition to take up Gerald's cause. And certainly not the good Abbot Iorwerth of Talley!

His devotions at an end, Gerald closed the heavy wooden doors of the cathedral behind him and paused to allow his eyes to adjust to the bright morning light. The low sun was burning off the last coils of mist, sending them winging aloft from the gravestones like departing souls. Here might be buried a hundred bishops, and perhaps the forgotten remains of a score of archbishops reaching back to the time of Saint David himself. Here too, one day, would rest the bones of Giraldus Cambrensis, beneath a stone battered and worn by wind and fortune until the inscription of his name blew as dust into the soil of this ancient land. The immortality of Gerald of Wales lay elsewhere. His books, diligently copied, would disperse his mind and spirit the world over. Thus would his soul live on, not only beyond the gates of Heaven but in the thoughts and on the tongues of countless generations to come.

The River Alun, in summer little more than a stream, flowed but a few paces from the great door of the Cathedral of St David's. The bridge was a single slab of stone, polished smooth over six centuries by the feet of the faithful, and the Welsh called it Llech Lafar. Many years ago when a corpse was being carried across to the graveyard, the stone had cracked and burst into speech, and since that day funeral processions had avoided the bridge, crossing instead by the shallow ford. The story was conclusively proven, for the crack in the great stone could be seen to this very day.

Beyond the bridge sprawled the square courtyard of the Bishop's Palace, official residence of the Bishop of St David's. It was a poor place indeed, with but one substantial building of stone and a few sparse wooden huts to shelter and feed the pilgrims. It had seen little of Bishop Geoffrey, who had preferred for himself the security of the castle on those few occasions when his household was resident in St David's.

The Bishop was spiritual leader of a see encompassing half the lands of Wales and, like the Norman lords of the Marches, he also held lands of his own. From these estates he collected taxes and administered his justice, owing allegiance neither to the King of England nor to the Welsh Princes. This very independence had for years held St David's aloof from the wars that had torn at the remainder of southern Wales, allowing it to become the most peaceful and most prosperous corner of the country.

It had not always been so. In the time of Saint David there had been little more than a few huts and a wooden church where the cathedral now stood. Here had been the Celtic *clas* in which the holy men had lived their lives, tilling the land, preaching the Faith, yet ever in fear of the square sails of the Viking ships. The Norsemen had harried the coast for centuries, burning and pillaging the monastery time after time. Always the *clas* had recovered, building a new church, replanting the torn fields, until in the year 1089 the Norsemen had committed their greatest atrocity of all. They had broken asunder the shrine of Saint David and stolen away the reliquary containing his blessed bones.

To Gerald, this had been a portent of the disaster to come. As the Norman barons had consolidated their hold on England and turned greedy eyes Westward for new lands to conquer, so had the Norman Church looked upon the customs of its Celtic cousin and thrown up its hands in horror.

The Celtic monasteries had been mixed communities. Many of the holy men kept wives and children, and the abbots would often pass on their offices from father to son like the secular lords of the land. With the coming of the first Norman Bishop of St David's in the year 1115, the Celtic tradition had faced a more insidious and enduring threat than had ever been posed by the Viking long-ships. St David's was reorganised on the Norman English pattern, with a non-monastic community of canons installed as the cathedral chapter. Other *clasau* across Wales had persisted longer, traditions dying hard, but everywhere the Normans sought to reform and Anglicise.

Had the Norsemen, in their ignorance, brought about the downfall of a nation? If the bones of Saint David were ever found, would they herald a rise in the fortunes of the Welsh? The rebirth of a new Wales? A Church of Wales, with its own Archbishop, free of the yoke of Canterbury?

It was easy to dream in the Sacred Hollow.

The muddy track wound along the valley of the River Alun, on towards the motte with its simple wooden buildings. The old castle, in Gerald's eyes, was something of an anachronism. Built by an early Norman bishop who had feared attack from the Welsh, its meagre defences had never been put to the test. A high palisade of stout logs enclosed the outer bailey with its stables and smithy, bakehouse and brewery in the protective shadow of the motte. From a second set of gates at the foot of this mound, a steep path climbed to the great wooden tower. Over the past century, other castles had been strengthened by replacing vulnerable wooden structures with fortifications of stone. By comparison with the great round keep of Pembroke and the stone curtain walls of Haverford, the defences of St David's were feeble indeed. But what defence was necessary? Norman and Welshman alike, as Gerald was fond of saying, were too pious by far to attack those under the protection of the Saint.

. Like the palisade itself, the open gates were of split logs, braced and pegged together with the bark still clinging. Only at night would they be closed and barred. This day, as any other, the entrance to the outer bailey was guarded by a single sentry who served more to welcome visitors than to deter intruders. He leaned at ease on the wooden shaft of his halberd, but stood a little more alert as the Archdeacon drew near.

'Did you see the fire last night, my lord?'

Gerald's curiosity compelled him to stop. 'A fire? Where?'

'Out at sea, close by Ramsey Island. I was on watch up the tower, my lord. Just after dusk I saw it. I told Captain Nevern, but it had gone by the time he got up there. Said I'd been too long at the mead, he did!'

'A ship?'

'Wasn't from a ship's lantern, my lord. Much too bright, it was.'

'What, then?'

'You know what night it was? Midsummer's Eve! That's when the dragons fly over Ramsey!'

'Dragons?' Gerald smiled at such nonsense. He knew that the creatures were extremely rare. He had travelled widely and had not seen even one. They were probably extinct by now, for the few accounts he had heard at first hand had been from very old men. 'Perhaps your captain was right.'

'Good morning, my lord.'

The Archdeacon turned to see Anselm, much agitated, striding towards him across the bailey. 'Good morning, Squire Anselm, I'm surprised to see you ready so early.' He looked over Anselm's shoulder to see the half dozen soldiers from Pembroke waiting impatiently by their horses. An odd assembly in their motley selection of ragged clothes, makeshift sandals and borrowed weaponry, they were mostly of Anselm's age except for one scarred veteran who might have seen a hundred battles. Good soldiers were scarce enough, even in the Castle of Pembroke, but even so the Earl Marshal must have spared his most experienced sergeant to keep a watchful eye upon his youngest son.

'We've been ready to leave since dawn, Archdeacon. We had hoped to reach Pembroke before nightfall.'

'You would not have reached Pembroke in a day, not even if you had left at sunrise.' There was a murmur of protest from the group. 'Oh, it could be done,' Gerald added quickly, 'if you were prepared to run your horses into the ground. But these horses, you will recall, are not yours.'

'Is it so far?' asked Anselm, uncowed.

'Not as the raven flies. But there are the two branches of the Cleddau to be reckoned with. They cannot be forded without half a day's travel upstream.'

'There is a ferry.'

'There was a ferry, until a month ago. But some fools had dragged a great stone down from the Prescellys to serve as a monument to the Welsh victories, and they bribed the ferryman to take it down the Cleddau. The ferry sank under the weight at the first bend in the river, and the ferryman fled to escape the wrath of the castellan of Haverford.'

14

'So it will take two days, you say?'

'You'll have to spend the night at Haverford. I know the castellan. He is a hospitable man and famed for his generosity, though it could be more frequently directed towards the Church.'

'Then we must leave at once, my lord, and I thank you for your...'

'A moment!' Gerald halted them with a raised hand. 'I've a mind to travel with you.'

'May I ask why, my lord?'

Gerald hesitated. He was curious about the Earl Marshal's motives for attempting to bring the hostages into his own custody. He wanted to discover more about the present situation between the English and the Welsh, but he would not admit his interest to the squire.

'You said your father awaits you in Pembroke, Squire Anselm. Well, perhaps I may be able to stay his hand when you tell him of your failure.'

'You would do that for me, my lord? Then I... I would welcome your company.'

Gerald smiled grimly as he gathered together his few possessions. Of one thing he was quite certain. Whatever punishment the Earl Marshal might vent upon his son, there was no man living, not even Giraldus Cambrensis, who would be able to change his mind.

IV

For all their poor apparel, the men of Pembroke made a brave company. Gerald could fault neither their horsemanship nor their bearing, and would have wished for no finer escort. The younger soldiers rode close together, in high spirits now that they were on their way home, and boasted of the wives or sweethearts who awaited them, the great meals they would eat, and the vast quantities of ale they would quaff when they rejoined their families. Gerald offered only an occasional word of his own, a question here, an anecdote there, enjoying the atmosphere of

15

eager anticipation that had settled over the group. Only Anselm himself, and the old soldier who might expect to share the blame for his failure, remained morose.

They rode eastward from St David's, the road rising steeply out of the cathedral close through the prosperous little town that flourished on providing shelter and selling souvenir tokens to the pilgrims. Out amongst the fields, where wiry grass vied with the bracken to wrest its own living from the stony soil, the road strayed never more than a mile from the sea. There was an invigorating sharpness to the air, a tang of seaweed on the fresh westerly breeze.

'My lord, those are poor defences.'

Anselm reined in his horse to ride beside the Archdeacon as he pointed towards the dyke that ran north to south across the road before them.

'Have you not visited St David's before?'

Anselm bowed his head in shame. 'I never thought of it, my lord. There are churches enough in Pembroke.'

Gerald rolled his eyes heavenward. Such ignorance! Such impiety! But he might have expected as much, for the Earl Marshal had never been noted for his devotion to the Church, least of all the Church of Wales. 'It may please you to know that the dyke marks the old border of the sacred precinct. It was erected in the time of the first Archbishops of St David's, and the monks were forbidden to venture beyond it.'

'The first. . .Archbishops, my lord?'

'Oh yes, Archbishops indeed, and Saint David himself was the first.' Gerald smiled. Here was an excellent opportunity to pass the time of the journey, and a little education might not be wasted on this son of the Earl Marshal of Pembroke. 'When this place was first embraced by the Faith a monastery was established here, and David was its abbot. That is how some folk think of him still, just as Abbot David. Whereas the rest of us know that David's influence was far wider, that he was in truth Archbishop of all Wales.' Gerald saw to his annoyance that Anselm's attention had wandered again. As they neared the dyke, they saw a cluster of pilgrims breaking bread by a spring. 'That is *Dŵr Cleifion*, the Water of the Sick. It has healing properties. The pilgrims wash their feet there before they enter these sacred precincts beyond *Ffos y Mynach.*'

'Beyond what, my lord?'

'The monk's dyke, that lies before us.'

'You speak Welsh, my lord?'

Gerald cleared his throat in embarrassment. It was not a skill of which he would boast whilst in Norman company. 'I seem to have picked up a few words, through the years. . . .'

The road climbed steeply from the little harbour of Solva, with its fishing boats grounded on the low tide, before dipping once again to cross Brawdy stream. Anselm called a halt at the ford to rest and water the horses. The travellers ate their bread and cheese, and Gerald told of the terrible winter in King Henry the Second's time, when a storm had blown with such violence that both sea and sand were driven away from the beach at nearby Newgale. There had been revealed a veritable forest of ancient trees, felled as if by the axe of Noah, and folk had marvelled at the sight of them.

As ever, one story led to another, and the soldiers were content to stretch themselves on the grassy bank, revelling in the luxury of the warm midsummer sun and the blue sky, the vast freedom of the open air around them. They were surprised in the revelation that this old Archdeacon could be an entertaining and informative companion. He could speak with first hand knowledge of people and places of which they had heard only tavern tales. Ireland and France, Canterbury and Rome, all sprang vivid into their imagination in every detail from the unrivalled mildness of the Irish air to the breathtaking majesty of the snowy Alps. Great men, barely mortal, were brought firmly down to earth by Gerald's tales. His counsel had been sought by two Popes, two Archbishops of Canterbury, three English kings and countless Welsh princes, and he could recall their every minute particular with merciless insight spiced liberally with his own forthright opinions.

The hours trickled away with the stream, the shadows of the grazing horses lengthened. It was Anselm who realised the lateness of the hour, and urged the soldiers to their feet. Gerald hastened to agree that it was time they were leaving, and reminded them that in the latter part of their journey the country would become heavily wooded. None wished to take the risk of riding through the forest after dark, and they made all haste to follow the course of the stream down to the sea. It was a broad sandy beach, here at Newgale, and they allowed the horses to canter through the shallows before returning to the dry mud of the road as it cut inland towards Haverford.

Trees and dense undergrowth, hitherto confined to riverside and valley, encroached ever closer upon the road. Soon the travellers were riding not over open heathland but through the depths of a forest.

Branches of oak and hornbeam touched their skeletal fingers above the dusty highway, so that the party now rode through a tunnel of shifting patterns. The few splinters of weak sunlight that filtered through the hungry grasp of the trees brightened the dull colours of the riders' clothing, gilded the bronze buckles of bridle and stirrup and, once in a while, sparkled from the hilts of the swords so generously provided by Captain Nevern. Gerald did not grudge such liberal use of church funds. Not when they were dispensed in so just a cause as his own protection, for in the forest the safety of travellers was by no means assured.

Thieves and cutthroats abounded of course, but other dangers, darker and more sinister, had their roots deep in the imagination of man. To left and to right, the trunks of menacing trees faded into a darkness far deeper than the dappled shadows of the road. There, where the branches knit close above the forest floor, day became dusk and night was transformed into the utter blackness of a nightmare.

In every shadow might lurk a crouching dragon, a coiled serpent, a snarling tiger, or any of the demonic beasts of which the bards sang with relish in their fireside comfort. A fallen tree trunk, a rocky outcrop, a twisted net of crippled bramble, any one of these things could conceal a demon, or could even of itself become the demon. For, just as a barnacle goose would grow out of driftwood, or an eel would emerge from horsehair in a stream, who could say that more sinister beasts were not created out of the black dreams of the twilight forest?

'Tell me something, Squire Anselm. . .' Gerald spurred his

18

horse level with the squire's, anxious to divert his own mind from the deepening shadows. 'You said your father awaits you. Did the King order him to return to Pembroke?'

'I think not.' Anselm stared at the ears of his horse, flicking in their futile defence against the myriad midges.

'Well then, did he even permit your father to return? Would the King wish to lose his most trusted ally, at such a time as this?'

'The Earl Marshal does not take me into his confidence, my lord. I tended his horse, and polished his armour, and carried his messages. I did not sit in council with him, nor would I expect to.' There was mild reproof in the squire's voice. He was beginning to resent the Archdeacon's persistent questions.

'Anselm, you must know that the Welsh are attacking your father's lands.'

'Yes.' The squire stared ahead.

'Then. . . is that why he has returned? To defend against them?'

'I don't know. Believe me, Archdeacon, I just don't know.'

'Perhaps he believes his own fortunes will rise if he abandons the King. Perhaps he thinks John will soon be ousted from his throne. Is that why he sent you to bring the Welsh hostages to Pembroke, so that he himself could use them for bargaining with Llywelyn? I know that he already holds Rhys Gryg in Carmarthen. . .'

Anselm looked sharply at Gerald. Rhys Gryg was one of the most powerful men in southern Wales, and his capture had been a major triumph for the Earl Marshal. But how did an old Archdeacon, living at the isolated shrine of Saint David, come to know so much of the Earl Marshal's business? 'He is no longer held at Carmarthen, Archdeacon, it is too near the border, too open to attack. Weeks ago, the Earl Marshal had him brought to Pembroke. He does not wish to lose his hostages.'

'I can understand that well enough. Your father already had Rhys Gryg, and then he asked you to bring Llywelyn's son to him. Yes, I see it all now. The Earl Marshal sought to gain a hold over the northern Welsh, as well as those of the south. . . I wonder what King John would think of that.' Gerald smiled at the discomfort on the squire's face. 'I accuse your father of nothing, Squire Anselm. His behaviour intrigues me, that is all.'

'Is it possible to be traitor, Archdeacon, in such times as these?'

19

Gerald cleared his throat. 'I am not sure that I understand...'

'My brother William sides with the rebel barons. He says theirs is the just cause of God and freedom, but my father calls him fool and traitor and says that he will come to his senses ere long.'

'You have other brothers. What do they say?'

'Richard is in France, and so proves himself traitor indeed. Gilbert I can only envy, for he is in the Church and need be loyal only to God.' Anselm hesitated, wondering why Gerald was smiling. 'Walter is little older than myself...and as undecided. He remains in England, seeking some middle course.'

'So you are undecided, Squire Anselm?'

Anselm shook his head, tight lipped. He regretted his candour, and now picked his words with caution. 'Did you know that the King took hostages from his own people, even from his own liegemen, as well as from the Welsh and the Scots? Can you believe that a dozen of the Earl Marshal's own men were taken? Some were my friends.'

'I suppose the King does not know whom to trust. With so many enemies, how can he? With most of England in the hands of traitors, and the Welsh pouring across the borders...'

'The Welsh, yes.' Anselm's mood lightened, for here was a question upon which his loyalty had never been torn. 'Did you know that Llywelyn even dares challenge the border into England? He has pledged support for the English barons, and the town of Shrewsbury surrendered to him without any show of resistance.'

Gerald nodded, trying to conceal his pleasure at this news. Lord Llywelyn was a fine leader of men, worthy in every respect, and moreover he had often been Gerald's ally in his own long quarrel with Canterbury. 'Tell me of Llywelyn's son. I assume he has a name, other than that of his father?'

'My warrant named him as Griffith.'

'Misspelt in the manner of the English, no doubt.' Gerald swallowed his irritation. He could only pity this child grown to manhood in prison. A child whose name had been considered unimportant, whose only role had been to stand as a bargaining tool between the most powerful men in the land. 'Gruffydd ap Llywelyn is his name, then, Squire Anselm. I think we might do well to remember that.'

V

The Castle of Haverford

21 June, 1215

From the gibbet outside the town gate swung a human skeleton, long since picked clean by kite and raven. By its side a more recently condemned prisoner slumped within the bars of the iron cage that mocked the human form. By day the flies would feast upon his blood and the birds would feast upon the flies, and ere long he would match his fellow.

Gerald of Wales swallowed hard and looked away. It was not that he disapproved of just retribution against murderers and robbers, but he did not see why the justice of God and State must offend the stomachs of honest folk.

High on the hill within the town walls, torchlight sparked from the narrow cross-windows of the great rectangular keep, vying with the cooler brightness of the stars. In its own way, the castle of Haverford was as eloquent a warning as the grisly relics suspended from its gibbet by the gate. One emphasised the unassailable power of the Norman lords, the other the merciless force of their justice. Between these two harsh symbols, rough buildings jostled for space, and the stench of overcrowded humanity closed like a stale blanket above the travellers' heads.

The castellan of Haverford was delighted to welcome the weary travellers to his hall, and would not rest until they sat down to join him in a repast that was little less than a banquet. He was a scarred old veteran with all the tact and gentility of a wild boar, and throughout the meal regaled his guests with tales of the most bloody episodes of a life devoted to conflict.

'Those were the best times,' the castellan sighed as he recalled the tournaments of his youth. 'Not like your modern tourneys. It's all posturing and prizes, these days.'

'Rather than maiming and slaughter?' Gerald wondered mildly.

'But the weak died with honour! And what fortunes were made by the victors!' The castellan brandished his overflowing goblet. 'Take his father!'

Anselm, startled by the violent gesture in his direction, blinked at the castellan. What with the long day's ride, the copious wine and the tedium of the conversation, he had relapsed into slumber.

'William the Marshal! Look at *him*! He was born with nothing. Yet he fought like a lion in the French tourneys. The King won a fortune in wagers on him, and see him now! Earl of Pembroke! Marshal of the King's Armies! The King's Champion! Now there's a true knight for you. There's a man who really knows how to hold a tourney. My son's still at Pembroke. . . yesterday he won himself two horses and a fine axe. Would have been more, if the damned clouds hadn't opened.'

A tournament at Pembroke Castle. . . now *there* was a potent gesture on the Earl Marshal's part! At last Gerald understood the reason for his hasty departure from the King's court. The tournament would have taken weeks of preparation and cost the Earl Marshal a fortune, and he would be anxious to preside over it in person. It would be a gathering of the Normans in Wales to let them enjoy his hospitality and to show that he would not desert them, but at the same time it would be a display of military prowess to warn the native Welsh to be wary of his power. It would provide the opportunity to bring to heel any of his castellans who might be showing signs of waywardness or laxity. Not least, it would enable the Earl Marshal to observe the most aggressive and flourishing of the ascendent young knights, for among these would be his future castellans. . . and his future enemies.

The castellan of Haverford was still in full flood. 'Yes, he could have won more. A fine lad, he is. Takes after me. I'd have stayed on another day myself, but I couldn't stomach the company the Earl Marshal was keeping.'

'What company?' Anselm was fully awake now. 'Are the rebel barons at Pembroke?'

'Worse than that, lad! He entertains a Welshman!'

Gerald declined to take offence. 'Was it Rhys Gryg?'

'Couldn't put a name to him. They all look the same to me, and

I can't even say their heathen names, much less remember them! Their black eyes and their black hair. . .goes with their black hearts, I always say.' The castellan stared blackly into the ruby depths of his goblet, forgetful of the Welsh ancestry of his eminent guest. 'If I were the Earl Marshal I'd not have let them through the gates! There was one of them sitting with him, though. Right up on the high table, looking as if he owned it.'

'I'll warrant he'd *like* to own it,' Anselm muttered into his goblet.

Gerald elected not to hear. 'That must have been Rhys Gryg. So now the Earl Marshal begins to treat his hostages with respect. . .'

'His hostages?' The castellan belched. 'You don't understand me, my lord. There are no hostages now.'

'No hostages?' Gerald paled. 'All dead? So the King has finally. . .'

'Not killed, my lord, though that would have been his fondest wish. No, they have all been released.'

'Released?' Gerald did not attempt to disguise his delight. 'By what miracle, my lord?'

The castellan stared at the Archdeacon in astonishment. 'You've not heard of the charter of liberties?'

Gerald glanced at Anselm, who shrugged his shoulders.

'You've not heard of it?' The castellan burst into laughter. 'All England reels with the news, and Gerald of Wales has not heard of it!'

Gerald turned angrily to Anselm. 'You were attending the royal court in England. You must have known something of this!'

'No, my lord! I own there was much quiet talk before my father sent me to Corfe, but nothing was explained to me.'

The castellan grinned broadly, delighted to display his knowledge to such an audience. 'A week ago, it was, the fifteenth day of June. I wasn't there, but the Earl Marshal told me all. The rebels had seized London, there was no stopping them. They all came together on a meadow by the Thames. . .the barons, the Church, the Welsh, even the Scots. They set down their demands in writing, and the King had no choice but to set his seal upon it. Your father was there, lad.'

23

'Yes...he would have been.' Anselm shifted uncomfortably on the wooden bench. 'Er...did the Earl Marshal support the rebel barons, my lord? Or was he true to the King?'

'Both!' The castellan grinned at the surprise of his companions. 'The King had no choice but to accept the barons' demands. The Earl Marshal made him see that, though the King will not soon forgive him for it.'

'And what of the Welsh?' asked Gerald. 'What was Llywelyn ap Iorwerth's role in this?'

'His role, Archdeacon?' The castellan's goblet crashed down upon the table top. 'Llywelyn's role has been the slaughter of my people, him and his allies.'

'You must forgive me, but St David's is an isolated place and news is slow to reach us. Have the Welsh been threatening the Earl Marshal's lands?'

'Threaten! Already we are invaded.'

'Who leads them, my lord?' Gerald leaned forward slightly, despite his efforts not to show too much of an interest. It was possible, indeed it was very likely, that the leaders of this rising would be his own kinsmen. His mother's grandfather had been the lord Rhys ap Tewdwr, from whom the princes of southern Wales were also descended.

'You'll know! You'll know soon enough, Archdeacon, when I spike their heads above the gates!'

'I pass this way but infrequently, my lord Haverford. Do you know their names?'

'Rhys and Maelgwn it was, a pox on them! Rhys and Maelgwn, kinsmen of that same Rhys Gryg who sups even now at the Earl Marshal's table.'

'And what did Rhys and Maelgwn do, exactly?'

'Never dry of questions, are you, Archdeacon!' The castellan slaked his own thirst, and held out his goblet to be refilled as he settled back in his chair. 'They walked across the borders to the north, and the damned Welsh peasants received them with open arms. Only Cemais resisted, and what remains there now? Bones and ashes! Then Rhys goes marching on to the south coast. Swansea to Carmarthen, he's taken it all.'

Gerald was thinking once again of his kinsmen. He was descended from the Norman lords of the Marches as well as from

24

the Welsh princes, and this list of conquests was coming uncomfortably close to home. 'Is there no hope for peace, my lord? Does this charter not apply in Wales?'

'Give it time Archdeacon! At least there's been no trouble this week past. None that's come to my ears, that is.'

'But how long will peace remain in the mind of a Welshman?'

Gerald ignored this outburst from Squire Anselm. 'What exactly is contained within this charter, my lord Haverford?'

'More power to the barons and yet more power to the Church, Archdeacon. Repeal of the forest laws. Trial by jury. No imprisonment without just cause...now there's a fine thing so long as we keep it to ourselves! Can't have the serfs hearing of that one! Nor the Welsh, eh?' The castellan dissolved into laughter as he raised his goblet, empty again, in Anselm's direction. 'Inheritance tax, marriage of widows, restoration of stolen lands. The rights of man, it is!'

Gerald contemplated the grin of triumph on the castellan's red face. 'Soon, perhaps, the breadth and justice of the laws of the English may begin to approach those of the Welsh.'

'What? What laws do those savages have?'

'Savages, you call them? You might be surprised, my lord. Their laws are complex and precise, and administered with a fairness that the English would do well to emulate....' Gerald checked himself. Much as he resented the castellan's ignorant bigotry, he had no wish to be seen to extol the Welsh too openly.

'Yet these are the heathens who lay waste my father's lands!' Anselm was taking renewed interest in the conversation.

'The Welsh are as Christian as you or I, Squire Anselm! And they regard those lands as their own. It saddens me that so many lives have been lost, but....'

'They would not have been lost, had the Earl Marshal been allowed to remain in Pembroke to guard them.' The castellan dared say no more against King John, but Gerald knew that, thanks to John's insistence that the Earl Marshal stay at his side, the depleted forces of the Normans in southern Wales had suffered heavily under the onslaught of the Welsh.

The castellan found another vent for his dissatisfaction. 'In Richard's day there was no trouble with the Welsh!'

25

Gerald smiled into his goblet. So selective a memory was all too common when the Norman lords lamented King John's brother and predecessor! Gerald was old enough to remember well enough the bitter protests when Richard Lionheart neglected his own country to fight his interminable foreign wars.

'And Henry! You must remember Henry, Gerald. My father told me all about him. Henry and Rosamund the Fair, eh? You remember that story?'

Gerald did indeed remember. The extramarital associations of King Henry the Second were numerous and well known, and the Archdeacon had no wish to discuss them.

'And all the while, behind his back, the Queen was out seeking her own pleasures!'

'What?' Gerald was shocked out of his pious indifference. The adultery of a king was one thing, good for many a tavern yarn and only to be expected, but the same behaviour in a queen could not be countenanced.

The castellan beamed with pride. It was seldom that any man could relate a story not known to Gerald of Wales. 'My own father told me that the King's Champion. . . .'

'*The Earl Marshal*?' Gerald's astonished cry caught the attention of the assembly. He lowered his voice. 'Do you tell me that the Earl of Pembroke. . . and the Queen of England. . . '

'I tell you only this, my lord. It wasn't just the *King*'s favour that set William the Marshal where he is today!'

Anselm caught the Archdeacon's eye. He smiled and gently shook his head. 'The story is popular enough in the Pembroke guardroom, my lord Archdeacon, but few believe it. Least of all my mother.'

'Come, lad! What wife would want to believe it?'

'If you want the truth, my lord, it seems the story was first spread by my father's enemies. They wanted to set the King against him but. . . '

'But the Earl Marshal was too great a soldier, and the King needed him.' The castellan grinned artlessly at Anselm. For a moment, the wine had made him forget who the squire was.

The soldiers of Pembroke lay in oblivion, some sprawled across the broad table, some beneath it among the dogs on the straw-covered floor. The castellan eyed them, disappointed. 'Well now, there's a sight for you. Barely midnight, and they're all snoring like sows. When I was their age, we would drink all night and still be fit for a good fight at cock's crow!'

In dismay, Gerald realised that only he and the castellan remained sober enough to speak. He could stomach no more profane oaths, no more blow-by-blow accounts of past battles, no more boasts of drinking prowess, no more tales from the barrack room. As the castellan of Haverford took his breath for another onslaught, the Archdeacon swiftly counter-attacked with a detailed dissertation upon the life and achievements of Saint David. The old soldier attempted a spirited sally with a bawdy song, but he had met his match, and the engagement was brought to its conclusion by the dull crash of the castellan's head as it fell to the wine-soaked table.

Gerald smiled in deep satisfaction as he settled back in his chair and took a sip from his goblet. It had been a close run thing, but with Saint David's help, he had won the day.

VI

Next morning it was difficult for Gerald to goad his companions out of their sodden slumber. Harder still was it for them to take their leave of Haverford and the castellan's overpowering hospitality, and it was nigh on noon before they assembled at the castle gates, still cursing their sore heads.

'God's teeth!' groaned one of the soldiers. 'I'll never drink again.'

'I told you the castellan was a hospitable man.' The Archdeacon showed not a trace of pity.

The Western Cleddau, broad and shallow at this point, flowed close by the castle of Haverford. Indeed, the main reason for building the stronghold had been to guard this southernmost crossing place. The riders waded their horses across, pausing to allow them to drink of the fresh Preseli water before they entered the thick forest that dominated the land between the western and eastern tributaries of the river. As the soldiers talked in eager anticipation of reaching their homes before nightfall, Anselm still fretted as to how he would be welcomed at Pembroke without Llywelyn's son in his charge. Gerald tried, generously, to raise the squire's spirits.

'Will any of your brothers be at Pembroke, Squire Anselm?'

'I hope not.' Anselm was forced to smile at the Archdeacon's surprise.

'That is uncharitable.'

'It is hardly my place to be charitable. Five of us, and I the youngest! I'll not get an acre of the Earl Marshal's land, nor a penny of his fortune.'

'You can expect something, surely?' Rights of inheritance aside, Gerald could not doubt that William Marshal was too wise a man to bestow all his considerable fortune upon the eldest son alone. That was not the custom. It left too great a temptation to fratricide on the part of the others.

'William, being the eldest, will get Pembroke and all that goes with it. At least, that is what he expects. But I do not think the Earl Marshal will easily forgive him for siding with the barons.'

'Even now that the barons have won their cause?'

'My father's loyalty does not shift with the wind, Archdeacon.'

Gerald remained thoughtful as he recalled the scheme to gather the Welsh hostages together in Pembroke. He would give much to know the Earl Marshal's true motives.

'Do you think he will disinherit your brother William?'

'I doubt it. Even if he did, there still remain Richard and Walter. Gilbert was bought into the Church years ago. I believe you know him?'

'I know of him. Bishop Geoffrey dealt with such matters.'

'Richard knows that he can expect some land, but our father is unwilling to divide his estate any further. That leaves Walter and myself with nothing.'

'The Earl Marshal must be confident that you harbour no ill intent towards your elder brothers. Is his trust well founded?' Gerald did not expect a truthful or even a serious answer.

'I'd be grateful enough if he left me a good horse and armour. And may it serve me as well as once it served him!'

28

'You'd make your fortune at the tournaments?' Gerald asked the question with distaste.

'Even William may yet have to do that. I can see our father outlasting us all. He seems as impregnable as that great round keep he holds so dear.'

Gerald raised an eyebrow. 'Would you be so forthright to your father's face?'

'A son who expects nothing can be more free in his speech than one who seeks an Earldom.'

'You're right... yes, you're right. A silent tongue and a cool head might have made me Bishop of St David's.'

Anselm glanced at Gerald, but said nothing. The sombre words had not looked for a reply and were not, perhaps, even meant to be heard.

The forest, cleared here and there for grazing and crops, lay never far from the road. It maintained a lively conversation of its own, with the trills and chirps of a thousand incautious birds intent upon their own romance and tragedy, whilst more insistent sounds marked the passage of wolf or deer. Presently a more cheerful sound emerged, as if tugging gently at the travellers' sleeves. It beckoned like an old friend, the bubbling welcome of the Eastern Cleddau, swollen and extrovert having drunk its fill of heavy rains in the Preseli mountains.

The travellers forded the river downstream of the castle of Llawhaden, and soon left the forest far behind. The drove road led now through rich pastures and farmland, divided into narrow strips separated by deeply ploughed ridge and furrow. Gerald explained to anyone who would listen how this way of farming the good earth was so alien to the Welsh land and its people. Pembrokeshire, with its Norman name and its Norman lords, hardly remained a part of Wales at all. Even the peasants who tilled the fields were foreigners, speaking only Anglo-Saxon or Flemish.

The Normans' conquest of this part of Wales had been achieved simply by driving away the native people and replacing them with tenant labour imported from England or the continent. The new people of Pembrokeshire held no thoughts of rebellion, and regarded the native Welsh with fear and contempt. Attacks on the border castles were real enough, to be sure, but the rumours of appalling Welsh savagery were carefully nurtured by the Norman overlords.

These Lords of the Marches, noblemen who thought of themselves first as English, yet whose culture and language were so firmly rooted in France, were seen by their subjects as the highest power on Earth. They enforced their own laws, sat secure in their impregnable strongholds, and could muster great armies from their own estates. It was true that they owed allegiance to King John, yet, for many, their oaths were long forgotten.

Not so the King's Champion, Earl William of Pembroke, Marshal of the Armies of the King. No man was more powerful, none more respected, and none more loyal to the crown of England...whoever should wear it.

A fortunate marriage, arranged through the goodwill of King Henry the Second, had given William Marshal the title of Earl, the castles of Pembroke and Cilgerran to hold in his own name, and vast estates from which to draw his armies and his income. Two more Welsh castles had come to him in the January of 1215, when a fearful King John had awarded him the custody of Cardigan and Carmarthen. Yet of all his possessions, Pembroke was ever uppermost in the affections of the Earl Marshal. Upon this fortress he had lavished the skills of the finest architects in Europe, and Pembroke had become the very embodiment of the power of the King's Marshal.

When William the Marshal had first assumed his Earldom, the castle of Pembroke had owed the greater part of its strength to its position on a lofty promontory, protected to the North and West by a tidal creek extending from the great estuary of Milford Haven. In those days it had been a timber structure, and the Earl Marshal's first action had been to replace the stockade with a stone curtain wall to close off the landward side. Into this he had set a lofty gatehouse with wooden gates and iron portcullis. Only then had he turned his attention to the buildings within, and the great circular keep, towering five storeys high, had been completed within the last decade.

The town gates of Pembroke stood open, manned by Flemish guardsmen who snapped to attention as the squire's company drew near. Anselm had grown ever more silent and withdrawn as he neared Pembroke, and did not meet the men's curious stares. Gerald wondered how much the guards knew of the squire's errand. Had they been told to watch for the arrival of Llywelyn's son?

The long, narrow street stretched in silence towards the castle, the houses of wattle and daub stood empty, a gaggle of geese represented the entire population.

'Did you expect so enthusiastic a welcome?'

'They will all be at the tournament, of course.'

'Of course.'

As the travellers reined in their horses upon the noisy cobblestones of the gatehouse, Anselm did not dismount but held steady below the portcullis. With the Archdeacon by his side, they could see quite clearly across the vast outer ward. Anselm nodded towards the high table. 'My father.'

Even from this distance the Archdeacon could recognise the grey haired old soldier presiding over the tournament. Gerald of Wales and William Marshal would never call each other friend, but they harboured a deep and wary respect for one another. Each knew that the other, in his own field, might well be considered the greatest man of his time.

At the Earl Marshal's left was seated a bearded, powerfully built man, laughing and loud in good humour.

'And that is Rhys Gryg? He seems in good health. . . for one so long a prisoner.'

'He may have been the King's hostage, Archdeacon, but Rhys Gryg has never seen the dungeons of Pembroke, nor those of Carmarthen. Even in his confinement my father ensured he was treated with courtesy and respect, and he ate as well as we. The Earl Marshal is not like King John, Archdeacon. He believes that one day Rhys Gryg may be a powerful ally.'

'More than likely. These southern princes have ever fought amongst themselves. It was the treachery of his nephews Rhys and Owain that first sent Rhys Gryg into the Earl Marshal's custody.'

'I must confess, Archdeacon, that I find the sheer numbers of these Welsh lords confusing. And when they share the same few names. . .'

31

Gerald smiled. 'Allow me to explain. Rhys Gryg is brother to Maelgwn, and is an uncle of the brothers Rhys and Owain ap Gruffydd. The four of them are the main leaders in the South. And then in Powys we have Llywelyn's old rival Gwenwynwyn, whilst Llywelyn ap Iorwerth himself remains unchallenged in the North.'

'You have no need to remind me of Llywelyn!'

'Yes. . . I imagine that all Europe must know his name. Even if they cannot pronounce it.' Gerald looked around, irritated to be left waiting with his horse in the gatehouse. 'Is there no one to greet us?'

The question found its answer as a neatly garbed little man emerged from the crowd and approached to welcome the new arrivals. He was an oddly civilised figure amid the carnage of the tourney, and it was clear that the incongruous sword at his belt was nothing more than a badge of office. His reddish hair and beard were well trimmed, his tunic neat and expensive, and his pale blue eyes missed nothing.

'Squire Anselm! My lord Archdeacon! It is good to see you returned to Pembroke.' John d'Erley paused as Gerald and Anselm dismounted and handed their tired horses to an ostler. 'But what has become of the Welsh who were to travel with you? The Earl Marshal expected Llywelyn's son. . .'

'Then that is something of which we will speak to the Earl Marshal,' Gerald interrupted, before Anselm could reply.

'And you shall, you shall. Yet at the moment Lord Rhys of Deheubarth is with him, and. . .'

'Of *Deheubarth*?' Gerald stared in disbelief at d'Erley's puzzled face. Deheubarth was the Welsh name for the whole territory of southern Wales. Much of the land of Deheubarth was held by the Norman liegemen of King John, and even those parts held by the Welsh were shared between Rhys Gryg and his kinsmen. For Rhys Gryg to assume such a title, within this very bastion of Norman power in Wales, was a show of reckless audacity that Gerald could only regard with admiration. It meant, in effect, that he was claiming to be the sole and rightful lord of all the south of Wales. The Earl Marshal could not possibly be aware of the significance of the title. He would never allow so blatant an insult to pass.

'Yes, of Deheubarth.' D'Erley was as ignorant as his master.

32

'Lord Rhys was held in confinement, but as soon as the Earl Marshal returned from England he ordered his release. Lord Rhys has been free for two days now, but he expressed a desire to watch the tournament and the Earl Marshal saw no reason to refuse him.' As he spoke, d'Erley's eyes were upon the high table. Gerald could see no signal, yet d'Erley nodded quite distinctly and turned to Anselm. 'The Earl Marshal will see you now.'

'Now? In Rhys Gryg's presence?'

'Your father is not a patient man, Anselm.' There was affection in John d'Erley's voice, as well as warning, for he had known all his master's children from infancy.

Anselm gazed across the ward, and paled at the grim expectation on his father's face. 'If the Earl Marshal knew what I must tell him . . .'

'Faith, Squire Anselm.'

Gerald's smile had been intended to be reassuring, but John D'Erley had already set out at a brisk walk towards the high table. The squire and the Archdeacon had no choice but to follow.

VII

The Castle of Pembroke

22 June, 1215

This was the final day, the climax of the Tournament of Pembroke. William Marshal, with his favoured guests at the high table, presided over the broad outer ward which had attained by now the aspect of a battlefield. Crowds of spectators lined the walls, elbowed their way amongst the low wooden buildings and jostled for space with pedlars and strolling players. A feast day had been declared, and all manner of men had come from miles around to witness the victories and defeats, the triumphs and humiliations of their lords and masters.

The knights, their long shields, the caparison of their horses, all blazed resplendent with the coats of arms so jealously guarded within each of the great families. Beneath his loose surcoat, each man wore armour of chain mail from neck to toe, and heavy upon his head an enclosed helm to cover his face. From the tip of his blunted lance floated a coloured pennant, triangular for the majority of the knights but large and square for those *knights banneret* who led a company of their own men.

Whether accompanied by servants, kinsmen or friends, the experienced knight made sure that he fought within a group. Rare indeed was the man who would ride alone in a tourney, rarer still the one who might emerge at the end of the day with skin and pride intact. Such a man, once, had been William Marshal, but his like had not been seen since those tourneys in France half a century before.

As in any tournament, there were few rules once the *mêlée* had begun. It was common practice for a group of knights to search the field for some well equipped, inexperienced young cockscomb and to fall upon him all at once, to divide the spoils of victory between them. Once the man was captured, his horse and arms became the rightful property of the victor, and he would gain his release only upon payment of a fitting ransom. So might the successful combatant amass a considerable fortune. . . always providing that the bested knight had no brother, or cousin, or friend, to lead a small army of retribution later in the afternoon.

For all this, there was yet greater reward to be gained by the man who acquitted himself well upon the field. For a young knight might gain the favour of the Earl Marshal, and this would bring with it the prospect of appointment to some position of responsibility or, better still, the giving of lands in the fair hand of some eligible young heiress. All these things lay in the gift of the Earl Marshal of Pembroke, and there was not one man on the field today who did not seek to catch his eye as ardently as any peacock strutting before its would-be mate.

William the Marshal knew all this, and better than any man living. A younger son of an obscure family, he had at one time been poorer than the meanest on the field before him. But now he was master of them all. Master by means of his Earldom, aye, and master in battle if he chose to ride amongst them! If he chose.

This day the Earl Marshal wore no armour, but still the quality and colour of his attire outshone that of any of his knights. His tunic was of purple, perfect in cut and exquisitely embroidered, the hilt of his sword set with the finest gold filigree. William Marshal did not know how old he was, but he would lay claim to more than seventy years. The richness of his attire did not detract from his great age. Rather, it drew attention to the power both of his position and of the formidable height and bulk which had helped him achieve it. The squareness of his face was emphasised by a close-trimmed outline of beard which, like his hair, was not grey but silver. The lines etched around his eyes proclaimed his age with pride, and those eyes, clear beneath a steady brow, regarded the world with ferocious intensity.

The Earl Marshal might, on close observation, have been seen to smile a welcome as Anselm stood before him, but any open demonstration of affection was alien to his nature. As the youngest of five sons, Anselm would inherit nothing of his fortune, but in truth, and in so far as he loved any of his offspring, William Marshal loved Anselm the best. In his own youth, William had fought his way to success, setting out as a knight errant with nothing but his horse and his sword. It pleased him to think that Anselm might rise to become his true successor by

35

clawing his way to power in the same way. His voice, nonetheless, was gruff as he greeted his son.

'How fared you at Corfe?'

'I must speak of it in private, my lord.'

'In good time. And welcome to you, Gerald de Barri. What brings you to Pembroke?' William Marshal was one of the few who still called Gerald by the name of his Norman kinsfolk, perhaps in the vain hope of reminding the Archdeacon where his true loyalties should lie.

'I came in the company of your son, my lord. He told me of certain. . . certain developments in England, and I am not so old that I do not welcome a change of surroundings.'

'Of course. John, fetch a chair for our honoured guest.'

D'Erley bowed, and hastened to find a menial to carry out the task. Gerald noted, without surprise, that the Earl Marshal did not invite his son to the high table.

'You know Lord Rhys already, Archdeacon?' The Earl Marshal did not smile as he made the introductions. He knew of Gerald's kinship with the southern Welsh princes, and eyed both men closely to catch any fleeting expression that might hint of complicity.

Gerald could not resist the temptation to aggravate the Earl Marshal's transparent mistrust. 'I knew your father well, my Lord Rhys.'

'And you are well known to me, Gerald of Wales.' Rhys Gryg addressed the Archdeacon, surprisingly, in Norman French. An unexpected civility for a man of such ferocious appearance, though betrayed by a slovenly accent that, together with his hoarse voice, made his greeting barely intelligible.

Among a race not noted for its stature, Rhys Gryg was a giant, a shade taller even than the Earl Marshal, and with broad, stooping shoulders reminiscent of a great black bear. His hair, contrary to Welsh custom, hung long and lank, and his beard swarmed black into the wolfskin draped as a cloak. Already much the worse for drink, he slumped in his chair as he eyed the Archdeacon through drooping lids.

'You honour me, Lord Rhys of. . .' Gerald's voice stumbled in a diplomatic cough. He had taken an instant dislike to the man.

'We have something in common, my lord. Rhys ap Tewdwr was my great grandfather. He was also an ancestor of yours, I believe.'

'Aye, that he was, and in the male line.' Rhys Gryg was born of a race amongst whom noble descent was prized above all other things, and he had forgotten that Gerald too could claim Welsh royal blood. 'But you, Archdeacon...you are descended from the female side. And through that Princess Nest, of all...'

Gerald hastened to interrupt. 'Yes, indeed. But at least my side of the family has always remained within the grace of our Mother Church.'

Rhys' knuckles whitened on the handle of his tankard. He had been unwise to bait the Archdeacon, but he had not suspected that the old man would stoop so low in his argument. To thrust that unhappy incident before him, and at such a time as this...

Rhys Gryg took a long quaff of his wine, belched eloquently, and threw the dregs into the face of the huge Irish wolfhound sitting patiently by his side.

The Earl Marshal had watched the exchange with a frown. 'My son has returned with some countrymen of yours, Lord Rhys. They too were...er, guests of King John, though I fear the hospitality of Corfe could not compare with that of Pembroke.'

'Other hostages?' Rhys Gryg moistened his dry lips. Like everyone else in Wales he had oft wondered as to the fate of the son of Llywelyn. 'Here in Pembroke, you say?'

'Fetch them before us, Anselm.' The Earl Marshal glanced impatiently to his son. 'I have the best of tidings for them.'

'My lord, I...I cannot.' Anselm's voice came in barely a whisper, and trembled with fear.

'What do you mean, lad? Bring them here at once.'

Anselm's face, as he stared up to the high table, was deathly white. He opened his mouth, but no words came forth.

Gerald could not let the ordeal continue. 'My lord Earl, you may be proud of your son's initiative. Your good tidings are that all the King's hostages are to be released, is that not so?'

'Yes...'

'Then it will please you that, thanks to Anselm, and through the providence of Almighty God, Gruffydd ap Llywelyn and his companions are already on their way in freedom to their homes.'

37

The Earl Marshal frowned to see the confusion plain on Anselm's face. 'Is this true? You set them free? You heard of the events in England, and you had the wits to foresee my command?'

Anselm could find no voice. He bowed, and without meeting Gerald's eye, gratefully departed as the Earl Marshal's nod dismissed him.

'So Gruffydd ap Llywelyn lives.' Rhys Gryg was not a devious man. He muttered into his tankard, quite unable to conceal his disappointment that Llywelyn's son had not been among the many to die in King John's prisons.

'He does.' Gerald was careful to betray no opinion upon the subject.

'A pity that we could not have travelled in company. I would have liked to meet him before he rejoins Llywelyn.' The Welshman looked squarely at the Archdeacon. 'What road did he take?'

'By now he will have set foot on the fair shores of Gwynedd.' Gerald was astonished that any man could be so unsubtle. This man who would be Lord of Deheubarth could have done no worse if he had climbed the great round keep of Pembroke and proclaimed to all his intention to abduct Llywelyn's son.

The Earl Marshal concealed a smile, and raised his goblet in a toast to Gruffydd's health. Rhys Gryg, after a moment's sulky hesitation, did the same. 'He'll arrive safe home, my lords, have no fear. That one knows how to look after his own hide!'

Gerald found it hard to remain civil to the man. 'You are well acquainted with the royal house of Gwynedd, my lord?'

'No, not I.' Rhys Gryg lapsed into Welsh, to the Earl Marshal's irritation. 'But the stories I've heard!'

'What stories?'

'From time to time English bards, er...minstrels, find their way into Wales. It seems that Gruffydd was not idle in his four years in Corfe.'

'Indeed?'

'He attempted escape, and more than once. And they dared not lay a finger on him, so fearful were they of his father's revenge! He bribed his guards with promises, he had the whole castle believing that he was the future King of Wales and would make their fortunes! They even said. . .' Rhys Gryg lowered his voice to a conspiratorial whisper, 'They even said that Gruffydd feasted, while his men starved on the slops.'

'For myself, I would not be inclined to believe the words of travelling players. Least of all, English ones. They are not like your bards, Lord Rhys. They sing to eat, and not for singing's sake. Most of them are no more than beggars.'

'A man of your calling might have more regard for beggars.'

'The Church is expected to feed them. But there is no compulsion for us to relish their company.'

The Earl Marshal broke into the conversation. 'How old is Llywelyn's son, Lord Rhys?' He spoke in French, and with some impatience.

Rhys Gryg shrugged. He could not recall.

'I do not believe he can be more than twenty years old.' Gerald was embarrassed by his own ignorance. For some reason, Llywelyn had of late been reluctant to discuss young Gruffydd, other than to demand his release.

'Less than that, I should say. Much less.'

The Earl Marshal seemed to find Rhys Gryg's words reassuring. 'Then he is only a boy.'

'Only a boy?' Rhys Gryg rose at once to the challenge. 'Lord Llywelyn ap Iorwerth was but twelve years old when he came to power. The bards still sing of it! *Great was the number of his enemies, but they who fell before him were greater in number than the stars!*'

Rhys Gryg's eyes traced the figure of the serving wench who came to the table, a pitcher in her hands. She set down the wine before the Lord of Deheubarth, and picked up the silver coin. Not a word was spoken as she cleared the platters, but as she departed Rhys Gryg watched her every step to the kitchen doorway.

'And how is your good lady, my Lord Rhys?' asked Gerald. It seemed an opportune moment to ask. The Earl Marshal, unlike the King, well understood that the good treatment of hostages would likely reap some future reward, and had permitted Rhys Gryg every comfort, including the company of his wife.

39

'The woman has no stomach for sport,' grinned Rhys Gryg, unabashed. 'She rests in the tower.'

'I trust she is not unwell.'

Rhys Gryg shrugged. It was of no consequence. 'There's months yet before the child arrives.'

'Your firstborn?' asked Gerald politely. First by his wife, perhaps, but Deheubarth was already well populated with the illegitimate brats of its self-proclaimed Lord.

Rhys Gryg yawned and reached for his tankard. The hound flinched.

A mere handful of knights remained on the torn and bloody field. To an armoured man, the summer sun could be his greatest enemy. The chain-mail would grow hot and heavy, the padding beneath soaked with sweat, and the air would grow stale within the furnace of the closed helm. It was a mercy to all the weary knights when the sun sank redly to its own defeat among the dark distant clouds beyond the waters of Milford Haven.

Gerald de Barri wondered idly if the sweat of a man might cause his armour to rust. He had never regretted his decision to enter the Church, and rued it less as he watched the spent knights slash and stab at one another in final desperation to prove their worth. Beside him, the Earl Marshal watched with a half smile of nostalgia. He no longer cared to ride into battle himself, but his greatest pleasure was to watch and spur on the gallant endeavours of others. Two of his own sons had been on the field today, and their strength, their determination in conflict, their magnanimity in victory, had been a fine example to all.

From the thinning tangle of combat, a knight mounted upon a heavy grey mare broke free to canter to the foot of the bank before the high table. He dipped his lance to the Earl Marshal, set it upright at his stirrup, and tilted the helm from his face with a gauntletted hand. His features were those of the Earl Marshal himself, lacking only the years and the strength of character. His coat of arms bore a red lion emblazoned across a green and gold ground, and was marked with an emblem resembling a horizontal letter 'E'. This, by his shield, was the eldest son of William Marshal, heir apparent to the Earldom of Pembroke.

'With your permission, my lord Earl,' said William the Younger, 'I will call the halt.'

'Do so,' the Earl Marshal nodded his assent. 'And invite the victors to join us in the great hall.'

VIII

The great hall of Pembroke Castle did not bear comparison with the splendour of those of Windsor and Corfe, but it was undoubtedly the finest in Wales. Its outer stone walls soared two storeys high, the hall itself being the upper floor with great oaken roof beams arching into the dim obscurity of dust and cobweb. The single large window was shuttered against the cool night air, and a huge log fire roared in the hearth at the centre of one long wall, close by the wooden stairway from the undercroft beneath. Blue woodsmoke curled up the chimney, or wafted gently into the room, rising to filter out through the cracks and chinks between the roof tiles.

The sweet aroma of burning applewood masked a multitude of other smells. In a society where bathing was regarded as a reckless abberation, any gathering was accompanied by a stench proportional to the number of persons present and as varied as their individual occupations, from tanner to tinker, from soldier to swineherd. Monks, it must be said, were required to wash every evening, and on occasion were even known to endure total immersion in river or sea. The layman would throw up his hands in horror at such an idea, and shake his head in wonder at the harsh deprivations of the monastic life.

The long table seated fully four score guests. Here in the great hall of Pembroke the Earl Marshal lived, ate and slept, along with his closest followers, while guardsmen and servants occupied the dark undercroft beneath. Talk was loud and boasts louder still. Serving wenches scurried to and from the kitchen bearing ever more jugs of wine and ale to slake the prodigious thirsts of the revellers, while dogs prowled beneath the tables, snarling and fighting over scraps to the delight of the onlookers.

41

Gerald de Barri wondered, as he came late to the table, how the Norman English could ever boast of being more civilised than the Welsh. Oddly, there was an empty chair next to William Marshal, and at his beckoning, Gerald found himself seated between the Earl Marshal and a graceful Welsh woman. She wore a green gown of becoming simplicity, and her dark hair cascaded about her shoulders in what might have been a conscious affront to the elaborate headwear of the Norman ladies.

'The Lady Regat, wife to Lord Rhys Gryg,' said the Earl Marshal by way of introduction. 'And this, my lady, is the renowned Gerald de Barri, former Archdeacon of Brecon. A kinsman of your husband.'

'I have heard much of your writings, Gerald of Wales,' said Regat in slow, hesitant French.

Gerald was surprised that she could speak the language at all, and said so. The lady blushed to the roots of her raven hair, and turned her attention to the dish of mussels that had been set before her.

'And you have already met my lady.' The Earl Marshal gestured to his wife at his left.

The Lady Isabel wore a gown of the same purple as the Earl Marshal's cloak, her greying hair caught up in an ornate head-dress. A small and slender woman with the fading charm of a primrose in May, she had borne him their eighth child thirteen years ago. He expected no more of her.

Isabel smiled most cordially at Gerald. 'I must thank you for the trouble you have taken over our son. I begged him to join us here.' She glanced sharply at her husband. 'But after what you said to him, my lord, it is little wonder he stays away.'

'My little brother skulks in the gatehouse through shame!' Her eldest son William interrupted rudely, already the worse for drink. 'It takes a rare incompetence to fail in so simple a task.'

'You say that Anselm failed?' Gerald feigned confusion.

The Earl Marshal smiled grimly, his voice in a whisper to avoid Regat's hearing. 'Anselm has confessed to me how Llywelyn's son escaped him. You may have deceived Rhys Gryg, Archdeacon, and I thank you for that, but you did not deceive me.'

'Then what is to be done, my lord?'

'With Anselm?' The Earl Marshal looked narrowly at the old Archdeacon. 'Do not trouble yourself over Anselm, Gerald de Barri. You did not come to Pembroke out of concern for my son.'

'No. Not entirely, my lord. I also seek news of a new charter upon which the King is said to have set his seal. I gather that it has caused the King's hostages to be released, that it is a treaty for peace, and that it enshrines the rights of Church and barony. I hear that this charter constitutes the most important event since William of Normandy set his foot upon English soil at Hastings. And yet I wonder why the Bishopric of St David's was left to hear of it by chance. You, my lord Earl Marshal, were present at its signing, I believe?'

'Er...I was.' William Marshal, for once, was at a loss. 'I must apologise for not informing St David's sooner, Archdeacon. I have been much occupied with...with more pressing matters. D'Erley will see that it is copied for you. Did you hear, John?'

'Yes, my lord.' D'Erley had appeared at his master's elbow with another errand in mind. 'The bard of the court of Deheubarth asks if you would honour him by choosing a ballad.'

'That is most courteous,' said the Earl Marshal, clearly surprised that the Welsh could be anything of the sort. 'But...'

'A bard? Here at Pembroke?' Gerald could scarce credit it.

'A few of Rhys Gryg's household shared his captivity, and paid well for the privilege.' The Earl Marshal leaned forward to catch the eye of Rhys Gryg's wife. 'What would it please you to hear, my lady?'

Regat blinked at the Earl Marshal, her eyes wide and ingenuous as those of a doe. She had, it appeared, not been attending to the conversation.

'Your bard is to sing for us,' Gerald explained in Welsh. 'The Earl Marshal invites you to choose.'

Regat considered for a moment, and broke into a cunning smile. 'Have him sing the ballad he composed last month. My husband suggested the tale it tells.'

'Indeed?' said Gerald politely as he watched d'Erley hurry to relay her wish to the bard. There had been a question nagging at his mind since he had taken the empty chair between Regat and the Earl Marshal. 'Where, by the way, is Lord Rhys?'

'He has retired to his chamber in the tower,' said Regat with an odd smile.

'I trust he is not ill?' This was a fine banquet, and such abstinence did not seem to be in the character of Rhys Gryg.

'He has retired, my lord, in the company of his latest harlot.'

Gerald choked on his wine. It was not the adultery that shocked him. That was common enough, to Gerald's despair, amongst Normans as well as Welsh. It was the calm, almost amused fashion in which this gentle beauty spoke of it, as though revelling in the knowledge of her lord's weakness. It served only to prove, as Gerald had always believed, that the innocent appearance of the fair sex was merely a mask for the duplicity of their nature.

The Earl Marshal glanced at the old Archdeacon in some surprise, but forbore to ask what revelation could possibly have deprived Gerald de Barri of speech. Conversation, indeed, was subsiding throughout the hall, for the Earl Marshal's men had been strictly briefed upon the importance of appeasing the Welsh, and it would be the height of ill manners not to listen attentively to the words of a bard.

The bard appeared from amongst a knot of Rhys Gryg's men by the door, his step graceful, his clothing in contrived disrepair, his eyes fixed upon the rafters as he wandered the length of the hall. His harp uttered a simple melody, soon to be blended into the contrasting tune of his song in the strictest metres of *cynghanedd*. It was a form of verse that flowed from the tongue, with a rhythm and quality of sound that could beguile even those with no knowledge of its meaning, but the eyes of the Earl Marshal glazed almost before the bard had finished the first verse. He loathed above all things the language of his enemies, the language that could turn so swiftly from song to battle cry. Gerald saw his head begin to nod, and for the sake of the fragile peace began quietly to translate the bard's words.

'He sings of Rhys ap Tewdwr... my great-grandfather, you recall. He tells of how King William the Conqueror marched with his army through Rhys ap Tewdwr's lands on his pilgrimage to St David's, and how ill the Welsh received his provocative show of strength.' Gerald paused, for the bard's song touched upon things that the Earl Marshal would not wish to hear. 'Er... and he goes on to relate how Rhys ap Tewdwr bought from the

44

English King the right to rule his own lands, and how well he ruled, and how he and the King at last became friends. But when Rhys ap Tewdwr died and the Norman lords of the Marches treacherously invaded his Welsh lands . . .'

'*Treacherously?*' The Earl Marshal, now fully awake, barely retained the self control to keep his voice down. 'If there was treachery, then it was that of the Welsh! They betrayed our trust, it was they who attacked us!'

'But this was over a century ago, my lord. Perhaps the chroniclers . . .'

'It is the thrice-accursed Welsh who hide the truth! Always it has been so!' The Earl Marshal turned to glare at the bard, but the man smiled in his sublime ignorance of the French tongue and sang on.

Gerald abandoned his translation. He did not think the Earl Marshal would respond well to an account of the glorious victories of the men of Deheubarth over the Norman barbarians. Mercifully, d'Erley came to his master's shoulder, distracting him from the song.

'My lord, the captain of the guard has brought in a Welshman, and asks what is to be done with him.'

'Brought in, you say?' The Earl Marshal's voice was as quiet as that of d'Erley, for neither wished Regat to hear.

'Your seal hunters were returning from Ramsey Island, my lord, and fished him out of the sea. They thought it best to bring him here.'

'And why do you trouble me with this?'

'There is a madness in him, my lord. He speaks nothing but the names of Gruffydd ap Llywelyn and . . . and of Anselm, my lord.'

IX

'Release him.'

The Welshman stumbled slightly as the soldiers stood aside. A greater contrast to Rhys Gryg of Deheubarth could hardly have been imagined, and the Earl Marshal could scarce credit that this slight and trembling wretch could be of the same race. His limbs

45

were pale and wasted, his eyes downcast, and the remnants of his clothes were rimed with salt and reeked of rotting fish. His close-cropped hair, and one side of his sallow face, were seared as if by flames.

'Welcome!'

The Earl Marshal's sudden remark broke the silence and caused the Welshman to start in alarm.

Unbidden, John d'Erley acted as his lord's translator. '*Croeso.*'

The Welshman raised his eyes first to d'Erley, then to the Earl Marshal, but did not seem reassured by the greeting.

'You have nothing to fear in Pembroke. England is at peace with Wales, there are no prisoners, no hostages now.' The Earl Marshal spoke quietly for his squire to translate.

'*Maen nhw i gyd wedi marw!*' The Welshman spat forth the words like venom, his voice torn between tears and rage. The soldiers backed away, the assembly recoiled without even knowing what he had said.

'All dead. . .?' Gerald heard his own voice, feeble and distant.

'Who is dead?' Regat rose from her chair, and placed her hands upon her countryman's shoulders. 'Regat is my name, I am a kinswoman of Llywelyn ap Iorwerth of Gwynedd. Who is dead?'

The Welshman stared at her. 'Gruffydd. . .son of the Lord Llywelyn ap Iorwerth. And all who sailed from Corfe, all slain.'

'Slain?' Gerald would not of choice have spoken Welsh in such company, but for this purpose. . . 'A strong word, my friend. Whom do you accuse?'

'*Y cachgi o Sais* who took us from Corfe.'

John d'Erley repeated the exchange, diluting nothing of the Welshman's insult.

The Earl Marshal's brow darkened. 'You will repeat that to my son's face!' He lowered his voice, conscious of Regat's sharp glance, and turned to his wife. 'Fetch Anselm! He will give the lie to this dog!'

As Isabel departed in silence, the Earl Marshal's stony gaze rested upon the Welshman. Regat had poured wine for him, but the goblet trembled in his hands. His eyes darted around the hall, seeing only enemies.

'You have nothing to fear while I am here,' said Regat gently.

The Earl Marshal's fingers drummed his impatience upon the

wooden table. 'You must be exhausted, my lady Regat. In your condition you should not deny yourself sleep.'

Regat's eyes flashed her contempt. 'And at your ripe age, my lord Earl, you should have been long abed! Shall we allow this poor fellow to speak, while breath remains in his body?'

Without looking again at the Earl Marshal, Regat returned to the table, leaving the Welshman to stand alone between the guards. He took a long, slow drink from his goblet, and wiped his mouth upon a tattered sleeve as he waited for silence from his audience. Every ear strained to catch the soft-spoken words as Regat translated his narrative.

'My name is Elidyr ab Idwal. My kinsmen farm the foothills of the Eryri below Dinas Emrys, the ancient fortress of my lord Llywelyn ap Iorwerth.'

'The fortress was built before even King Arthur's time,' Gerald whispered to the Earl Marshal. 'There was a prophecy. . .'

'Pray let him continue, Archdeacon.' The Earl Marshal was not interested in Welsh folklore and knew, moreover, that it was a subject upon which the Archdeacon would expound for hours.

Elidyr ab Idwal glanced from one to the other, waiting for their silence before he dared continue. 'Four years ago the armies of your King marched into Gwynedd, and took many castles along the Conwy before they met their inevitable defeat. I chanced to be in one of those castles, and that is how I came to forsake the great mountains of my home for the blackness of an English dungeon.' He paused, and the Earl Marshal could be heard to utter a prayer for patience.

'Yes,' said Gerald tactfully. 'But we are anxious to hear the fate of the hostages.' How typical of the Welsh, to turn a testimony into a ballad. He supposed he should be thankful that it was not framed in song. They were all bards under the skin.

'Then I will not tell you, my lords, of the long months and years we spent at the mercy of our gaolers. They fed us only the rotting scraps from the English table, and little enough of that. To keep ourselves alive, we used promises to bribe a woman of the castle to bring us more food. When the gaolers found out, they hanged her. But not at once. First they. . .'

'When you have finished *not* telling us of your imprisonment,' Gerald interrupted, before the narrative should become too grisly

47

for the ears of the fair Lady Regat, 'perhaps you would proceed to the events following your release.'

'When our prison doors were opened, we had no memory of the day nor of the season. It was then we were met by your Norman lord, with his orders to bring us to Pembroke.'

'You speak of Squire Anselm?' asked Gerald.

'I do. At first we refused to go peaceably with him, but my lord Gruffydd ap Llywelyn said the Norman had the look of a fool, and this was our best chance of escape. And even if we could not gain our freedom, we thought a Norman prison in Wales could be no worse than a Norman prison in England. He took us down to the harbour, and set us down below the deck of a galley. And there he left us, bound hand and foot amongst the rotting fish and the bilge water, and he wondered why we grew sick!'

'*Get on with it, man!*'

'I know not how many days we were at sea. For a time we lacked the spirit to think of escape, but then the crew began to show us more kindness than did our captors. They were Cornishmen and understood a little of the language, and they hated the oppressors as much as we. They said they dared not raise their hands against the Normans, but one night they cut us free. We could have killed our captors, but we chose to let them live. We set them ashore close to Tyddewi and then. . .'

Elidyr's voice cracked. It was as if all the breadth and detail of his story had been but a means to delay its ending. 'We were well out from land when the fire took hold. The flames spread from below, they ran along the planks, they leapt into the sail and devoured the rigging. I trusted my life to the sea, rather than wait for the fire to take me. Would that my comrades had done the same.'

'So that was the light in Ramsey Sound!' Gerald turned to the Earl Marshal, to all the Norman lords who would rather believe nothing of the Welshman's testimony. 'My lords, a burning ship was indeed seen from the castle of St David's on that very night!'

Elidyr looked sharply at the old Archdeacon, wondering what he could have said to create such a stir. '*Be' ddywedsoch chi, f'arglwydd?*'

Gerald smiled at the courtesy of the Welshman's question. Clearly the fellow had wits enough to recognise the one man in the room who deserved his respect! 'I only confirmed that the fire was seen from my home at Tyddewi.'

'When my lord Llywelyn hears of this, the heat of it will be felt all across Wales.' Elidyr ab Idwal raised his voice, emboldened by the Archdeacon's words. 'For I swear before Almighty God that the fire was kindled by Squire Anselm to kill us all.'

'Enough of this!' The Earl Marshal would hear no more. 'D'Erley, are we to wait until dawn for Anselm? See what detains him.'

D'Erley returned within moments, hands raised to stay his lord's wrath. He came to the Earl Marshal's side, and spoke a few quiet words.

'Gone!' William Marshal's rage shattered all d'Erley's attempts at discretion.

'Yes, my lord. Anselm has fled the castle.'

There was a clamour of excited voices. To many, Anselm's disappearance served to lend the ring of truth to an unlikely story. If he were innocent, why did he not step forward to denounce his accuser?

'Rouse the guard!' The Earl Marshal was on his feet now, yet Gerald saw the weariness in his eyes. 'A hundred pennies to the man who finds Anselm. We will hear his account of this, and any man who harms him will pay dear!'

At the promise of this vast fortune, the hall erupted into a frenzy of activity. The Welsh were first to be gone, but a good many of the Normans leapt to their feet, the long benches crashing backwards to the floor as they jostled one another to be first to their horses.

William the Younger bowed briefly to his father, and left with greater dignity than most.

God help us.' It was the voice of young William's wife, but her words echoed the dread thoughts of every man and woman who remained in the great hall of Pembroke.

This wretched Welshman, so worthy of pity, so secure in the victim's role, would incite a new war with his soft words.

X

The fire collapsed into its own dying heart, taking with it William Marshal's hopes for peace.

The Earl Marshal's careful plans to increase his power in Wales had been doomed from the moment Gruffydd ap Llywelyn escaped his son's custody, but now matters had taken a far graver turn. Guilty or no, how could Anselm have been so stupid as to run? Now that he could give no account of himself, the inevitable accusation would not be slow in coming. . . the accusation that the Earl Marshal had plotted from the first to murder the son of Llywelyn ap Iorwerth.

Against that charge, however false, the fragile peace offered by the charter of the barons could not hope to endure.

Lady Regat leaned forward in her chair, her chin cradled in the fingers of one slender hand, her green eyes eager. The Earl Marshal sat motionless, impassive as the weathered stones of his great keep. Gerald de Barri watched, waited, and for once knew that his own wise counsel was not wanted by any of those present.

Elidyr ab Idwal had not moved when the bulk of the assembly rushed to obey the Earl Marshal's rousing cry. He stood where the guards had left him, gazing at the faces of those remaining in the hall, and not at all displeased by the reaction of his audience. Indeed it had been an audience of which any bard might be proud.

The depleted mob of the Earl Marshal's liegemen moved forward, and ranged themselves about the head of the table like spectators in an arena. Gerald took the crucifix from about his neck, and with great deliberation set it down upon the table before Elidyr ab Idwal. 'I am. . .I was once Archdeacon of Brecon, in the see of St David's. Now, by the Cross. . .'

'*Gerallt Gymro ydych chi?*' The Welshman could not conceal his awe.

'Yes, my son, some call me Gerald of Wales.' Gerald did not allow himself to smile, though such recognition was always a delight to him. 'Now. By the Cross upon which our Lord allowed His son to suffer, swear to the truth of what you have told us, in peril of your soul.'

With a calm strangely noble, Elidyr placed his blistered right hand upon the silver crucifix. '*Yn enw Duw a Dewi*, I so swear.'

Gerald kissed the crucifix and replaced it around his neck. He wondered what the Earl Marshal would do now, but it was Regat who broke the silence.

'Speak, any man who doubts the truth of what we have heard this night.'

The Earl Marshal rose to his feet, his face without expression, and turned to Regat with cold, rigid courtesy. His voice was infinitely tired, his words indistinct as though spoken in sleep. 'My dear lady, this is not the place for such a question, nor is it your place to ask it.'

'Is it not? And who better, tell me?' Regat's eyes flashed her anger as she stood face to face with the Earl Marshal.

'This accusation, my lady, is the concern only of your lord Rhys Gryg, and until he is informed, I fail to see what it profits us to pursue the matter further.' The Earl Marshal raised his voice only a fraction, but the hall fell silent to hear him. 'A trial will decide the truth of it. When Squire Anselm returns, then he will answer this fellow's testimony and give his own account. Until then, the Welshman will remain in Pembroke under our protection.'

'No!' Regat cried at once.

'Under the protection of the Earl of Pembroke, my lady, with my word upon his safety. For the moment he will be placed in the care of my physician, who may find that something can be done for his injuries.' At this, John d'Erley escorted Elidyr from the hall. The Earl Marshal smiled thinly. 'Of course, my lady, if you are so concerned, then you are welcome to stay in Pembroke yourself for as long as it may please you.'

Hiding her own indecision, Regat turned away from the Earl Marshal. 'I will speak with my husband.'

'And high time that she did.' The Earl Marshal scowled after Regat as she left the hall. He would never have tolerated such outlandish behaviour from his own wife. How could Rhys Gryg be so weak as to allow this woman to act on his behalf?

Gerald poured more wine for himself and the Earl Marshal. 'Elidyr ab Idwal must count himself fortunate to have such an ally.'

'Do you believe his story, Archdeacon?'

'Yes, I do. The burning ship was seen in Ramsey Sound. The guard who saw the fire took it for a dragon, and at the time I thought nothing of it, but now. . . I must believe it.'

'Even if a burning ship was seen, there can be no proof that my son was responsible.'

'We dare not take lightly what the Welshman has said. If Anselm is innocent, then why has he fled?'

'You do not know my son!'

'Do you yourself know him, I wonder?'

The Earl Marshal subsided, slouching back in his chair, no more the great soldier but a tired old man faced with an impossible dilemma. 'No, Gerald, perhaps I do not know him. I could not say that Anselm is incapable of such an act. To my knowledge he has never killed a man, but neither would he allow a slight to go unrevenged.'

'He told me that Gruffydd ap Llywelyn stole his sword.'

'Yes. . .I saw it was missing. It was my gift to him when we set out for England. He valued it highly.'

'Well then, my lord? Would he have killed to avenge his loss?'

'He. . .he might have acted blindly, by the only means he could. He always did lack the wits to foresee the consequence of his actions. . .'

Gerald nodded in agreement, surprised that the Earl Marshal would confide in him upon such a matter. 'Have faith, William. There is, as you say, no proof. If there was a fire aboard the ship, there is no proof that Anselm or any of his men started it. Nor is there even proof that Llywelyn's son is dead.'

'The word of any Welshman will be proof enough for Llywelyn, however we argue against it. He will want to see Anselm hang. I come to think that it might be better for us all to give him his wish, whether Anselm be guilty or no. . .' The words would have seemed callous, were it not for the strain showing in William Marshal's voice.

Gerald allowed a pause before his next question. 'You would have no objection if I were to speak to this. . .Elidyr?'

The Earl Marshal was on his guard immediately. 'For what purpose?'

Gerald shrugged. 'I speak his language. Who knows, he may confide to me what he would not dare say in your presence.'

'The confessional?'

'No! You know me better than that, my lord.'

'He recognised you by your title.' The Earl Marshal did not attempt to conceal his suspicion.

'Who would not?'

'Go and speak with him then, Giraldus Cambrensis, for what good it may do. And remember that you are only a quarter Welsh. The rest of you is Norman.'

There might have been a smile in the Earl Marshal's eyes, but it was hard to tell.

XI

The infirmary of Pembroke Castle was a tiny hut that would have served equally well as a pigsty. From the wattle and daub walls hung feathers and bones, hooves and antlers, dried snakes and toads, and a variety of unrecognisable fragments of plant and animal collected by the physician in his mystic apprenticeship half a lifetime ago. On the rough table in the middle of the room flickered the tiny yellow flame of a tallow lamp. Beside it lay a stone bowl which might have been carved before the time of the Romans, and in the bowl fermented a potion of the same grey-green hue as the dried herbs which hung in bunches from the rafters above.

From the shadows emerged a tiny, grotesque fellow with matted white hair that fell as cobweb beyond his hunched shoulders and tangled with the amulets about his throat. If this creature were the physician of Pembroke, then his medicine surely owed more to Merlin than to Hippocrates. The Archdeacon's hand instinctively sought his crucifix as he announced his business, and to his immense relief the apparition left his den to disappear into the pre-dawn darkness, muttering in pre-dawn Welsh.

53

As Gerald's eyes became accustomed to the dim light, he saw against the far wall a tangled pile of skins, and amid these relics lay Elidyr ab Idwal.

Elidyr stared at his visitor with suspicion, but not surprise. 'Are you here as another leech, or as my confessor?'

'I am here to talk.' Pushing aside the lamp and the bowl, Gerald sat himself on the edge of the table. It creaked alarmingly, but held his weight. 'Has the physician seen to those burns?'

'He gave me a salve for them.'

'Is this it?' Gerald looked with distaste at the contents of the bowl.

'No. That is for a more grievous ailment, so the physician says. He has told me that a black demon lies caged within my ribs, gnawing at my heart to make me tell such lies. He spoke his incantations to the skull of a toad, steeped it in that foul brew and bade me drink.'

Gerald could well understand the disgust in Elidyr's voice, and cast the bowl to the floor. 'No doubt he acts on the Earl Marshal's orders.'

'But you, Gerallt Gymro . . . you believe I spoke the truth?'

Gerald could not answer the question. Not yet, at least. 'You said you chanced to be in one of the castles that fell to King John's army. Were you there to defend it?'

'Every man, woman and child was there to defend it!'

'You have not the bearing of a soldier.'

'Every Welshman will fight when the need arises. You should know that, you write of us in your books. Is that all you want of me, Gerallt Gymro? A new story?'

'I want the truth, Elidyr, nothing more. How can you be so sure that all your comrades died in the fire?'

'The men who pulled me from the sea searched until well past dawn for other survivors, but could find no one.'

Gerald nodded grimly. 'Still, you cannot be certain they are dead. And where is your proof that it was Anselm who set the ship ablaze?'

'The fire began below decks, and none were there but the Normans. Anselm was their leader, the responsibility was his alone.'

'So you said, when you told your story before the Earl Marshal

54

and the Lady Regat. So you said in anger, seeking only your own revenge.'

'A just revenge, you cannot deny!'

'Revenge is not the path of a true Christian, my son. I cannot help but wonder whether you seek retribution upon Anselm because of his crime, or because of his race.'

'I do not understand, my lord...'

'Because a man has been wronged, that does not make him incapable of sin! Four years you were held hostage, and now you must despise the Normans...all of them. I could hardly blame you for that. But I can blame you for acting so blindly against an innocent man.'

'So now you are accusing *me*?'

'You acknowledge that you did not see the fire start, and in truth it could have been nothing more than accident. Yet you would have your revenge upon Anselm and his father even though it was not they who held you captive...'

'I did not choose to come to Pembroke, my lord. The seal hunters brought me here. They gave me clean water to drink and the best food I've tasted since I left these shores. I thought they were my friends until I saw the towers of this castle! They must have expected a good reward for delivering one of the enemy into their lord's hands.'

'Did you not realise they would bring you to Pembroke?'

'They told me their master was the Bishop of St David's.'

'What?' Gerald was torn between outrage and laughter. Yes, the seal hunters might well have said such a thing to whoever they met, for Ramsey was part of the Bishop's estate and the Earl Marshal's men had no business to be poaching it.

'In the hall, my lord, I did not mean to say what I did... But once they bade me speak, I had to speak the truth.'

'And the truth is that all the hostages from Corfe are dead...'

Gerald paused as he recalled Anselm's account of the Welshmen's excited chatter about Dewi Sant. How would Elidyr react to the name? 'So it seems that not even Saint David could save them.'

'What do you know of Dewi Sant?'

Gerald smiled affably. 'Well, my son, I was once his Archdeacon. I mentioned our Saint only because Anselm said you were speaking of Saint David before you set him and his soldiers ashore.'

'All the time we were on that ship, we prayed to God and to Dewi Sant for deliverance, and it seemed as if our our prayers were answered. When we put in to Porth Clais to set the Normans ashore, I wanted to go to the shrine to give thanks. But my comrades were too eager to enjoy their new freedom. They wanted no delay in returning to their homes.'

'And then came the fire?'

'Yes, my lord.' The Welshman's voice was barely a whisper.

Gerald remained silent, regarding Elidyr closely as if to read in his face more than his words would convey. With one slender hand, Elidyr was clutching at a simple bronze cross that hung by a leather thong about his neck. Gerald saw in surprise that it was not of the Celtic form, that there was no circle supported by the arms of the cross.

'Where did you come by that?'

'It.. it was given to me.'

'In England?'

'Yes...'

'In prison?'

Elidyr gazed long at the old Archdeacon, unable to trust this man of God who spoke Welsh so confidently with a Norman accent, who conversed with a Welsh prisoner, yet who sat by the Earl Marshal in a Norman hall. He slipped the cross out of sight beneath his shirt and would say no more.

XII

The tall ship sailed the midsummer night with death in her wake. Her prow, swept up as that of a Viking longboat, was carved into the snarling head of a savage beast, nostrils agape, eyes astare, teeth bared and bloody. Her sails of scarlet caught the wind, but were not content with that alone. The masts and spars shivered and resolved themselves into the skeletal hands of a bat, crooked fingers webbed with the diaphanous membrane of nightmare wings. The dragon stretched its neck, uncoiled its sinuous body from the rigid outline of the ship's hull, and sprang to the air with a scream of fiery breath. But the flames, flung back on the wind, caught the taut wings even as the beast soared aloft. The dragon roared its anguish, consumed in its own fire, and fell to its funeral pyre in a valley strewn with bones. The screams were those of dying men, and a raven descended to scavenge its prey...

Gerald de Barri jerked back to consciousness, his heart thumping in his chest, his breath roaring loud as the dragon of his dream. And what a dream! He sought to recall it, but it slipped through the fingers of his mind, elusive as the morning mists of the Sacred Hollow. He opened his eyes. Sunlight streamed through the open window of the great hall, brightening the swirling clouds of dust and stale woodsmoke, and the lady Regat leaned over him, quiet and disconsolate.

'Good morning, my lord Archdeacon.'

'And to you, my lady. I trust you slept well.'

'Hardly at all. I will be blunt, my lord. I must beg a favour of you.'

'It will be a pleasure, my lady. Last night you acted with laudable compassion towards that unhappy liegeman of Llywelyn. And all the more remarkable, since Llywelyn has long been at odds with your lord.'

'But I am Llywelyn's kinswoman, Archdeacon, and the ties of blood run deep. Am I to blame, that he married me to a southerner to try to forge bonds of loyalty between Gwynedd and Deheubarth? Llywelyn has always sought his allies where they suit him best... be it in Wales or in Ireland, even in England or in Rome.'

'If Llywelyn seeks peace, my lady, I can find no fault in him for that. Blessed are the peacemakers.'

'Peacemakers!' Regat smiled at the old man's naïvety. 'Years ago, when my Lord Rhys' father led the men of Deheubarth against the Normans, Llywelyn joined with King John's army to oppose him. Now Gwynedd has made allies of the Norman barons against King John. Llywelyn has seized Shrewsbury, and the Welsh rejoiced at the taking of an English town. And then what did he do? He returned it to his Norman henchmen! There are those who say that, in his quest for power, Llywelyn forgets his own people.'

Gerald could barely believe that he had heard a woman speak thus, but it confirmed his dawning suspicion that it was Regat who was the true driving force behind the Lord of Deheubarth. Rhys Gryg, with all his bluster, lacked her intelligence, and she must... Gerald firmly put aside his train of thought, it was unworthy of an Archdeacon. 'My lady, what did you come here to ask of me?'

'Last night, my lord, I spoke with Elidyr. With our bard at hand I stayed by him while he slept, lest the Earl Marshal had some treachery in mind.'

'And did the Earl Marshal make any attempt to harm the prisoner?'

'No.' Regat admitted the truth reluctantly. 'But I am sure that Elidyr will be in danger the moment we leave Pembroke. That is why I have come to you, my lord Archdeacon. My Lord Rhys wishes to leave at once, so that he can tell Llywelyn of the events that have come to light here. He also wishes, as I do, that Elidyr be allowed to travel with us.'

'Why?' Gerald doubted Rhys Gryg's concern for the health of any man of Gwynedd.

'Llywelyn may not accept the word of my husband...that is what makes Elidyr of such importance. Only by speaking with him directly would Llywelyn believe his son was murdered. If we leave him here in Pembroke, there is nothing to prevent the Earl Marshal from silencing him for ever.'

'For myself, I would be inclined to trust the Earl Marshal's word.'

'But I would not! Elidyr will not live beyond today if he remains here. You, my lord Archdeacon, can save him.'

'How?' Gerald was curious, though he had no intention of involving himself with Regat's scheming.

'Speak with the Earl Marshal and my Lord Rhys...they have been arguing since dawn. Lord Rhys wants Elidyr released to him, but the Earl Marshal insists that he remain here until Anselm is brought to give his own account. It seems impossible that they can ever reach agreement, but you, Archdeacon, with your devotion to both nations... Well, I see no reason why you could not arrange a compromise.'

'I can see several reasons, my lady Regat, but I am willing to try.'

They picked their way through the sleeping bodies littering the floor of the great hall, and stepped out into the fresh morning air. It was raining, and would doubtless continue to do so all day, but the cool rain was a blessed relief from the rank odours that pervaded the hall. They passed the high prison tower, where the stench would be worse still for the old sergeant who had shared Anselm's humiliation on their return from Corfe, and circled the broad base of the Great Keep. Even as they approached the imposing wooden stairway to the first floor, they could hear angry voices from above.

The lady Isabel stormed down the stair, her long gown sweeping the steps, her drawn face damp with tears of anger. Regat, with a solicitude much at odds with her previous behaviour, tried to comfort the older woman, but Isabel sniffed and turned her face away.

'Is something amiss, my lady Isabel?' Gerald asked.

'My lord the Earl is in council, but he has no need of me there. I am a hindrance to him.' Her voice was bitter, and with good reason. The castle, and the Earldom that went with it, had been her father's. William the Marshal had acquired his power through marriage, and had never allowed his wife to share it. 'And you? You are on your way to see him?' She addressed her words to Gerald, but looked coldly at Regat.

'We are.' Regat met her stare.

Gerald regarded the two women in embarrassment. 'I hope to settle the dispute between your... er, your husbands.'

'The dispute over that...' Lady Isabel paused, mindful of her language before the Archdeacon, and lowered her voice to a level befitting a lady of her standing. '... that villain? Who could even consider setting him free to... to spread his poison! He told nothing but lies.'

Regat bridled at this. 'How can you be so sure?'

'My son is not a murderer!'

'Of course not,' Gerald interrupted. 'Let us pray for Gruffydd's deliverance, and for Anselm's return so that his innocence may be proven to all.' He searched the lady's evasive eyes, and was

59

disturbed by what he saw. Isabel was worried to distraction for her youngest son, but behind this he could see nothing but deceit. Lady Isabel paled, sensing that he had guessed her thoughts, and hurried on down the last few steps to disappear round the curved wall of the keep.

Regat and Gerald, thoughtful after this encounter, continued upwards in silence. There was a narrow spiral stair just inside the doorway, and as they climbed, they became aware once more of the rising clamour of voices from above. As they emerged onto the third floor, the sounds of disagreement were abruptly quenched.

The Earl Marshal and Lord Rhys Gryg sat glaring at one another across a circular oaken table. John d'Erley stood behind the Earl Marshal's chair, a silent witness to the quarrelling of his betters. A broad shaft of morning sunlight brightened the dust on the table top. With it came a chill salt breeze from Milford Haven, but colder by far was the atmosphere between the Earl of Pembroke and the Lord of Deheubarth.

'What are you doing here?' Rhys Gryg had sent his wife away an hour ago, and had not expected such disobedience.

Gerald de Barri gave her no time to reply as he stepped forward from the doorway, 'If I may offer my counsel, my lords. . .'

'There will be no compromise,' snarled the Earl Marshal. 'Unless you can devise some miracle to keep this Elidyr in Norman and Welsh custody at the same time.'

'Norman and yet Welsh?' Gerald smiled broadly. The Earl Marshal must be losing his wits to play so easily into his hands. 'You describe myself perfectly, my lord Earl. I am Norman and yet Welsh. I am Welsh and yet Norman. Deliver Elidyr ab Idwal into my care, and he will be secure.'

The Earl Marshal looked long and intensely at the old Archdeacon. 'And what would you do with him, my lord?'

'I would place him under the protection of my own kinsmen at Manorbier. There he will be held in safety until this unhappy matter is settled.'

Rhys Gryg, while reluctant to be seen to accept any solution proposed at the behest of his wife, was anxious to leave Pembroke and could think of no better compromise. 'I've no objection to that, Archdeacon, on your oath that he will be brought to testify when Anselm is found.'

William Marshal cursed his own folly. Gerald de Barri was a quarter Welsh, his mixed ancestry derived from the Norman lords of the Marches and from the southern Welsh princes. The Lord of Manorbier was Gerald's nephew, and he had a Welsh wife. Could the prisoner be trusted to their guardianship?

'Very well,' the Earl Marshal nodded at last. 'Elidyr will remain at Manorbier.'

'We have your word on his safety?' Rhys Gryg asked of Gerald.

'Elidyr will come to no harm at Manorbier.'

That, it appeared, was good enough for the Lord of Deheubarth. 'We'll be on our way north then, my lord Earl, with thanks for all your . . . hospitality.'

'You'll speak with Llywelyn?'

Regat smiled graciously. 'Have no doubts upon that score, my lord Earl. I will speak to Llywelyn myself.'

'My respects to him, then, though I shall be sending my own messengers to Gwynedd.'

Rhys Gryg laughed loud as he followed Regat from the room, his good humour restored. 'I'll warrant you will!'

The Earl Marshal listened grim faced as Rhys Gryg's laughter, twisted into a savage, distorted echo, receded down the spiral stairway. 'Follow them, John,' he told his squire. 'See that no man of Deheubarth remains within our walls. And then arrange an escort for the other Welshman to Manorbier.'

'At once, my lord. Will you be riding with them?'

'No,' said the Earl Marshal wearily. 'I must wait here. Soon the hunt for Anselm will be over.'

'Without success, I hope!'

'Do you?' The Earl Marshal's voice was bleak. At d'Erley's astonished glance he shook his head as if stung back to reality. 'You go with them, John.'

'Yes, my lord.' D'Erley was clearly pained by the exhaustion on the Earl Marshal's face. He turned, with respect, to Gerald. 'Will you accompany us to Manorbier, my lord Archdeacon?'

'Of course, though my visit must of necessity be a short one. St David's cannot be without its Archdeacon for long, whilst its Bishop has yet to take office.' Events at Pembroke had quite convinced Gerald that St David's needed him, whether the new Bishop was there or not.

The Earl Marshal rose from his chair as the Archdeacon turned to the door. 'My lord, I suppose His Grace Bishop Iorwerth will be on his way to take office, by now. I hope he will break his journey at Pembroke, there is much I wish to discuss with him.' He paused, obviously troubled by some new thought. 'Tell me, Archdeacon, is Bishop Iorwerth related to Llywelyn ap Iorwerth?'

Gerald laughed. 'Only in so far as every Welshman is related to every other, should you look back far enough. Iorwerth is a common enough name. They may be cousins ten times removed, but then . . . even the Welsh and the Normans are all sons of Adam.'

The Earl of Pembroke gave a faint smile as the Archdeacon left the room. He cared little who wore the mitre of St David's, as long as it was not Gerald de Barri. He looked forward to the arrival of the new Bishop Iorwerth, for he was uncomfortable in the knowledge that Gerald had been administering the see since the death of Bishop Geoffrey. Much as he respected the learning and wit of the Archdeacon, William Marshal could not help but be wary of Gerald's ambitions, both for himself and for Wales.

Some would dismiss Gerald, these days, as a mere irritation, a tiresome figure too old to pose any real threat. William the Marshal knew better. He knew that Giraldus Cambrensis would be a danger to Norman supremacy in Wales until the day he died. Or even, given the power of his books, for years beyond.

XIII

To Manorbier

23 June, 1215

Manorbier had been the birthplace of Giraldus Cambrensis, and was still the home of the de Barri family. Gerald himself had had three older brothers, destined to be knights all, and on the death of their father it had been Phillip who inherited the manor. In his middle years the Archdeacon had often sought retreat in his old home, for Phillip had been Gerald's favourite brother and they had remained on close terms throughout their lives. Phillip's death, fully fifteen years ago now, had come as a bitter blow to Gerald, but his grief had been softened a little by his affection for Phillip's elder son and heir.

William de Barri, now Lord of Manorbier, had almost from the cradle been like his father in his exceeding prudence, his wisdom and his good character. So like his father. . . and so different from his brother!

Gerald's pleasant thoughts were marred, his distant smile faded, as he recalled this younger nephew. With the fond expectation that the boy would one day follow in his own illustrious footsteps, Gerald had lavished all the fruits of his own learning and experience upon him. He had appointed learned tutors, he had provided his nephew with every opportunity to make his way in the Church, and ultimately he had even given up to the young man the title to his own Archdeaconry of Brecon, albeit on the understanding that the monies and the actual responsibility of the office would remain with Gerald himself. And how had his outstanding generosity been repaid?

The perfidious little scorpion had neglected his education, preferring to indulge himself in such temporal pleasures of the flesh as hunting the forests, the copious swilling of ale and the singing of bawdy Welsh ballads. Eventually he had entered into a conspiracy with the very tutor appointed by Gerald, and had succeeded in diverting all the income of the Archdeaconry to his own purse. It seemed, with hindsight, the cruellest of ironies that this younger nephew had been christened after Gerald himself.

Young William too had been sent to his uncle to further his education, but he had not scorned the Archdeacon's wisdom. Gerald recalled that even as a child William had never behaved childishly. When at the age of twelve he had accompanied Gerald and Archbishop Baldwin on their journeying throughout Wales to enlist support for the Crusade, he had amazed all with his powers of observation. Indeed, it had been young William's sharp eyes and keen memory that had provided so many of the interesting little asides in Gerald's celebrated account of that journey.

William had spent much of the remainder of his youth in Ireland, where many of the de Barris lived still, but on the death of his father Phillip he had returned to Wales. And now, a Norman lord, William de Barri was raising his own family in Manorbier...just as his father and his grandfather before him.

Gerald realised that he had little idea what to expect of William. He had visited his old home all too rarely, these past few years, but suspected that his nephew might well have become too enamoured of the Norman side of his heritage now that he was Lord of the Manor.

Gerald would say that it was difficult for others to tread the middle path between two great nations as successfully as he himself had done, but he knew better than anyone that, in truth, he had failed. The Welsh saw him as a Norman lord and mistrusted him accordingly, and he could sympathise with their feelings. But the Normans called him Welsh and had thwarted his ambitions at every turn. They had refused him the bishopric of St David's, and Gerald had become so embittered by continual, unrelenting frustration that he was beginning to wonder if he had any true friend in either camp.

Elidyr ab Idwal, riding a led horse, was immersed in his own melancholy. Gerald explained to him where he was being taken, but had his doubts as to whether Elidyr believed his reassuring words. The prisoner plainly trusted neither the Earl Marshal nor any of his race, and for this Gerald could hardly blame him.

'There is no prison at Manorbier,' he remarked, to no one in particular.

'No prison? None at all?' John d'Erley, riding by Gerald's side at the head of the mounted soldiers, found this difficult to comprehend.

'We never needed one. You forget that Manorbier is not one of the Earl Marshal's castles. It is but a manor. . .one might almost call it a farmhouse.'

'I would never venture to do that,' d'Erley smiled. Gerald's books had eulogised Manorbier, and he knew better than to belittle it before the Archdeacon. 'But where is the prisoner to be kept? Surely there is somewhere secure?'

'I remember a small storeroom that could be used.' Gerald could see little justification for keeping Elidyr in confinement, but there was no point in arguing the matter with the Earl Marshal's squire. Once d'Erley and his guard had left Manorbier, Gerald was certain that a more civilised arrangement could be devised. He was aware of the possibility that Elidyr might have the ear of Llywelyn ap Iorwerth, and he was anxious to maintain the goodwill of the Lord of Gwynedd.

'A storeroom? That should serve the purpose.' D'Erley was clearly glad to have done with the distasteful subject. 'What of your family at Manorbier, Archdeacon? I trust they are all in good health?'

'I hear little of them. I imagine they are well enough.'

'I gather they plan to build a new gatehouse.'

Gerald nodded, his hand covering a yawn.

'Yes indeed, my lord. Soon the manor will indeed become a castle befitting the House of de Barri!'

The one-sided conversation carried on unabated as the Earl Marshal's squire asked too many personal questions about the Archdeacon's family in Ireland, and touched upon the sensitive subject of the appointment of the new Bishop of St David's. Gerald barely heard him, for the palace of Lamphey was not far away now, and the chanting of the monks at prayer echoed faintly across the forested deer park.

Lamphey was a palace of the Church, a country retreat where the Bishop of St David's would retire for hunting and leisure whenever the rigours of administering the see became too much for him. Gerald recalled only too well how much time the late Bishop Geoffrey had spent at Lamphey. Given the spartan accommodation at St David's, this was scarcely surprising, but Gerald frowned as he thought of the weak will, the lack of dedication, the unashamed self-indulgence of those irresolute men who had occupied the bishopric so richly deserved by himself.

The road divided, one branch continuing eastward towards the well fortified castle of Tenby, while the party turned south to Manorbier. The air freshened now into that sweet breeze, fresh from the Irish sea, of which Gerald had written with such eloquence. It was surely true that nowhere else in Wales did the air have quite the same quality. Not even in the clear peaks of Snowdonia, the Eagle Mountains, the *Eryri*, did the wind carry with it this very breath of life.

No sooner had the breeze ruffled the manes of the travellers' horses than the castellated walls of the great hall of Manorbier came into view. The manor was sited atop a low hill, and flanked by two streams running into a narrow bay between steep cliffs. On that sandy beach, Gerald de Barri had played as a child. He had climbed those cliffs for gulls' eggs. He had stolen apples from the orchard beyond the manor walls and, once, had nearly drowned in the deep fishpond in which were bred carp and pike for the lord's table. And the small church, just across the valley, had been the setting for the first, most basic instruction that had inspired Giraldus Cambrensis to follow the life of the priesthood.

Manorbier. The place was so thronged with childhood memories that Gerald could scarcely bear to see the changes that had been wrought. As they drew near, John d'Erley could not resist the temptation to remark that the new gatehouse was already nearing completion. '. . . and in these times, I would call it a wise precaution.'

Gerald frowned at the sight of the structure as though it were a scar on the face of a dear friend, but he had to admit that it would be a significant improvement in the manor's defences. 'Manorbier has never been attacked, Squire d'Erley, though the Welsh came close. I remember that after the storming of Tenby I had to run into the church for sanctuary.'

'The Welsh stormed Tenby? I cannot recall such an event.'

'Perhaps not. But then, William Marshal has only been Earl of Pembroke for these past thirty years.'

66

'For how long has your family lived in Manorbier, Archdeacon?'
'The name of Manorbier itself dates back six hundred years,
d'Erley, can you comprehend that? On this site stood the house
of Abbot Pyr of Caldey, *Maenor Pyr*. The monks of Caldey farmed
these lands for centuries, until the Conqueror gave the estate into
the care of Odo de Barri for services rendered. That was in the
Year of Our Lord 1090, if I recall. . .' Gerald stopped himself, and
smiled. 'But I bore you, Squire d'Erley, when your own eyes tell
you all that need be known of my birthplace.'

A deep moat surrounded the manor walls, but the portcullis
was raised, the drawbridge down. The gatehouse stood open to
all, its newly quarried limestone gleaming silver in the rain, and
there was no challenge as the horses' hooves clattered noisily
across the stout timbers. They halted within the gatehouse,
surveying the one other building of stone that served both as the
great hall and the lord's private chamber, and a dozen smaller
buildings of wattle and daub.
      Servants, peasants and a scattering of tradesmen hurried about
the courtyard, each intent upon his own business. None paid
them heed until a small woman dressed in a plain grey gown
descended the stone stairway from the hall. She crossed the bailey
to greet them.
      'Good morning, Squire d'Erley.' She gave a slight frown as she
looked towards the soldiers bearing the Earl Marshal's colours.
      'Good day, my lady.' D'Erley replied stiffly. He did not like
Lady Angharad. Her perfect French, with its deliberate Welsh
accent, unnerved him beyond measure.
      Gerald had fallen to the rear of the group as he looked around
him at the alterations that were being inflicted upon his old home.
Angharad broke into a broad smile as she saw him. 'And a warm
welcome to you, my dear uncle.'
      She was not, Gerald recalled, his true niece, but the wife of his
nephew. The Welsh wife, of his nephew William. Yes, he had
almost forgotten about Angharad.
      'What brings Gerald of Wales to Manorbier in such company?'
      Gerald was interrupted by the talkative d'Erley before he could
make his greeting.

67

'Our business is with Lord William de Barri. With the lord of this manor, Lady Angharad.'

'Lord de Barri is at home to no one at the moment. You may tell me what fortune brings you here.' Angharad's voice did not conceal her dislike for the Earl Marshal and for all who served him.

Gerald graciously removed the problem from d'Erley's hands. 'My lady, would you see to it that the weapons store is made ready to receive our guest? This is a delicate matter. Please do as I ask, and I will explain at a more suitable opportunity.'

Angharad stared with compassion at the bewildered Elidyr. Unable to understand their French, he was aware only that he was being discussed. At a sharp prod from d'Erley, he slid awkwardly from his horse to the ground, but no one moved to untie his hands. Angharad's gaze took in his wasted limbs, his scorched face, his downcast eyes and the foul condition of his clothing. He was of her own race and, moreover, she suspected that he had been cruelly used in the dungeon of Pembroke. She turned upon d'Erley, her dark eyes blazing. 'You have brought us a prisoner, Squire d'Erley, is that it? Are the dungeons and charnel houses of Pembroke so full that you must foist your captives upon us?'

'Angharad, this man is not a criminal,' Gerald told her quietly.

'Perhaps you are mistaken, my lord Archdeacon. Perhaps his being Welsh is crime enough. Is that not so, Squire d'Erley?'

'Please, my lady,' d'Erley protested. 'He claims he was witness to a murder! He has accused the son of the Earl Marshal, and we ask only that you keep him here for his own protection until the matter is settled.'

'Very well. The weapons store is below the hall, through the doorway by the stair. You may tell your men to clear it out.'

'Yes, my lady.'

Angharad had second thoughts. 'No, wait here.' She could not permit strangers to take charge of the weapons upon which the safety of Manorbier depended. She turned to a guardsman of the manor, who had been watching the proceedings from a doorway of the gatehouse. 'You, man. Take this prisoner to the kitchen. See to it that he is fed, and find him some better clothing. . . but stay by him until the storeroom is prepared.'

Angharad's eyes followed Elidyr as the guardsman escorted him across the bailey, and it was not until they were out of sight that she returned her attention to her visitors. 'Will you take some refreshment, Squire d'Erley, before you leave us?'

D'Erley hesitated, embarrassed by the clear dismissal. 'Thank-you, my lady, but the Earl Marshal expects our return to Pembroke before nightfall.'

'Then you had best hurry.'

D'Erley had no notion of how to deal with such treatment from a woman. He bade Gerald and Angharad a hasty farewell, and led the Earl Marshal's guard in their disorderly retreat across the drawbridge.

Angharad, having disposed of d'Erley and his guard, turned to Gerald. 'Is it true, my lord? A son of the Earl Marshal accused of murder? Which one?'

'Anselm, it was. He is accused of the murder of Gruffydd, son of Lord Llywelyn of Gwynedd. The man we have brought here claims to have been the only survivor after Anselm set their ship ablaze.'

Angharad shuddered. 'And is this story to be believed?'

'Who can tell? But it does seem odd that Anselm fled the castle. Nothing can be done until he is found to speak for himself. Until then, our witness is to be kept closely guarded for his own safety.'

Angharad paused, thinking long upon the possible consequences. She could not banish the dread spectre of war from her mind. 'I see that I have done the Earl Marshal an injustice. It was not in Pembroke that the fellow received his injuries. You must tell me the full story. Over supper, perhaps.'

'It will be a great pleasure, my lady Angharad.'

Gerald followed Angharad to the broad stone stair which led up to the great hall. As he approached the familiar old building, his eyes rose to the enormous window, and above the window to the array of square holes set below the eaves of the castellated roof. Doves murmured from within, and launched themselves to waft their noisy way across the courtyard. He smiled happily at the smells and sounds of his childhood.

Gerald liked pigeons. And he loved pigeon pie.

XIV

There were thirteen steps in the stairway that led to the hall. Gerald counted them anew as he climbed, and felt a thrill of pride that his memory served him so well. The stout door at the top of the stair was new to him, and intricately wrought with black iron hinges that blossomed into dragons as they uncoiled their way across the wood. Everything at Manorbier bespoke the care that had gone into its making, to proclaim that this was not a castle, not a garrison or a place of combat, but the home of a family.

The hall itself was not large, yet imparted an impressive sense of scale by its lofty height. Two storeys from rush-strewn floor to vaulted roof, it was a light and airy place. More richly ornamented than its larger counterpart at Pembroke, shields and tapestries bedecked the walls, and central among them blazed the gold and red bars of the arms of de Barri. A large window looked out over the headland to the dull greens of heather and gorse, the yellow grey of the stony beach, the shifting blue of the restless sea flecked with foam. Gerald climbed to the first of three deep steps to the window ledge. He would have been content to stand and stare, as often he had stood there as a child, but other matters demanded his attention.

'Where is my nephew?' Stepping down, Gerald realised that Angharad had disappeared.

'What?' Angharad called from the adjacent buttery, 'I was just telling cook that you are staying for dinner.'

'I asked what has become of young William.'

'Young William?' Angharad smiled a little sadly to hear her husband so described. She gestured to the room above the buttery, with its inner window looking down into the hall. 'Young William is resting in the solar. Had you not heard? He was almost killed at the Earl Marshal's tourney. I'm surprised that d'Erley was not aware of it.'

Gerald wondered if the Earl Marshal himself realised that William de Barri was ailing. The strain of the past few days must be telling upon the old soldier. 'Is his life in danger? May I see him?'

'Of course.' Angharad knew that Gerald would see him whether she forbade it or not. 'But, he may not be awake. They carried him home from Pembroke yesterday, and he has neither stirred nor spoken since.'

Gerald followed Angharad up the narrow spiral stairway to the solar. This room held more memories for him than any other. He stared at the fireplace, at the windows, the bed and chairs carved in fine oak, the tapestries bearing scenes of Arthurian legend, old friends all, and the fresh flowers strewn among the rushes on the floor.

Gerald de Barri had been born here. He had lived and slept in this room for the first ten years of his life. It was difficult indeed to brush the dust and cobweb of these lingering memories from his mind, to see the room as it was this evening, with his nephew pale and motionless upon the skins that covered the wood-framed bed.

As the Archdeacon approached to look closely at William's ashen face, the wounded man stirred a little, and with a barely perceptible groan, he opened his eyes.

'Uncle? Why have they brought you here?' William's voice was feeble, his words clipped with pain. 'Am I dying?'

'Calm yourself! I am not here to administer the Last Rites.' Gerald did not bother to ask how the injury had been acquired. The only thing that William loved more than fighting in a tournament was to boast of his brave deeds afterwards. 'Has the wound been tended?'

'Yes, by the leech at Pembroke. He was much in demand that day . . . but he vowed it's not so grievous as it looks. I took it from the Earl of Gloucester's son, damn his blood! Right on the collarbone.' William spoke through his pain with clinical relish, but curiosity triumphed over the temptation to describe his battle in every detail. 'So, uncle, if I'm to live to show my scars, then what brings you to Manorbier?'

'The Earl Marshal's business, it grieves me to say. He has sent a Welshman for your safe keeping. Angharad will explain.'

'Is the Earl Marshal here? I must greet him.' William made as if to rise.

'No,' Angharad explained. 'He sent d'Erley, along with a small escort. I took charge of their prisoner and they have returned to Pembroke. The man can be secured in the old weapons store, if the Archdeacon thinks it necessary.'

71

'You should have invited d'Erley to stay the night.'

'We need not entertain the vassals of the Earl Marshal.'

William looked to Gerald, and immediately regretted the unconscious attempt to shrug his shoulders. 'I could take issue with a knight in armour. But there is no defence against this woman!'

'You must rest now.' Angharad tidied her husband's bed by way of dismissing the Archdeacon, and though William was disposed to argue with her, Gerald was not.

Gerald wished his nephew a speedy recovery and hurried down the stair to attend to more pressing business, towards the unmistakable smell of pigeon pie.

The pie was not the only delicacy to grace the Manorbier table. There was a stew of mussels, cockles and small crabs, a large stuffed carp, and a roast saddle of mutton, all served on trenchers of hard bread that would suffice to eke out the provisions of the guards and servants when the meal was over. Gerald took the proffered place of honour, and Angharad sat by his side, the long table stretching before them flanked by empty benches. Every nobleman of the district was at Pembroke for the Earl Marshal's tournament, and Gerald was the only guest at Manorbier.

The Archdeacon spoke Grace, his prayer of thanks for the food set before them perhaps a little more hurried than was seemly, but more than compensated by the depth of his feeling. Angharad made to carve up the pie, but hesitated as she glanced across the hall. Gerald followed her gaze, and saw that they were being watched from the doorway.

'Our children. David and Nest.'

'Your daughter is the elder, if I recall?'

'By two years, yes. David is only twelve.' Angharad frowned. 'They know they are not to come here when we have guests.'

'No,' Gerald protested. 'Let them join us.' He liked children, if only because in their innocence they were ignorant of the trials and disappointments that had marred his own life.

'David, Nest, come here and meet your great-uncle. Archdeacon Gerald of Wales, the most renowned of all our line.'

David and Nest obeyed, more reluctantly than Gerald had expected. The boy said nothing, avoiding Gerald's eye, and

72

seemingly absorbed by the expression on the face of the stuffed carp. Clearly, thought Gerald indulgently, overwhelmed to be in the presence of an Archdeacon.

Nest found her voice. 'Welcome to Manorbier, my lord.'

'Thankyou, child. You will not remember the last time I was here, you must have been but five years old.' Gerald recalled the occasion well, and was astonished by the change that had come over the children in nine short years. He noted that the girl's French was perfect, without trace of a Welsh accent.

'Why do they call you *Giraldus Cambrensis*?'

Gerald's mouth was too full of hot pigeon pie, his attempt at solemnity spoiled as he was compelled to lick the gravy from his fingers. There was a long pause, as if he sought to find the answer among the growing pile of pigeon bones. 'Because that is what I am.'

'Gerald the Welshman?'

'Gerald of Wales. There is a difference.' The Archdeacon dismissed the subject with a wave of his hand as he returned to his pie.

Angharad challenged the children. 'Where have you been? I've not seen you since breakfast.'

'We walked along the cliffs to Swanlake Bay.'

'We saw some knights!' David spoke for the first time. 'They seemed to be looking for someone.'

'They were indeed,' Gerald said gravely, and explained to an eager audience the events of the previous night in Pembroke.

'Do you believe what they say about Squire Anselm?' Nest's blue eyes sparkled with excitement.

'I would not sit in judgement until I had heard his side of the story.'

'Will they find him?'

'If they have not found him by now, I doubt that they ever will.'

'Do you think he meant to kill the Welshmen when he set fire to the boat?'

'I cannot imagine.' Gerald was beginning to be irritated by Nest's questions, and wished he had not broached the subject of Anselm. He would speak no more of murders, nor of Welsh princes or Norman squires, and steered the conversation towards the more interesting subjects of his own travels and his eminent acquaintances.

As the rush torches began to sputter and burn out, the food long since devoured, Nest and David yawned mightily, and with the blessing of the Archdeacon left the hall by the spiral stairway. Angharad and Gerald assumed that they were on their way up to the solar where the whole family would sleep, and did not notice as they trod quietly down the stair to the undercroft.

Angharad smiled wearily. 'I am sorry, uncle. They should not have disturbed us. Least of all when I have so many things to ask of you.' She hesitated, yet Gerald waited patiently for her to speak. 'Was Lord Rhys Gryg allowed to leave Pembroke freely?'

'Certainly! The Earl Marshal had already released him from confinement, it was his own wish to stay for the tourney. But then, after what happened yesterday, he was eager to go. He will relish breaking the news to Llywelyn.'

'Rehearsing his weeping and wringing of hands all the way to Gwynedd, no doubt.' Angharad gave a wry smile. 'Rhys Gryg can never have been more happy than when he heard Gruffydd ap Llywelyn was dead, take my word on it. I knew him, many years ago . . . he is distantly related to my own parents, as well as to the de Barris.'

'Is he influenced by his wife?'

'By Regat?' Angharad did not attempt to hide her dislike. 'Be wary of that one. She has good reason to despise Llywelyn and all his kin.'

Of course. It was clear, now that Gerald thought of it. Llywelyn had risen to power in Gwynedd only by supplanting his father's two half-brothers. Regat must have been the child of one of them, brought up in exile, nurtured on stories of the cruelty and injustice of the Prince of Gwynedd. 'Yes, I can see now why she is so loyal to Rhys Gryg. She uses him as a tool of her own revenge against Llywelyn. I wonder . . .'

'What is it?' Angharad was surprised by the troubled expression on Gerald's face.

'I was just recalling Elidyr ab Idwal . . . the Welshman confined below. He spoke to Regat in Pembroke. I hope he does not come to regret his trust in her.'

XV

Nest and David paused at the foot of the spiral stair by the narrow doorway of the undercroft. Outside, heavy rain pounded from the blackness of the night into the sodden turf of the courtyard, invisible but for the stray flicker of a torch from the hall above. Nest took the initiative, and David cursed her for her courage as she stepped forward and tapped lightly upon the door of the small armoury that adjoined the main storeroom. Their eyes had become used to the shadows, and now they could just discern the faint glint of swords and halberds, the dark shapes of longbows and sheaves of arrows piled around the walls outside the door. The weapons were usually kept secure, of course, but now that they had been removed to make way for the prisoner, the tools of death seemed ill at ease beside the jars of honey, the pigeons' eggs and the salted fish.

David reached forward and tapped on the door again, as loud as he dared. 'Can you hear me?'

'Not in French, you fool!' Nest moved closer to the door, and spoke in quiet Welsh. '*Ydych chi'n gallu fy nghlywed?*'

'*Gallaf. . . pwy ydych chi?*' The voice was faint and startled, and bore an accent they had not encountered before.

'Who are we. . .' Nest repeated the question to David, who had shown neither enthusiasm nor aptitude in the practise of his mother's native tongue.

Something stirred on the other side of the door. The prisoner's voice was louder when it came again. 'Who are you? You speak Welsh as the Archdeacon does. Are you his kinsfolk? Where is he? He said I would be safe at Maenor Pyr, but he did not tell me that I would be a prisoner! Is he still here? Can you fetch him?'

'The Archdeacon isn't lord of Manorbier. Our father is.'

'Then can you fetch your father here?'

'What would you wish to say to him?' Nest, as ever, was curious.

'I would tell him that it's stifling in here. I would tell him that the walls are cold, and there are rats in the straw. I would tell him that he is risking much by treating me so!'

'You would dare threaten him? You?' Nest giggled at the thought, but the prisoner's voice was grim and insistent.

'When Lord Llywelyn takes Pembroke, then the threat will be real enough. I could save Maenor Pyr with a word. Or I could destroy it.'

Angharad sobbed, her face buried in her hands.

Gerald regarded her in dismay. What was one supposed to do? He patted her shoulder awkwardly. 'My dear child, please! What troubles you?'

'He has taken many wounds in the past, but never have I seen one so bad as this. I think he does not realise. . .'

'Give him time, Angharad. I will pray for him. I am sure he will be recovered before the week is out.'

'But that is the trouble! He will never rest for as long as he should, he will put on his spurs and ride for Pembroke the moment he is summoned. And he *will* be summoned, won't he? When Llywelyn hears about his son, when he sends his army. . .'

'Even if Gruffydd ap Llywelyn really is dead, Angharad, I do not believe Llywelyn would go to war over it. It would profit him best to demand lands from the King in compensation. And even if the worst should happen, Manorbier would never be in danger from him. He has been my ally for decades, I could even call him my friend. He would not besiege my home!'

'Not whilst you are here, perhaps. If you could stay with us. . . then at least my children would be safe.'

'You will be safe because you bear the name of de Barri. I am sorry, but I may stay for only a few days. I will be needed at St David's to assist Bishop Iorwerth in my. . . in his new office.'

'If they need you so much, why do they never honour you as you deserve? Why are *you* not Bishop?'

'It is not for want of trying! The Chapter of St David's would have it so, but it is the Archbishop of Canterbury who has ever stood in my path.'

Angharad knew full well Gerald's deep resentment of Canterbury, of the Pope, of the cruel wheel of fate that had begun its downward turn thirty years ago. 'Why go on, my lord? Why not abandon so thankless a task? You could live here at Manorbier. You could devote all your time to your books. . .'

Gerald smiled and gently shook his head. It was a recurring dream that must be put speedily from his mind.

'Yes, retire. Before you drive yourself to your death!'

'Better that, than to rot out my days in obscurity!' Gerald sighed as he gazed at the familiar trappings of the hall. 'Still. . . it will do no harm to pass a few days here. There is the charter of the barons to be read. I have brought a copy from Pembroke, but there has been little opportunity to examine it closely.' Gerald warmed to the idea. 'Yes, I could stay for a few days, and I could continue with my book.'

It was inevitable. Angharad had long since realised that there came a time in every conversation when Gerald de Barri would begin to talk about his books.

'It is called *On the Instruction of a Prince*. My treatise on King Henry the Second and his sons.'

'I hope you will not offend King John.'

'I doubt that he will even hear of it. I doubt that he would ever find a monk willing to read to him! No, King John is not the enemy of my book. It is time that dogs my heels! But, God grant me the days, I may yet finish it before the year is out.'

'Then all the more reason for you to stay in Manorbier where you may work in peace!'

Gerald appeared not to have heard. 'I *will* have the time, if Bishop Iorwerth can shoulder his responsibilities.'

Once the new incumbent took the Bishopric of St David's, Gerald would lose all responsibility for the see. He would be able to devote more time to his books. He would be able to forget the ambitions and defeats of the struggle for St David's. He would be able to live out his remaining years in peace, and yet he did not know whether to mourn or to rejoice.

XVI

Gerald de Barri felt an overwhelming contentment as he watched the manor busy itself about its morning tasks. All was at peace. Along the wooden fence that marked the boundary patrolled a handful of men-at-arms, and they smiled and chatted to one another as they passed. Here was a laxity that would never have been countenanced at Pembroke! The new gatehouse, still garlanded in its scaffolding, was coming on apace, and the masons were working hard to extend it into the adjacent tower. Nearby lay the stable and smithy, while closest of all, at the foot of the slight bank that divided the two levels of the courtyard, was the place that perhaps Gerald held most dear. Blue woodsmoke stole through the wooden roof tiles of the wattle and daub kitchen, and the heady aroma of the daily bread had not changed these sixty years.

Gerald settled once more to his task, and suppressed a yawn as he bent forward to read.

'My lord?' Angharad hurried down the narrow spiral stair from the solar, and paused at the end of the table. 'Is that the new charter of the barons?'

'It is.' Gerald welcomed the interruption, even though he was surprised that Angharad should show an interest in such things.

'Would you tell me what it says?' Angharad had lowered her voice as she drew closer to peer at the writing. It meant nothing to her for she could not read, and in any case it was in Latin, yet she regarded the parchment with awe. 'William told me that the charter means peace for all Britain, but he would say nothing more. He explains more to our son than he will to me!'

'Well, David can expect to be lord of Manorbier one day.'

'What does this say?' Angharad pointed to the first few lines. 'Is that the Earl Marshal's name . . .'

Gerald sighed. He supposed it could do no harm. He bent over the parchment and began to read aloud.

'John, by the Grace of God King of England, Lord of Ireland, Duke of Normandy and Aquitaine, and Count of Anjou, to his archbishops, bishops, abbots, earls, barons, justices, foresters, sheriffs, servants, and to all his loyal subjects. Greeting.'

'Why do the King's titles not mention Wales?'

'Perhaps he does not wish to be reminded of his defeats here!' Gerald paused as a new thought occurred to him. 'Yet he still clings to his French titles, even though he lost those lands years ago...'

'What else does it say?' Angharad settled herself upon the bench next to the Archdeacon as she craned to look at the incomprehensible script.

Gerald continued with ill grace. He disliked reading aloud anything that he had not written himself, and the penmanship of this copy was so poor that he was hard pressed to decipher it at all. A prolific writer himself, Gerald could well imagine the terrified clerk as he had hastily copied out the endless clauses, trying in vain to concentrate upon his task while an impatient John d'Erley peered over his shoulder and exhorted him to finish by sunrise.

'The King declares that the following clauses have been granted for the sake of his soul, the exaltation of the Church and the better government of his Kingdom. King John has made his peace with the Church, and the first concession confirms its rights and freedoms. No doubt he is eager to show his gratitude to Rome for lifting the interdict, and even more so for rescinding his excommunication.'

'What was the interdict?'

Gerald smiled at Angharad, obviously delighted by her puzzlement. 'There, now...your question in itself explains why the interdict was lifted.'

'How so?'

'The interdict was an order from the Pope. He commanded the Church of England to cease all services but for the baptism of infants and the absolution of the dying. It was a ploy to turn the people against the King, but many clergymen disobeyed and continued to preach outside their locked churches. Like yourself, most people have not even heard of the interdict, because it was ineffective and did King John little harm. Indeed, it might have made him the richer, because it gave him an excuse to seize Church land. Now he will be able to demand payment for its return.' Gerald did not think it worthy of mention that King John had also kidnapped the mistresses of supposedly celibate priests, and had held them to ransom too.

'So excommunication did not trouble the King?'

'It placed his soul beyond the protection of the Church, but what does that mean to a man such as John? One who is excommunicate is despised by his fellow men, but the King was despised anyway. It is the Church's ultimate sanction, but it has been used too often. Indeed, perhaps I have used it too often myself. . .'

Angharad knew very well the oft recounted stories of the Archdeacon's earlier years. 'Is it true, then. . . about the Bishop of St Asaph?'

'That was a long time ago, yes, when Henry the Second was King. I was Archdeacon of Brecon at the time, but I was also Bishop-elect of St David's. The Chapter had put my name forward, and I was administering the see while Canterbury plotted how best to deny me the Bishopric. Even King Henry. . .'

'But what about the excommunication?'

'Oh, that. . . I had heard news that the Bishop of St Asaph was on his way to consecrate a new church. It was within my see. . . well, within the see of St David's, so I went with all haste to occupy the church before Bishop Adam could steal it and lay claim to its income. In Ceri, it was, close to the English border on the road to Shrewsbury. On the way I was joined by two Welsh cousins of mine, Einion and Cadwallon, along with their men. We arrived barely minutes before the Bishop. He came to the gates and made his claims, and I made mine in return. We argued for hours, until finally he threatened to excommunicate me.'

'He would have excommunicated *you*?'

'He began to read the verses, but his ceremony was a poor affair. I read the same lines to excommunicate him in return, and as I had possession of the church bells, I made a thorough job of it. I could read much more quickly than he. . . being a more accomplished scholar, and when he realised that I would finish first, he gathered together his company and fled.'

Angharad laughed in delight.

'I regret to say,' Gerald recalled with a frown, 'that my companions stoned them out of sight!'

'I would have given much to see it! But to use force against a bishop. . .'

'That is the only thing some of them understand. They are not

allowed directly to shed blood, of course, not Christian
blood...but still they fought in the Crusades! They favoured a
spiked metal ball on a chain. It seems that crushing a man's skull
does not count as shedding blood...not, at least, when it is only
the heathen head of a Saracen. I too might have fought, for it was
I who preached the Cross in Wales. Myself and Archbishop
Baldwin of Canterbury. He died for his faith at the walls of Acre,
whilst I was forced to remain behind.'

'You took the Cross, my lord?'

'I did. You did not think that I would preach the Cross to all
Wales, without being prepared to fight for it myself? I set out with
the rest of them and travelled as far as France, but then Richard
was crowned and he ordered me back to Wales. He said I would
better serve him by preaching the Cross than by dying in
Jerusalem. I suppose he was right. Yes, he *was* right, though I
disagreed with him strongly at the time.'

Gerald sighed. Interesting though this might be, he must return
to the question of the charter. 'Er...yes, to continue. It was
barely two months ago that King John made his peace with the
Pope. He has not been a well man, and perhaps he feared to die
excommunicate. He placed himself...and England...completely
under the command of Rome, and His Holiness most generously
accepted.'

'Did his bargain include the charter?'

'No... No, it takes many weeks to communicate with Rome, as
I once learned to my cost. I do not think that His Holiness can
even have heard of the charter, as yet. It was surely the work of
the traitorous barons...and perhaps also of Archbishop Steven
Langton.'

'And the Welsh?'

'The Welsh, the Scots, even the French had a hand in it, but
they would not have dared interfere with English affairs had the
country not been divided. As for the rest of the charter, it is
simply a long list of concessions, mainly in favour of the barons.'

'Please read them, uncle.' Angharad met his eyes, and he saw
the anxiety that had prompted her questions. Her husband's
grave injury had made her think upon the future.

Reluctantly, for they were tedious indeed, Gerald read out

clause upon clause of the intricate laws of debt and inheritance, trial and taxation.

'Clause thirty-nine. No one shall be arrested or imprisoned, except by the lawful judgement of his equals or by the law of the land.'

Clause followed clause. The restoration of confiscated lands. The return of moneys seized by the King. Gerald scarcely paid heed to what he was reading, until one particular sentence caught his eye. He leaned forward and spoke out the words anew.

'Clause fifty-eight. We will at once give up the son of Llywelyn and all hostages of Wales. . .'

At last, Gerald finished reading. He released the parchment and allowed it to roll up on itself.

Angharad stared long at the yellow calf-skin. 'If the Earl Marshal had read and understood his own copy of the charter, he might have thought twice about sending an innocent man into prison.'

'Whether Elidyr ab Idwal be innocent or a wicked liar, Angharad, we dare not set him free. I have given my word to the Earl Marshal. But even so. . .I see no reason for him to be imprisoned all the time. I think he could be given a measure of freedom within the confines of the manor.'

'I will see to it.' Angharad rose to her feet, but Gerald caught her arm.

'You must consult William first.'

'I know what he would say.' She looked up towards the dark window of the solar. 'Nest is watching over him. . .I told her to call me should he wake. I will not disturb him.'

'Very well.' Gerald looked gravely at his nephew's wife. 'But I should prefer to give the order myself. I would not have you flout the authority of your lord. . .nor that of the Earl Marshal.'

David de Barri crouched in the shadows of the undercroft, his ear to the iron-studded door of the armoury. He was the son of the Lord of the Manor, soon to be a squire at the castle of Pembroke, thence to join the ranks of the knights. But he was also the son of a Welshwoman, and the great-nephew of Gerald de

Barri, with an insatiable curiosity that had drawn him once again to whisper through the prison door.

'Elidyr! Elidyr ab Idwal!'

'*Pwy sy 'na?*'

David started, in spite of himself. The voice had been louder than he had expected. 'I was here last night, with my sister. You will have to speak slowly if you have only Welsh.'

'Your father. . . did you speak to him?'

'No.'

'Listen. . . .' The voice began low and urgent, then broke off with a muffled curse. 'What is your name?'

'I am David, son of Lord William de Barri. And my sister is Nest.'

'Did you say David and Nest?'

'Yes. Why?' In spite of the door between them, David was sure that the prisoner was smiling broadly.

'You are well named! The Welsh Saint and the fair Helen of Wales.'

'Helen of Wales? What do you mean?'

'There was another Nest, it must be near a hundred years ago. She was a Welsh princess, daughter of Rhys ap Tewdwr, but she married a Norman, Gerald of Windsor. He was castellan of Pembroke, long before William Marshal became Earl. Nest was a fabled beauty, and of, er. . . a wandering nature. And generous with her favours. It's said that she was seduced by every high-born man in the country. Or she seduced them, it's not for me to say. But she was *notorious*! It is even said that she bore a child by King Henry the First of England!'

'What became of her?'

'She persuaded the Lord Owain ap Cadwgan to abduct her from the castle of Cilgerran. In the struggle, her husband barely escaped with his life by lowering himself down the soil chute of the garderobe!'

David giggled. This part of the story appealed to him, even if the rest did not.

'In the end Nest was restored to her husband, but Gerald of Windsor was to have his revenge. Seven years later he laid an ambush and slew Owain. For a time, this put paid to all thoughts of peace between the English and Welsh. That is why Nest

83

became known as the Welsh Helen of Troy.' Elidyr paused as he heard the scurry of footsteps. 'Are you still there?'

The answer came in the turning of the well greased lock. Gerald de Barri stooped to enter the low doorway.

Elidyr stood at once, and bowed deeply. 'My lord, may I speak...'

'You have spoken more than enough already. Is it your custom to tell such scandalous tales to the ears of children?'

'Perhaps in years to come it will serve as a lesson to the boy...'

'Enough! Do you not know who Princess Nest was?'

'She was a...' Something in the Archdeacon's expression halted Elidyr.

'Princess Nest was my grandmother!'

'Oh. I...I meant no offence, my lord.'

'I came here to offer you a measure of freedom. But now...'

Elidyr spoke quickly. 'I know you to be a good and just man, my lord, a loyal friend to the Welsh. Why can't you just give me your blessing and help me on my way? It will go well with Llywelyn, when he hears...'

'I have no need to buy favours of Llywelyn. We were friends before you were born! I gave my word to the Earl Marshal that you would stay in Manorbier, and stay you shall.'

'For how long?'

'At least until news comes of Squire Anselm.'

Elidyr looked with distaste at the musty straw and the damp walls. 'Very well, my lord, I give you my parole that I will not escape. Now will you release me from this dark, filthy, stinking place?'

'Perhaps. On certain conditions...'

'But you already have my word!' Elidyr took an angry pace forward, yet he was conscious that his liberty, his food, his drink, even the very clothes he stood in, were all in the gift of Manorbier. 'You don't trust the word of a Welshman, is that it?'

It was not a wise accusation, not a thing to be said of Gerald of Wales, but the Archdeacon would not be goaded. 'Be quiet and listen. You will be free to leave this chamber by day, but on your honour you will make no attempt to escape. You will not approach the gates, nor the boundary fence, nor will you enter the great hall or the solar. Each evening after supper you will return here to be secured for the night. You will comply with all these things on pain of excommunication.'

Gerald could not help but to smile wrily to himself as he walked across the courtyard. He had not excommunicated anyone for years.

XVII

Elidyr did not stray far from the cooking pots. He was content enough to sit by the bubbling cauldron outside the kitchen, to savour the aroma of mutton stew and to watch the cook and the serving maid go about their business. Whenever either woman paused by the cauldron, the Welshman would continue in the telling of his tales. Already this morning he had told them the history of the Magical Mound at nearby Narberth, of Pwyll, Prince of Dyfed, who for a year changed places with King Arawn of the Otherworld, and of the Cauldron of the Lake that could restore dead men to life. Soon he would reach his own favourite part of the story, that of the giant King Bendigeidfran, Bran the Blessed, *the blessed raven.*

'*A sut mae heddi*', Elidyr ab Idwal?' Nest spoke brightly, her brother sullen at her side.

The cook escaped to her kitchen as Elidyr stopped mid-sentence. He looked up to see the round, innocent face of the child, her long fair hair carefully plaited, her bright gown dappled with mud at the hem. She, and the boy beside her in the tunic and short cloak of a Norman squire, were staring at him with rude curiosity.

'You must be Nest and David.' Elidyr paused to wipe a scrap of bread around the shallow bowl from which he had been drinking. Satisfied that the last trace of stew had been accounted for, he settled himself more comfortably on the steep bank by the kitchen fire and smiled at the children. 'Did you hear of the time the Welsh waded the sea to Ireland?'

'Waded the sea?' David's attention was captured at once. He squatted down beside the Welshman. 'When was that?'

85

'Oh, many years ago. Before even King Arthur's time. Bendigeidfran was lord of the lands that Llywelyn now rules, a giant in stature as well as in wisdom. One day a starling flew into his hand, carrying a message from his sister in Ireland. The lady's name was Branwen, and she told him that her husband, the Irish king, was treating her ill. Bendigeidfran loved her dearly, and felt that his own honour had been slighted. And so he led his men across the sea.'

'He waded?' Nest, still standing, felt herself too old for such fables.

'He waded.' Elidyr held her eyes. He was smiling gently, and she could not have guessed whether he laughed at himself, at the ancient author of the tale, or at her. 'There was no ship large enough to carry him, so he had no choice. At first it seemed that the quarrel with the Irish might be resolved amicably, and Branwen was brought to meet her brother. But there was a breaking of faith on both sides and war was not long in coming. Bendigeidfran stood by his sister, holding her behind his shield, but at last the sheer numbers of the Irish prevailed, for they possessed the Cauldron of the Lake and no force could diminish them. Only seven of the Welsh army survived, and they carried Branwen and the head of her royal brother back to the Island of Prydain.'

'The Island of Britain.'

'The seven survivors fell to much lamenting upon their return, for in their absence a new king had seized the crown and there had been great changes in the land. Branwen, her heart broken, died on the shore of Ynys Môn, and there they buried her with her face towards the West. The Seven debated at great length what was to be done, for they had neither the heart nor the strength to challenge the usurper.

'At last the head of their dead king Bendigeidfran opened its eyes, and he spoke his wise counsel as clearly as he had in life. Following his directions they journeyed southward and, coming to the very spot where the castle of Pembroke now stands, they found a great hall with three doors. For many years they lived and laughed and feasted well in that hall, while the starlings of Rhiannon sang above and the head of Bendigeidfran entertained them with song and story.

86

'In all that time the Seven aged not a day, nor did any thought of grief enter their minds. But one morning they awoke to find a door in the West wall, a fourth door that none had made note of before. It seemed fitting that the door should be opened, and through it they looked out upon the shores of Ireland and saw anew the sorrow of Branwen, the pain of their fallen comrades, the shame of their defeat. And from that moment they could find no rest until they followed again the words of the Head of Bendigeidfran.

'They forsook their country and their dreams of regaining the lands stolen from them. Into Lloegr they travelled, bearing the Head in honour before them until they came to London, to the White Mound, and there they buried Bendigeidfran's head with his face to the East. And while the head remained, no enemy could cross the seas to Prydain.'

'Is the White Mound still there?'

'Upon it is built the Tower of London.'

'But the Normans built the Tower.' David was insistent. 'Didn't *they* cross the sea to Britain?'

'It is said that King Arthur had already removed Bendigeidfran's head from the White Mound, for he wanted none but himself to defend the realm.'

David giggled, thinking that this had been rather foolish of Arthur.

Nest was staring at the Welshman, her brow creased in a frown. 'Are you a bard, Elidyr?'

'Do you think I am a bard?' The Welshman smiled, a challenge in his eyes.

'I think. . . I think that you would like to be.' Nest looked past Elidyr as she spoke, for she could see her mother and the Archdeacon descending the steps from the great hall.

Gerald called to the children at once. 'Your father is asking for you.'

'Is his wound much worse?'

'No, David, he feels a little better. Go up to the solar now, both of you.'

Elidyr rose to his feet as Archdeacon Gerald de Barri and the lady Angharad approached.

The Archdeacon's mood had improved considerably. 'Which story was it this time?'

'The history of Bran the Blessed and the sorrow of Branwen.'

'I am not sure whether *history* is the correct word, but at least it is a tale more suited to the ears of children.'

Angharad smiled at the chagrin on the Welshman's face. 'You are fond of your stories, Elidyr?'

'Of that story above all, my lady.'

Angharad knew the legend well herself. 'The Welsh are defeated, and yet they endure. I think you see much of yourself in the Seven.'

'You are Welsh, my lady?'

'The Princes of Deheubarth and Gwynedd are my kinsmen. Distantly, it is true, but I am of the blood of Gwenllian ferch Gruffydd ap Cynan.'

'Gwenllian? Daughter of the King of Gwynedd, she was. Wife to Gruffydd ap Rhys ap Tewdwr, King of Deheubarth! It is said that while her husband was away, she herself would lead his armies.'

'You are a northerner, Elidyr ab Idwal, I can hear that.'

'I was born in Gwynedd. And never left there, until the English came, though I travelled the length of Dyffryn Conwy in search of...' He hesitated, but the gentle smile on Angharad's face put him at ease. 'In search of the greatest bardic school.'

'Ah...you sought to be a bard! I had a nephew who followed the path. Cadell was his name.'

'Cadell? Meurig's son? Yes, I knew him...he was another who never wasted an opportunity to boast the names of Gwenllian and Rhys ap Tewdwr!'

To Gerald's surprise, Angharad laughed with the Welshman instead of taking offence. He stared at them in mild irritation. The Archdeacon had always felt that the Welsh shared some kinship forever closed to the Normans. Once, he had put it down to the peculiarity of their language, but even now, when he considered himself fluent in Welsh, he did not think he could ever feel fully at home in their company.

'And how fares Cadell?' Angharad stilled her laughter, conscious of Gerald's silence.

'He is dead, my lady. An English arrow in his throat in the defence of Degannwy.'

Angharad's eyes were sober now. 'How long did you stay in the bardic school, Elidyr?'

'Not long enough.'

'So you are not a bard?'

'No, my lady. The English did not allow me that. Many of the masters were slain, for they fought as bravely as any warrior, and the rest were imprisoned.' Elidyr gave a heavy sigh. 'I hoped to be *pencerdd*, to sit at the heir's side at the three great feasts, to recount the great deeds of my lord in song... Well was I rewarded for my presumption.'

Gerald nodded in sympathy. He could well understand Elidyr's frustration. His own work in chronicling the events of his time afforded him a similar satisfaction, though he had often wished that great deeds were as common in real life as the bards always seemed to suppose. 'I thought to myself, as you spoke at Pembroke, that you have the true heart of a bard.'

'But, alas, I can boast few of the skills.'

'Is there so much to learn?' Gerald cast his mind back to his own education. For as long as he could remember he had wanted to join the Church. Heedless of his older brothers' childhood games of knights and battles, of dragons and maidens in distress, he had eagerly sought to follow the example of his uncle David FitzGerald, the then Bishop of St David's.

Latin had come slowly at first, but when at the age of ten he had been sent to school in Gloucester, far from the diversions of Manorbier, he had progressed rapidly under the guidance of the good Master Haimo. At the age when his brothers had been fighting their first tournaments, Gerald de Barri had entered the University of Paris, and there he had honed to perfection his skills in Latin, rhetoric and logic...

'... a great many years of study, my lord. And even then there are those who never achieve greatness. The learning is necessary, but it is not enough.'

'No, it is not enough...' Gerald sighed, his mind far distant. For an archdeacon also, the learning had not been enough.

XVIII

The Archdeacon sat alone at the long table, absorbed in the great task of committing the thoughts of Gerald de Barri to parchment. He had written barely a dozen lines when the noisy arrival of the children made him set down his goose quill and stare in annoyance.

'I'm sorry, my lord, but our father is much better now and we. . .' Nest stared curiously at the manuscript upon the table. 'What is that?'

'Is it your new book? Mother says you're writing about King John!' Eagerly, David pushed forward to look at the mysterious lettering upon the pages.

'Er, yes.' Gerald hastily piled together his manuscript and pushed it to one side, along with the unfinished page of his morning's work. He hated anyone to look at his writings before they were finished. 'It tells of King Henry the Second and all his sons. . . Geoffrey and Richard as well as John. But there is much yet to be done. I began the writing of it almost thirty years ago, but always it has to be put aside for more pressing matters. I have so little time for my own work. In Manorbier it seems I have none at all!'

'Do you know King John well, my lord?'

'I knew him when he was little older than you are now, David. I was chaplain to his father's court, you see, and. . .'

'You were?' David's eyes widened. He had never imagined that anyone could be so old. Except for the Earl Marshal, of course. Like most of the children of Pembroke, David de Barri firmly believed that William Marshal must have fought by the Conqueror's side at Hastings.

Gerald closed his eyes as he leaned back in his chair. 'Yes, I spent a year following the court. What a time that was! The stories I could tell. . .' With difficulty he restrained himself. The stories from Henry's court were hardly suited to the ears of children. 'But then King Henry decided to send his youngest son. . . John . . . to Ireland, and I was to go with him. I knew the country well, of course. I had spent some time there with my uncles, the FitzGeralds. It was largely they who had conquered Ireland.'

'All by themselves?'

Gerald smiled. 'Not entirely, Nest. They had their armies but, alas, so did the Irish. It was a bloody business. It was an Irish king who had sent for the FitzGeralds in the first place, you see, to quell his own rivals, but so successful were my kinsmen that they seemed set to turn the whole country into their own empire! King Henry was horrified. He had for long been wary of the power of the Marcher lords, and so he declared Prince John *Lord of Ireland* and sent him there to ensure his own claim to the lands. I was to accompany the Prince as his chaplain and advisor, but I fear John's mission was not a great success. He knew nothing of the Irish, and he cared nothing for their land or their customs. He was too arrogant to heed my counsel, and in his ignorance he offended them at every turn...'

'But do you know King John *now*, my lord?' David had already heard the tales of the FitzGeralds from his father a hundred times before.

'No, I know him hardly at all now. Since those days he has become the most tyrannous whelp of all his line, the most tyrannous of bloody tyrants... Er, one moment, if you please.' Gerald seized his quill, inspired, and wrote in haste before the thought could leave his mind. He set down the feather and beamed at the drying ink. 'Do you know, I had been struggling all morning for a generous and fitting phrase to describe King John.'

'What will happen when he reads it?'

'I doubt that he will even hear of the book, Nest. He is no more literate than his predecessors. I dedicated two books to them... Henry and Richard... but I cast my pearls before swine!'

'Poor King John, I feel quite sorry for him.'

'I don't,' muttered David.

Gerald smiled. 'John does seem to have been beset by ill fortune. As to whether he deserved it... well, your opinion must rest upon which stories you believe.'

'Stories?' The children sat up with renewed interest.

'The murder of Prince Arthur of Brittany springs to mind.' Gerald recalled the event with distaste. 'It was a sordid business. The boy was Prince John's nephew, and when King Richard died he was no older than you are now. There was much debate as to which of them should succeed Richard. Arthur was too young to rule without a regent, yet his claim to the throne was strong. His name, more than anything, made him popular among the Welsh and the Bretons. . . all Celts, you understand. They rejoiced at the prospect of a new King Arthur, and if Arthur of Brittany had been crowned King of England, we might even now be living in a united kingdom. Wales, England and France, all at peace.' Gerald smiled. A vision so delightful, but so utterly unattainable. . .

'But Arthur of Brittany was not crowned King,' Nest reminded him.

'No, he was not. John was of the right age and, most important, it was said that King Richard named him as his successor. That was enough for the loyal barons. . . men such as William Marshal . . . and they rallied behind Prince John. Prince Arthur, for his part, raised an army in Brittany and allied himself to King Phillip of France, and together they began to drive Prince John's English out of France.'

'Was that how John got the name *Softsword*?'

'It was. The English barons mocked his failures and planned their own treachery, but just as Prince John felt his power slipping away, his fortune changed. One of the Norman lords in Wales . . . William de Braose it was. . . somehow captured Prince Arthur and turned him over to John. The boy was imprisoned in a monastery near Rouen, and was never seen again.'

'What happened to him, my lord?' David showed a rare interest, for this had more of the sound of a grisly ballad than of boring history.

'Years later William de Braose began to spread rumours that the King himself had killed Prince Arthur, and it was even said that John had strangled the boy with his own bare hands. This was the first step in John's downfall. The stories led to trouble with the Welsh, and they became a great problem to him. His strategy was to rule them by means of their own dissent, to pit the princes of Gwynedd, Powys and Deheubarth against each other. The Welsh had fought amongst themselves for centuries, and now John sought to worsen their squabbles by offering his own soldiers to help the princes quell their rivals. At times he supported Llywelyn against the south, while at other times King John's soldiers fought side by side with the men of Deheubarth.

'The Norman lords in Wales, too, were often rebellious. William de Braose in the end was turned out of his lands. But he bided his time, and when King John journeyed once again into Ireland to quell the growing powers of his barons there, de Braose set to scheming behind his back. He managed to ally himself with Llywelyn ap Iorwerth in a rebellion. The uprising soon crumbled, but it was perhaps because of this that John hardened in his resolve to destroy the threat of Gwynedd for ever.

'King John rallied together all the Welsh enemies of Llywelyn. To all the malcontents and the power-hungry he appealed, and the princes of Powys, Gwynedd and Deheubarth declared themselves his allies. Rhys Gryg was one such man . . . your father would have seen him at the tournament in Pembroke. They joined ranks with John's own English soldiers and foreign mercenaries, and formed such an army as had never before challenged the heart of Wales. They seemed set to defeat Llywelyn, but he retreated into Snowdonia just as the Lords of Gwynedd have always done in time of greatest danger, and King John's mighty army was left to starve in the foothills. Come the summer, John rallied the survivors with more generous provisions, and the English advanced down the Conway driving Llywelyn's men before them. When they came to Bangor they torched the episcopal city, and the King's foreign mercenaries abducted the Bishop from the very foot of the high altar!'

'Why?'

'Why, Nest? Because Bishop Robert was a pious and honourable man and had refused to meet with John, declaring that he would have nothing to do with an excommunicate king. A fine of two hundred hawks secured the Bishop's release, but he never recovered from his ill-treatment and did not live another year. King John's army seemed invincible, and in desperation Llywelyn sent his wife Joan to plead with her father . . .'

'Her father? Who is he?'

David gave his sister a superior glance. 'King John himself, of course.'

'King John's daughter wedded to Llywelyn of Gwynedd?' Nest looked at the Archdeacon in astonishment. 'Is it true, my lord?'

'Why yes, did you not know? Joan is one of King John's bast . . . that is, not one of his legitimate children. She was married to Llywelyn some years ago. It was supposed to be a profitable alliance for both sides.'

'Is...was Prince Gruffydd the grandson of King John, then?'

Gerald smiled tolerantly. Given the tale he had just told about Arthur of Brittany, the children must think there was no villainy beneath King John of England, including the holding of his own flesh and blood as hostage. Indeed, Gerald had often thanked God that he was no relative of the King. 'No, child, he is the product of an earlier...alliance.'

'An earlier marriage, my lord?'

Gerald cleared his throat in embarrassment. 'Er...that is a matter of some confusion. Gruffydd's mother was high-born. She was Tangwystl, daughter of Llywarch the Red, but I could not say whether she was ever actually *married* to Lord Llywelyn. In any case, the laws for succession in Wales are disgracefully lax. It matters little whether a son is born in wedlock, all that matters is whether or no his father chooses to recognise him. But, as I was saying...' Gerald hastened to abandon so distasteful a subject. 'At Joan's intercession a truce was agreed, but the terms were severe. King John took four cantrefs around St Asaph, and large tributes of cattle and horses, dogs and birds. He also took thirty Welsh hostages, and Llywelyn's son Gruffydd was among them.

'A year later...that would be three years ago now...King John felt confident that he had honed his military skills to perfection, and he raised an army to regain the lands he had lost in France. At the same time, his policy with the Welsh seemed to be working well. Llywelyn was becoming increasingly isolated from the other princes, whose lack of resistance allowed the Normans to build their castles right into the very heart of Wales. Soon, though, none could doubt that John's intent was the total conquest and settlement of Wales.

'Llywelyn must have realised this when he spent the Easter with his wife and his father-in-law King John at Cambridge, and soon dissent was sweeping the whole country. Welsh princes who had hitherto allied themselves with King John against Llywelyn changed their allegiance yet again and attacked the new Norman castles. Rhys Gryg and his brother Maelgwn burned Aberystwyth, and Llywelyn's men captured the forts that King John had built along the Conway.

94

'King John regarded this as the blackest treachery. His great army was already poised to invade France, but he resolved instead to turn all his forces against Wales. Some say that John was sitting down to dinner, in good appetite after witnessing the hanging of some Welsh hostages, when...'

'But you said they were released last week!' David was confused.

'The *survivors* were released, yes, but as I was saying, just when John was sitting down to dinner, two messengers arrived. One was from his daughter Joan, the other from the Scottish King. They warned that if Wales were attacked, then all Britain would rebel in outrage. Even the English barons would take arms against their King.

'John called off the attack, and to maintain his power he seized castles in England and Norman Wales and took yet more hostages ... from his enemies and his loyal followers alike. Even William Marshal's men were not safe!'

'The King mistrusts William Marshal?' David could scarce believe it. The Earl Marshal was his hero, the greatest of all knights, the very flower of Norman chivalry...

'John once said he had as many enemies as he had barons! And of course, for a time, even the Earl Marshal's eldest son had sided with the rebel barons. The King did not know whom he could trust, but he soon realised that William Marshal was the one man in Britain upon whose loyalty he could truly depend.'

XIX

The toadflax garlanding the walls of Manorbier wilted beneath the noon sun, with not a breath of wind to stir it into life. In the solar, William de Barri sweltered and cursed the itching of his unhealed scars. In the courtyard below, Elidyr ab Idwal had been set to work to draw water from the well, and bathed in an unaccustomed sweat as he laboured at the handle of the winch. The cook watched with hands on hips and a grin on her broad face as he paused to catch his breath.

'Working hard today, Elidyr?' Nest laughed as she and her brother crossed the courtyard from the gatehouse. They had finished their lessons in the church, high on the opposite hill, and welcomed the thought of a cool drink.

Elidyr smiled and leaned on the winch handle. 'The water from this well comes forth cool as the snows and fresh as the Irish breeze.'

'If it ever comes forth at all!' cried the cook impatiently, and went back to her pots.

'There's as fine a well where I come from.' Elidyr turned to his work again. 'But no one dares use it.'

'Why not?'

Elidyr refused to answer David's question until the bucket rose brimming to the stone rim of the well. The children fetched earthenware bowls from the kitchen, and for a moment all three drank in silence.

'It is an old story. . . ' Elidyr sat on the coping, with a cautious glance into the still depths below. 'And it begins hundreds of years ago, when a child named Emrys lived in the city of Caer Fyrddin. The City of Merlin, you French would say.'

'That's Carmarthen!'

'We've stayed in the castle there.'

'Ah, but this was many years before the castle was built. Emrys lived long before the Normans came, in the time when the Welsh. . . the Britons, we were then, were fighting the Saxons. Now the boy Emrys had the gift of second sight. One day a messenger came to seek him out, and took him back to Gwynedd to stand before the King of the Britons. Gwrtheyrn was the King's name. He had suffered a great defeat, brought about by the treachery of the Saxons and by his own folly, and had retreated into the mountains of the Eryri. . . just as the Welsh have always done in their time of greatest hardship. The mountains are our fortress, the cold winds our arrows, the winter snows our shield.'

'But what about Gwrtheyrn and Emrys?'

'Gwrtheyrn had planned to build a stronghold in the Eryri, close by Afon Conwy, but the very soil was accursed. All the work done by day would be swallowed into the ground by night, and no mortal culprit could be found. Gwrtheyrn's magicians had told him that they could solve the problem through the boy Emrys.

They were to sprinkle his blood over the soil to drive the demons away. . .'

'His blood?' David stared in horror. 'They wanted a human sacrifice?'

'They did. But Emrys was wise beyond his years and showed no fear of them. He pointed to a great flat stone among the scattered foundations, and vowed that beneath it would be found the answer to the curse. It took a score of men to drag the stone aside, and there beneath was revealed an ancient well. In the depths of the waters were coiled two dragons, one white as ivory, one scarlet as blood.

'As Emrys and Gwrtheyrn watched, the dragons stirred and began to fight a great battle, and it seemed that the white one would prevail. But almost at the moment of victory, the scarlet dragon gathered its strength and drove the white dragon from the well. The white dragon fled on tattered wings, and Gwrtheyrn replaced the stone to secure the red dragon in its conquered realm for all time.

'The white dragon was the invader, the red dragon was the Welsh people. And the well was the Kingdom of Prydain.'

Nest frowned, incredulous. 'Do you really believe that?'

'I have seen the stone that covers the well.'

'And did you lift the stone?'

'Of course not. That would have allowed the red dragon to escape. And if ever the dragon should leave the well, then my people will be driven even from their land of Wales.'

David, far from sharing his sister's scorn, was enchanted by the story. 'What happened to the boy Emrys?'

'Emrys attained such powers that he succeeded Gwrtheyrn as King. They say that Gwrtheyrn himself had gained the throne only through treachery, and that Emrys was in truth the son of the king whom Gwrtheyrn had slain. Many years later Emrys became known as Myrddin. . .'

'Merlin. . .'

' . . . and *Myrddin* was in turn succeeded by Arthur Pendragon. Thus it was that the ancient lineage of the princes of Wales continued unbroken. It is a lineage that can be traced to the fall of Troy and to the Garden of Eden.'

'To the fall of Troy?' David knew something of Homer, thanks to his father's teaching. 'Then you are descended from Ulysses and Achilles and...'

'Not from the Greeks with their gifts and treachery! Not the Greeks, David, we were the Trojans!'

David was astonished that the Welshman could take such obvious pride in this. 'I thought they were all killed in the sacking of Troy.'

'The Greeks slew all within the city walls, but many of the Trojan cavalry were outside when the city fell. Their leader Aeneas rallied the survivors, and together they escaped the Greeks and took flight westward across the sea. Some settled, eventually to found the city of Rome, but others sailed onward through the Pillars of Hercules on a great voyage that brought them to the shores of Cornwall and Brittany. There they prospered, and in time they could lay just claim to the whole Kingdom of Prydain.'

'The whole of Britain...?' Nest was thoughtful. 'So once, the descendants of the Trojans were the only people here.'

'Yes. All this land was ours, long before the Saxons and the Normans drove us into the West and the North. And it shall be ours again, God willing.'

'Do you expect King Arthur to return to lead you?'

'Perhaps.' Elidyr's mind was far away, he did not hear the mockery in Nest's voice. 'Perhaps he will follow his uncle, Dewi Sant, as once he did before, and together they will drive the English into the sea. When the sign comes, then King Arthur will awaken. We have only to wait.'

'For how long?'

Elidyr looked at the children, his sad eyes as deep, as black as the still waters of the well. 'Now that my lord Gruffydd ap Llywelyn is dead, I cannot even guess.'

'What has Gruffydd's death got to do with it?' Nest spoke with a new interest.

'Oh, I...I meant nothing. I have spoken too much of legend today, I begin to forget where the old tales end.'

'Where do they end?'

Elidyr's eyes were evasive now. He glanced in apprehension

98

towards the hall. 'Your kinsfolk will wonder what keeps you. It will go ill with me if they learn of the stories I have told you.'

'What makes you think we shall tell them?' Nest looked keenly at Elidyr, as eager in her pursuit of a secret as the Archdeacon would have been. 'You spoke of a sign, and of the return of Saint David. Do you mean the finding of his bones. . . would that be the sign?'

'I cannot speak of that.'

'The Vikings stole them, didn't they? Did Gruffydd know where they were hidden? Do you know where they are?'

Elidyr stared long at the girl's eager face. He remembered who she was, and who her father was. 'Quite an imagination you have, isn't it? Do all the kinsfolk of Gerald of Wales dream of the bones of Dewi Sant?'

'The Archdeacon says they are very important! He wishes. . .'

'He wishes he could find them for himself, I know. And if the great Gerald of Wales cannot find the holy relics, how do you imagine that I could?' Elidyr smiled humbly, though there was a devious look in his eyes. 'It is the bards and seers, all greater men than I, who say that King Arthur will return with Dewi Sant.'

Nest was sure that the bard was hiding the truth, and she resented it. 'It seems that every Welshman who is not a bard must be a seer.'

'Emrys and Taliesin, yes. But even Gerald de Barri, even your Norman Archdeacon, says that victory shall be ours!'

'I don't believe you!'

'Then ask him yourself,' Elidyr challenged, as he fled the approaching Archdeacon.

For Gerald de Barri the morning had passed swiftly, despite the stifling heat in the great hall. He had written an entire chapter and admitted to himself, in all humility, that it was superb. The atmosphere of Manorbier had inspired him to the heights of his literary prowess, but now it was time to take a brief break before his midday meal. The sky was clear, the breeze fresh, and the cliffs and the beach beckoned as strongly as ever they had in his childhood.

'My lord!' Nest and David came running, halting the old

Archdeacon in his tracks. David spoke eagerly. 'Did you ever make a prophecy, my lord?'

'I am a chronicler, not a prophet.'

The children looked at one another, disappointed.

'However,' Gerald curbed his impatience to set out upon his walk, 'there are times when an astute observer might, by interpretation of what he has seen of the past, er. . . *anticipate* a certain course of events. What manner of precognition did you have in mind?'

'Concerning the Welsh, my lord. Did you not write a prophecy in one of your books?'

'Well. . . there is no need to ask where you heard of that.' Gerald looked across to see Elidyr peering from the shadows of the kitchen. 'Yes, I may have said something in my *Description of Wales*. Now what was it. . .'

Gerald took much pleasure in the quotation of his own works, and this was not a matter to consider in haste. 'Ah yes. I said *Come the Day of Judgement, I do not believe that any nation, or any language, other than the Welsh, will answer for this corner of the Earth.* Yes, that was it.'

'Which corner of the Earth did you mean?' Nest asked urgently.

'Why, Wales, of course.'

Nest relaxed. 'I thought you might have meant all Britain.'

'All Britain?' Gerald laughed. 'No, I doubt that even the great Llywelyn ap Iorwerth could have such ambition.'

'Julius Caesar did. And William of Normandy!'

Gerald opened his mouth to say something to Nest, but thought better of it. He was not going to let this child spoil his day. He turned instead to David. 'My own ambitions were of a less warlike nature.'

'Your ambitions, my lord?'

'Oh yes. I was quite a patriot. It was my undoing, of course. I would be Bishop of St David's now, were it not for my Welsh blood. Or, rather, for my willingness to boast of it. But that was many years ago. I have my books to occupy me now. . .' Gerald paused, reflecting upon how Archbishop Langton might receive his *Rights and Privileges of St David's*.

'But when you prophesied. . .'

'What I wrote was not a prophecy! It was an observation of what

I know of the Welsh. They will recover their lands because they have the courage and the tenacity to do so, and because they are deserving in the eyes of The Lord Our God. But now I really must be going. . . .'

'You are not leaving Manorbier?'

Gerald smiled, flattered by the whining anxiety in David's question. 'No, I am only going for a walk along the cliffs.'

'May we come with you?'

'Oh. . . .' Gerald hesitated. He had intended to seek solitude, to think over events at Pembroke, but now he was not so sure that he wanted to be burdened with such worries. 'Oh very well. Come along if you wish.'

Nest had disappeared into the kitchen at the mention of the walk, but now returned clasping a bag of cakes. Gerald led the way towards the manor gates, not pausing for a moment as Elidyr ran up and fell into step with him.

'Are you leaving Manorbier, my lord?'

'Not yet.'

'I wanted to thank you, my lord, for what you have done for me. When I leave this place, you can be sure that Llywelyn will hear well of you!'

'If you wish to thank me, then see to it that you do not betray my trust.'

'I will not, I promise you. Indeed, my lord, I thought I might try to repay you for your kindness.'

'In what way?'

'I cannot claim to be a true bard, my lord, but. . .if you would allow me, I could sing for you in the evenings.'

'By which means you would contrive to sup with us.' Gerald was unimpressed. 'I think you would better demonstrate your gratitude by remembering your place.'

Elidyr stopped in confusion. He stared after the Archdeacon long after he and the children had passed through the manor gates.

As the trio descended the steep path, David shaded his eyes to look towards the sea. 'Are we to take the easy way across the fields by the church, my lord?'

Gerald frowned at the recollection of his last visit to Manorbier. 'Tell me, is Gregory of Kilgetty still Rector?'

'Yes, he instructs us in Latin and the Scriptures.'

'Then we will take the cliff path.' Gerald recalled with distaste that Gregory of Kilgetty was undoubtedly the most tedious man this side of the Severn. Even when he was not teaching Latin.

David grinned, finding a new kinship with his great-uncle. They walked by the shallow stream until it soaked into oblivion in the sandy beach, and turned to follow the tide line towards the cliffs rising from the far side of the tiny bay. Gerald found it tiring to walk on the soft sand and loose pebbles, and quite unconsciously reverted to his childhood game of trying to step from stone to stone without touching the sand. He cleared his throat gruffly as he noticed the children's amused glances, and was grateful for the distraction of a most interesting object amid the tangled flotsam of the beach.

'What is it?' Nest was intrigued.

The driftwood, a tree branch perhaps three paces long, was twisted and gnarled like the severed limb of an ancient ogre. Fronds of drying seaweed played host to a myriad sand flies, and dense colonies of strange, greyish creatures, each the length of a finger, drooped sadly as they baked to their death in the hot sun. Each had a delicate fringe, and a long, dark stalk to anchor it to the wood.

'I know!' David cried in his excitement. 'I know, I know! I've heard about these. They're tiny birds, joined to the wood by their heads. Look!' He bent to examine one of them, poking the whithered, reddish tuft at the end with a tentative finger. 'There are the tail feathers! They sprout from trees like this, and when they're big enough they break free and fly away! This branch must have fallen into the sea before the birds were ready.'

Nest regarded her brother with scorn. 'Don't be silly, David! They look more like shellfish than birds.'

Yet more proof of the folly of all females. Gerald watched with a benign smile as the children argued. The origin of barnacle geese was well known. Even Pliny had written of them a thousand years before. Although the birds were common enough, they were never seen to breed, but here for all to see were geese in the making! It was obvious, the evidence before their eyes! *Quod Erat Demonstrandum!*

XX

The path to the clifftop was steeper than Gerald remembered, and narrower by far. He could not recall how many years it was since he had last come this way. Perhaps ten, perhaps fifty, and he saw something of his own youth in the children who ran heedlessly ahead. Pausing to take breath, he looked back across the bay towards Manorbier. Perched on its hilltop, enclosed secure in its wooden palisade, a tendril of smoke from the kitchen fire curling into the perfect sky, the manor was a picture of contentment.

Only as the Archdeacon turned to follow the children did he remember the chasm. 'Be careful!' Gerald shouted his urgent warning, just as his older brothers had done in his own childhood. He recalled quite clearly the narrow cleft that sliced into the cliffs, clean as a knife through butter. Barely a good pace across, and half concealed in the bracken, the smooth, perpendicular walls fell to a terrifying confusion of rock and funnelling surf a hundred feet below.

Nest and David were waiting for him as he came to the chasm, and Gerald was unaccountably irritated in the knowledge that they knew the path as well as he. They held out their hands to assist the old man. 'Take care, my lord, this is a dangerous place.'

The Archdeacon's reply was short and ungracious.

The reddish mud of the path was baked to the texture of unglazed pottery, and a delight to walk on with its border of thistles, bracken and heather entwined with the delicate blooms of honeysuckle. Butterflies bobbed heedlessly across the path, as though they, and not the family of de Barri, owned these cliffs. As, perhaps, they did. A small blue butterfly settled upon Gerald's sleeve, and as he inspected the insect he marvelled at the perfect hue of a summer sky, at the minute symmetry of black eyes and trembling feelers, at the wonder of God's creation that He should lavish such care upon even the smallest creature. The butterfly flicked its wings and flew away inland across the bracken towards the pale gold of a distant meadow, and Gerald found himself standing beside the King's Quoit.

The great capstone, three paces across and fully five good paces long, rested at one end upon the steeply sloping ground, the other end upon two tall upright stones so that it lay almost level, with a dark, damp place beneath. This ancient burial chamber, gathering its pelt of lichen long before even the coming of the saints to Wales, had looked out upon the Severn Sea for countless centuries to watch with equal detachment the passage of raft, coracle and Viking longship.

Gerald felt a twinge of conscience he had never had as child, as he sat down beside Nest and David upon this ancient monument. Nest produced the bag of cakes, Gerald's favourite, and handed him the flagon she had carried from the manor. He drank gratefully.

The heat would have been unendurable, were it not for the westerly wind blowing in from the Irish Sea. There was always such a breeze on the cliffs of Manorbier, or so Gerald imagined. It must contribute to the healthy atmosphere of the place, for the sweet air of Ireland was so pure that no poison could work in that land, and the Irish never suffered from any of the three plagues that tormented the unhappy souls of the British.

'Some say this was the burial place of one of the old Welsh kings,' said Gerald through a mouthful of cake, as he brushed his crumbs from the surface of the stone.

At once, David jumped down from the capstone. Not, as Gerald first thought, from guilt, but to peer into the shadows beneath. 'There's nothing in there now!'

'The grave would have been robbed long ago. They used to bury their kings in all their regalia of gold and silver. . . as offerings to their pagan gods, I imagine. The Welsh are not pagan now, of course,' Gerald added hastily. 'They were brought into the fold many hundreds of years ago. Some by Christian Romans, some by the Celtic saints. . . Patrick, David, Justinian and the like. Saint David was the first Archbishop in Wales, as you know, and some believe he was the uncle of King Arthur.'

'Yes. . . Elidyr told us about that.'

Far below, a gull floated on wings of carved ivory. Gerald drank once more from the flagon, disappointed that the well-water of Manorbier was already losing its chill. 'You seem to have made a friend of our Welsh guest.'

'Did we do wrong?'

Gerald frowned at the challenge in the girl's voice. 'If I did not wish you to speak to Elidyr, child, you would not have been allowed near him! You could learn much from Elidyr, but hear his words with caution. The Welsh are a lyrical race, they bend the truth for beauty's sake.'

'Only the Welsh?' David spoke up, with a mischievous edge to his voice.

Gerald cleared his throat. 'Few have challenged the veracity of *my* writings.' He was careful not to say *none*.

'Elidyr told us a story about Gwrtheyrn and Emrys, and the dragons in the well. Is it true?'

'Gwrtheyrn? Yes, that is the Welsh name for Vortigern. And Emrys is called Merlin by some. All the bards tell of it.'

'But is it true?'

Gerald found it hard to admire David's persistence. 'A good question. And, like all good questions, no easy matter to answer. No doubt Elidyr has his own sources, but I learned of the story from the writings of Geoffrey of Monmouth.' Gerald spoke as though he expected the boy to grasp at once the significance of this.

'Was not Geoffrey of Monmouth a great historian?'

'I have heard the story told of a young man of Caerleon who was so gifted of second sight that he was able to *see* lies. He would see a demon dancing upon the tongue of the liar. When this fellow was given a copy of Geoffrey's *History of the Kings of Britain*, demons danced upon the manuscript and all over the body of the reader!'

'But Archdeacon, when does an untruth become a lie?' Nest asked her question eagerly. 'Would the demons have danced on the manuscript if Geoffrey did not know it was untrue?'

Gerald, almost against his own stubborn will, began to feel a certain respect for Nest. She was a true sceptic after his own heart. She would have made a good chronicler herself, had she

105

not had the misfortune to be born female. 'Geoffrey of Monmouth has been responsible for more confusion than any so-called historian I can think of. He was an irritating little man, with more imagination than veracity. A man who regarded the truth as. . .as more of a hurdle than a stepping stone in accounting for the events of history.'

'You met him?' David spoke with awe. Geoffrey's great book was so well known that his father had taught him whole sections of it by rote.

'It was years ago, when I was very young, and he was as old as I am now. He boasted that he had access to some great work of history, the hidden source from which he drew his own book. But he would never allow anyone to see it!'

'Do you think Geoffrey invented it all?'

'There is a fine thread of truth running through the story, I have no doubt of that. I am sure there was a king named Vortigern, and that he was defeated by the Saxons. And I believe that there was a King Arthur who drove the Saxons away again.'

'But surely there are Saxons in England now.'

'Of course there are, Nest, else the Norman English would have no one to enslave. But in Arthur Pendragon's time there were none. He drove them out of Britain in twelve battles, the final victory at Mount Badon. That is recorded by Nennius, and I have no doubts as to *his* veracity. He lived through the events he described, and that is more than can be said of Geoffrey of Monmouth.'

'What happened then?' asked Nest. 'After this last battle?'

'Mount Badon was not King Arthur's last battle, but it was his last great victory. Arthur over-reached himself. He tried to extend his empire so far beyond the Island of Britain that he fell prey to treachery at home. He was killed, his empire was divided and the Saxons returned yet again.'

Nest looked at the blue stone of the King's Quoit, at its scarred surface, its growth of lichen, its unimaginable age. 'Elidyr doesn't think Arthur is dead. He believes that Arthur sleeps somewhere, waiting to return.'

'Of course he does.' Gerald laughed aloud at the children's astonishment. 'What I mean is, I am sure that Elidyr believes what he says! Most of the Welsh, in their ignorance, share that

106

belief. Near St David's there is a stone burial chamber, much like this one, save that it is still covered by a mound of earth. They call it *Coetan Arthur*. Even here at Manorbier I have heard tales that this very chamber on which we sit was King Arthur's tomb. Every town, every village claims to have Arthur Pendragon buried nearby. There must be scores, hundreds, of such places.'

'But King Arthur must be buried somewhere,' Nest retorted.

'Of course he must. And thirty years ago they found his tomb.'

The children stared in amazement.

'I should have said,' Gerald smiled, 'that a tomb was found. Whether or not it belonged to Arthur, you may decide for yourselves. The story of the tomb first came to light when King Henry the Second was travelling through Deheubarth... through South Wales. A wandering bard told him that King Arthur lay buried in Lloegr, in the Vale of Glass. The Normans call it Glastonbury. On King Henry's orders the monks from the nearby monastery searched for the tomb, but they found nothing. Some years later, after Henry had been succeeded by Richard, the abbey of Glastonbury fell upon hard times. There was a fire, and much of its wealth and holy relics were destroyed. Fewer and fewer pilgrims came, so less money was donated to the abbey. It was then that the miracle happened. The monks found King Arthur's grave.

. 'The body, within a casket of oak, rested between two stone pyramids. Beneath the casket lay a stone slab with a cross and an inscription which said that Arthur lay buried there, with his second wife Guinevere. The monks took up the casket and carried it into the church, where it was reinterred with great ceremony. Glastonbury became a centre of pilgrimage once again, and this brought much wealth flowing into the abbey.'

Nest smiled. 'Do you think the monks made the tomb themselves?'

'They may not have been above such things. The Abbot of Glastonbury has even claimed that the bones of Saint David are buried in the abbey.'

'Is that possible?' David's quick interest surprised the Archdeacon.

'I do not believe so. The relics of the Saint were lost many years ago, when the Norsemen stole them from his shrine at St David's.

How could the bones have come into the hands of Glastonbury? And, if they did, why did the monks of the abbey not return them at once to their rightful place? No, I do not believe that Glastonbury holds the bones of our Saint. I journeyed there, years ago, but they could show me no proof of their claim. The proof of Arthur's grave was there for all to see, of course, and the old tombstone still lies upon the new shrine they built for him.'

'And the stone says that Arthur is buried with his wife Guinevere?' Nest asked eagerly.

'That is what the inscription says.'

'Then the monks' story must be false!' cried Nest. 'Arthur's wife... her name was *Gwenhwyfar*. It was the French who called her Guinevere, hundreds of years after she died.'

Gerald nodded his approval. 'Exactly. The tombstone was carved by a Norman.'

'You already knew that? But you must tell everyone, you must challenge the abbey and prove them liars!'

'I fail to see what purpose it would serve. Between you and me, child, there are relics in many a great shrine that might not bear close inspection. It would be a foolish man who pried too close into the fabric of our Church!'

Nest and David, Gerald was sad to note, appeared shocked. 'No, wherever King Arthur may be, he is not at Glastonbury. There is another legend that he was carried to the Isle of Avalon, there to be cured of his wounds after the last great battle. The name is derived from the Welsh, as you know, and it means *The Isle of Apples*. Think of your vision of Paradise, my children, then compare it with that of the Welsh. A green island lost in an endless sea, where the apples are ever ripe on the trees.' Gerald paused. It was an attractive vision. 'A strange idea of Paradise, for a race they tell us is so savage. And Arthur... Arthur their King, sleeps there still. Or so they believe. It is said that, from time to time, the island floats into view and can be seen from St David's. Alas, I have never seen it.'

'I thought King Arthur was flying around Wales in the form of a raven,' said David. 'Watching over his people, waiting for the time to lead them to victory.'

'Waiting first for Saint David to return...' Nest murmured, almost to herself.

'Is that something else Elidyr told you?' The Archdeacon spoke with sudden interest, remembering once again the things he had heard on the night of the Welshman's appearance at Pembroke. Elidyr seemed to show far too much interest in Dewi Sant for a mere layman.

'It was only one of his stories, my lord, I'm sure he meant nothing.'

Gerald looked in concern at Nest, sure that she was defending the Welshman. 'I think Elidyr ab Idwal has told too many stories.'

XXI

Manorbier had awoken to a chill grey morning, a capricious change of humour so typical of the Welsh climate. A sharp wind rose from the bay, stealing through the window of the great hall to ruffle the sheets of parchment as they lay upon the table before the Archdeacon.

Gerald absently placed his ivory ink pot to secure the pages more firmly. He paused as he reached across with his quill, and with a guilty smile removed the inkpot to a safer place. He would have scolded Brother Hugh for courting an accident by such carelessness.

'My lord?' The voice spoke quiet from the doorway.

Gerald completed his sentence, but dipped his quill twice more before he set the page aside and looked up. 'You were instructed to stay away from this place, Elidyr.'

'I must speak with you, my lord Archdeacon.'

Unconsciously, Gerald glanced up to the dark window of the solar far above, from which the lord of the manor could overlook the interior of the great hall. There had been no sound or movement from the solar since daybreak, but he knew that Angharad kept vigil by her husband's side. William must surely be still asleep. 'Very well. What troubles you?'

Elidyr looked around him at the fine trappings of the hall, and cast his own wary glance at the solar window above. 'I wondered if you had heard anything of the Earl Marshal's son.'

'Patience, Elidyr! It has only been three days.'

'Then another three days, and threescore more after that! By now I could have reached my home, I could have told my lord Llywelyn what has happened.'

'Have no fears on that score. The day we left Pembroke, Lady Regat was already on her way to tell Llywelyn, and I have little doubt that she will do so. Either she, or her husband.'

'Her husband? Who is he?'

'How can you not know? He was at Pembroke. . . though I recall now that he was, er. . . occupied with another matter when you arrived. Regat's husband is Rhys Gryg. He calls himself Lord of Deheubarth.'

'Rhys Gryg? *Rhys Gryg? Nen' Tad*, what have I done? My lord, I *must* go to speak with Llywelyn.'

'I have given my word to the Earl Marshal. . . and to Rhys Gryg, for that matter, that you will stay in my custody.'

'My lord, I said things to Regat that should never have come to the ears of Llywelyn's enemies. I beg of you, as you value his friendship, help me undo the harm I have done.'

'I could send a courier. You have only to tell me the message.'

'I. . . I cannot tell you, my lord.'

'You have said things to Regat of *Deheubarth* that you will not trust to the ears of an archdeacon from the very shrine of Saint David? You make a strange choice of confessor, my son. . .' Gerald toyed with his goose quill. The Welshman's eyes had become evasive at the very mention of the name of Saint David. 'Or perhaps it is not so strange. You seem to have a particular aversion to any mention of our patron Saint.'

'Forgive me, my lord.' Elidyr was on his feet now, edging towards the door. 'I should not have troubled you.'

'Elidyr, wait!' But Gerald saw that he was calling only to the grey sky beyond the open door.

With a sigh the Archdeacon bent anew to his manuscript. Some means must be found to loosen the Welshman's tongue. He was grateful now that no news had come from Pembroke. At least it gave him more time. . .

It was not a day for walking on the cliffs, nor for hunting crabs on the beach, and the children came to watch the archery practice

110

in the courtyard. They found Elidyr sitting upon the steps, gnawing at the remnants of a saddle of mutton and casting an occasional wary glance towards the bowmen's sorry display.

'Is something wrong?' David was not accustomed to being ignored.

Elidyr let the bones slip through his fingers, to be snatched up by a patiently waiting hound. 'I will never be free of this place!'

'Have you spoken with the Archdeacon?'

'I asked him if there was news from Pembroke, but it seems the Earl Marshal has hidden his son well.'

'No, Anselm ran away from Pembroke. Didn't you know?'

Elidyr looked up at Nest's innocent face. 'Can you believe that the Earl of Pembroke would hang his own son on account of a Welshman?' In the children's silence, he watched the arrows fly to their straw targets. 'Your archers. . . why do they practice so long?'

'It is the King's command that all able men must improve their archery.'

'And perhaps the Archdeacon is anxious lest his prisoner escape.'

'Our guards would not shoot you. Our mother has given strict orders.'

'Has she, now?'

The children did not notice the quick interest in the Welshman's reply.

The Archdeacon sat upon the broad sill of the window of the great hall, enjoying the cool evening breeze as he looked across the bay of Manorbier towards the distant monument of King's Quoit. The path along the clifftop traced a fine red thread amid the greens and greys of leaf and stone, and along the path ran the tiny figure of a man.

Gerald's fingers drummed upon the window ledge. Perhaps his old eyes deceived him in the failing light. The slight figure seemed to have a familiar look to it. . . but it would be foolish to call out the guard on so feeble a suspicion.

Gerald of Wales turned to the table and took up his manuscript. He would write a little more before he slept.

XXII

William de Barri slumped moodily in his high-backed chair at the head of the table. Breakfast had been an uncomfortable affair, and not merely because of the lingering pain of his healing wound. The kitchen maid, distraught for Elidyr, had underbaked the bread, whilst the mutton resembled nothing so much as the charred wood in the hearth and the pigeons' eggs would have better served as slingshot.

William stared balefully at his family. 'Dead? The Earl Marshal's prisoner?'

Angharad's eyes brimmed with tears as she bowed her head. 'He tried to escape along the cliff path, my lord, but he ran too fast. He did not see the cleft near King's Quoit. It is a hundred feet down to the sea. No man could have survived.'

'And you saw this?'

'From the solar window, my lord, while you slept.'

'And why is it only now that you tell me?'

'I did not wish to disturb you. There was nothing any of us could have done.'

'We could have searched the shore for his body. Good God, woman, do you imagine the Earl Marshal will believe this tale without proof? He will say that I gave the prisoner his freedom, that I disobeyed him to help a Welshman! He has never wholly trusted me, with my Welsh...'

Gerald had tried not to intrude into the argument, but now he must. 'William, I too saw Elidyr on the cliff path.'

'Did you see him fall?'

Gerald could only shake his head. He was surprised when Angharad looked sharply at him. Did she expect an Archdeacon to lie to support her story?

'How could the guards be so careless?'

'If you recall, my lord, at your order the guards were engaged in practising their marksmanship. Perhaps their vigilance was not what it should have been...'

'So you lay the blame at my door! Then tell me this... how did the fellow escape from a locked storeroom?' William turned upon his wife. 'Is there some Welsh sorcery, my dear, that could bring about this miracle?'

'Does it matter?' Angharad was sobbing now.

'Of course it matters! Manorbier and all within it belong to me. All that passes within its walls is my responsibility. It is I who must stand before the Earl Marshal to give an account of this! But first I will have the truth of it . . . how did he escape? Tell me!'

'He was only locked in by night.' Angharad glanced uneasily between Gerald and William.

'Only confined by night? And by whose permission did he roam free by day?' William's voice was quiet now. Dangerously so. Only this morning had he felt well enough to leave his bed, and he had not expected to find his authority usurped during his few days of illness.

Gerald knew that his nephew's pride was easily bruised. 'It was at my request, my lord. I thought the Welshman deserved better treatment . . . but now it seems I was mistaken in trusting him. I am entirely to blame, and I will tell the Earl Marshal so.'

'You should have consulted me!' Crocks leapt from the table as William's fist crashed down. 'By God, but the guards will pay dear for this! They are *my* liegemen! This is *my* castle!'

'But surely you would have agreed the futility of keeping him prisoner? Elidyr ab Idwal is not . . . was not a criminal. He was a freeman loyal to Lord Llywelyn of Gwynedd, and his only blame was that he survived the shipwreck in which all his comrades perished.'

'So that is why you allowed him to escape . . . he was Llywelyn's man.'

'I knew nothing of his flight until it was too late.'

William swore, unashamed by the Archdeacon's presence, and drained his tankard of ale.

'I shall be leaving Manorbier soon,' Gerald said quietly. 'I must go back to St David's.'

'Then I wish you Godspeed and a safe journey. And pray for me, Archdeacon, that if we ever meet again, I will still be Lord of Manorbier.'

It had been his own fault, of course. Gerald had spent too much time with Angharad and her children, and had forgotten that William did not share their sympathies. Lord William de Barri knew that he could not afford to display his kinship with the

Welsh. He had more Norman blood in his veins than did Gerald and he was, moreover, a nobleman in a land governed by the zealously Norman Earl Marshal of Pembroke.

As Gerald pushed back his chair to take his leave, there came the sound of a hurried tread in the doorway. The guard was breathless. 'A. . . a messenger from Pembroke, my lord.'

'Well? Where is he?' William snapped.

'Already gone, my lord. He had to reach Tenby by nightfall. His message was that the Earl Marshal requires you to attend him at Pembroke, my lord. There's to be a council.'

'What has happened?'

'He did not say, my lord.'

'Has Squire Anselm been found?' This was the first thing to cross Gerald's mind.

'He did not say.'

'Very well.' William rose painfully from his chair. 'See to it that my horse is saddled. My escort is to be prepared to ride within the hour.'

'And ready my horse also,' said Gerald, before the guard could hurry away. He turned to his nephew. 'I will ride with you to Pembroke.'

'I thought you were going to St David's.'

'So I am. . . but Pembroke is on the way.'

William shook his head as he strode out of the hall to make his preparations. Pembroke was miles away from the road to St David's.

As Gerald busied himself in collecting together his few belongings, Angharad lingered in the hall. Now that her husband was gone, her tears had swiftly dried. Her hand rested lightly on the table top, and her gaze did not leave the Archdeacon's face.

'My lord?'

Gerald rolled his manuscripts and packed away his quills. 'What is it, child?'

'Did you truly see Elidyr on the cliff?'

'Do you think an Archdeacon would lie?'

Angharad seemed lost in distraction. 'You do not ask if I know anything more of. . . of what happened.'

Gerald stared long at her troubled face. 'If there is something

114

you have to confess, then go to your own priest. Gregory of Kilgetty can shoulder the burden of your troubles. I must not!'

Angharad looked at the Archdeacon, surprised by his lack of curiosity, but then she understood. Gerald was to go to Pembroke, and he could not lie to the Earl Marshal. He did not dare learn anything more of Elidyr's death.

Left alone in the great hall, the Archdeacon stood awhile at the window to take one last, lingering look upon the sandy beach of Manorbier, the tumbling sea, the steep cliffs, the path to King's Quoit. So often as a child he had gazed upon the view from this window.

And one thing Gerald de Barri remembered very well. From nowhere in the manor was it possible to see the deep chasm where poor Elidyr had met his death.

XXIII

The Castle of Pembroke

27 June, 1215

'Your names!'

The voice barked from the gatehouse of Pembroke Castle, and was closely followed by an ill-tempered and ill-shaven guard. Torchlight glinted from his drawn sword, his helmet, the whites of his eyes. A dozen of his fellows stood back in the shadows, crossbows at the ready.

Gerald and William de Barri reined in on the cobbles beneath the portcullis, both taken aback by the challenge. It was an hour past dusk, and it was the guardsman's duty to be wary, but surely...

'Do we look like Welshmen?' The journey had been a slow and painful one for William de Barri, and he was in no mood to argue with the Earl Marshal's vassal.

'Hard to tell, in this light.'

'This is Archdeacon Gerald de Barri, and I am Lord of Manorbier. The Earl Marshal is expecting me.'

The guard peered narrowly at him. 'Aye, I recognise you now, m'lord.'

'We know the way,' said the Archdeacon. 'Take our horses to the stables and show our men to the kitchen.'

The guard grunted, but did as he was bidden.

As they crossed the moonlit outer bailey, Gerald marvelled at the change that had been wrought since the tournament. The central square of churned mud was crowded with makeshift huts and tents to house the hundreds of men at arms and all the accoutrements to accompany a small army. Smithies and field kitchens, butchers, bakers, tailors and cobblers, bowyers and fletchers, swordsmiths and wheelwrights, and all manner of camp followers plied their business among the caged hens and geese, the tethered pigs and goats.

The pavilions squatted still where the lists had been, their

116

colours bled from them by the cold moon, their pennants hanging idle. Here camped the minor nobles and squires, whose bounden duty compelled them to bring their serfs to serve their liege lord Earl William Marshal in time of war.

On the battlements, where the harsh grey of the curtain wall faded into the softer blackness of the night, the grim spectres of guardsmen paced, ever watchful.

'They must have trebled the guard.' William de Barri's voice was little more than a whisper as he peered around him in awe at the defences of the great castle.

'A wise precaution.' Gerald was wondering whether he would be well received at the council, acutely aware of how high the feeling must be running against the Welsh and anyone seen to be in sympathy with them. As they approached the great hall, Gerald cautioned his nephew. 'I think we might be wise to avoid the Earl Marshal, if possible.'

'Because of the escape?'

'Partly because of that.'

The great hall was crowded with castellans, knights and sundry officials, all liegemen of the Earl of Pembroke. In the odd stillness there was no revelry, no ribaldry, no serving wenches bustling to and fro with food and wine. Only the ringing voice of the Earl Marshal echoed into the respectful silence.

The Earl Marshal had been speaking for some time. Already he had told his liegemen of Elidyr's accusation, for not all had been present at the tourney, and of Anselm's flight from Pembroke. 'From St David's to Carmarthen, from Tenby to Llawhaden, nigh on a hundred men have scoured the country. They have questioned everyone and have found nothing. I cannot believe, now, that Anselm will ever be found. Perhaps he is already dead.'

'Your pardon, my lord.' The castellan of Carew, close by the Earl Marshal's right hand, rose to his feet and immediately drew the attention of the gathering. He was a tall, bearded man of conscious elegance, a distant relative of the de Barris' who flattered himself that he was the most loyal of all the Earl Marshal's followers. 'All of us pray that your son is safe. None believe that Llywelyn's son is dead. That the Earl of Pembroke should be placed under duress by the wild rantings of a . . .'

117

'I thank you, my lord.' The Earl Marshal disliked Carew, an obsequious fellow whose opinion of himself far outstripped his stature. He dressed too well, and it was evident from the blandness of his smell that he washed too often. It was even said that he *bathed*. 'I should have thought it self-evident that even if Gruffydd is alive, there is no certainty that he will let it be known. From what I have heard of him, I'll warrant he would like nothing more than to incite a war...by whatever means.' The Earl Marshal raised his voice to address the hall.

'What matters, my lords, is what Llywelyn chooses to believe. He could use the boy's disappearance to demand Norman lands and castles as compensation. He might use it as an excuse to break the peace agreed at the signing of the charter. Rhys Gryg is eager for war, that I know. So, I believe, are the other southern princes, but thus far Llywelyn's good sense has restrained them. But what if he believes the story of his son's death? Worse, my lords, what if he hears that it was I who took the boy from Corfe, and believes that my intent was to murder him? Then we might face the whole Welsh nation united against us under Llywelyn. That is the one thing I have always feared. The one thing the King has always feared. And that is the one way that Pembroke might fall.'

William Marshal paused, allowing his cold gaze to roam about the hall, looking every man in the eye. He noticed the Archdeacon, and frowned as he did so.

'But I have not summoned you here to Pembroke, my lords, only for a council of war. Here in Wales we feel ourselves far removed from the troubles of England. But we must not forget that we are all liegemen of the King.'

The Earl Marshal held up a loosely rolled parchment upon which could be seen a scarlet seal. 'I have received this message from King John. The King believes that the charter of liberties will fail, he believes that some amongst his barons still seek to usurp his power. Indeed, he tells me that these traitors now disobey the very clauses that they themselves forced upon him!'

The assembly roared their disapproval. William Marshal waited for silence. His heart was gladdened by the sight of these loyal men. By their strength of limb and character, by their respect for himself, by their eagerness to hear his words, he felt his own powers redoubled.

'Yet the King is generous to those traitors amongst his barons. He gives them now the opportunity to meet with him, to discuss again any provisions of the charter that cause them grief. Council will be held next month at the town of Oxford, and the King has commanded the presence of William Marshal to stand by his side.' The Earl Marshal had to wait for silence once again.

'My lords, once before I neglected my Welsh lands in order to advise the King. I was with him in England for weeks before the signing of the charter, and you know well enough the consequence of my absence. We were attacked upon every front. Giles de Braose...'

There was an obedient mutter of dislike for this son of the hated William de Braose. But Giles had seen his exiled father die in penury, and his mother and elder brother had starved to death in the King's prison at Corfe. It was small wonder that he had been among the foremost of the rebels against the King.

'... Giles de Braose sought to make allies of the Welsh by having his brother Reginald betrothed to the daughter of Llywelyn. Reginald seized back the castles that the King had confiscated from his traitorous father. Abergavenny he took, Skenfrith and Pencelli, White Castle...all of them. And he was not content to rest there, as you well remember.'

The castellans fell to silence. It was as if the Earl Marshal sought to humiliate them by flinging past defeats into their faces.

'And the princes of Deheubarth did not stand idle. They took Maenclochog, Cemais, the Gower... How many castles did we lose? How many acres of land? How many lives? It will be decades before we can regain what the Welsh have stolen. And now my King calls me to England! I put it to you, my lords. Am I to go to Oxford to stand as a prop for an ailing king? Or am I to stay in Pembroke to hold the castle ready against the Welsh and the traitorous barons?'

William the Younger, seated at his father's right, regarded the sudden uproar in the hall with eager anticipation. His wishes were written clear on his face. If the Earl Marshal were to go to Oxford, then this would leave him, the eldest son, in command of Pembroke. Perhaps the Earl Marshal would die in England, felled

119

by a stab in the back in Oxford, or by a brigand's arrow on some dark highway. William the Younger had waited a long time for his inheritance, and he was not a patient man.

The castellan of Carew rose to his feet once more. 'My lord Earl, without your leadership our task against the Welsh will be all the harder. But an order from the King cannot be disobeyed.'

The castellan of Haverford was quick to speak against Carew. 'My lord, you are not a counsellor. You are a soldier, the finest in Christendom! The King has courtiers aplenty. They fawn at his feet, all begging to advise him. King John does not need you, but Pembroke has never needed you more! If you go to Oxford, my lord, we shall be slaves of the Welsh within a month.'

There was a murmur of agreement. Though none would dare speak of it aloud, there was a common feeling that the Norman English had brought their problems upon themselves. They had no right to call upon their kinsmen in Wales for assistance.

The Earl Marshal could not allow himself to think in this way. He owed everything to the King of England. The decision, for him, was an impossible one.

A gaunt, bearded figure near the head of the gathering rose painfully to his feet. The hall held silence for him, for this was the Lord of Cemais.

'I know nothing of this meeting in Oxford, my lords, I know only that a month ago I saw men and women and their children slaughtered before the burning towers of my home. That was but the beginning! The Welsh will not be sated. They will press on eastward, and to the south! Who will be next to fall? Llawhaden? Carew? Tenby? Pembroke?' He glared at each castellan in turn. 'What I say, my lords, is that the danger to us, to our wives and children, is real. We need our whole strength, our *whole* strength, to survive the onslaught.'

'Let the English fight their own wars, and leave us to ours!'

Gerald de Barri was astonished, and not displeased. It was his nephew who had spoken.

The uproar was silenced by a great crash from the centre of the gathering. The castellan of Haverford beat upon the table with the flat of his broadsword, and rose to command the attention of the assembly.

'My lord Earl, you say that the King has summoned William

120

Marshal to join him in council at Oxford. Stay in Pembroke, my lord, yet obey his command! Let the King have his William Marshal, and let us have ours. Send him your son!'

The silence in the great hall gave way to a clamour of approval. William Marshal, Earl of Pembroke, threw back his head and laughed.

William the Younger did not. Was this, then, his father's way of punishing him for his open alliance with the rebel barons? 'I. . .I would go, my lords, and gladly. . . but dare we disobey the King?'

'The King will be glad enough to see you lad,' bellowed Haverford. 'If you're your father's son, you'll deal sharply with those traitors!'

William the Younger dared muster no argument. In truth, the more he pondered the idea, the more the opportunity appealed to him. It would allow him to make his own peace with the King, or to conspire with the barons, or both, whichever course promised the best advantage. 'Very well, my lords, I shall go as proxy for the Earldom of Pembroke. If that is your wish, my lord Earl?'

The Earl Marshal did not look at his son. He knew well enough what must be passing through the boy's mind, but the security of his castles, and indeed of the whole Norman presence in southern Wales, was uppermost in his own thoughts. He smiled grimly. 'Then I will stay, my lords, while my son goes to Oxford to attend King John. John, King of England. . .aye, and long may he reign as the true King of Wales!'

As one, they assembly took up the Earl Marshal's warcry. 'John, King of Wales! John, King of Wales! John, King of Wales!'

Gerald de Barri closed his eyes as the rhythmic chant shuddered through him. He leaned back against the door pillar, unwilling to be seen to differ, unable to voice either protest or agreement. Through his mind rang the echo of another cry. . .heard years before in a gathering not so different from this one.

'*Llywelyn Fawr, Brenin Cymru!*'. . . Llywelyn the Great, King of Wales.

XXIV

Wine and ale flowed freely, now that the Earl Marshal's dilemma had been laid to rest. He forsook his place at the head of the table and moved amongst his liegemen, speaking to each one in turn. The strengths and weaknesses of every castle, plans for their defences, their immediate needs in the forthcoming crisis, all these things he could discuss in the most minute particular. The lords and castellans jostled for their turn, jealously noting the order in which the Earl Marshal spoke to them, as if this in itself were some indication of their rank.

Just as the Earl Marshal moved around the hall, so too did Gerald de Barri, for the Archdeacon was intent upon business of his own. His progress was slow, for he felt obliged to stop and converse with every man whom he recognised, and to make the acquaintance of those few he did not. He was ever eager to exchange news and gossip, to offer his own good counsel, and the knights for the most part were flattered by his patronage. Soldiers, more so than any other class, were ever anxious to better their souls, and Gerald of Wales was no ordinary ecclesiastic! Author, chronicler, confidant of princes and kings and himself of noble blood, he had travelled to Rome, he had spoken even with Pope Innocent himself.

Gerald's purpose in this was to learn the whereabouts of the men at arms who had returned from Corfe Castle with Squire Anselm. The stories told by Elidyr and Anselm as to the loss of the ship had served only to confuse matters, and the Archdeacon wished to obtain a less biased testimony.

He found one of the soldiers standing guard by the stairway from the undercroft, and was not surprised to learn from him that the sergeant was still not recovered from his flogging.

'Then *you* may answer my questions,' Gerald said generously.

'Yes, my lord.' The soldier stared stoically ahead.

'I would like to know the fate of the Welshmen who travelled with you from Corfe.'

'I told it all to the Earl Marshal yesterday, my lord.'

'And now I would like to hear for myself. What happened on board the ship?'

The soldier frowned, his eyes seeking his master in the crowd, anxious lest he be seen in dereliction of his duty. At length he reluctantly replied. 'Quite a set-to there was, my lord, when the Welshmen got free. Most of us were asleep, and we woke to find our own swords at our throats! And there were the crew, just standing with grins on their faces while the Welshmen paid them off with our money! They stick together, my lord, these Celts.' The soldier lowered his voice. 'Fools we were, to take a Cornish galley. My sergeant tried to get Squire Anselm to take a different ship, but he wouldn't listen. Oh no, he knew best. Only the swiftest in the harbour was good enough for him. So there we were, out at sea with a crew of traitors, and *him* in command. And now the sergeant's wearing stripes across his back that would better suit Squire Anselm, were he not the Earl Marshal's son . . .'

'So the crew helped the Welsh seize the ship. What then?'

'Instead of bringing us to Pembroke, my lord, like they'd been paid to do, they sailed straight on past Milford Haven and across St Bride's Bay. We were all saying our prayers, I can tell you. We thought we'd be thrown to the fishes, can't understand to this day why we weren't. If I'd been in their place . . . Well, they sailed the boat up a small creek, Porth Clais I think it's called, close by the castle of St David's. There they stripped us and gave us their own filthy rags to cover ourselves, then they let us go.'

'What happened to Llywelyn's son?'

'The last I saw of him was when we were floundering in the shallows as they sailed away. There he was on the stern, jeering at us, wearing the fine clothes he'd took from the Squire.' The soldier gave a laconic grin. 'I tell you one thing, my lord. If the ship really did go down, I'd like to have seen that little bastard trying to swim wearing the Squire's chain mail!'

'Would that be possible?'

'Well, our sergeant used to say that some soldiers are trained for strength that way . . . swimming in their armour. Can't see the use of it myself. The iron would all rust, seems to me. But looking at Gruffydd . . .' The soldier shook his head, still smiling. 'Not a chance, my lord. If the ship was on fire . . . not a chance in the world.'

'The Welshman . . . Elidyr ab Idwal . . . he said that Anselm set the ship afire.'

'I heard his story, my lord, but as God is my witness I saw no fire.'

'Do you understand the Welsh tongue? Do you recall what the Welshmen were saying before they set you ashore?'

'I could follow some of it, my lord. That Elidyr repeated it oft enough! Children's stories and tavern tales, most of it, but they swallowed it like gannets. Argued amongst themselves for hours on end, they took it so serious.'

'What was it they talked about, mostly?'

The soldier hesitated. The Earl Marshal had not asked about such things. 'Well...much of it was stories about King Arthur. They listened to those tales as if they were parables of Our Lord, blasphemous heathen that they are. They think he lies sleeping, waiting for the time to awaken and lead Wales to greatness, or some such...'

'And when would be that time?'

'I didn't understand it all, but they seem to believe that if Saint David were to return, then King Arthur would soon follow.'

'What else was there?'

'There was much harping on about Saint David himself. Now then, what was it...'

'Think, man! Was it the bard saying this? Was it Elidyr?'

'Yes, it was him alright. He did more talking than all the rest of them put together! Now...he was saying as how the bones of Saint David were lost from the shrine, centuries ago.'

'One hundred and thirty six years ago,' Gerald corrected him with an encouraging smile. 'The Vikings raided the village and burned the church of Saint David to the ground, and the holy relics have never been seen since.'

'Yes...yes, that's what they said. The raiders found a stone chest in the church, and thought it must be treasure...gold or jewels or some such. They took it back to their ship, meaning to open it once they were safe away, but then there was a great storm and the ship was driven ashore somewhere. They took shelter in a cave, and it was there they opened up the stone chest. When they found nothing they valued, they cast it aside and it shattered into pieces, and the bones of Saint David still lie where they fell. Well, that was the story, but I don't see...'

The soldier rambled on, but Gerald de Barri was no longer listening.

So that was it! Elidyr must have heard the story, perhaps while imprisoned in Corfe. Perhaps he even knew where the relics might be found. And what if they were found? What then? *King Arthur will follow Saint David.* Could the Welsh really believe it. . . that if the holy bones of Saint David were found, then King Arthur would return to lead them to victory? Or could it be that they would bestow Arthur Pendragon's name upon whichever leader held the relics, believing that the great King was reborn in him?

What a talisman those blessed remains would be! The Welsh would take their finding as a sign of God's favour. They would unite behind the relics, they would feel themselves invincible. They would drive the Norman oppressors into the sea, and at their head would have been Gruffydd ap Llywelyn, the new King of Wales, the new Arthur of Britain. If Gruffydd had not died. . .

'Did they. . .' Gerald's throat had tightened so that he could scarcely speak. 'Did they say where the Vikings found their cave?'

'You believe the story, my lord?'

'*Did they say?*'

'No. At least, never in my hearing.'

'You said they argued about the story?'

'It was all. . . all nonsense, my lord. Oh, that Elidyr claimed he knew where the bones could be found. He wanted to go and search for them, but even the other Welshmen knew what a fool's errand that would be. Only Gruffydd seemed to listen to him, he and a few of the other young lads. The rest just wanted to get home, back to their Gwynedd. They argued about the story even as they set us ashore, I thought they would come to blows! Do you want to know what I think, my lord?'

'Very much.'

'I think they did come to blows, after we had gone. Gruffydd and Elidyr wanting to sail close inshore to search along the cliffs for the Vikings' cave, trying to force the others to take the risk. What if there had been a fight? There were torches on board. Easy enough for one of them to be knocked over, and there's your fire!'

'But Elidyr said. . .'

125

'I know what he said, my lord, but that one has the heart of a bard, and the imagination to go with it! Truth or lies, history or legend . . . they're all one and the same in that stewpot of a Welsh head!'

A loud belch warned, too late, of the approach of the castellan of Haverford.

'Terrible business, eh, Archdeacon?'

'Yes, indeed.' Gerald wondered how best he could make his escape.

'All credit to Squire Anselm, I say! A few less of the Welsh swine for the rest of us to slaughter!'

Gerald abandoned all thought of retreat. 'But it is foolish, surely you agree, to condemn an entire nation for the folly of its leaders.'

The castellan knit his brows. This was a difficult concept for him to grasp, but Gerald gave him no time to ponder. 'Have you yet spoken with the Earl Marshal? What are his plans against the Welsh?'

Haverford swelled with pride. 'He sought me out before all the others! We are to place watchmen on the battlements and in the church towers, and stay on the defensive. No point in chasing 'em, when they can run backwards faster than we can run forwards, eh?'

'But surely they will just lay siege to the outermost castles and take them one by one?'

'No, the Earl Marshal has thought of that. He has arranged that we may each send for reinforcements, the moment we are threatened. We will each take back a basket of pigeons. We can bind messages to their legs, and they will fly straight back to Pembroke.'

'An excellent scheme.' Gerald felt as reassured by this as he had been by the Earl Marshal's decision to stay in Pembroke, though nothing would have induced him to say so. 'I wonder if the Earl Marshal has thought of including the Bishop's lands in his plans? Perhaps I should speak with him . . .' Gerald made to move away, but the castellan lurched after him.

'Will you be staying long in Pembroke, Archdeacon?'

'I must return to St David's in the morning.'

'Then I would be honoured to escort you. I have to attend to the defence of Haverford, but my men will accompany you the rest of the way. Can't trust the roads, you know. Not these days.'

'Most generous, my lord.' Gerald administered a hurried blessing, and took his leave. He had seen the Earl Marshal speaking to William de Barri, and knew he would be sorely needed.

'...dead, you say? While trying to escape? Couldn't be better, de Barri! It seems I can depend on you...' The Earl Marshal was speaking in a conspiratorial whisper, while William de Barri appeared bemused by the whole business. Gerald could only smile in his relief that the Earl Marshal had accepted Elidyr's death in this manner.

William Marshal looked up at Gerald's approach. 'Good evening, my lord Archdeacon. I hear that your prisoner met his just end.'

'God's will be done, my lord Earl.'

'No matter. The Welshman is of no further consequence now that Anselm cannot be found.'

William de Barri, wearied by the lingering pain of his wound, interrupted. 'Forgive me, my lord Earl, but if you have no further need of me here, I would ask your leave to return to Manorbier.'

The Earl Marshal frowned for a moment, then remembered. 'Ah yes. The wound still giving you trouble, eh? Go back to your castle by all means. But remember what I have told you. Get the gatehouse finished...and stone walls would serve you better than those wooden palisades!'

William de Barri bowed to his liege-lord. It was easy for the wealthy Earl of Pembroke to talk, but stone walls cost money. He turned to Gerald. 'You are not returning with me, my lord?'

'No,' said Gerald sadly. 'Convey my blessings to Angharad, and to David and Nest.'

'They will want to see you return to the manor soon. As I do, uncle.'

'I will do my best. Perhaps I will retire to Manorbier. But not yet.'

'Farewell then, and to you, my Lord Earl.'

'A fine soldier.' The Earl Marshal's eyes followed the Lord of Manorbier as he limped from the hall. 'And a brave man. I've seen my sons take to their beds for weeks on end with lesser injuries than his. A pity about his castle, though...'

'The *manor*?' Gerald asked drily.

'The manor...er, yes. In all honesty, I doubt that it will withstand a serious attack.'

'Manorbier has always looked to the protection of Pembroke. It would be my earnest wish...'

'Manorbier may continue to rely on us, you have my word on it,' the Earl Marshal conceded heartily. 'On Pembroke, and upon my other castles. That is why we are here.'

This promise was a great relief to Gerald, but now he looked keenly at William Marshal. 'I am surprised that there is no representative here from the castle of St David's.'

The Earl Marshal frowned. 'I have not forgotten the Bishop's castles, my lord. The castellan of Llawhaden accepted my invitation, though he seems confident that the Bishop's soldiers can hold the border without my aid. As for St David's...I beg your pardon, my lord Archdeacon, but it did not occur to me to send for anyone. Surely you do not believe that the Welsh would be so barbarous as to attack the shrine of their own Saint?'

'I do not expect to have to defend St David's, my lord, but that does not mean that the castle cannot be of service to Pembroke. It commands a fine view of the Western seas, as you know, and on a clear day to the shores of Ireland! No invading fleet could sail from Gwynedd round to Pembroke without our notice.'

'An invading fleet from Gwynedd? That's a preposterous idea!'

Gerald thought so too, but he was determined that his castle should be taken seriously. 'I wonder, my lord Earl, if King Harold thought the same of William of Normandy? With a little forethought on his part, none of us Normans might be here today.'

The Earl Marshal of Pembroke looked long and hard at the Archdeacon, unable to decide whether this old man was mocking him, or whether he himself had overlooked something in his strategy. His experience told him that he could not allow any eventuality, however outlandish, to go unconsidered. 'Very well, Archdeacon, perhaps you are right. Take with you some of our pigeons, and loose them to return to Pembroke when this fleet of yours is sighted. But pray do not alarm yourself over the prospect. Our concern for the moment is with the border castles.'

The Archdeacon gave his blessing to the Earl Marshal of Pembroke, and left him to his castellans. He had no delusions as to the position of St David's in William Marshal's scheme of things. It was remote, and although an important place of pilgrimage, it was of little strategic value and of no interest to the Marshal of the King's armies. If St David's were to be attacked, its fall would be regrettable, but no more than that.

As for sending messages through the air, Gerald de Barri could think of far better use for a basket of pigeons. . .

XXV

The Cathedral of St David's

30 JUNE, 1215

The sun streamed in through the tall windows, painting all the splendid hues and patterns of their glass upon the ranks of carved columns. The colours stirred languidly with every transient cloud that veiled the face of the sun, dimming to oblivion, ever to reappear brighter than before. Surely this pallette of nature held more beauty by far than the lead and the glass of the windows themselves, and yet, without the inspiration that had fashioned them, even the sun could not have wrought such artistry upon the stone. The stone, the columns, the windows, the light, all combined to make a whole that was far more than the sum of all the parts.

The Archdeacon noted the thought for use in some future book. Never wanting for ideas, he had many books planned in his mind. Some he had begun, but rarely now could he find the time to complete them. If only he had the time. . .

Gerald made his way through the nave, walking silent among the villagers and pilgrims who knelt at prayer in the great tiled space between the columns. There were no benches upon which to rest. The faithful could stand, or they could kneel, or they could prostrate themselves before their saints, but they could not sit. Indeed there was nowhere to sit in all the cathedral, but for the stalls reserved for the Chapter. There in the choir, isolated from the worshippers by the ornately carved rood screen, it was possible to look upwards into the heights of the tower, and to hear the chatter of jackdaws that had chosen to dwell in the House of the Lord.

The choir was empty now, but even so it was dominated by the Bishop's chair, the *cathedra* that squatted resplendent among the lesser stalls. The Bishop of St David's was head of the Chapter, and by tradition would join their meetings whenever he was in this corner of his considerable estate. Here, many times, Gerald had stated his case to be appointed Bishop, but however strongly the Chapter had supported him they had always been overruled by Canterbury.

Gerald's first defeat had come with the appointment of Bishop Peter de Leia, forty years before. The second defeat, more bitter still, had come after Bishop de Leia had been killed in the Crusades. On the twenty-ninth day of June in the Year of Our Lord Eleven Hundred and Ninety Nine, with the support of the newly crowned King John, the Chapter had been unanimous in their election of Gerald de Barri as Bishop of St David's. Gerald had believed this to be the first great step in his ambition, and seeing it as an opportunity to petition for an *archbishopric*, he had made the long journey to Rome to ask Pope Innocent the Third, rather than Archbishop Hubert Walter, to consecrate him. What might have passed between Canterbury and Rome, Gerald would never know, but he had met with a blank refusal from the Pope. Worse was to come, for his return from Rome was bedevilled by danger, poverty, debt, imprisonment and finally despair. He had returned to England barely recognisable, and there had found Bishop Geoffrey consecrated in his stead.

It was this crushing disappointment that had caused Gerald de Barri to announce his intention to give up all ambitions to the see, and had further prompted him to resign the office of Archdeacon of Brecon in favour of his nephew. This highly irregular succession to the office was readily agreed by Archbishop Langton and Bishop Geoffrey, neither of whom could quite believe that they might finally be rid of this most turbulent priest since Saint Thomas à Becket met his martyrdom in Canterbury.

In truth, Gerald still remained Archdeacon in the mind of many, for his unlettered, idle nephew had done nothing to merit the title. Few had shown surprise when Gerald of Wales emerged from this supposed retirement to offer his assistance following Bishop Geoffrey's death. There had, indeed, been some talk of Gerald as successor to Bishop Geoffrey, but he had not truly expected to be given a third chance.

Had he been a few years younger, then things might have been different. If only he had had the time . . .

131

Upon entering the presbytery, the Archdeacon felt obliged to offer prayers for forgiveness of the sins of the many castellans and knights of Pembrokeshire. Gerald had not wasted his time at the Pembroke council. The threat of war had caused even the most unholy to give a thought to the wellbeing of their souls, and the Earl Marshal's liegemen had vied with one another in their generosity towards the Cathedral of St David. Gerald had been given so much gold to carry back that he had been truly grateful for the company of Haverford's escort.

The altar was a single slab of stone, carved with the five crosses that represented the wounds of Christ. In its centre stood a jewelled and gilded crucifix, donated after the Third Crusade by a wealthy and anonymous pilgrim in gratitude for his deliverance.

Such riches, such conspicuous wealth, and only the clergy permitted to see! Here, in this most Holy place, not even the pilgrims were allowed to enter. They might view the presbytery and choir through the tiny squint, but they could not come close, nor venture to touch the altar. It was a pity, in a way, thought Gerald as he concluded his prayers, but he held no illusion as to the frailty of human nature. Perhaps the bishops had been right, perhaps it really was impossible to have so much gold on open display. But still, it was a pity.

Gerald tarried long before the altar with its jewelled cross. In a small, wooden church, upon this very spot, had rested the bones of Saint David. A poor building by comparison with the great cathedral, but at least the old church had been *Welsh*, and it had sheltered the greatest symbol of Welsh Christianity. Without the relics of David, perhaps the Church of Wales never could hope to stand free of the yoke of Canterbury.

Gerald shook his head sadly. So much had happened in the great council of Pembroke, that only now did he consider fully what the soldier from Anselm's escort had said to him. *Elidyr ab Idwal had known where the bones of Saint David lay hidden.* So too, most likely, had Gruffydd ap Llywelyn. Had the knowledge come to them from another prisoner at Corfe? Or had it been by divine revelation? The truth of it could never be known, now, though the former seemed improbable. But Gruffydd was dead. Elidyr was dead. It no longer mattered.

Elidyr was dead. Gerald frowned as he walked slowly back

through the choir. Here was another mystery he had pushed to the back of his mind. When Angharad told how she had seen the bard fall down the cleft, she had been lying, there could be no doubt of that. She had been lying. . .

The Archdeacon paused to give his blessing as he walked back down the long, gentle slope of the nave. Pilgrims knelt with heads bowed in their own quiet prayers, or stared to marvel at the wall-paintings of saints and martyrs, the stained glass of the windows and the carvings of the wooden rood screen. A nobleman, richly dressed, eyed with impious envy the quality of the paintings. A knight, of mournful countenance, knelt deep in prayer. A woman, hands clasped before her drawn face, prayed earnestly for her sick child. A young squire, gaunt and dishevelled, did not admire the cathedral nor offer prayer, but watched with haunted eyes as Gerald stumbled in his blessing, his raised hand frozen in its unfinished benediction.

'Squire Anselm!'

'My lord. . . I was wrongly accused!'

'Undoubtedly.' Gerald stared hard at the youngest son of the Earl Marshal. 'But why did you run away?'

The squire seemed surprised that the Archdeacon was ready to believe him. The cathedral of St David's had offered him a short period of sanctuary willingly enough, but no one had seemed interested in asking whether he were guilty or no. 'Do you need to ask? You all believed I was a murderer! It would have served you well enough that Llywelyn's son was dead, and with no blood on *your* hands.'

'Lord Llywelyn is my friend, Anselm. Do not class Gerald of Wales with the King's barons in this!'

'I am sorry, my lord. But am I wrong?'

'About the rest of them? No. They believed you had acted in a way none of them would have dared.'

'And my father?' Anselm stared piercingly at the old Arch-deacon. 'Would he have sent me to the gallows? You must know, you sat at his side.'

Gerald hesitated to answer. Which would serve Anselm best? To know the truth, or to believe in his father's affection?

'It might have been argued that your death could prevent a war.'

'You have not answered my question.'

'How can I? I doubt that the Earl Marshal himself could answer it. But I am sure you would be well received if you were to return now to Pembroke. To some, you would be a hero. The castellan of Haverford was generous in your praise.'

'My praise? Rather than his own? You astonish me, my lord.' Anselm smiled sadly. 'So what has happened? Have the Welsh attacked in vengeance for their prince? Or has the boy been found?'

'Let us just say that the matter may soon be forgotten. I am convinced now that the fire on the ship was started by accident after the Welshmen set you ashore. Their deaths were tragic, but their blood is on no man's hands.'

'None but his hands.' Anselm's voice was low, and Gerald barely caught the words.

'You blame Gruffydd ap Llywelyn?'

'He was the one in command of the Welshmen...and of the Cornish crew for that matter. He was the one who caused every argument, even among his own men...none of them wanted to go to Ramsey. We heard their voices raised in anger even as they sailed away from us at Porth Clais.'

'Wait, Anselm! You say Gruffydd ordered the ship to Ramsey Island?'

'So my men tell me...I do not speak Welsh. I thought nothing of it.'

'But there is nothing on Ramsey.' Gerald looked away, and his eyes rested upon the lofty window from which Saint Justinian stared down in frosty benediction. 'Nothing on Ramsey Island to tempt those poor souls to tarry for a moment on their journey home.'

'Gruffydd ap Llywelyn seemed to think there was, my lord.'

XXVI

The old Archdeacon sat at the table in the Bishop's chamber, the room he looked upon still as his own. Soon the new Bishop would arrive, and Gerald of Wales would be relegated once more to work in his own tiny cell. Until then, he was determined to enjoy his position as acting-Bishop to the full, savouring the sometimes onerous responsibilities as well as the privileges of rank.

Gerald spent much of his time in the administration of the Bishop's see, an area that included much of southern Wales. The collecting of tithes, the appointment of deans and local priests, the commissioning and funding of new buildings, all these things were within the gift of the Bishop of St David's, and all now fell, to a greater or lesser degree, upon the Archdeacon. Much of the business would of necessity be delayed until the new Bishop's arrival, but Gerald still found enough work to occupy his every waking hour and, to their dismay, every waking hour of all those around him. He loved his vocation, he thrived upon the work, he relished the power it gave him, but he never ceased to complain of how it robbed him of the time he needed for his books.

This day Gerald de Barri was absorbed in his history of King Henry the Second, his *On the Instruction of a Prince*. In a few hours time it would be his duty to welcome the latest group of pilgrims to the shrine of St David's, but first he was determined to finish the fifth chapter.

He was working well. Elegant phrases sprang so easily to mind that every dip of his quill into the small ivory inkwell was a maddening delay in the setting down of his thoughts. If only some means could be devised to speed the task of writing, what a gift it would be to the scholars of the world! To write for hours without pause, with no need to trim the quill, to mix the pigment, to rule out the page. . . Gerald shook his head, and berated himself for the contemplation of such ungodly haste as he bent anew to his parchment.

A knock at the door, and the lucid flow of Gerald's thoughts fled from his mind. He set aside his quill and bade the vandal enter.

Captain Nevern was well accustomed to the Archdeacon's capricious ill-temper, and braved the baleful stare that invited him to leave.

'I hope I am not disturbing you, my lord.'

'Indeed you are, but now that you are here. . . .'

'It is the Earl Marshal's son, Anselm. Will you speak with him?'

'Upon what matter, Captain, the Instruction of a Prince?' Gerald immediately regretted his ill humour, and bade the bemused Nevern continue. The captain was, after all, only doing his duty.

'I told him that you were occupied, my lord, but. . . .'

'Oh, send him back to Pembroke, Nevern.'

'As you wish, my lord.' The Captain bowed and half turned to go, but hesitated in the doorway. 'My lord. . . are you aware that he believes Llywelyn's son may still be alive?'

'Does he indeed? And what brought about this revelation?'

'He says he will find Gruffydd for us, if we will provide him with an escort and a boat to Ramsey Island. Yesterday he troubled my men enough, what with all his questions about the fire they saw on the night he came here in rags, but now he goes too far! He stands even now in the courtyard, declaring to all that the Welsh are going to attack the castle.'

'Pembroke?'

'*This* castle, Archdeacon.'

Gerald snapped upright in his chair. 'St David's! Are you mad?'

'It is not I who is mad. Squire Anselm is like a man possessed. He has sworn to find Gruffydd and to take him to Pembroke. . . in chains if need be.' As always, Nevern had chosen his words with care. Gerald never could determine just how Welsh the captain felt himself to be. Or, indeed, just how Welsh the captain considered the Archdeacon to be.

Gerald walked to the window, and could see Anselm holding forth to the small gathering of idlers in the outer bailey. 'He has been wronged and is anxious to clear his name, nothing more. Why do you bother me with this?'

'Well, my lord, what if he is right?'

'You too, captain!' Gerald shook his head. He was beset by fools, his book would never be finished. 'Very well, bring him here. He has troubled St David's long enough.'

Anselm looked neither mad nor possessed. He was afraid.

'Well? What is it? What causes you to inflict this commotion upon the peace of St David's?'

'I have seen the Welsh, Archdeacon. Lord Rhys Gryg is here!'

'Calm yourself, Squire Anselm. Tell me from the beginning.'

'This morning I rode to the Chapel of Saint Justinian. As you know, it overlooks Ramsey Island, and I thought the fishermen who live by the inlet might tell me something of the night of the fire.'

'But they speak only Welsh.'

'That had not occurred to me when I set out. In Pembroke even the peasants have a civilised tongue! As I was walking past the chapel, down the steep path to the beach, I heard a clamour of voices from the cliff top above. I hid behind a rock and saw a large band of armed men. Lord Rhys Gryg of Deheubarth, it was! He was marching at the head of his army!'

'An army, you say?'

'They were equipped for war! They carried swords. . .'

'How many men were in this army?'

'It could have been hundreds! Their numbers were hidden from me by the fold of the cliffs.'

'How many did you see, Anselm?'

'Fifty at least. . . Well, a score, perhaps. I did not have the time to count them! Rhys Gryg saw me and they gave chase, but I outran them!'

'Most people would, on a horse,' Gerald observed drily.

'You had best prepare for a siege, my lord.'

'They could be here on pilgrimage. It is not the Normans alone who fear God and His saints.'

'Rhys Gryg? A *pilgrim*?'

Gerald rolled up his parchment, and sighed deeply as he set it aside. 'It must be self evident, Squire Anselm, that Lord Rhys Gryg would not waste his time in attacking St David's. This castle has but a small garrison and presents no threat to him. It is not well fortified, and if he occupied it the Earl Marshal's army could retake it within a day. If he burned it, then he would earn the condemnation of his own people and he would be excommunicated by myself. If Rhys Gryg is here, then it is not to attack St David's. It would avail him nothing.'

'Perhaps he seeks something else! I wanted to see the numbers of his army, so when I was well away from St Justinian's I climbed a great outcrop of rock by the roadside. I could see over the cliff top and right out across Ramsey Sound, but the only thing in sight was a small boat being rowed out to the island.'

'Was Rhys Gryg aboard?'

'I could not tell from that distance, but I saw him nowhere else.'

'So perhaps he went to St Justinian's only to charter a boat to the island...that would be quite possible. Ramsey Sound is a dangerous place. The fishermen make a good living in summer by ferrying pilgrims across. Only they can navigate those waters in safety.'

'What is to be done, Archdeacon?'

'What need be done? The castle is not in danger, I am sure of that. Why should we trouble Lord Rhys Gryg?'

'He is up to no good, else why did he not come to the castle? He and his men must have slept out on the cliffs last night, when they could have sheltered here.' Anselm hesitated, waiting for Gerald to speak. 'My lord...is it not clear? Gruffydd is not dead, but sheltering on Ramsey Island. And Rhys Gryg has come to find him!'

Gerald's eyes betrayed no emotion, but he continued to look narrowly at the squire's excited face. 'What would the Lord of Deheubarth want with Gruffydd ap Llywelyn?'

'Why...' Anselm thought only for for a moment. 'Because he could use the boy to gain a hold over Llywelyn.'

'Yes, even at Pembroke the thought was in Rhys Gryg's mind, I could see that plainly enough. He may have a difficult task in regaining his power in Deheubarth, having been a prisoner for so long. It was his own nephews, Owain and Rhys ap Gruffydd, who first betrayed him into King John's hands, you understand, and they have not been idle during his captivity. With Gruffydd as his hostage, Rhys Gryg would be able to bargain with Llywelyn for help against his kinsmen. But what I cannot see, Anselm, is why Rhys Gryg would search for the boy on Ramsey?'

'Did Rhys Gryg speak to Elidyr after I left Pembroke?'

'No...Elidyr was not fool enough to have trusted a southern lord. But...' Gerald's voice faltered. Could this have been the great secret that haunted the bard? Merely the whereabouts of

138

Gruffydd ap Llywelyn, and not the relics of Saint David after all? Gerald remembered the words of the guardsman at Pembroke. *I know what he said my lord. . .truth or lies. . .they're all one and the same in that stewpot of a Welsh head!*

'What is it, my lord?'

'Elidyr confided in Regat, believing her loyalty lay in the north. It was only later, in Manorbier, that he learned who Regat was. . .then he was desperate to escape and put things to rights.'

'To protect Gruffydd from Lord Rhys Gryg!'

Gerald paused. To accept this explanation would be to forsake all hope of finding the holy relics. Yet he could not bring himself to speak openly of the blessed bones of Dewi Sant. . .not to the Norman squire standing so impatiently before him. 'I. . .I cannot be sure. Elidyr ab Idwal swore upon this very cross that you had murdered Gruffydd ap Llywelyn. If he lied, then he has perjured himself and has placed his very soul in peril. I do not. . .I cannot believe that he would have done such a thing.'

'There is a simple means to find the truth of it, my lord Archdeacon. Send your soldiers with me to Ramsey!'

XXVII

'It was good of you to come with us, my lord Archdeacon. But I would not have kept you from your duties.'

'You are not the only one to have an interest in what may be found on Ramsey Island.' Gerald spoke quietly as their horses carried them towards the Chapel of Saint Justinian, but his thoughts were as turbulent as the sea tearing at the cliffs beneath.

Anselm glanced back at the dozen men who plodded behind them on foot. 'If Rhys Gryg is on the island still, I fear we may have need of the soldiers.'

Never one to seek the Archdeacon's company, Captain Nevern rode alongside his men. He met the eyes of the young squire, but did not reply.

'Not a man for idle words, our good captain. But a fine soldier, so I'm told.' Gerald spoke reassuringly to Anselm, thinking over the squire's words. 'I doubt that there is anything for us to fear.

Even without the guard, Rhys Gryg would not dare act against me.'

Anselm shook his head, unconvinced, but made no reply.

They rode on in silence for a while as the breeze freshened and the roar of the sea grew ever more insistent. The rough grassland was spotted by the clean white backs of newly shorn sheep and, here and there, was broken by great outcrops of grey rock that sprang from the flat land like bubbles in a cauldron.

Gradually Gerald became aware of the soft voices of doves coming from a basket slung by the saddle of the squire's horse. 'Is that to be our supper on the island?'

Anselm laughed. 'No, my lord, they are homing pigeons, the ones my father gave you in Pembroke. I brought them in case we should discover Gruffydd.'

'You would treat him to a feast, after all you have said?'

'Each bears a message tied to its leg. Brother Hugh draughted it for me. It says *By the Grace of God Gruffydd ap Llywelyn is alive and well.* I thought it would be wise to send three, with so many peregrine falcons about. We have only to release them when Gruffydd is discovered, and they will fly straight back to Pembroke.'

'And then?'

'Then, the peace will be assured.'

'Nothing else? Is that all the message says? I will not tolerate any action against Llywelyn's son while he is on my...on the Bishop's lands. Not from you, nor from your father's soldiers. If Gruffydd is on the island, he is to be treated with all respect, you understand?'

'Respect! For that little...'

'Whatever harm he has done you, Anselm, you must try to forgive. He has suffered much at the hands of the Normans.'

'So must we all now suffer because of him? I showed him every consideration on the journey from Corfe, just as if he had been my equal. When he seized the ship, he could at least have returned the courtesy. But no! He stole my sword, my armour, my every possession.'

'He gave you your life.'

Anselm appeared not to have heard. 'He left me to walk the pilgrims' path in those filthy rags, with a stench that fetched me

140

insults from fifty paces away. I tell you he obeys no one, he respects no one, he trusts no one!'

'A prudent attitude, I should say, for a man in his position. He has little enough cause to trust the Normans.'

Anselm cursed beneath his breath. 'Do you not hear me, Archdeacon? Gruffydd would stop at nothing to injure us.'

'Us, Anselm?' Gerald smiled sadly. 'I have heard much of Gruffydd ap Llywelyn, and little of it inspires me with confidence. But I must keep my own counsel. In all my years, I have learned that even the most truthful witness has his own bias, his own prejudice, his own interest at heart. I will not judge Llywelyn's son upon your words, nor Lord Rhys Gryg's words, nor Elidyr's, nor those of the Earl Marshal. I will wait, and I pray that we find our answer on the island.'

As they neared the Chapel of Saint Justinian, the four mounted soldiers of Captain Nevern's advance guard approached. 'Nothing in sight, Captain. We scoured the clifftops, but there's not a sign of Rhys Gryg or his men. Oh, and all the boats have gone.'

The soldiers fell silent as they halted by the gabled end of the little stone chapel. Some cast wary glances through the single square window, others shuffled their feet by the door. None were eager to enter without their captain's direct order.

'What troubles them?' Dismounting, Anselm handed his reins to Nevern and pushed his way to peer through the window. There was nothing to be seen but a plain stone altar with a crudely carved cross, but the damp chill of the air made him shiver.

'There's nothing to fear from the ghost.' Gerald's voice echoed cheerfully from within.

'The ghost?' Anselm hunched his shoulders, and hugged himself against the sea breeze that seemed to grow suddenly more chill. He cast a brave glance into the chapel to show his men that he was not afraid, then as the Archdeacon emerged to walk to the cliff top, he followed as closely as his pride would allow.

'You said . . . a ghost, my lord?'

'A most benevolent spirit, Squire Anselm. You need not fear.'

'It is the soldiers who are afraid, Archdeacon. I ask only so that I may reassure them . . .'

141

'Oh, I see.'

'Well, Archdeacon? What lies within the chapel?'

'The bones of Saint Justinian are buried beneath the altar.'

'But why do the soldiers fear that? There are such relics in every chapel.'

'Perhaps not in every one.' Gerald spoke in mild reproof. 'Justinian was a very great man. . .the friend and confessor of Saint David himself. While David settled his monks in the valley, over there where the cathedral now stands, Justinian established his *clas* on Ramsey Island. For a time all was well. . .but the harsh conditions and deprivations of the island became too great, the resolution of the monks too meagre. The Devil seized upon the frailty of their resolve, and visited upon them such a madness that they fell upon Justinian and smote his head from his shoulders.'

'So why doesn't his ghost haunt Ramsey?'

'By God's good grace, Justinian did not die. He picked up his severed head and, carrying it in his hands, he walked across the waters of Ramsey Sound to the very place upon which this chapel now stands. Whereupon he set down his head, and from that spot a holy well sprang forth.'

'And. . .and the ghost, my lord?'

'They say Justinian still follows that final journey.' Gerald gestured across to the island. 'From the ruins of his monastery he walks across the waters, and over these very cliffs to the holy well.'

Gerald and Anselm looked down into the steep, narrow cove that served as harbour. The pilgrims' journey to St David's was long and perilous, and often in the urgency of a storm the tiny ships had little choice of landing place. By every possible haven, even here on the treacherous Ramsey Sound, stood a chapel to allow the faithful to offer their thanks for a safe journey. Visitors from Ireland would sometimes land here at St Justinian's, but more often would choose the safer waters to the north where the Chapel of St Patrick stood sentinel over the windswept sands of Porth Mawr.

Gerald eyed the swirling currents, the rip tides, the sharp rocks jutting from the angry waters in the middle of the Sound. 'Your ship must have foundered out there.' He bowed his head and made the sign of the cross. It was difficult to believe that anyone could have survived in such waters.

Nevern had followed, unnoticed. 'There was some wreckage, my lord. The guards saw the broken hulk of a ship on the rocks over yonder, out towards the island. *The Bitches*, the fishermen call them, and you can see why.'

'When was that?'

'It was the morning you left for Pembroke, my lord. They couldn't see any sign of life, not at that distance, and the wreck was lost from sight on the next high tide.'

Anselm was impatient, spoiling for action. 'Are we to talk all day, my lord? Or shall we set out for the island?'

'It might profit us best to talk all day.' Gerald was finding the prospect of a voyage less attractive by the minute. 'Consider. . . Lord Rhys Gryg must still be on the island, and from these cliffs we can see all that passes in Ramsey Sound. We have only to wait, and he will deliver himself to us.'

'There is no need for you to come, my lord. This is a task for soldiers!'

Gerald laughed and shouted after the eager young squire as he strode away. 'I should say that, since there are no boats, Anselm, it might rather be a task for Saint Justinian himself!'

XXVIII

The fire burned bright on the floor of the Chapel of Saint Justinian, and the soldiers of St David's clustered close around to escape the darkness of the shadows beyond. Archdeacon Gerald de Barri had long since returned to the castle, confessing that a man of his age could not be expected to spend a night at the mercy of the elements, but he had ordered that a vigil be kept until dawn. Captain Nevern was inspecting the watch on the clifftops and Anselm, disdainful of the company of common soldiers, had left the firelight to join him.

It was a hazy night, the stars barely visible, the pallid moon peering infrequently through its thin veil of high cloud to cast a shimmer of light upon the waters of Ramsey Sound. On such a night the most sober of men might dread the coming of the headless wraith of Justinian. Squire Anselm shivered. How many more ghosts must now haunt the island?

'Do you see anything, Captain?'

Nevern did not glance in the squire's direction, and the darkness hid his smile. 'Worse things than Justinian's ghost have been seen over Ramsey Island, Squire Anselm. Have you never witnessed the flight of a dragon?'

Anselm followed the captain's gaze and saw the tiny point of light shining fitfully across Ramsey Sound. It did not move, but flickered from time to time as if figures were passing before it. 'That's not a dragon. It must be Lord Rhys Gryg...and I hope he's heard the story of the ghost.'

A squall from the west brought the first splinters of rain as Anselm and Nevern turned back towards the shelter of St Justinian's Chapel. The muffled sound of their footsteps on the loose cliff path vied with the murmur of the waves below until they came once more to the chapel, into the warm circle of firelight.

Only as the fire returned the feeling to their fingers did they realise how cold it had been out on the clifftop. They sat upon the bare stone floor as the soldiers shuffled round to make space, and drank deep as the wineskin was passed round. The chill of the night, and the warmth of the wine, had soon made the soldiers forget their fears.

Nevern ordered four of the men to take watch upon the cliffs, and two more to guard the chapel door. With a curt nod to Anselm, he folded his rough cloak about him and settled down to sleep.

Some of the soldiers were already snoring, others exchanged bawdy stories with occasional bursts of muted laughter. Anselm watched them with deepening gloom. Even though he had been born in Pembroke, he was still a Norman, and to be sitting among these men of St David's, upon the floor of a Welsh chapel, in the land of the Welsh Saint, made him feel very much an alien.

'What shall we do when Lord Rhys Gryg comes ashore?'

Nevern did not open his eyes. 'That will depend upon Lord Rhys Gryg.'

'Will you fight him?'

'If need be.'

'But he is Welsh. . . '

'I am bound to defend the Church.'

One of the older soldiers chortled from the fireside. 'And there's worse infidels in these islands than ever you found in the Holy Land, eh, Captain?'

Amid the laughter, Anselm addressed the Captain with a new respect. 'You fought in the Holy War?'

'There was nothing *holy* about it at all. Disease and vermin, wilderness and starvation, they were the real enemies. Our horses died in the sand beneath us, weighed down by our armour in the heat. We wandered lost in the desert, dying from thirst, blinded by the sun and the flies. When we found a village. . . any village, we slaughtered all within. Saracens and Jews, women and children, even the goats and the dogs. We were all mad with the poison of the Church.'

'Yet now you serve the Church.'

'There was no greater misfortune than to return alive from the Crusades. The true heroes were the men who died. We who returned were despised! I came home, wounded and penniless, to find my father dead and my younger brothers squabbling over his land. There was no place for me, and I lacked the spirit to fight for it. I was fortunate to be given a post here.'

'By Gerald de Barri?'

'Yes. A real Archdeacon he was then, and not just in name, like he is now. He gave me charge of the garrison. He owed me that much.'

'Owed it to you? Why?'

Nevern's smile was devoid of humour. 'Have you not heard of the great *Journey Through Wales* of Giraldus Cambrensis? The most famous of all his books, it is. He tells the tale of his travels. . . near thirty years ago it was, when he was helping to raise support for the Third Crusade. He is a great orator, our good Archdeacon, and we Welsh were much prized as soldiers in your King Richard's army. Few men who heard Giraldus preach could ignore his message. Scores of us came forward to take the Cross. Hundreds, thousands of us, all across Wales. A whole generation going forth to die in a foreign land, while our own country was laid waste by the English.'

'Yet you serve the Archdeacon now, and of your own free will.'

'He believed in what he preached, I'll give him that. So did I, I suppose. At the time.'

Anselm stared into the fire, his back chilled by the draught from the door, his feet roasting before the flames. The soldier next to him gave a nod of recognition as he passed on the wineskin. Anselm drank gratefully, and now he felt at ease. He was beginning to forget why they were waiting in the Chapel of Saint Justinian, and it did not seem to matter that these men were born of Wales, while he remained a Norman.

'Are you looking forward to the coming of the new Bishop?'

Nevern did not answer immediately, but the soldiers were losing their distrust of the young squire and his question brought forth a peal of sardonic laughter. 'Of course we are! He's a Welshman, isn't he!'

'This is a great event for St David's,' Nevern explained. 'The Chapter fought like lions to win Iorwerth's appointment. . .the whole of Wales seemed to be behind them. I heard that even Llywelyn of Gwynedd lent his support.'

'So now you have the first Welsh Bishop of St David's since. . .when was it?'

'I forget the year. The Archdeacon would be able to tell you.'

'I suppose he is eager to welcome Bishop Iorwerth.'

Nevern scratched at his chin. 'That's the strange thing about it. He showed no pleasure at all when the news came.'

'I'd have thought Gerald of Wales would be glad to see any Welshman as Bishop. His ambitions for the Church in Wales are well enough known.'

'Some say, Squire Anselm, that the good Archdeacon's ambitions have always been too much for Gerald, and too little for Wales.'

XXIX

The distant clatter of horses' hooves, the clash of arms, the clamour of angry voices, all these sounds of conflict came through the low blanket of morning mist in portent of the horrors of a war to come. They grew louder as Gerald de Barri neared the cathedral of St David's, then ceased with the abruptness of a dream shattered by the dawn.

A black cloud of birds burst from their roost in the cathedral tower, the ever present jackdaws scattered by a solitary raven in their midst. The cloud wheeled and twisted high over the gravestones as the jackdaws mobbed their larger cousin until, with a harsh cry, the raven beat his great wings and rose from the ranks of his persecutors to soar far away towards the mountains of the north.

Gerald's gaze followed the fast-diminishing speck beyond the cathedral tower, but as he walked down towards Llech Lafar his thoughts were brought firmly back to more earthly matters.

There were a dozen sweated horses grazing amid the gravestones of the Sacred Hollow.

From the cathedral came the unaccustomed sound of sandalled feet at the run. The heavy doors, left ajar, were flung back on their hinges as a terrified rabble burst forth. They fled as if their very souls were in peril, leaping through the shallow ford of the Alun, not sparing even the few extra steps that would take them over Llech Lafar. The Archdeacon did not stay to watch as they fled like rabbits into the shelter of the Bishop's Palace. He strode to the cathedral doorway to witness with his own eyes the unholy scene within.

Armed men rushed here and there, sword in hand, looking behind every pillar, searching every dark corner. And from their midst, incredibly, came the frantic scream of a horse, tortured by the spur, forehooves flailing at the delicate carvings of the rood screen while the rider swung a naked sword above his head to the peril of the carved saints who stared down from their niches in mute reproach. The gates of the screen broke from their hinges as the grey stallion plunged forward, scrabbled for grip and fell kicking to the smooth red tiles of the choir.

147

The rider clambered free and brandished his sword to rally his men. 'Follow me, you dogs! The bastard runs, there's nothing to fear! He cowers above us like an old woman! Up into the tower with you!'

Gerald knew that voice as well as he remembered the huge frame and the wolfskin draped across those ursine shoulders. Stunned, he watched the scene unfold in the finest particular as the figures of the Welshmen were painted in a dozen colours by the sunlight stealing through the windows. He saw every intricate detail of the fine glazed tiles, cracked now by flying hooves. He saw the broken gate leaning awry against the rood screen. He saw the sword hilts pounding against the narrow wooden door that concealed the stairway of the tower, and the splinters as they fell from the finely carved panelling. He saw the Welshmen betray their ancestors, *his* ancestors, in every blow against the tower door. He saw the heavy plumes at the fetlocks of Lord Rhys Gryg's horse, as the terrified animal clattered down the long slope of the nave to make its escape into the sunlight of the sane world that must surely await beyond the cathedral doors.

'Rhys Gryg! This is the Devil's work!'

The door shuddered still to the assault of Rhys Gryg's men.

'In the name of Almighty God, be still! As you pound upon that door, so do you knock upon the very gates of Hell!'

Rhys Gryg turned furiously. 'Get back, you old fool. This is no concern of yours.'

But even as he spoke, Rhys Gryg's voice faltered before the Archdeacon's stare. Not only anger, but sadness and pity were in the old man's grey eyes. Rhys Gryg saw in them the repudiation of his own father, his grandfather, the contempt of a hundred generations of the princes of the South. His lip trembled, his sword arm fell to his side, he could not meet the truth of the unspoken accusation.

'It is my duty to excommunicate you all!'

The cathedral was suddenly silent. Even Rhys Gryg's soldiers stood still and fearful, for Rhys' father, Lord of all Deheubarth, had himself died excommunicate. He had died excommunicate because of the folly of his wicked brood of sons, and the horror of it was even now spoken only in whispers.

Rhys Gryg and his brothers had abducted Bishop Peter de Leia from his bed one chilly April night, and had dragged him half naked through the woods below Dinefwr Castle in vengeance for his intervention in their affairs. Rescued by William de Braose, de Leia had promptly excommunicated the old Lord of Deheubarth along with all his sons.

Soon afterwards, Rhys Gryg's father had died of the plague. Divine retribution, many had believed, and as an excommunicate his body had lain unburied whilst his sons went humbly to Bishop de Leia to make their repentance and to petition for the saving of their father's soul. The Bishop of St David's had referred the matter to the Archbishop of Canterbury, and the Archbishop of Canterbury had pondered at length, and all the while the corpse of the Lord of Deheubarth lay rotting.

At last had come the pronouncement that the Mother Church was always ready to receive sinners back into her bosom, provided there be a just and fitting penance. That penance had been the scourge, and not only of Rhys Gryg and his brothers, but also of their father's rotting corpse.

Eighteen years ago it had happened. Rhys Gryg would have been little more than a youth, but those scars would last him a lifetime.

'It is my duty. . .'

The Archdeacon spoke more quietly now, acutely conscious of the danger should he carry out his threat. Rhys Gryg might not be a man to be deterred by excommunication. Perhaps he had not learned his lesson. Perhaps he was still too young, too head-strong, to think of the peril to his soul, too foolish to repent his sins. Were Gerald to excommunicate Rhys Gryg now, he would have no further sanction. . . and Rhys Gryg, like a cornered rat, might do his worst and be damned!

'And excommunicate you so I shall. . . if you remain within the Shrine of Saint David.' There, he had given Rhys Gryg a means of escape. Now God grant the fellow the wits to seize upon his chance. . .

Rhys Gryg only smiled at what he saw as the Archdeacon's weakness. 'No need for that, my lord Archdeacon. We can both profit from this. Just turn your back while we fetch the bastard down. . .'

'I will not deny him sanctuary.'

149

'Turn your back, and I'll give you my word. . . '

'Your word?' Gerald assumed an expression of mild surprise as he paused to look about him. At the men with their reddened faces, at the broken gate to the choir, at the filth left by Rhys Gryg's horse upon the floor of the Shrine of Saint David. 'Did you say *your word*, my Lord Rhys Gryg?'

'Let us talk, Archdeacon. . . out of the hearing of these dogs. . . '

'I can think of nothing to discuss.'

'There is much to discuss, Archdeacon. You are fond of a good story, eh? Then give heed to this. You recall Llywelyn's bard, the one you took quietly away to your Manorbier? Remember him? Killed at the Earl Marshal's behest by your kinsmen. . . '

'They did not. . . '

'At Pembroke he squealed before my wife like a hog at the slaughter. Do you know what he told her, Archdeacon? A pretty tale, it was. About a miracle in a stinking Norman cell. About a vision of a dead man's bones. A vision brought to a Northern brat by the grace of Dewi Sant.'

'Elidyr ab Idwal told this to Regat?'

'He trusted her, see.' Rhys Gryg gave a low laugh. 'He told Regat, and she told her lord and master, and so I came to Ramsey Island for the bones of Dewi Sant.'

'You found the relics?'

'Better than that, Archdeacon. D'you know what it was that I found? A Welsh lad in the armour of a Norman squire, and with it the arrogance to say that I was his vassal. His *vassal*, do you hear. . . a Welshman using a Norman's words.'

'Gruffydd ap Llywelyn?'

Rhys Gryg nodded with a slow smile. 'The son of Llywelyn. He and four others who had struggled to the island when their ship foundered. *Duw*. . . but if you could have seen their joy when a fellow Welshman came to their rescue!'

'But the holy relics. . . had Gruffydd found them?'

'I couldn't say, Archdeacon. . . I didn't question him. I wanted him to trust me, see, and I'd only taken a few men to the island. I'd seen that son of the Earl Marshal nosing around St Justinian's Chapel, so I sent the others to Porth Mawr to guard our return in case his father's soldiers might be near.'

'You landed at Porth Mawr? How did you get the ferryman. . . '

'I gave him something more to fear than the rocks and currents! But the minute we touched shore the damned *gogs* turned on us. Llywelyn's son made a run for my best horse, and the other four fought like lions to cover his escape! I never saw such courage, Archdeacon, I cannot deny it. They were like men possessed! I lost some of my finest warriors this morning.'

'Then let it be a lesson to you upon the wages of treachery!'

Rhys Gryg glowered, yet he would not be roused to anger. His eyes narrowed, and his voice dropped lower still. 'We could both profit from this, Gerallt Gymro. Let me have Llywelyn's son ...you have only to walk from the cathedral. The boy knows where the bones of Dewi Sant are hidden. He must know. Two weeks on the island he had, and with nothing to do but search for them! He hid them away when he saw me coming to rescue him.'

'Rescue him?'

'Gruffydd cannot escape us, Archdeacon. Give him to me and I will soon have the secret out of him. Then you can have your relics, and I will return in peace to Deheubarth with *my* prize.'

'Rhys Gryg! You are a villain beyond redemption . . . but worse, you are a fool!'

Gerald paused, and he knew that he was wrong. Rhys Gryg was not a fool. Rhys Gryg knew the prize of which Gerald of Wales had always dreamed. Rhys Gryg believed that, for such a prize, there was nothing that Gerald would not do, no depths to which he would not sink. Gerald felt the Devil at his shoulder, and his voice shook with fear. 'Can you believe that Giraldus Cambrensis would sell the life of his friend's son?'

'Nobody need know, Archdeacon. None would dispute it, if you said you found the relics yourself, that you were guided by a miracle! *None would know!*'

In years to come, Gerald would tell himself that the temptation had not troubled him, that the decision had been an easy one. But in truth it was a fearful burden. He concentrated his mind upon how ruthless a man was Rhys Gryg, how ludicrous the offer of a trade. He told himself that only Rhys Gryg of Deheubarth could have the audacity to put such a bargain before a devout man of God. Yet the vision of the relics hung still before his eyes. He saw not the dry bones, but Saint David himself. The man living, the man standing upon the Sacred Mound of Llanddewi Brefi, the

151

Dove of the Holy Spirit upon his shoulder, his hand lifted in benediction... Or was it reproach?

'You disgrace the Welsh nation, Rhys Gryg! You dishonour the name of your... of *our*... ancestor Rhys ap Tewdwr!' Gerald had raised his voice so that all could hear. 'What would it profit you to betray Llywelyn and gain his throne? With you as King, Wales would fall within the month! Treachery against the Lord of Gwynedd is treachery against all the Welsh people. Betray Wales and you betray yourself. For if the Welsh fight amongst themselves, brother against brother, then will the Normans assuredly defeat us. Your own future greatness lies with that of Gwynedd, my lord Rhys Gryg. Can you not see that?'

Rhys Gryg said nothing.

'It was your wife Regat who told you to come here, I know. But what does a woman know of such affairs? Would you let her wiles and petty jealousies ruin you? Tell me... who is truly Lord of Deheubarth?'

Rhys Gryg could take no more. 'Not that damned northern bitch!'

Only as Rhys Gryg rode from the Sacred Hollow did he realise the true cost of his ambition.

His men were whispering amongst themselves. Some were laughing. They had seen Lord Rhys Gryg of Deheubarth, their mighty leader, Pretender to the throne of the ancient kingdom of southern Wales, revealed as the pawn of his own wife.

Rhys Gryg savagely spurred his horse to a gallop. Worst of all, he had been bested by that old fool of a priest who could have been his grandfather.

XXX

The Archdeacon did not feel at ease until the sound of Rhys Gryg's horses had faded far down the road towards Haverford. He sat himself in the nearest choir stall, his legs unwilling to support him as he realised what he had achieved. He had succeeded in driving away the desecrators of the cathedral, he had saved the son of Llywelyn ap Iorwerth and he had, perhaps, done much to foster peace between Gwynedd and Deheubarth. Gerald noticed, with an ironic smile, that he had chanced to sit in the Bishop's place. He was not entitled to do so, but he did not move. No one was more deserving. He would allow himself this one indulgence.

The sound of a light tread on the stone steps and the drawing of the bolts of the tower door reminded Gerald that his task was not yet complete. He looked up at the figure in the doorway, and had to shake himself free of the delusion that he was thirty years younger, when a journey through Wales had brought him to the mountain fastness of Gwynedd.

There before him was the same drawn, weary face. The same blunt nose, the same dark hair with its trace of curl. The same dark, deep eyes, penetrating and unforgiving. Dear Lord, the resemblance to his father, these thirty years later, was incredible! Yet this lad was thinner, and there was a set to his jaw that had something of the sulky child about it. And perhaps, after all, they were not so alike. . . Llywelyn ap Iorwerth had assuredly never worn the chain mail of a Norman squire.

'You are not injured, I trust?'

'*Be' ddywedsoch chi, Archddiacon?*'

Gerald cleared his throat. What had he been thinking of! He adjusted his thoughts into Welsh, and repeated the question.

Gruffydd ap Llywelyn nodded as if applauding the efforts of a slow learner. '*Da iawn. Dwi'n eich deall chi rŵan.* No Gerallt Gymro, I am not injured. For that I have my comrades to thank. And now yourself, of course.'

'Gruffydd ap Llywelyn. . .' Gerald could think of little else to say. 'I believed. . . we all believed that you were dead. Yet there you were on Ramsey Island.'

'Hunting for gulls' eggs and seals, finding what shelter we could among the caves.' Gruffydd smiled with a sudden dark humour. 'Our ordeal was not as onerous as you might suppose, Gerallt Gymro. Nor as fruitless.'

'What did you find?' Gerald could not disguise the anxiety in his voice.

Gruffydd ap Llywelyn stared mockingly at the old Archdeacon. 'Well. . . I do believe you already know. Or *think* you know. Come then, Gerallt Gymro, Great Chronicler of our race. Tell me what you would write about the son of Llywelyn ap Iorwerth.'

'First answer my question, my lord. What could anyone hope to find on Ramsey?'

Gruffydd ap Llywelyn's low laugh echoed into the recesses of the great tower above. 'Justinian found his Martyrdom.'

'Did you seek yours?'

'I was seeking Dewi Sant. Why else do the pilgrims flock to this holy land?'

'And. . . and did you find him?'

'Archdeacon! Are you there?'

The voice came from the great doorway at the far end of the nave. Gruffydd recognised it well. He did not move, but his glance to the Archdeacon was questioning.

'Stay where you are, Gruffydd. For the moment, it would be best if you were not seen.'

The Archdeacon walked through the broken gateway of the rood screen and down the long central aisle to find Squire Anselm standing between the half-open doors.

'What has happened, my lord?'

'A visit from Rhys Gryg, mercifully brief. . . he will not trouble us again.'

'He may not trouble you, Archdeacon, but my father must still find ways to deal with him. Where has he gone?'

'Back to his own land, if God wills it.'

'And you let him go? He did *this*, and you let him go? Archdeacon, he may be a kinsman of yours, but. . .'

'What Rhys Gryg has done within these walls is my concern, and that of the Bishop when he comes. Pray do not trouble yourself with it, Anselm.'

In truth, Gerald had no intention of telling the new Bishop what had happened. He did not want to create any greater rift between Gwynedd and Deheubarth, least of all when Rhys Gryg appeared ready to concede his loyalty to Llywelyn.

Anselm bowed his head to the Archdeacon. 'I'm sorry, my lord. I just came to tell you that the boat has returned to St Justinian's.

154

We questioned the ferryman, but could get no sense out of him. Do you wish to accompany us now to the island?'

'No need for that, Anselm. Not now. There is nothing to be found.'

'Then we shall pursue Rhys Gryg.'

'It would serve no purpose. It would deplete our own defences, and regardless of that, I believe he is no longer a threat to St David's.'

Anselm was troubled by the weariness in the old man's voice. 'You drove away Rhys Gryg of Deheubarth, Archdeacon? You alone?'

'No man acts alone in the service of the Lord our God.'

'How many men were with him? Was... was Llywelyn's son amongst them?'

Gerald lowered his voice. 'Do you still have the three doves with the message to your father?'

'Yes... Why do you ask?'

'Listen to me. Loose them now, then ride with all haste for Pembroke.'

'Why?'

'No questions! Go now, make your peace with the Earl Marshal, and tell him that Gruffydd ap Llywelyn is alive. And God be with you!'

The Archdeacon watched the doves, and felt his own spirits rise with them as they leapt into the air above Llech Lafar. The Earl Marshal would be swift to send word to Llywelyn that Gruffydd was alive. Then would Llywelyn's mind be set at rest, and Wales might fully enjoy the peace which the charter of liberties had promised.

XXXI

Wearily, Gerald de Barri turned as Gruffydd ap Llywelyn emerged from the cool shade of the cathedral. 'He is gone. You have nothing more to fear.'

'I never was afraid of Squire Anselm.' Gruffydd pushed the unkempt hair back from his face, narrowing his eyes against the brightness of the morning.

'I asked him to convey to the Earl Marshal the glad tidings that you are alive.'

'And you say I have nothing to fear! The Earl Marshal will send his dogs after me!'

'Not now. . . didn't Rhys Gryg tell you what has been happening in England? The King has set his seal to a new charter, freeing all hostages.' Gerald found himself speaking only to fill the silence. 'It guarantees your safety, Gruffydd. . . from the Earl Marshal, at least. Even if you do not trust the King's word, you can be sure that William Marshal will honour the charter.'

'I would sooner not put him to the test. I will rest here tonight, and start out tomorrow for my home. I will need a strong escort. . . plenty of good men and horses.'

'You shall have them,' Gerald gestured for Gruffydd to precede him across Llech Lafar, 'but first I can offer you the hospitality of the Bishop's Palace. . . or his castle, if you prefer.'

'The castle, then.'

'I thought you might say that.'

Gruffydd laughed. 'Every Welshman is a soldier, that is what you say in your books.'

'Am I wrong? What was it the bard said? *Turn peace away, for honour perishes with peace.*'

'Very good, Gerallt Gymro. But if you know my people only through our bards, then you know us not at all.'

Gerald frowned as they crossed the stone bridge. 'My grandmother was Welsh. . . and I knew your father before you were born.'

'Yet you speak of the Earl of Pembroke as a friend.'

'Even enemies may harbour respect for one another.'

'And what do you say to the Earl Marshal when he seeks your counsel as to the Welsh? Do you tell him that you respect us?'

As they entered the bailey of the castle of St David's, both men became uncomfortably aware of the curious stares of the bystanders. Gruffydd ap Llywelyn looked as Celtic as any of these folk could imagine, yet he wore the rusting chain-link armour of a Norman. And although he walked as an equal in the company of Archdeacon Gerald de Barri, his cloak was torn and stained, his boots more hole than leather.

Despite Gerald's reassurances that Gruffydd had nothing more to fear, they had quite unconsciously quickened their pace until they passed through the gateway to the inner bailey. Pilgrims and pedlars left behind, interest in the young stranger now became less obvious, and the guards knew better than to challenge anyone in the Archdeacon's company.

In the blessed quiet of the Bishop's chamber, Gerald invited Gruffydd to be seated and stared at him for a long moment across the breadth of the table.

'The likeness. . .it is almost beyond belief. . .'

'What likeness?'

'You are so like your father, Gruffydd. And perhaps not only in your appearance. Time will tell.'

'Where is he now?'

'In Gwynedd, I should think. I expect he will be biding his time after the signing of the charter. . .to see if it has any effect.'

'This *charter*. . .' Gruffydd spoke the Norman word with distaste. 'Apart from freeing your King's hostages, how does it touch upon Wales?'

'It restores to the Welsh the right to live by Welsh law. . .and the Marches by Marcher law and England by English law.'

'How generous, to bestow upon us rights that were always ours!' Gruffydd's sarcasm bit deep. 'Did my father have a say in it?'

'It must have been at his insistence that the clause securing your release was included.' Gerald looked at the litter of parchments spilling across the table and onto the floor. 'I have it here, somewhere.'

'No matter, my lord. . .'

'Your father had been prominent amongst the rebels.'

'What rebels?'

'The Norman barons, mostly.'

157

'He sided with the Normans?'

Gerald nodded, surprised at Gruffydd's anger. 'Some of the Norman lords have been good allies to Llywelyn, didn't you know? Take Reginald de Braose, for instance. Now that he is to marry your sister...'

'What?'

'Your sister, Gwladus the Dark-Eyed...'

'I know my own sister! But Reginald de Braose! You call him our ally? Don't you remember the treachery of his father?'

'Well...' Gerald feigned confusion. He knew well enough the atrocities laid at the door of William de Braose, but this was not the time to speak of them.

'How many hundreds died at his hand? Trahaearn of Deheubarth...he was a man of noble lineage, but de Braose had him bound by his heels to a horse's tail and dragged to the gallows through the streets of Brecon.'

'That is but a story...'

'But one of many!' Gruffydd seemed eager to recite them all, but Gerald was quick to interrupt.

'Reginald and his brother...he is Bishop Giles of Hereford... they have been generous and loyal to their allies. They have even given over some of their recaptured castles into the hands of the Welsh. The building of such alliances can only bode well for the future...'

'And that is not the only alliance, is it, my lord Archdeacon? My own father took an English woman to wife. A bastard daughter of the King...'

'Joan...' Gerald spoke the lady's name with emphasis, for he pitied her Gruffydd's enmity, 'Joan is a good wife to Llywelyn, by all accounts.'

'Well and good, but...' Gruffydd hesitated, as he saw the troubled look in Gerald's eyes. 'What is it, Archdeacon?'

Gerald opened his mouth to speak, but struggled to find the words.

'Something has happened while I was imprisoned...'

'Much has happened, Gruffydd, and would that I knew the whole truth! I have heard so little from Llywelyn these past few years...'

158

'Yet there is something you hide. Is he not well? Have the traitors of Powys and Deheubarth. . .'

Gruffydd started at the quiet knock at the door. Two servitors entered at Gerald's bidding. They spoke no word and looked neither man in the eye as they set down the food and ale and hurried away.

Gruffydd forced a smile. 'Archdeacon. . . I want no surprises when I return to Gwynedd. I must know what has happened.'

Gerald chewed thoughtfully at his bread. He needed time to collect his thoughts, to think how best to frame his words. 'Will you not eat something, Gruffydd? The Bishop's hospitality would not be so generous if he were here to dispense it himself.'

'Damn your Bishop! And damn you with him, if you do not. . .' Gruffydd stumbled in his speech. He pushed the platter away from him and leaned forward on the table, his face buried in his hands. 'Forgive me, my lord.'

'For Llywelyn's sake.'

Gerald began to feel a genuine pity for the son of his old friend. In a supreme act of self-sacrifice he pushed the brace of roast pigeons closer to his guest. 'Now. You shall eat, and I shall talk. I am truly sorry for what I have to tell you, Gruffydd, but I beg you to remember that Llywelyn has acted for your sake and not through cowardice, nor treachery, nor folly.

'Four years ago, as you must well know, Llywelyn was in despair. King John's army occupied the foothills of Snowdonia, they had overrun the castles along the Conway, and you had been taken as hostage into England. Llywelyn believed himself to be at the mercy of the English. He feared for his rule, he feared for his country, and he feared most of all for you, Gruffydd.

'Llywelyn could think of but one course of action which might ensure the safety of all three. He promised King John that, should he die without legitimate heir, *without legitimate heir*, Gruffydd, then all his lands would pass to the King.' The silence pressed hard upon the old Archdeacon, yet he waited for Gruffydd to speak.

'Without legitimate heir? What are you trying to say? I am his legitimate heir!'

'By the laws of England. . .'

159

'What are the laws of England to me? My mother was Llywelyn's wife!'

Gerald shrugged his shoulders. Nothing would be achieved by pursuing that argument. 'Gruffydd, I must tell you now that Llywelyn has denied your legitimacy. He believed it was the only way...'

'My own father betrayed me?'

'What else was he to do? King John was executing his hostages whenever it pleased him, and there was the best of all reasons for being rid of you. Imagine your father's position, Gruffydd. By giving this promise...'

'By disinheriting me!'

'By giving this promise your father saved your life! There was no need for your captors to kill you, once you were out of line for succession to your father's power.'

'So now when Llywelyn dies, he will give Wales into the hands of the English for ever! How could he have promised that? How could he have been such a fool?'

Gerald took a slow sip of his ale. He met Gruffydd's gaze firmly as he spoke. 'And that is why there was great rejoicing in the court of Gwynedd, when Lord Llywelyn was blessed with a second son.'

Gruffydd stared in disbelief. Gerald felt as though Gruffydd's dark eyes scoured his very soul in their anguished search for falsehood or betrayal.

'Another son...by that English king's bastard?'

'Dafydd, he is named.'

'Dafydd ap Llywelyn...heir to the Kingdom of Gwynedd? Then what am I?'

Gruffydd's voice had barely escaped his lips. Nothing in all his four years in Corfe Castle had come so cruel.

XXXII

The oaken table, the silver candlesticks, the finely penned books, the rich tapestries, all had lost their reassuring familiarity. It was as if the presence of this stranger, back from the dead, had made alien the comfortable surroundings of the chamber of the Bishop of St David's.

The door was pushed open to reveal the captain of the guard.
'Forgive me, my lord Archdeacon. . .' Nevern frowned to see this oddly-attired Welshman in the Archdeacon's company, but made no remark upon it. 'I would not have intruded, but I bring grave news.'
Gerald glanced towards his guest. Gruffydd was staring fearfully at the captain, as if he guessed what the news must be but dreaded the hearing of it.
'Speak, captain. In Welsh, if you please, for our guest.'
'It was past dawn, my lord, when the ferryman returned to the cove at St Justinian's. He was in a state of terror and babbling beyond reason. When we had poured some wine into him and calmed him down, he told us his tale in some manner of sense. He said a band of cutthroats. . .'
'That would have been Rhys Gryg.'
'Whoever it was, my lord, they'd promised him good money to take them to the island. Once there, they met with five more and made him take them all back. . . but further along the coast to avoid St Justinian's. He said they had barely set foot on the sands of Porth Mawr when his passengers set to fighting, and he was lucky to escape with his life. I took my men along the cliffs to have a look, but we found nothing but the bodies of the slain.'
'How many?' Gruffydd's voice was heavy.
'Four.' Nevern stared at him, surprised to hear a northern accent.
'Rhys *y bradwr* left them to rot.' Gruffydd turned away so that his tears should not be seen.
'They must have fought with great valour. . .' Nevern spoke quietly and would have said more, but Gerald waved him back towards the doorway.

161

'You will arrange an escort for our guest, Nevern, as many good men as you can spare. He is anxious to be on his way home.'

'Yes, Archdeacon. But. . .who is he?'

Gerald smiled despite himself. Even the grave Captain Nevern was not immune to curiosity!

The boy faced Nevern and lifted his head proudly. 'I am Gruffydd ap Llywelyn ap Iorwerth ab Owain ap Gruffydd ap Cynan ap Iago ab Idwal ap Meurig ab Idwal ab Anarawd ap Rhodri Mawr ap Merfyn. . .'

Forgetting all else, Gerald de Barri reached for his inkpot and quill. He had always been a little confused as to the genealogies of the northern princes, and was tempted to ask Gruffydd to repeat the names there and then. . .but perhaps this was not the time. He wrote frantically from memory as Nevern bowed low before Llywelyn's son.

'You are well come, my lord. Your deliverance is a miracle indeed.'

'My friends, captain. Where are their bodies now?'

'Lying where they fell. . . Shall I send a burial party, my lord Archdeacon?'

'No, captain, have them brought here, all of them.' Gerald dipped his quill, and with barely a glance at Gruffydd said brusquely 'And you can give me their names. . .I will have them buried in the cathedral close.'

'They should rest well there.' Gruffydd smiled with bitter irony. 'By the shrine of Dewi Sant.'

'Captain Nevern will arrange your escort, and it would be well if you were to leave in the morning as soon as you have made your farewell to your comrades.' Gerald looked up from his manuscript, his brow creased in a frown. He really would have to ask Gruffydd to recite those names again. . .

Gruffydd ap Llywelyn settled back in his chair as he gazed thoughtfully at the Archdeacon's face. 'So now it has come to pass, just as I feared. I alone survived, from a score of the King's hostages. Is it just my good fortune that I was the one to return to Wales? Or am I delivered by the hand of God? What do you think, Gerallt Gymro?'

Gerald remembered Rhys Gryg's words at Pembroke. *That one*

knows how to look after his own hide. 'I think...I think you were fortunate to have been blessed with such brave companions.'

'And now they are lost. I have no friends, no allies, no advisers. When I return home I will have to act for myself, among men who remember me only as a child. I must know everything that has passed in my absence.'

'I will tell all I know, but you must strengthen your knowledge with Faith, my son, and temper your deeds with compassion.'

The sky beyond the window of the Bishop's chamber was beginning to darken, the snakeskin cloud bloodied by a tiring sun. Gerald de Barri felt that he had been talking without pause since dawn, so weak and hoarse had his voice become. He had told Gruffydd ap Llywelyn all that had passed in four years, in Gwynedd, in Wales, in Britain, in all Christendom, and still the boy had more questions.

'And where is King John now?'

'The King, I imagine, will be on his way to his council in Oxford.'

'With no plans for Wales?'

'He has summoned William Marshal to attend him, no doubt to advise upon the Welsh problem.'

'A problem, are we?' Gruffydd's sudden smile was startling.

'To the Normans...yes, you are a problem. But isn't that what you want?' Gerald could not restrain his temper. He was tired and thirsty, and sorely in want of his supper, but he would not be first to bring an end to the discussion. He knew that Gruffydd needed to ask his questions, and he was flattered by so avid a pupil.

'It is common knowledge that King John grows more insecure and unstable by the day, and old beyond his years. He does not want to embark upon any new campaigns, he wants only to keep his kingdom together and to preserve his own neck. His barons despise him, his knights despise him and I should think that when he falls, all England will rejoice. They would accept any king in his stead. English, French...'

'Welsh?'

Gerald's pause spoke more eloquently than any words. 'Well, who can tell? Perhaps even Welsh.'

163

There was a knock at the door. A young serving maid came in, a bundle in her arms. She curtseyed clumsily before the Archdeacon, without daring to look at Llywelyn's son. 'Captain Nevern said you...er, *he*...might welcome a change of garments, my lord.'

Gruffydd stared at the fine linen, the wool and fur in the girl's arms, and only now did he seem to notice the poor state of his Norman attire. The fine iron links of the mail shirt were congealed in rust, and he would not be sorry to be rid of the weight that had near cost him his life in Ramsey Sound. 'I am most grateful.'

The girl curtseyed again, her face colouring to crimson as she set down the garments upon the corner of the table.

Gerald too had noticed the quality of the clothing, and frowned as he considered Nevern's over-generous use of Church funds. 'One more thing, girl...our guest will sleep here this night. See to it that he is provided with a jug of my own good wine.'

'He's sleeping *here*, my lord? In the Bishop's chamber?'

'The son of Lord Llywelyn can hardly sleep in the hall among the pilgrims.'

'But my lord...' The girl trembled, torn between her terror of the Archdeacon and the unknown menace of the new Bishop to come. 'But...what if the new Bishop should arrive tonight?'

Gerald dismissed the girl with an impatient wave of his hand, and turned to Gruffydd. 'Bishop Iorwerth will not come today, we can be sure of that. He will send word in advance of his arrival to ensure his welcome. And if Iorwerth of Talley did find his room occupied;...then he would do nothing. He would simply apologise for being a nuisance and sleep in the hall. That is the nature of our new Bishop. He does not assert himself, he will not complain. He expects nothing, and so he will achieve nothing, not even the respect due to his office.'

'And that is the new Bishop of St David's?' Gruffydd's voice betrayed his disappointment. 'Yet he bears a great name.'

'He is Welsh by birth, but his sharing of your noble grandfather's name is a bitter irony indeed. Bishop Iorwerth is born of the Welsh, but at the same time he is more of a Norman than I am.'

164

'But you, my lord. . .you could persuade him where his true loyalty must lie. If he really is so weak, he would bend easily to the will of Gerallt Gymro.'

'Perhaps. . .' Gerald closed his eyes to dwell upon the notion. Gruffydd was right. Here was the golden opportunity to be Bishop in all but name. Unseen, he could wield all the power of that office, and by his influence. . . He was startled as Gruffydd came closer and whispered in his ear.

'Gerallt Gymro, you must make it known to Iorwerth of Talley what his appointment means to us. The people of Wales will expect much of their new Bishop. Ensure that he acts always in our interest. And when the time comes, we will show that we are grateful to our next *Archbishop.*'

'Archbishop? Surely you mean. . .'

'I know what I mean, my lord! And so, I think, do you.'

For a moment, Gerald de Barri was drawn to share the burning ambition in the dark eyes of Llywelyn's son. Only for a moment. The Archdeacon was tired, tired in body and tired in spirit. He could not rise to the challenge, he could not even begin to wonder what made Gruffydd ap Llywelyn speak of the dream that had both blighted his career and ensured his unacknowledged prominence in the Church of Wales.

'I will bid you goodnight, Gruffydd ap Llywelyn. I think that we are both in need of rest.'

Gerald paused at the foot of the tower to gaze down across the outer bailey. The market stalls lay like skeletons in the twilight, crooked limbs bared and beckoning, now that their shrouds had been removed. The distant River Alun shimmered through the willowed banks, a thread of beaten silver running through the crumpled cloth of the land.

The Archdeacon had intended to retire to his own chamber, yet he knew that sleep would not come. The events of the day spiralled within his mind, and would allow him no peace. Had he been mistaken in permitting Lord Rhys Gryg to leave St David's without the just punishment of excommunication for his crimes? Had he treated Llywelyn ap Iorwerth's son with too much respect? Or too little? Had he placed his own soul in peril for

165

listening, just for a moment, to the temptation of this young Pretender?

And for all his talking with Gruffydd ap Llywelyn, he had quite forgotten the most important question of all. *Where, in the Name of God, were the bones of Dewi Sant?*

XXXIII

'There's gold eagles up there in Gwynedd too, not just the kites and buzzards.'

'And they say the eagles can talk!'

'The mountains are so high there's snow on top.'

'Even in summer!'

'There's gold and silver just lying there waiting to be taken!'

'The sheep are as big as cows.'

'And the cows are as big as. . .as. . .' the man floundered.

'As Megan of Brawdy!'

'I'll wager the cows are not as ugly!'

Gales of ribald laughter rose from the soldiers lounging by the gates.

'And Llywelyn owns the lot. Lucky bastard!'

'Lucky? You've not seen that son of his! They say Gruffydd is going to raise an army and oust this so-called King of the Welsh from his throne!'

'Where did you hear that?'

'From the sister of his serving maid.'

'Take care that he does not lead you into his glorious battle. You know how we reward deserters.' Nevern's grim warning effectively ended all such speculation.

'Good morning!'

All turned in anticipation to the familiar voice of Gerald de Barri as he came striding down from the inner bailey. The Archdeacon frowned as he drew near. 'Is Llywelyn's son not with you?'

'Perhaps he still sleeps, my lord.'

'Sleeps, captain? But he wanted to leave at dawn. I thought I might have missed him.'

'I would have sent a man to rouse him, my lord, but. . .'

166

'Never mind, Nevern, I will go myself. . .there is something I have to ask of him.'

Gruffydd ap Llywelyn stood by the window of the Bishop's chamber, comfortable in his new garments, his face washed and his hair cropped short. He did not turn as the Archdeacon came in. 'You see the raven?'

'There is always a raven over the valley. He haunts the place.'

'King Arthur. Watching and waiting.' There was a silent mockery in Gruffydd's smile. 'Waiting for Dewi Sant, Elidyr would have said.'

'Elidyr? Who would that be?'

'Come now, Archdeacon. Rhys Gryg told me many things on the boat from Ramsey, it cannot all have been lies. I think you know Elidyr well enough.'

'I've known many a man by that name. There was an Elidyr I knew of once, who told everyone that he knew of a cave that led to an underground realm of little people. They rode on horses the size of dogs and. . .' Gerald smiled innocently. 'He died many years ago, though. I don't suppose it was he. . .'

Gruffydd did not return the smile. 'Elidyr ab Idwal is his name, Archdeacon. You spoke with him at Pembroke. You took him in your custody to Manorbier. And then he disappeared.'

'Was. . .is he a friend of yours?'

'He was the only one to stand by me when the others rebelled.'

'When was this? On the ship?'

Gruffydd looked away. 'They were all happy enough when I spoke to the Cornishmen and won our freedom. . .and happy enough when I cast the English ashore. But as soon as they had the taste of freedom they lost interest in landing on Ramsey, they just wanted to go on home. They challenged my authority. . .I could not submit to that.'

'And so. . .?'

'There was a fight. Only fists, it was, but a lamp was knocked over and fell below decks. You know the rest.' Gruffydd's tone did not invite further questions, but Gerald had to be sure.

'The fire was no fault of Anselm's?'

'How could it have been? Oh, I know what Elidyr told you all at Pembroke, but why did you believe him? Surely it was plain

167

enough to see that Anselm hadn't the wits or the courage to act against us.'

'But Elidyr swore upon his oath that you were all slain.'

'We were dead for all he knew. What was the difference?'

'The difference is that he swore Anselm started the fire!'

'Well, Elidyr never could see the need for the truth, if a lie would serve him better.'

'But he perjured himself, Gruffydd! Do you not understand what that means?' Gerald was angered that the boy could take this so lightly. 'He took his oath upon this very cross!'

Gruffydd stared for a moment at the old Archdeacon. 'Rhys Gryg told me that you acted as Elidyr's gaolor.'

'I took him to Manorbier to protect him from the Earl Marshal. . .and from Rhys Gryg.'

'Rhys also told me that Elidyr was killed while under this *protection* of yours.'

'He was seen to escape, his fate is in God's hands now.'

'You are a cunning old man, Gerallt Gymro. You could have murdered him yourself, and I would never wrest the truth from you.'

'You owe me your life. Do not forget that!'

'Only a jest.' Gruffydd smiled. 'No, I will not forget. And one day you may find that I can be a powerful ally.'

'I have always counted Lord Llywelyn as my friend. It would be my hope that his son and heir. . .' Gerald's voice died in his throat as both men remembered, and the name of Dafydd ap Llywelyn hung unspoken in the air.

'Continue to hope, my lord Archdeacon, and to pray. And we both know full well that there are many in Wales who would not suffer a half-English mongrel to take my place.'

'You cannot. . .' Gerald stared uncertainly at his guest. 'My lord, you must not incite civil war among the Welsh. The English wait like crows for such easy pickings! What would it profit you to be king of a conquered race?'

'Do not fear for us, Gerallt Gymro. Now it is the English who fight amongst themselves, and it is time for the Welsh to stop running into the mountains! Why should we stay west of the Dyke, when all England trembles in fear of us?'

'The Dyke. . .?'

168

'Have you forgotten that all Britain was once ours?'

'And so was the Kingdom of Troy! Would you take your ships back there? You are a fool to think of taking Britain, Gruffydd ap Llywelyn, when half of Wales lies in English hands, when you have seen for yourself how the southern Welsh princes ache for the chance to betray your father!'

'They need a sign, the people of Wales. They must have a sign to unite them under one banner. Just think what it would have meant if I had found the bones of Dewi Sant!'

Gerald's heart sank. 'But I thought you had . . .'

'A miracle, it would have been. I alone . . . Gruffydd ap Llywelyn Fawr of Gwynedd . . . I alone would have been the one with the courage, the vision, the God-given power, to bring him home. You know this well enough, Gerallt Gymro. You must know it, you of all men. The man who found the bones of Saint David would become as a saint himself!'

The Archdeacon rounded upon Gruffydd, who seemed now to be upon the verge of blasphemy. 'A saint you would be now, is it? I thought you saw yourself rather as a new King Arthur?'

'With the bones of Saint David carried before me, I could do anything. *Anything!* With those relics, with God's help . . . with *your* help, Archdeacon . . .'

Gerald de Barri said nothing. Was it inspiration or was it madness that drove the boy? Was it the Holy Spirit or the Devil's hand? Gruffydd had spoken in a voice so calm. Yet his knuckles shone white on the table's edge, his eyes astare and never leaving the Archdeacon's face. Gruffydd's voice had fallen to little more than a whisper.

'Even the Normans revere King Arthur.'

King Arthur. . . . Saint David . . . the images of raven and dove intertwined in the Archdeacon's anguished mind. He knew that to anticipate the relics' recovery could lead only to further torment. He knew that to allow himself the smallest hope would be to expose himself yet again to defeat and to disappointment. And he knew, as the boy held his eyes, that Gruffydd was possessed only by his own ambition, consumed only by his own pride.

'I do not understand why you say these things, Gruffydd ap Llywelyn.' Gerald felt his sanity returning in his own calm voice.

169

He saw that Gruffydd's right hand gripped the table still, his nails bitten and bloody. 'If you have the relics, then you must return them to the cathedral where they belong. The Word of Our Lord lies there upon the table. Will you place your hand upon the Book and swear that you have never seen the bones of Saint David?'

Gruffydd gazed at the Bible and remained silent.

'I tell you this, son of Llywelyn. Not a hundred years ago lived Caradog, who is now a Saint. His dying wish was to be buried here in our cathedral, but the Earl of...well, I will not say, but a nobleman tried to steal the body. He hoped that the relics of Caradog would perform miracles for him, but at once a fierce illness descended upon him, and he enjoyed not a moment free of torment until he brought the body here. Now Caradog's bones lie in their shrine and bring their blessings upon all deserving souls who pray before him.'

Gruffydd laughed outright. 'But can you truly believe that Dewi Sant would punish a Welshman for returning his remains to his own people? Can you possibly believe that he would rather rest upon the altar of a Norman cathedral? And a Norman cathedral built upon the ruins of a true Welsh church by the very bishops you yourself despise!'

Gruffydd ap Llywelyn walked to the door, but his eyes never left the Archdeacon's face. 'Think well upon this, Gerallt Gymro... You are respected by Welshman and Norman alike, your counsel is sought, your advice is heeded. You are a man of God, and none knows better than you the power of true Faith.'

'Yes, but...'

'Spread the word that the relics are found, my lord Archdeacon. And one day...one day...Dewi Sant may come home. But only when his home is fit to receive him.'

Gerald sat back feebly in his chair, his mind spinning as he listened to Gruffydd's departing footsteps. Gruffydd had found the bones of Saint David. Of that there could be no more doubt. He had them hidden, and he would use them to further his own reckless ambition.

And there was nothing that Gerald of Wales could do to stop him.

XXXIV

The mists had long since lifted from the valley beneath the castle of St David's. Captain Nevern was not a man easily bored, but even he was beginning to find the wait unendurable. The soldiers slouched in their saddles or leaned easy against the palisade, and scarcely stirred as Gruffydd ap Llywelyn made his unhurried way from the Bishop's tower.

'Captain Nevern! Your Archdeacon delayed me, you know how he loves the sound of his own voice.'

Nevern bowed stiffly.

'Are you riding with me, captain?'

'Alas I cannot, my lord. These good men will be your escort.'

'Are they Welsh?'

'Some are Welsh, my lord, and the rest know something of the language.' The captain looked towards the tower. 'Is the Archdeacon coming down to the gates?'

'I think not, captain. I left him in thoughtful mood.'

Nevern held Gruffydd's stirrup, noting the awkwardness with which the boy heaved himself into the saddle. Not a skilled horseman, it was clear, but the captain smiled grimly as he remembered that there would have been little opportunity to practise the art in the dungeons of Corfe Castle. The soldiers were mounted up and eager to be off, but Gruffydd hesitated to give the word. He twisted the leather reins between his fingers.

'Captain...' Nevern came closer as the boy leaned down from his mount to speak in confidence. 'You have been here for many years?'

'I have, my lord.'

'Then you must know Gerallt Gymro as well as any. Which is he at heart...Norman or Welshman?'

'He is a man of God, my lord. I wish you God speed!' Nevern slapped the horse's rump hard as he turned away. 'And good riddance.'

Captain Nevern lingered by the gate as the horsemen rode from sight. Though never one to leap to a hasty judgement, he could not suppress the uncharitable notion that it might have been better had Gruffydd ap Llywelyn been left to rot in the King's

171

dungeon. He sighed as he kicked the dust of the pathway. Peace was a fine thing for the women and the monks, but the relentless inaction of the garrison of St David's gnawed at his very soul.

The courtyard was less crowded than usual as Nevern began his inspection of the guard. Rumours of war had begun to deter all but the most devout of pilgrims from the long journey to St David's, in favour of the more accessible shrines of Canterbury, or Glastonbury, or Walsingham. Nevern wondered how well the rumours were founded. He wondered if any true Welshman ever would attack the shrine of his own Saint. And then he remembered Rhys Gryg. If the man who called himself Lord of Deheubarth could threaten murder in the Cathedral of St David, then surely no perversity was beneath him. Nevern looked up to the inner bailey, where the Bishop's tower sat brooding over the smaller wooden buildings like a hen with her chicks. How pitiful were the defences of St David's! How archaic they were by comparison with the great fortresses of Kidwelly, or Haverford, or Pembroke.

Nevern was a soldier, not a nursemaid for this graveyard community. He yearned for action, yet he would never see it here. By God, how he wished that he could have made the journey into Gwynedd with the escort of Llywelyn's son! Yet if he could not see the fabled wonders of the Eagle Mountains, then any journey would suffice. Perhaps St David's might send out a party to meet its new Bishop, to escort him with all due pomp and ceremony to his new throne, and it would surely be fitting and right for the Captain of the Guard to command so vital an escort.

The captain continued his inspection, yet contrived never to let the door from the Bishop's chamber out of his sight until at last the Archdeacon emerged. Nevern, resolved to ask him at once, readied his arguments as Gerald walked across the bailey, but he changed his mind as he saw the old man's dark scowl. Deep in thought, as Gruffydd had warned, Gerald de Barri was clearly in no mood to discuss the sensitive subject of Bishop Iorwerth.

'Has he gone, captain?' The Archdeacon's question was abrupt. He was more angry than Nevern had anticipated.

'Llywelyn's son? Yes, my lord, as soon as he had taken his leave of you.'

'And what did he say to you?'

172

'Nothing of consequence, my lord. He was glad to be gone.'
'I share his joy. You gave him his escort?'
'Five men, my lord.'
'How many guards does that leave us here?'
'Thirty men at arms, all told, though two are not fit for duty.'
'St David's could ill afford its five best soldiers.'

Nevern hid a smirk. His garrison was well rid of its five worst loiterers and wastrels, and he cared not if they never returned.

'Under duress we could raise another threescore men and boys from the villages, my lord.'

Gerald nodded, his eyes following the road into the distance.

'Is something wrong, my lord? Should I have detained Gruffydd?'

Gerald shook his head. That might have been one way, to let the captain use his skills to wrest the truth from the boy, but it was not his way. 'He was hiding something, captain.'

'If you wish it, my lord, I shall fetch him back. But if I have the measure of the boy, he would suffer much before...'

'No! For pity's sake, no.' Gerald could not look the captain in the face. Nevern had confessed much on his return from the Crusades. He had seen and done things that had made the Archdeacon fear for his very soul.

'It was the relics, Nevern. The holy relics of our Saint David. Somehow Gruffydd discovered where the Vikings had left them ...after their attack on St David's. And now he has gone, and the knowledge has gone with him. Can you understand what that means? Can you understand what I have lost?'

Nevern looked about the courtyard. The stalls were busy now, the traders loud in their cries. He lowered his voice. 'If it will ease your mind, Archdeacon...that little bastard was lying in his teeth. There was a story my mother used to tell me. Her great-grandfather was a Norseman who took fancy to a Welsh woman and settled near Fishguard...well, at Nevern, it was. He forsook his pagan ways and accepted the True Faith. But he had been to Wales before, see? He had been among those who pillaged St David's, Archdeacon, at the time when the relics disappeared...'

'Why have you said nothing of this before?' As Gerald stared at Nevern, he felt as if those pale blue Nordic eyes were the very

173

ones that had looked upon the burning ruins of the church of Dewi Sant and the broken bodies of its brother monks...

'There are still those who would hound a man for the deeds of his ancestors, as well as for the colouring of his race.'

Gerald remembered the castellan of Haverford, and felt ashamed.

'My mother told me much of what had happened here in St David's, my lord. It was a tale handed down in the family from her great-grandfather's time. The Norsemen would have taken everything they valued from the church, true enough. But they would not have bothered themselves with the relics... *even if they had found them.*'

'What do you mean, captain? Why should they not have found them?'

'From St David's you can see for miles. When the Norsemen used to come here, they found only the things the locals couldn't carry away with them. They burned everything to the ground, yes, but all they ever took from St David's was a few stray sheep from the fields.'

'I don't think that...'

'They didn't get away with half as much as people say. Think on it, my lord. If you thought you were going to be attacked, you would hide your most precious things, wouldn't you?'

'I suppose so. If I had fair warning...'

'Well, I reckon that if the relics disappeared, then they had been hidden somewhere not far away by one of the monks. And perhaps he didn't live to tell the tale.'

XXXV

On most of his days in St David's, Gerald de Barri would enjoy the celebration of Mass as a quiet opportunity to think upon his own duties, or to plan the text of his latest book. This day there was much for his mind to dwell upon, but the hammering of the blacksmith rendered concentration impossible. The hapless fellow had been told to complete his work without the slightest delay and, taking his orders all too literally, he pounded at the choir gates in a slothful attempt to straighten the hinges without removing them first from the wooden framework of the rood screen. It was a great relief when Mass was over.

The old Archdeacon stood still as the columns of the nave, watching quietly as his congregation began to disperse. A small group of monks, pilgrims perhaps from some other see, came to speak with him, but he waved them away with an excuse even though they were in the company of their abbot. How he despised these monks of the cloister, these pious, bland, blameless men whose only thoughts were for the wellbeing of their own souls, who disguised their own selfish ends in deeds of conspicuous charity, each to ensure his own place in Heaven. Gerald consoled himself with the thought that, while their memory would perish with the corruption of their bodies, his own would endure as long as sober men sought wisdom in books. Yet at the same time he knew too well that his own thoughts were unworthy, his own ambitions ultimately selfish. The Good Lord, all seeing, all knowing, must be aware that His archdeacon had sought the relics of Saint David in order to further his own ends.

The words of Gruffydd ap Llywelyn still plagued Gerald's conscience. The boy had been right. The man who possessed the bones of Saint David would be revered throughout Wales, he would seem favoured by God, he would, in truth, almost become as a saint himself. Gerald had thought Gruffydd's ambitions bordered upon the blasphemous, yet now he realised that his own thoughts, his own dreams, were no less sinful.

Gerald de Barri did not pray for forgiveness. He prayed for guidance. The finding of the bones of Saint David would be of great moment for Wales, whoever should recover them. Was Gruffydd ap Llywelyn even now carrying the holy relics north into Gwynedd? Was this indeed the path ordained for them? Would the bones of Saint David, through Gruffydd, lead the Welsh to the glory they had awaited for six centuries past?

'Archdeacon. *Archdeacon!*' A cowled figure plucked at his sleeve. 'Is something wrong, Archdeacon? Are you unwell?'

'Hugh?' Gerald stared vaguely at the clerk, his mind returning but slowly to the ordered world of the cathedral. 'Brother Hugh, it is! How can you be returned so soon from Canterbury?'

175

'You forget, my lord Archdeacon. His Grace Archbishop Langton was at the consecration of Bishop Iorwerth. I left the ship at Lymington and was fortunate enough to reach Winchester before the Archbishop departed.'

'What did he say about my book?'

'He charged me to tell you that he was gratified to receive it, and that he expected to find it most. . .' Brother Hugh hesitated.

'Most what?'

'Er. . .I'm sorry, Archdeacon, but I didn't quite catch the rest of His Grace's words. There were a great many people in attendance and he spared me but a moment. I'm sure your arguments will give him much to think on.'

'I should hope so! The Pope himself keeps copies of my books by his bedside, so indispensable does he find their company!' Gerald laughed at himself, his good humour restored. 'Well, Brother Hugh? What news from England? How fares the great charter of liberties?'

'Oh. . .' Hugh's eyes widened in awe. 'You know of the charter, my lord? Even here? On the journey back we saw knights on the road and armies on the move, but none bothered us. No one in England would challenge a Bishop's entourage! Oh, what a glorious sight we made! All the horses, the carts, the fine robes, and a splendid new cross borne before the Bishop. . .'

'You travelled with Bishop Iorwerth? Is he here now?'

'Yes. . .er, no. He was tired and will abide a few days at Llawhaden before completing his journey. He sent me on to announce his coming.'

'Llawhaden?' Gerald gazed thoughtfully at the jewelled cross upon the altar, remembering what the Earl Marshal had said at Pembroke. Llawhaden Castle was close to the border between the Norman lands and the Welsh-held region of Deheubarth. Its position on the Eastern Cleddau, but a few leagues from Pembroke and Haverford, would make it a valued addition to the conquests of the southern princes. Only a decade ago, indeed, had the castle of Llawhaden been recaptured from the Welsh and restored to the Bishopric of St David's. 'We must pray that the Bishop arrives safely in St David's. And, Brother Hugh, you must see to it that he is received with all the ceremony befitting his office.'

'But...but surely, my lord, you will be here to receive him yourself.'

'So that I can teach him how to be a good Bishop? I am but an old archdeacon, Brother Hugh, I cannot work miracles.' Gerald could not disguise the bitterness in his voice. 'Forgive me, brother. Too much has happened, these past few days.'

'What is it, my lord? I can see something troubles you.' There was a genuine anxiety in Brother Hugh's voice.

'The son of Llywelyn ap Iorwerth has been here. He may have the blessed relics of our Saint in his possession.'

The clerk's eyes grew wide. 'The bones of Saint David...found at last?'

'It is not quite the good news we prayed for, Brother Hugh. I fear that young Gruffydd ap Llywelyn may try to use them to fire an uprising of the Welsh...'

'You must explain it all to Bishop Iorwerth when he comes. He will need your...'

'No, Hugh. I am going to Manorbier. I am too old, too set in my ways.' The Archdeacon turned away so that his face could not be seen, and spoke in a barely audible whisper. 'And perhaps too vulnerable to temptation. I am going home to Manorbier, there to retire and to die in peace.'

'Retire, my lord? But there are so many of your books yet unfinished! You've not completed your *Instruction of a Prince*... and what of your *Topography of Britain*? And you haven't even begun...'

'I can write at Manorbier. Indeed I shall write all the better without the worries of St David's to distract me.'

'Please, Archdeacon! You *cannot* leave so soon before the new Bishop arrives! People will say that you shun him, think of the scandal, and him a Welshman too!'

'I am leaving today.'

'Then stop at Llawhaden on your way to Manorbier, my lord. You could at least offer him your blessing. Bishop Iorwerth will want to see you... He will *need* to see you for your wise counsel!'

'You think so, Hugh?'

'I know he will, Archdeacon! I have spoken with him. No man living admires you more than he!'

177

Chapter XXXVI

Ͳhe Castle of Llawhaðen

4 July, 1215

The Bishop's castle at Llawhaden was almost as outdated as its counterpart at St David's. It had only a single, circular courtyard enclosed by a wooden palisade and a deep moat, and among the scattered wooden buildings within stood a tall, square tower of stone. In the uppermost chamber of this tower, the new Bishop of St David's had made his temporary home. And the new Bishop of St David's was not comfortable.

Like the great keep of Pembroke, the tower was designed to withstand a siege, and would be the final retreat should the castle walls be breached. The solar, adjacent to the wooden hall, was far more suited to the abode of a bishop, as the castellan had most respectfully advised His Grace, but the Bishop was a cautious man. In the few days since his consecration at Winchester, his long journey had shown him far too much of the new aggression amongst the southern Welsh. Several times he had been stopped, and the Bishop firmly believed that only his Welsh name had saved himself and his entourage.

It was not going to be easy for a Welshman to be Bishop of St David's. Iorwerth was fully aware of this, and he was not the kind of man to rise to a challenge. He had, in all honesty, been first shocked and then dismayed to receive the Archbishop's summons to Winchester. He had been happy enough in the undemanding post of Abbot of Talley. He had enjoyed the greatest comfort in his living quarters, and the most beautiful countryside upon which to rest his eyes. He had been afforded every respect but, best of all, he had faced no adversity. Everything that went on in the small Abbey of Talley was easily administered, easily capable of being handled by himself or delegated to others. But the Bishopric of St David's was another matter entirely.

The responsibility of administering St David's, the most hotly disputed, the most infamous of the four Welsh sees, made Iorwerth sweat with fear whenever he thought of it. He knew that all would look upon him as successor, not to Bishop Geoffrey, but to *Giraldus Cambrensis*. Gerald de Barri was a towering personage whom Iorwerth both feared and revered, and he knew himself far too weak a man to be worthy, or able, to fulfil Gerald's ambitions for the Welsh Church.

What Iorwerth did not know, and could not have guessed, had been as plain as daylight to Gerald de Barri. His very weakness had been the precise reason for which the Archbishop of Canterbury had chosen him as his new Bishop. Iorwerth of Talley was Welsh, and this would salve some of the rebelliousness of his countrymen. He was well known in Pembrokeshire as a passive and undemanding churchman, and would therefore be accepted willingly by the Earl Marshal. And, most important of all, he was irresolute enough to be easily manipulated by the English Church.

Bishop Iorwerth's heart missed a beat as there came a furious pounding upon his door. At the Abbey of Talley, all had knocked with a single, respectful tap. He had yet to become accustomed to the rough ways of soldiers, and raised his hands in alarm when a chain-mailed figure strode in.

'Begging your pardon, Your Grace, but there is a Welshman here to see you.'

'A Welshman?' Iorwerth stammered. 'Why did you let him past the gates?'

'He says he is sent by Llywelyn ap Iorwerth, Your Grace, to convey his lord's welcome.'

'He. . . he carries Llywelyn's seal?'

'No, he claims he was robbed of it on the way. Will you see him, Your Grace, or no?'

Bishop Iorwerth calmed himself with an effort, using, as ever, the example of the great Gerald de Barri as his model. He loathed mixing with the laity. Earlier this day, he had been required to join an assembly of knights for dinner, and had despised their rowdy company. Even the knowledge that they were his own liegemen from the lands around Llawhaden, ready to provide military service should their Bishop demand it, had done nothing

179

to ease Iorwerth's discomfort. He had left them, barely an hour ago, when they had become too drunk to hold decent conversation. It was to be hoped that no attack would come, for half the defensive force of the Bishop's estates lay snoring in the great hall.

Iorwerth reminded himself that he would need every ounce of goodwill, even from the Welsh, to succeed as Bishop, and this would be an easy way to begin. 'Very well, send him in. And stay close by...just outside the door.'

The soldier bowed and left, leaving the door ajar. Iorwerth wished he had closed it. A cruel draught howled up that accursed stone stairway. Up the stair, through the door, and out of the narrow window behind him, chilling the Bishop's feet on its way. Iorwerth loathed the idea of such narrow windows, even though they were in the shape of the cross. He was more accustomed to broad lancet windows, fittingly decorated with stained glass, or opening onto mile upon mile of the broad Llandeilo hills. Already he missed his home at the Abbey of Talley. The Bishop's Palace, his palace at Lamphey, where he had spent the previous night, had been more to his taste than Llawhaden, but even Lamphey had borne an unpleasantly martial air. It was to be hoped that the palace of St David's would match the comfort and tranquility of Talley. If not, then surely the treasury of St David's could afford a few improvements worthy of a...

'*Prynhawn da i chi, f'arglwydd.*'

Bishop Iorwerth started nervously, then frowned at the man's use of his own native Welsh. How dare the fellow address an abbot...no, the *Bishop*, in so...so ungodly a language?

'*Elidyr ab Idwal ab Owain ydw i. Aelod o lys Llywelyn ap Iorwerth, Arglwydd Gwynedd a...*'

'Yes, I know who Llywelyn is.' Bishop Iorwerth had winced to hear his own name, shared as it was with Llywelyn's father. 'And I would have expected his courier to have the courtesy to speak French.'

'*Dwi ddim yn deall, f'arglwydd.*'

Iorwerth's frown deepened. He disliked the speaking of Welsh, just as he disliked anything that reminded him of his own ancestry. Yet if it was the only way to communicate... 'You don't understand French? That makes you a strange choice for Llywelyn's courier.'

'Not when I travel through Wales to meet a Welshman, my lord.'

Iorwerth reddened. 'What is your master's message?'

A sly smile crept over the bard's face. 'There is no message from Llywelyn, my lord.'

'Then why...' Iorwerth began to stammer.

'I heard tell that the new Welsh Bishop of St David's was breaking his journey at Llawhaden, so I came to see for myself. And to pay my respects, Your Grace.'

The Bishop looked doubtfully at his visitor. He supposed that he should have been afraid of this man who had tricked his way into his company, and yet his curiosity prevented him from calling the guard. 'What happened to your face?'

'A Welshman must be careful in these parts, Your Grace. The Normans are a treacherous race. Have you not found it so?'

'They have always treated me fairly, and with respect.'

'Perhaps it is different for men of God. I have not yet learned your name, Your Grace.'

'I am Bishop Iorwerth...' He was sorry to see that Elidyr expected more, but refused to follow the Welsh custom of citing his kin. 'I was Abbot of Talley.'

'And now you are Bishop of St David's, Your Grace. That is a great achievement for one of our race. Is Gerallt Gymro known to you?'

'We have met.'

'Will he be at St David's to greet you?'

Bishop Iorwerth avoided Elidyr's eye. That would be the worst part of it, the one thing he had been dreading above all else. Of all men in Wales, of all men in the whole of Britain, Iorwerth most feared Giraldus Cambrensis. He feared Gerald more than he feared Archbishop Stephen Langton of Canterbury, more even than King John himself. Gerald knew the problems Iorwerth would have to face, yet he would seek to double and redouble those problems. Gerald would endeavour to place upon the new Bishop's shoulders a mantle of responsibilty which Iorwerth feared to wear, an awesome challenge to which the former Abbot of Talley would never dare rise.

'... will the Archdeacon be at St David's to greet you, Your Grace?'

'Er...yes, I expect so.' Bishop Iorwerth peered narrowly at his guest, wondering what prompted his precocious questions, noting the care with which the Welshman seemed to commit each reply to memory. 'Is there some particular matter that brought you here?'

'There is, Your Grace.'

'Well?'

Elidyr looked away. He had reached his decision the moment he heard of the new Welsh bishop. Yet still he hesitated, fearing that the weak man before him was not worthy of his trust. He swallowed his doubts. Iorwerth was Welsh, and he was Bishop of the Shrine of Saint David. There could be no turning back.

'Your Grace...Dewi Sant was born in the midst of a great storm on the cliffs east of Porth Clais, where the chapel of his sainted mother Non now stands. He was the most resolute of missionaries, the holiest of men, it was he who wove the many strands of our language into a united whole. Even before Dewi's birth, Gildas prophesied his future greatness. And when Dewi preached at Brefi, the very ground upon which he stood lifted him on high, and the Dove of the Holy Spirit settled upon his shoulder. All this you know, Your Grace.'

'Who does not?'

'Then know this! I am possessed of a secret that is known to no other living man. I shared the knowledge only with the lord Gruffydd ap Llywelyn Fawr of Gwynedd. He was my friend. We were determined that the revelation of it must be for the glory of Wales. But two weeks ago I saw Gruffydd die, and then I wished the knowledge to die with him.'

'Gruffydd ap Llywelyn dead?' Despite himself, Bishop Iorwerth was intrigued by Elidyr's story.

'Now I see only one true course.'

'And what course is that?'

Elidyr lowered his voice, so that the Bishop had to lean forward to catch his words. 'Listen well, Your Grace. I bring you the greatest good omen for your rule as Bishop of St David's. I offer you the most powerful talisman that our people of Wales could ever imagine.'

Iorwerth's eyes stared wide from his pale, plump face. 'I am listening, Elidyr ab Idwal.'

'Across the sea, within sight of Tyddewi, lies an island that the Welsh call *Ynys Dewi*. They say it was smitten from the mainland by a giant's blow. Once, the island was home to Saint Justinian, and his ghost haunts the channel still. There are two great hills on the island. Look to the west and north of the greatest of these, and you will find a cave that lies open to the sea. The name of the cave is *Ogof Colomennod*. Make of that what you will.'

The Bishop licked his lips. 'The Cave of Doves. . .'

'The cave is strewn with the accursed remains of the Viking heathens who burned Saint David's shrine. There they have lain for a century past, and among them rests the stone casket wherein are the bones of Dewi Sant.'

Bishop Iorwerth's jaw dropped. His was not a quick imagination, and he had not anticipated this. 'The bones of Dewi Sant? On Ynys Dewi, you say? But. . . but that is Ramsey Island, isn't it?' Iorwerth's eyes became furtive. He rose from his chair, walked quickly to the doorway and dismissed the guard.

'Who else knows of this?'

'I have told only you, Your Grace.'

'How did you learn of it?'

'It was revealed to me.'

'By what means?'

'By God's grace.'

Iorwerth frowned. He was well accustomed to playing with words, but he felt that this Welshman would have the measure of him in such a contest. 'Why do you not go to Ramsey for the relics and claim the glory for yourself? Why tell me of this revelation?'

'Because I am nothing, Your Grace.'

'Well, then what of your master Lord Llywelyn? Why do you not carry this joyous news to him?'

'The relics belong with the Church, Your Grace, and so I give them to you. They should rest in the shrine of Dewi Sant. . . the Cathedral of Saint David.'

'I see.' Bishop Iorwerth looked up at the cobwebs on the ceiling, examined his perfect fingernails, rubbed thoughtfully at the callus that writing had placed upon the middle finger of his left hand. 'How do I know that the story you have told me is true?'

'The proof lies on Ramsey Island, Your Grace.'

'Perhaps. . .but there are many such stories. I have it on good authority that Saint David rests in Llandewi Brefi. The Abbot of Glastonbury will tell you that the grave lies within his precinct, and the people of Ireland know equally well that the relics are there!' The Bishop sat back in his chair and laughed. 'Every charlatan, every gullible fool, thinks he knows where the relics are to be found. They lie at the bottom of the sea, beneath a mound, down a well. . .'

'They are in the Cave of Doves on Ramsey Island, Your Grace.'

'A man would waste all his days if he were to chase every wild goose that flew across his path. Or every white dove.'

Elidyr took an angry step towards the Bishop of St David's. 'I came here in all good faith, Your Grace! I came here seeking a man of God and a man of Wales, but it seems I have found neither!'

The loud knocking at the door shattered the tension between the Bishop of St David's and his seemingly unhinged guest, but for Iorwerth the worst was yet to come.

XXXVII

Bishop Iorwerth stood awkwardly. 'How good of you to come to meet me. . .er, my lord.'

The tall, angular figure in the doorway ignored the Bishop completely.

Elidyr retreated until the sweating palms of his hands pressed against the cold stone of the window ledge. In the shape of Archdeacon Gerald de Barri he could see only the spectre of excommunication, the just reward for breaking his parole at Manorbier. 'Archdeacon! Let me explain, I beg of you!'

'Very well. What brings you before the good Bishop? Have you given His Grace the great secret you would not entrust to me?' Gerald, quite unconsciously, sat in the Bishop's chair. He made himself comfortable, arranged the folds of his robes about his knees, and sat back with his hands upon the chair arms. Bishop Iorwerth was left standing by the table. He made no protest. He dared not speak.

Elidyr had not trusted Gerald at Pembroke, nor at Manorbier, and he could not wholly trust him now, yet he steeled himself to tell the truth. 'My lord Archdeacon, I have made the most momentous discovery, the most powerful portent for the destiny of our people, the greatest . . .'

The Archdeacon's fingers drummed upon the chair arm. 'Do not try my patience, Elidyr ab Idwal.'

'This will come as a great shock to you, my lord, but . . .' Elidyr paused, giving the Archdeacon time to prepare himself for the news, '. . . but I know where the bones of Dewi Sant are to be found!'

Gerald was not shocked, nor did he mask his smile at the disappointment written clear upon the bard's face.

'You already knew, my lord?' Elidyr stood in awe of the Archdeacon's calm.

'Pray tell me from the beginning. Just how did this momentous revelation come to you?'

Elidyr hesitated but a moment. 'Four years ago it began, my lord. When first they brought us to the castle of Corfe, I was . . .'

'Elidyr! No more tales of the dungeon, we do not wish to offend His Grace.'

'Your pardon, my lord, but my story will mean little if I cannot mention the prison at all.'

'Very well.'

'At first I was imprisoned in the common dungeon. There I found an old Saxon, half out of his mind. For a time he did nothing but curse and spit at me, and it took many weeks for him to realise that I was not his enemy. He knew he was dying, and almost with his last breath he spoke to me.'

'In Welsh?' Gerald was finding the story less credible by the minute.

Elidyr nodded, his hand at the bronze cross about his neck. 'It was he who gave me this cross. And with it he told me how the Vikings pillaged the shrine of Dewi Sant, how they carried the relics away in their long ship, how they were wrecked on Ramsey

185

Island when the storm was raised by God's wrath against them...'

'This fellow must have been a long time dying.'

'His will to pass on his great secret surely kept him alive, my lord Archdeacon. But if you do not wish to hear it, then I will not burden you...'

'No, no...' Gerald forced a smile. 'Forgive me, Elidyr. What happened after the great storm?'

'The Norsemen struggled ashore onto Ramsey. They dragged themselves and their plundered treasures into a sea cave, and there they died. The cave is called Ogof Colomennod, and Dewi Sant's bones lie there still among the heathen who despoiled his shrine!'

Gerald looked thoughtful, but was not impressed. 'Why did you not tell me this story when we were in Manorbier?'

'What does it matter now! My lord, I spoke to Lady Regat at Pembroke, and she will have told Rhys Gryg of Deheubarth every word of it. They may even now be searching the island! The relics must not fall into their hands, my lord...'

Elidyr turned to implore Iorwerth, not noticing as the Bishop stifled a yawn. 'Your Grace...I beg of you, send your soldiers to Ramsey before it is too late!'

Gerald smiled grimly. Elidyr plainly suffered agonies of guilt, and would continue to do so until he knew that Rhys Gryg had not laid hands upon the relics. But this wretched little Welshman had never once taken the Archdeacon into his confidence, and Gerald saw no reason to be generous in return.

'I could have gone to Ramsey to claim the relics for myself, my lord, but I did not!' Elidyr was desperate to redeem himself. 'I vowed that they must come to the Church. Is that not so, Your Grace?'

Bishop Iorwerth shrugged his shoulders. He was perplexed and quite exhausted by this encounter.

Gerald did not give the Bishop time to answer. 'It would have saved us all much time and trouble if you had told me in Manorbier. The relics would be safe in St David's by now, and you would be safely home.'

'Would you have let me go free?'

'Once the relics were found the Earl Marshal would not have

held you captive. He would not have *dared*, Elidyr. The man who recovered the bones of Saint David. . . he might almost come to be regarded as a saint himself.'

Elidyr swallowed hard as he stared at the Archdeacon. 'I have heard those words before, my lord.'

Gerald said nothing. He would not explain, not yet, and his uncustomary silence unnerved the bard.

'I. . . I am sorry, my lord Archdeacon. I should have told you in Manorbier, but then I had not learned to trust you. How could I? When I first saw you in Pembroke you sat by the Earl Marshal's side, and when you spoke to me your Norman accent showed heavy through your Welsh. Even at Manorbier you had the bearing of a Norman lord, you treated me no better than Llywelyn treats his slaves! How could I have confided in you? For the love of God, my lord Archdeacon, I acted only as I thought best!' Elidyr's words had tumbled forth without pause, almost without thought, and still Gerald kept his silence.

'Archdeacon. . . Your Grace, I ask you. . . is it Norman justice to excommunicate a man for doing what he thought best in the eyes of God?'

The Bishop of St David's sat uncomfortably on the edge of the table. All this was beyond him. 'Archdeacon, what is going on?'

Gerald might not have heard his Bishop speak. 'It was not just the breaking of your word, Elidyr. You importuned my family, you won the friendship of their children, and then you betrayed their trust. Angharad deceived her own husband for your sake, and to defend her he has lied to the Earl Marshal. Can you comprehend what will happen to them when the Earl Marshal learns that you have made fools of them all?'

At last, Bishop Iorwerth felt that he must assert his authority. 'Archdeacon! Explain to me this talk of excommunication. It is a serious matter, and not to be threatened lightly.'

'Your Grace, this fellow has been through a great ordeal. He cannot be held responsible for all he says.'

Iorwerth looked with suspicion at the bard. 'That would explain a good deal.'

'Your Grace, it would best serve us all if he were to leave now and follow his lord's son home to. . .'

'What?' Elidyr took a pace towards the Archdeacon. 'What did you say, my lord?'

'Gruffydd ap Llywelyn...he showed a touching concern for your welfare when I spoke with him yesterday.'

'Gruffydd is alive?'

'I have just said so.'

'Thanks be to God!' Tears welled in Elidyr's eyes. Not only for Gruffydd, but for the future of his country. Gerald de Barri had always felt that Elidyr's grief at the death of Llywelyn's son had been genuine, and so now was his breathless joy to hear of his salvation. 'Was he injured? Is he with you now?'

'He is well enough, and on his way to Gwynedd with an escort from the garrison of St Davids.' Gerald smiled sardonically. 'And I pray they will have greater success in their commission than did Squire Anselm of Pembroke.'

Elidyr turned his back upon Gerald and looked out of the window, out over the forests of Deugleddyf. 'Tell me, my lord ...does he have the bones of Saint David? Did he find them on Ramsey?'

Gerald could only shake his head. 'I do not know, my son. But through God's good grace, that is something you may discover for yourself.'

The Archdeacon had, of courtesy, offered his chair to the Bishop, but Iorwerth declared himself quite comfortable as he shifted, stiffly, from the corner of the table to the great wooden chest by the wall.

Iorwerth leaned towards the Archdeacon and spoke quietly in French to exclude Elidyr. 'Brother Gerald, how much credence do you place in these stories of the holy relics?'

'The Norsemen did plunder St David's, and the bones of Dewi...Saint David...were lost, all that is common knowledge. But if my years have taught me anything, Your Grace, it is that all accounts are clouded by the ambitions and prejudices of the men who utter them. Perhaps the Norsemen did carry the bones of our Saint to Ramsey Island. Perhaps Gruffydd ap Llywelyn did find them. Perhaps even now they are in Gwynedd.'

'If Gruffydd has the relics, then we will hear of it soon enough!'

The old Archdeacon shook his head doubtfully. 'If, in a few

months time, the rumour spreads that a great miracle has come to Wales, then it will fall to Canterbury to decide whether the relics are the true bones of Saint David.'

'And if they are not?'

'If they are not, as I suspect will be the case, then Canterbury will be only too pleased to denounce the Welsh Church and cast the sacred name of Saint David into the dust.'

'How will Canterbury prove whether they are the true relics?' Iorwerth's awe of Gerald de Barri was growing with every minute he spent in the old man's company.

Gerald smiled gently. 'Proof is in the eye of the beholder, Your Grace. What the Archbishop decides will depend entirely upon what is expedient.'

'I . . . I cannot condone so cynical a view, Archdeacon. What of the reliquary? Elidyr said there would be a reliquary.'

'Oh, of course!' Gerald wondered how he could have forgotten. 'Yes, there was a reliquary, it is mentioned in the old records. It was a stone chest, the length of a man's arm, and finely carved with scenes from the life of the Saint. I believe I once saw a drawing of it in the palace of St David's. Indeed, the base of the shrine that once held it stands in the cathedral still. If the bones were found within the casket, then there could be little doubt . . .'

'No doubt at all,' said Iorwerth.

'Of course, there would have been another way to ensure the finding of the relics was accepted by all. But it is too late for that now.'

'What would that be?' Iorwerth was tired, his interest was flagging, and he could not disguise a yawn.

'Forgive me, Your Grace, for so exhausting you. I would not keep you from your bed, it is a matter of no consequence.'

Bishop Iorwerth was thankful to quit the Archdeacon's company. So thankful, indeed, that he did not think to question Gerald's motives for wishing him gone.

Elidyr, for his part, was not thankful at all to be left alone with the Archdeacon. He turned from the window, to look sullenly at Gerald de Barri. 'You were about to say something to the Bishop, my lord, then thought better of it.'

'In Manorbier,' Gerald observed gravely, 'you kept a more civil tongue.'

'I learned in Corfe to treat my gaolors with respect.'

'And in Manorbier you betrayed their trust and broke your parole.' Gerald held up his hand to stay any further argument. 'Now, as to what I was going to say to the Bishop. It was only a passing idea . . . it simply occurred to me that if the bones of Dewi Sant came to light by a divine revelation, then few men would dare question such a miracle.'

'A divine revelation, my lord? Surely it would be seen as a miracle however the bones were restored.'

'Yes, of course it would. I am tired, Elidyr, and my mind wanders. In my youth I dreamed that I myself might find the bones of Saint David, but all came to nothing. I prayed for the intercession of his sainted mother Non. I kept vigil for days at the place where he was born. There is a well by the Chapel of Saint Non, it sprang forth when Dewi was born, and the altar stone bears even now the marks of Non's fingers. I prayed that her blessed son might return to the place of his birth. I was younger then, and with the confidence of youth I expected an answer. An answer clear in my mind, or spoken aloud, or written upon the stones.'

Elidyr looked with sudden suspicion at the tired face of Gerald de Barri. 'Why do you tell me this, my lord?'

'Merely the reminiscences of an old man. It is not sinful to lament for what might have been.'

'The relics of Dewi Sant, to return once more to Non's Chapel . . .' Elidyr smiled. He believed he understood what the Archdeacon was trying to tell him, 'a lluman glân Dewi a ddyrchafant.'

Gerald de Barri softly repeated the words. ' . . . and they will uplift the Holy Banner of David.'

'It is from the Armes Prydein Fawr, my lord.' Elidyr gazed out through the dark cruciform of the window. 'From the Book of Taliesin. It calls upon the Welsh to unite under the banner of Dewi Sant, to ally themselves with the Scots, the Cornish, the men of Northumberland, even the Vikings . . . with anyone who can help them defeat the Saxons. It means the same as it ever did,

190

my lord... except that the English now go under a different name.'

The bard fell silent, his attention held by the scene beyond the window, beyond the confines of the bailey, towards the rolling hills of Deugleddyf lit only by the cold light of the stars. And by something else...

Elidyr ab Idwal stared, transfixed, and his eyes held the light of the hundred torches that flickered amid the trees beyond the moat.

XXXVIII

The specks of fire crept ever closer, until they were joined by their flickering reflections in the moat. Soon came the excited cries from the bailey beneath as men at arms were roused from their sleep. The attackers themselves would become visible as they kindled their fire arrows and then, within range of the long-bowmen lining the parapets, they would be at their most vulnerable.

Heavy footsteps sounded upon the stone steps. Captain Nevern stood in the doorway, and half a dozen men of the garrison of St David's crowded behind him, their arms laden with wood and kindling. 'Not in here, you fools! Go on up to the roof and light the beacon!'

Nevern had accompanied Gerald de Barri to Llawhaden, and was to escort Bishop Iorwerth back to St David's. 'My lord, where is the Bishop?'

'He has retired to his bedchamber... the room below. Who threatens us?'

'The castellan thinks they may be led by the brothers Rhys and Owain ap Gruffydd, my lord. The man is an ass! There have been rumours for days that the Welsh were growing restless, yet he mounted no extra guard! His watchmen are an undisciplined rabble... they were asleep at their posts, and now he leaves it to me to light the beacon when it should have been done the moment the enemy were sighted!'

191

'The beacon?'

'On top of this tower, Archdeacon. If we are fortunate it may bring help from Haverford.'

'But...but what of Pembroke? The Earl Marshal's scheme to send pigeons to every castle...'

'Oh, the castellan has released the pigeons, my lord.'

'Thanks be to God...'

'He has released them, but he sent no message with them. It seems no one explained to him that the birds cannot *speak* their errand.'

'Then our fate depends upon the castellan of Haverford...'

'Stay in this chamber, my lord. And keep away from the window when the arrows begin to fly.' Nevern looked at the Archdeacon's companion with undisguised suspicion. 'You, man...they tell me you claim to be Llywelyn's messenger?'

Elidyr started at the captain's sudden use of Welsh. 'I do...I am. But I swear I know nothing of this.' He glanced to Gerald for support, but the Archdeacon chose to remain aloof. He would not interfere in the captain's business.

Nevern supposed that Gerald had good reason for allowing this wretch into his company, yet he was uncomfortable at the thought of a traitor within the gates. 'Take care you do not cross my path, Welshman!' Nevern reverted to French. 'Archdeacon, may I rely on you to see that the Bishop does not leave the tower? And if the Welsh should breach the palisade...'

'... then we must tell them that they attack the Bishop of St David's, the *Welsh* Bishop of St David's. If they are God fearing men they will come no further.'

Bathed in the bloody light of the beacon, the bailey was a scene of confusion as the garrison prepared for the attack. Long chains of women and children passed buckets of water from the well, to dampen the thatched roofs against the expected hail of fire arrows. The castle gates were double barred and reinforced with extra props, and heavy wooden shields were dragged forward to provide a last line of protection for the archers, should the portcullis be breached. Sergeants distributed weapons from the armoury to footsoldiers roused from their sodden slumber, and shouted until they were hoarse to bring about a semblance of

192

order that, in a well run garrison, should have come as second nature.

Crossbowmen manned the high catwalks behind the palisade, ready to fend off the attackers as they reached the moat. Longbowmen with their bows of French yew took the higher vantage points to pick off the enemy at longer range. These men were the élite, much envied by lesser soldiers. The longbowman could loose five or six aimed shafts while the crossbowman was laboriously reloading his weapon. He fought at longer range, keeping himself in the least vulnerable position, and at his lofty post atop the castle, the longbowman would be spared the intimate horrors of hand to hand combat until all the lesser ranks had fallen.

Gerald and Elidyr were joined by a longbowman from the garrison, a Flemish immigrant who crouched, eyes straining, by the window slit. He set his sheaf of arrows ready to hand, and neatly coiled beside them the second string for his bow. His only word was a command that the candles be doused, and smoke curled still from the dying sparks of the iron braziers on the walls.

The chamber was in darkness now, save for the faint golden flicker as embers rained down past the window from the roaring beacon above. Elidyr paced the room without pause, his agitation growing with every moment.

'Look at me, Gerallt Gymro. Just look at me. I tell the heroic tales of Arthur Pendragon, of Gwrtheyrn, of Emrys, yet here I hide in this lofty tower like some helpless maiden. What shall I tell my children when they ask me of my role in the great fight for freedom?'

'If you go down to the courtyard, Elidyr, Nevern will kill you. He dares take no chances, with the Bishop's safety at stake. He knows only that you are Welsh, and that you arrived here with the flimsiest of excuses.'

'I wished only to give the relics to the Church. Do you not believe me, my lord?'

'What I believe now is immaterial to the defence of this castle. I am not a soldier, thanks be to God.'

'But the Bishop. . . what if they should kill him, the first Welsh bishop for centuries?'

A fire arrow sang past the window. The Flemish archer jolted back with an incomprehensible curse, and loosed the first shaft from his bow.

The hungry roar of flames came now from below, louder and more insistent than the comforting crackle of the beacon. The shrill whinny of horses mad with terror mingled with the furious cries of men and the screams of their women.

'They have fired the stables!' Gerald was already at the door.

'Where are you going?'

'If an old Archdeacon cannot wield a sword, then he might at least take issue with a fire!'

The stables were a vision of hell. Untended horses plunged against their tethers as the burning thatch rained down. Men hurried by, too intent upon the saving of their own skins to intervene. Arrows poured over the palisade, trailing smoke and flame, striking men and women, wood and thatch without discrimination. The soldiers retaliated with their own arrows, and the sound of their flight made an unending banshee wail amidst the cries of terror.

It seemed now that the whole castle was alight. The Archdeacon found himself in the midst of a score of men and women fighting to save the wooden buildings. He thought he glimpsed Elidyr running from the tower, and shouted a warning, but the bard was lost to sight as a burning beam fell in a great cascade of sparks. A pale young woman thrust the reins of a terrified horse into Gerald's hands, and he looked in panic for somewhere safe to lead the beast whilst striving to keep it in check. He turned back to speak to her, but now she lay before him with a Welsh arrow in her heart. Gerald turned away, sickened. The Last Rites would have to wait.

The summer had been unusually hot, and there had been little rain. It had seemed a blessing at the time. Now the tinder-dry stables burned furiously. The leaping flames had already seized hold of the great hall and were beginning to spread along the palisade. Monks fought the fires alongside serving maids, or dragged the wounded to whatever sparse shelter they could find. Gerald strove to rally them, and badgered the idle and the panic-stricken into action, knowing full well that any task would ease their minds from the contemplation of their fate. He turned as he heard someone shout his name, to see Captain Nevern as he ran back from the gate, sword and dagger in hand.

'Archdeacon...let the stables burn! *For Christ's sake save the palisade!*'

'Have you seen them, Nevern? Are they drawing closer?'

'They must be coming now...the arrows have stopped.'

Gerald had not noticed. Only now did he see that the air was clear.

'If they breach the palisade, my lord, go into the tower. Take with you the women and children.'

'No! I must be here...I will try to reason with them.'

'Their blood is up! Once they are among us they won't be turned back with words! They will kill you, you old fool!' Captain Nevern did not stay for an answer.

Gerald peered through the widening gap in the burning palisade. The forest lay sullen, silent, but the black waters of the moat shivered in the moonlight. Ripples spread lazily from the opposite bank. Dozens of ripples, each radiating from a dark figure whose nature he could guess too well.

Rarely now did an arrow fly down from the tower, for the archers were running short of shafts and must choose their targets with care. The crossbowmen on the palisade had long since shot their bolts, and fought with their daggers and short swords against the crude weapons of the attackers.

A man staggered against Gerald and clutched at his sleeve. He made a curious, gurgling noise as his knees buckled and he subsided gently to the ground. Gerald stooped to help the man to his feet, but he saw the short Welsh javelin that transfixed his neck and realised the futility of it. All about the courtyard soldiers were falling. The brave party who had fought the fires did so no more. They battled for their lives with staves or fists, else ran to the tower for shelter. Through the doorway, Gerald could see them packed onto the stair, women and children and monks. Men of God, true enough, but there were able bodies among them too. '*Cowards!*'

The Welsh seemed to be everywhere. Skins darkened with daubed mud, heads shaven, their armour nothing more than toughened leather, they fought with all the courage and skill of which their bards sang so proudly. Yet Gerald de Barri could see nothing to admire, no poetry, no grace in this dance of death.

The Archdeacon did not notice the final clash of arms, nor the last cry of anguish, but the men of Deheubarth had fought and died in the blood-soaked mud of the bailey until no more came to replace them. Gerald heard only the miserable clamour that followed the onslaught, the moaning of the wounded, the weeping of the women, the muffled neighing of injured horses. The soldiers of the garrison wandered the bailey, swords unsheathed, halberds lowered, looking for the last wounded Welshman to despatch. When none remained alive they picked over the bodies of the slain enemy, looting their weapons, lamenting for their own fallen.

The suffering of the wounded was terrible to hear. Their cries brought down the women and the monks from the shelter of the tower, and the physician from his hiding place. The Archdeacon wandered about the bailey, senses reeling, with no thought for anything but to absolve the dying.

The wind had dropped with the coming of dawn, but the fires continued unabated and the smoke from the dampened thatch hung heavy within the courtyard. Gerald de Barri knelt in the mud of the bailey of Llawhaden and prayed. He prayed for the souls of all these good men, for England and the English, for Wales and the Welsh. He prayed for Bishop Iorwerth and for Captain Nevern, for William the Marshal and for Anselm, for Gruffydd, for Llywelyn, for the princes of Deheubarth, for his kinsfolk at Manorbier.

Gerald prayed even for the soul of Elidyr ab Idwal, but of him there was no sign.

XXXIX

'My lord?'

Gerald de Barri concluded his prayers, crossed himself, and climbed unsteadily to his feet. He could see that already the watery sun was brightening the sky beyond the gates. 'Are they gone, captain?'

Nevern regarded the Archdeacon with concern, but the captain himself was more in need of rest and seemed not to have heard the question. His face was smeared with blood, as was his right shoulder and arm. Whether it was his own blood or other men's, he could not himself have guessed.

Gerald could see no expression in the captain's eyes, they were as empty, as distant, as reddened, as the dawning sky. 'Are they gone?'

'Yes, my lord.'

'It seems my prayers were answered.'

'A score of the enemy got through into the bailey, but once we had slain them no more followed. There must have been hundreds waiting across the moat, but by some miracle none of them came.'

Gerald nodded wearily. 'Llawhaden was within their grasp, yet they spared us. A miracle indeed!'

'Gerald! Gerald!' Bishop Iorwerth hurried across the bailey from the tower, his pale face whitening as he took in the scene around him, his hands wringing their dismay. 'We feared you dead. Why did you not remain in the tower?'

'I thought my time better spent in giving what help I could.' Gerald was too tired to control the edge in his voice. 'This, Your Grace, is Captain Nevern of the garrison of St David's. He came to lead your escort. It was he who mustered the defenders last night, by default of the captain of Llawhaden's guard. We are much in his debt.'

The captain took a step forward and fell to one knee before his Bishop. 'Your Grace, I must tell you that many of the soldiers of Llawhaden were lost, the captain among them.'

Iorwerth nodded, not prey to any great sense of loss. 'Yet the fault was not yours. Rise up, my son. You have our gratitude.'

197

Nevern wearily obeyed. 'The captain's body lies with the others in the ruins of the chapel, awaiting your blessing.'

Bishop Iorwerth grimaced at the thought of so disagreeable a task before breakfast, but he nodded his agreement. 'Lead on, captain. You must give me their names.' He paused and looked to the Archdeacon. 'What became of the young Welsh fellow? Llywelyn's man . . . I forget his name. He is not in the tower now.'

'Elidyr? I last saw him across the bailey when the stables were burning.' Gerald was too weary to think further. His head swam with fatigue as he walked unsteadily towards the keep. 'Perhaps you will find him laid out in the chapel.'

'Do you think he is dead?' Iorwerth could not conceal his alarm. 'Llywelyn's man, dead?'

'Llywelyn has lost so many, I doubt that one more will make a difference.' Gerald stumbled, and leaned for support against the cold wall of the stone tower. 'Your Grace, I must ask you to excuse me.'

Without waiting for reply the Archdeacon climbed the steps to the Bishop's chamber. He lay atop the Bishop's bed, and there fell into the dreamless sleep of utter exhaustion.

There were forty dead in the chapel, their bodies strewn hastily upon the floor like so many sacks of grain. Iorwerth gagged as he entered, too many horrors assailing his sensibilities, yet he could not turn back. The monks of Llawhaden and those of his own entourage stood in the shadows by the altar, as still as the dead before them. Outside were gathered the surviving soldiers of the garrison, all bearing the marks of battle in the weariness on their faces or in their roughly bound wounds, and among them the servants and women passed quietly with baskets of bread and jugs of ale. There was a weary silence, broken only by the sparse whimpering of the children.

'Your Grace? Will you begin?'

The Bishop of St David's swallowed hard and hurried his way through a perfunctory blessing of the men who had fallen in his defence, and of those who had survived to fight for him tomorrow.

All the while a single raven perched upon the charred cross of

198

the chapel roof, awaiting its turn. The burials would have to be soon.

The hot noonday sun was shafting through the window as the sound of laughter jolted Gerald de Barri from his uneasy sleep. It was a laughter that could not be ignored, it seemed to shake the very stones of the keep. Gerald gave forth a sigh of resignation as he trod stiffly up the narrow spiral stair to meet the castellan of Haverford. Bishop Iorwerth's relief was obvious when Gerald entered the chamber.

'Archdeacon!' The castellan's voice would have carried the breadth of the bailey. 'I heard of your part in the battle, you proved yourself a hero!'

'You are too generous, my lord. The true hero is the one who persuaded the Welsh to abandon their attack.'

'God's will be done.' Bishop Iorwerth crossed himself.

'I came as soon as we saw the beacon, but still we arrived too late. It was two hours quick march, you know, even after the garrison were mustered.' The castellan of Haverford grinned. 'My men are disappointed with those Welsh cowards. They have sweated in training for too long, and with not a scar to show for it. Spoiling for a fight, they are. Still, if you would allow us to escort you to St David's, Your Grace, I'm sure we could root out a few on the way!'

The Bishop looked alarmed. 'What do you mean?'

'The forest between the rivers is crawling with Welshmen. We never got them to stand and fight, but we glimpsed them often enough.'

'Does it occur to you,' Gerald inquired idly, 'that they may even now be marching on Haverford?'

The castellan laughed. 'Then they'll find a warm welcome! I left my sons in command of the better part of my forces. They'll have no trouble defending themselves. The Welsh have not the stomach to storm a strong castle, Archdeacon, and they lack the patience for a siege. One charge, and that's their courage exhausted. They flee like women before a stout resistance, just as they did last night!'

'I do not believe it is true to say that they fled, my lord. They simply ceased their attack and went away.'

199

'Why would they have done that, Archdeacon?'

'I think, perhaps, they realised that the Bishop himself was in residence. They would not have wished to harm His Grace, I am sure of that.'

The castellan shrugged dismissively. Perhaps, he thought, the Earl Marshal might best be served by an army of bishops.

Gerald de Barri had guessed more than he dared relate. The brothers Rhys and Owain ap Gruffydd were thoughtful men, and ever willing to cast in their lot wherever it would profit them best. They were not subject to Rhys Gryg's blind rages, nor were they deaf to persuasion. Gerald gazed through the window, over the green hills of Deugleddyf, and wondered what had become of Elidyr ab Idwal. Elidyr had come to Llawhaden resolved to give the holy relics of Dewi Sant into the hands of their rightful keeper, doubtless thinking that this might atone for his perjury at Pembroke. Now perhaps the bard had found another means to redeem himself, by saving the lives of the men and women of Llawhaden.

'So what's to be done, Your Grace?' The castellan looked eagerly at the Bishop, as anxious as his own soldiers for a taste of battle.

Iorwerth was growing more anxious by the minute. 'If. . . if the forest is as dangerous as you say, my lord, perhaps we could make our way to St David's by some other route?'

'A wise suggestion, Your Grace.' Gerald agreed entirely. There was little to be gained by making a hazardous journey solely to satisfy the castellan's lust for Welsh blood. 'The Eastern Cleddau flows into Milford Haven, and then it is but a short way by sea across St Bride's Bay. You could accomplish the journey within two days with a fair wind.'

'But you must come with me to St David's!'

'I would not wish to be in your way. . .'

'You would be of the greatest help to me.' Bishop Iorwerth was genuinely anxious for Gerald's company now, at least until he had gained confidence enough to impose his own authority upon the chapter of St David's. 'You have had as much influence upon the see, and indeed upon the Church in Wales, as any bishop.'

Manorbier would have to wait. Gerald wondered how he ever could have thought of retirement. He had quite underestimated the high regard in which he was held by Iorwerth of Talley, and he realised now that he could indeed wield the greatest influence upon the affairs of St David's.

There was also the matter of the bones of Saint David. The strange events at Llawhaden had made Gerald de Barri anxious to return to the cathedral. And what was more, he felt an undeniable calling to pray once more before the altar in the Chapel of Saint Non.

Chapter XL

St David's

8 July, 1215

It was a steep and winding path from the beach to the Chapel of Saint Non. Far below, the galley had already embarked upon her return journey across St Bride's Bay towards Milford Haven, her square brown sail filled to the light westerly wind. Gerald de Barri was not sorry to see her go. Two days of misery on the boards of that ship had done nothing other than to reinforce his own prejudice that travel upon the sea was meant only for the livelihood of fishermen and the martyrdom of saints. The unease of his stomach had cleared almost as soon as he waded through the shallow waves to the sanctuary of the sandy beach but now, as he paused for breath, his brain still voiced its protest as the cliff path seemed to rock gently beneath his feet.

'Your Grace! A moment, if you please!' Gerald cursed the youth of the Bishop and his entourage as they stopped in silence to wait for him. There had been near a dozen passengers aboard the ship, all told, for Iorwerth had brought his favourites from Talley as well as his servants and the three surviving soldiers of Gerald's escort to Llawhaden.

The Archdeacon could not help but feel a little sympathy for Brother Hugh, who would most likely be thwarted in his hopes for an easy post close to the Bishop. But not all were disappointed. Captain Nevern had been given charge of the garrison of Llawhaden, the gift of a grateful Bishop at the behest of his Archdeacon. Llawhaden was a castle worth the defending, and one that would likely be challenged again. Nevern had pledged himself to double its strength. He would train new men for the garrison, he would improve the fortifications and, no doubt, he would demand funds from the Bishop for the replacement of palisades with curtain walls of stone. Gerald wished him good fortune, and well deserved.

The Archdeacon rejoined his companions at the top of the cliff path, and noted with satisfaction that Bishop Iorwerth was gasping for breath as painfully as he. Iorwerth's good living as Abbot of Talley had afforded little incentive for exercise, and he was clearly not accustomed to walking far.

Gerald pointed towards the square stone building but a hundred paces from the cliff path. 'The birthplace of Dewi Sant, Your Grace.' He had quite deliberately used the Welsh name.

Bishop Iorwerth paused to look at the scene before him in the failing light. The lush pastures of St David's, the multitude of grazing sheep whose wool and mutton would provide much of his income, and the small stone Chapel of Saint Non.

'Upon that very spot, Your Grace, Dewi Sant was born of Non.'

'Yes, Archdeacon.'

'In the midst of a great storm, it was, and the altar stone bears even now the marks of Non's fingers.'

'We know the story well enough, Archdeacon.'

'And over there beyond the Chapel is the Holy Well. It sprang forth from the rock at the very moment of his birth, and . . .'

'I have been here many times before, Archdeacon.'

High on the cliff above St Bride's Bay, the Chapel of Saint Non had stood for six centuries past, its impassive face ever turned towards the anger of the sea. But now the single square window winked with candle light as the Bishop and his Archdeacon drew near. The sun had long since dipped to oblivion between the twin peaks of Ramsey Island, and evening was heralded as ever by a new chill to the wind.

'There will be a thunderstorm soon.' Gerald was surprised by the sound of his own voice. In the lee of the Chapel it was too loud, too harsh, and it brought a startled glance from Bishop Iorwerth.

'The clouds are gathering surely enough, Archdeacon.'

'In the midst of such a great storm, it was, six centuries past. In this very place . . .'

Bishop Iorwerth stopped in the narrow doorway of the Chapel of Saint Non. Gerald stretched to peer over the Bishop's shoulder, and his breath caught in his throat as he beheld the sight within.

A single candle flickered in the centre of the crude stone altar. The flame guttered in the wind, and a wraith of smoke curled gently upwards like a departing spirit into the cool chapel air.

In the soft inconstant light, pale shadows danced to the song of the wind upon the pitted greyness of weathered human bones.

XLI

'And there, brothers. . . there upon the altar before us, lay the very bones of our Blessed Saint!' Gerald de Barri's triumphant words concluded a breathless account which had lasted so long that rumour had already spread the length and breadth of St David's.

'The true bones of Saint David, my lord Archdeacon?'

'To whom else could they belong?' Bishop Iorwerth was quick to counter the Doubting Thomas. 'The Chapel of Non was filled with the voices of angels, and the bones shone of their own divine light!'

The Bishop's chamber in the castle of St David's seemed smaller than ever before, so many were the people crammed within. Bishop Iorwerth sat regally in his broad, high backed chair, whilst the Archdeacon perched on a stool beside and slightly behind him. The Bishop's retinue and many of the clerics of St David's stood in close array, and dozens more crowded the stair beyond. Some had prayed and waited half their lives for the return of their Saint. Few could comprehend the significance of it at once.

'A miracle, Your Grace!'

'A miracle indeed, brothers!' Bishop Iorwerth's voice rang clear and strong, unclouded by doubt.

Gerald de Barri leaned forward to speak into the Bishop's ear, his voice unheard by the chattering assembly. 'For the present, Your Grace, I would suggest that the relics be placed in the safety of the cathedral. We can only guess as to how the news of their finding will affect the people of Wales.'

'All the world must know! The recovery of the relics can be

nothing other than a Sign! Our Lord's blessing upon the first Welsh bishop for a hundred years!'

'You are proud enough to be Welsh, now that it profits you.' Gerald spoke too loudly and in haste, and regretted at once his acid words. They earned him some murmurs of reproof, but he also saw a wry humour in the few Celtic faces in the chamber. Indeed, many of those present must have shared his feeling, though none would have dared admit to it. 'Forgive me, Your Grace, it was the sin of envy that made me speak thus. This miracle does indeed confirm that God's will be done.'

'And through His Good Grace you will stay to help me in my task, Archdeacon.'

Bishop Iorwerth could not have uttered a wiser reply, thought Gerald with a private smile. 'I shall be pleased to remain in St David's for as long as I am needed, Your Grace. Now, as I was saying, there may be trouble as word of the miracle spreads. For the Welsh, it will raise their spirits, it will rekindle their patriotism, and it may inspire them to struggle all the harder against the Normans.'

There were nods of agreement from the Archdeacon's audience.

'If this were to come about, Your Grace, then I believe the English Church would do all in its power to discredit the holy relics. It would claim that they were not the remains of Saint David, and would denounce us as charlatans working for our own ends.'

'That is unthinkable, Archdeacon.'

'There is a solution, Your Grace. Send our swiftest courier to Canterbury, and he must arrive before the rumours reach the Archbishop's ears. He will announce our . . . your great discovery, Your Grace, and invite Archbishop Stephen Langton himself to look upon the bones and pronounce them the true relics of Saint David . . .'

'And then the Archbishop himself will declare it a sign for all the people of Wales, the Welsh and we Normans alike, to live together in peace and tranquility.' Bishop Iorwerth beamed in contentment. There could have been no more propitious beginning for his appointment.

Brother Hugh cleared his throat to gain attention, and gently elbowed his way between two of the Talley brethren to stand closer to the Bishop. 'Forgive me, my lords, if I play the Devil's Advocate, but what if it should emerge that the bones are *not* those of our Saint?'

'What?' Bishop Iorwerth, for the first time in Gerald's memory, appeared angered. 'I am satisfied that the relics are the true bones of Saint David, and that is enough.'

Brother Hugh, his face reddening, bowed his head in submission. 'I am sorry, Your Grace. A true man of God needs no proof.'

Gerald de Barri hid a smile. Poor Brother Hugh! This was not the time to be quoting his Archdeacon's words! It might be the best thing he could have said, or it might be the worst. Gerald had to come to the young monk's rescue. 'Your Grace, I know Stephen Langton, and I believe the Archbishop will require some verification of the relics.'

Bishop Iorwerth's brow darkened as he stared at the Archdeacon. 'What manner of verification would you expect Canterbury to demand?'

'There is the matter of the reliquary, Your Grace. It is well known that the bones were in their casket when they were stolen, and it would have helped our cause if it had been recovered with them.'

'Helped our cause?' Iorwerth lurched to his feet, his fists clenched. '*Helped our cause*? Shall we pray to the Good Lord and ask Him to send us the reliquary? Shall we tell Him that one miracle was not enough? Your scepticism serves you ill, Archdeacon.' The Bishop thrust his way to the doorway. 'Come, brothers, we shall offer up our thanks in the cathedral. Will you join us in our prayers, Archdeacon, or does your faith fail you now?'

Gerald tried to salvage his pride as the brethren made their silent way down the long path to the Sacred Hollow. He knew that he could not risk an open confrontation with the new Bishop. Iorwerth of Talley was beginning to discover the extent of his power, and now Gerald feared that his own influence might not be as strong as he had hoped. It would entail much effort, certainly, but he must recover his good favour in Bishop Iorwerth's eyes. That would be the most difficult part of it. Gerald de Barri had never been a flatterer. Not, at least, outside the pages of his books.

His books! Perhaps he should dedicate his latest work to the new Bishop of St David's...

'Archdeacon?' Brother Hugh had waited for Gerald de Barri by the Llech Lafar bridge. 'It was generous of you to defend me, my lord. I am sorry about...'

'About the Bishop's displeasure? I can deal well enough with his tantrums, though I confess I was surprised.'

'The finding of the relics has had a profound effect upon him, my lord.'

Gerald waved a reproving finger. 'Beware those who believe themselves touched by God, Brother Hugh! A few may become saints, but others are the most bloody of tyrants.'

'What you said about the relics, my lord... May we really believe them to be the true bones of Saint David? Or are we fools to accept them without the reliquary?'

'The reliquary?' Gerald smiled as he saw the troubled expression clouding the young monk's honest face. 'It is not the fine trappings that concern us, Brother Hugh, but the truth that lay within.'

Chapter XLII

St David's

21 August, 1215

It was a great day for Gerald of Wales, and a great day for St David's. Gerald set aside his quill, and placed the final page of *On the Instruction of a Prince* atop the untidy pile. Two books finished within the year! Admittedly the early pages of this book were already yellowing with age, but it was an achievement to be admired nonetheless. And if that were not enough, he had also revisited his old *Journey Through Wales*. He had brought the book up to date and, more pressing, he had made all those small amendments that would maintain its author's favour in the seats of power.

The Archdeacon smiled wrily at his own hypocrisy. When Henry the Second had been King, Gerald had never committed his true opinion of the English court to parchment. But King John was a feckless failure by comparison with his father, and in his *On the Instruction of a Prince*, Gerald had made little effort to conceal the contempt in which he held the King. In truth, Gerald did not believe that King John would ever hear of the book. If the rumours were to believed, and civil war was truly poised to tear England apart once more, then John would not likely live to see next Michaelmas. Why, it was even rumoured that the barons were plotting to invite Prince Louis of France to be King of England! Imagine that! Louis' father, Phillip of France, was the man against whom the Norman English had been at war for... well, for what seemed like generations. What irony, that Prince Louis might soon cross the English Channel to lead his armies against the King of England in the very footsteps of Duke William of Normandy a century and a half before.

There came a knock at the door. Gerald, as always, did not answer at once. He liked to let people wait awhile, and felt that the Bishop's chamber served admirably in imparting to God-fearing people a right and proper sense of humility. He sat back comfortably in the Bishop's chair and regarded the broad, beeswaxed table top that had been his for almost a year now, the clean stone of the walls, the finely tooled covers of his collection of books, the wide window that looked out upon the Sacred Hollow and the cathedral in all its majesty. The Cathedral of Saint David, *complete* in all its majesty. The holy relics rested upon the high altar now, in a fine new gilded casket commissioned by Bishop Iorwerth at his own expense. The bones of Saint David. The very bones of David, son of Non, returned at last.

Another knock. Louder, more insistent this time, and with a distinct quality of authority about it. Gerald scowled at the door. How odd. It was not Brother Hugh on one of his interminable errands from the Bishop. Brother Hugh always tapped with such diffidence that Gerald would often fail to hear him, and the hapless clerk would wait for an age before daring to knock again. No, it was not Brother Hugh. Nor could it be the new captain of the guard, an ignorant, lumpish Fleming who had yet to learn to knock at all in spite of Gerald's final, despairing threat of excommunication.

The door opened. Perhaps it was the captain of the guard after all.

'Did you not hear me?' William Marshal, Earl of Pembroke, regarded the Archdeacon with annoyance. 'I had expected to find the Bishop.'

Gerald swallowed his surprise as he half rose and gestured towards the chair at the other end of the table. The Earl of Pembroke visiting St David's? This was unheard of! William the Marshal never went on pilgrimage. Indeed, he despised all churchmen...with the exception, perhaps, of the Knights Templar who wore armour and rode into battle.

'Where is the Bishop?' The Earl Marshal spoke bluntly, ignoring the proffered chair. 'I asked at the gate for the Bishop's chamber.'

'His Grace will be in his chambers in the Bishop's Palace, down by the cathedral, my lord. He prefers the company of churchmen and pilgrims to the rigours of the temporal world.' The Archdeacon waved his hand airily. 'This was once Bishop Geoffrey's chamber, there is still confusion in some minds.'

The Earl Marshal glowered. 'Then I will bid you good day.'

'Er...I imagine you bring news of Archbishop Langton, my lord Earl.'

'I will conduct affairs of State with the Bishop alone.'

'At least you could tell me if Langton has accepted our invitation at long last. He will expect an elaborate welcome, and Bishop Iorwerth is sure to pass on the responsibility to me....'

'That is a part of it.' The Earl Marshal was angered more by Gerald's tone of voice than by his unsubtle questioning. 'The Archbishop of Canterbury deserves more respect than you accord him, Archdeacon. For the past year he has striven tirelessly to hold together what remains of England. He has mediated between Church and barons, and he alone held control over the city of London while they squabbled over its lordship.'

Gerald listened with interest. Rarely could the Earl Marshal be goaded into discussion of such matters so freely. 'I am surprised, my lord, that Canterbury employs so...so exalted a courier as yourself for so trivial a mission.'

The Earl Marshal controlled his anger with an effort. 'I have not come to St David's merely to announce the Archbishop's arrival, Archdeacon. I am here to oversee the preparations for it. There must be complete security.'

'The Archbishop of Canterbury is in no danger from the people of St David's, my lord.'

'I do not doubt it.'

'But that is why you are here, notwithstanding.'

'Merely a precaution. Even an Archbishop is not immortal.'

'I can recall the murder of only one archbishop in recent times, my lord. Saint Thomas à Becket...foully slain before the altar in Canterbury at the behest of your King Henry.'

The Earl Marshal looked hard at Gerald de Barri, but his eyes betrayed nothing. 'I think Archbishop Langton has every reason to be wary.'

'Do the Welsh challenge your borders again? I have heard nothing.'

'They have been quiet enough of late, but I do not trust them.'

'Then what of Pembroke, my lord Earl? Surely you should be there to. . . '

'Pembroke will not fall, I have seen to that. But other castles are less well fortified, other castellans less well prepared. Would Llawhaden have survived, were it not for the miracle of which you boasted? Could St David's withstand an onslaught?'

'The Shrine of Saint David will never be attacked by Welshmen.'

'Come now, Archdeacon, have you forgotten Rhys Gryg so soon?'

'Oh, him. . . How did you hear of that?'

'Anselm gave me his account of it on his return to Pembroke.' William Marshal smiled drily. 'And does your memory also fail you in the matter of Llywelyn's son, Archdeacon?'

'Not at all. I learned that he was alive, and was glad to pass on the news to you.'

'Having first ensured that he was safely out of my reach.'

Gerald chose to ignore the jibe. 'Tell me, my lord, how fares young Anselm?'

'He is at the Bishop's Palace with my men. They will pitch our tents in the courtyard.'

'You brought him here to St David's?'

'Why not?'

Gerald shrugged. 'I thought he might remain at Pembroke. In chains.'

The Earl Marshal snorted with laughter. 'Perhaps that is what he deserves, Gerald, but I must shepherd my sons with care. Anselm, at least, has never been disloyal to the King, nor to me, and I punish him only by requiring that he train all the harder. Soon he will take the oath of knighthood in the service of the King.'

'Is that wise at such a time? King John. . . '

'In the service of *the King*, my lord Archdeacon. Whoever the king may be.'

'Is. . . is the King dead?' Gerald was careful to betray nothing in his voice.

'He is not.'

'Then what has happened? Has your son William brought word from Oxford?'

'You must already know that the King's council was a failure. Now the barons gather their armies, they are fortifying the castles that the charter returned to them, and they have yet to give up the city of London to the King.'

'Er. . .have you changed your allegiance, my lord?'

The Earl Marshal looked in astonishment at the old Archdeacon. Few men would have dared ask such a question of William the Marshal. 'No! Not to that presumptuous whelp Prince Louis, if that is the way you are thinking.'

'But who else is there, my lord?'

William Marshal leaned forward, his voice quiet now. 'King John is not in good health, Archdeacon. If a traitor's dagger does not kill him soon, then his sickness will. Young William tells me he is aged beyond recognition, he has become an old man since last I saw him.'

'And twenty years younger than we are!'

'Yes, Gerald. King John will die before the year is out, I'm sure of it. But his son. . .his oldest *legitimate* son, that is. . .is not yet nine years old. Prince Henry is too young to rule, but if there were to be certain. . .*provisions*, then he might be accepted, even by those who despise King John. Think upon it.'

Gerald nodded. He was beginning to see what was in William Marshal's mind. 'The provision, for example, of a suitable regent?'

'A regent, Archdeacon. To rule until the boy comes of age. Such a man would need all the qualities of a king, and more, to recover the lost ground of King John's reign, to pull the country together into a united kingdom.'

'Yet King John would be the one to choose the regent. There can be few such men in England, fewer still who remain in the King's favour.'

'In England, Gerald, I'll warrant there are none at all.' The Earl Marshal's grey eyes were steady. They held a promise, and they held a warning.

'None at all in England, my lord Earl, as you say. But perhaps in Wales. . . Perhaps in Pembroke. . .'

The Earl of Pembroke smiled. 'You flatter me, my lord Archdeacon.'

212

XLIII

'Is it possible?' Gerald de Barri asked the question aloud as he knelt before the bones of Saint David in their gilded reliquary. Could it be possible that Earl William Marshal of Pembroke would, in all but title, be the next King of England?

One part of Gerald's mind dwelt upon the question of any offence he might have given to the Earl Marshal, any slight, any insult that might bring the Regent's vengeance upon the see of St David's or upon its Archdeacon. The other part was much occupied with the forthcoming visit of the Archbishop of Canterbury.

Gerald now firmly believed that Archbishop Stephen Langton would declare that the bones were not those of Saint David. He felt neither sorrow nor anger. Bishop Iorwerth had bathed in the glory of the relics' miraculous restoration, and it would be Bishop Iorwerth who was discredited along with them. Gerald's own doubts as to Canterbury's acceptance of the relics had made him distance himself from the 'miracle'. If anyone was going to be called charlatan, it was not going to be Gerald of Wales.

Gerald felt a light touch at his sleeve. The monk spoke with distaste. 'There is a Welshman waiting in the nave, Archdeacon. He seems to think himself above the common run of pilgrims, and demands to see you.'

'Croeso, f'arglwydd!' This time, Gerald did not forget his Welsh.

Gruffydd ap Llywelyn stood by the rood screen, idly fingering the clumsily repaired hinge of the gate. Gerald noted the ornate brooch at the neck of his fine cloak, the buckle of chased silver at his sword belt, the heavy ring encircling the fourth finger of his left hand. Llywelyn must have killed the fatted calf for his son's return

'Am I much changed, Gerallt Gymro?'

'In your appearance, certainly. As for your soul...'

'Upon that you reserve judgement?' Gruffydd ap Llywelyn was all amiable smiles now. Gone was the fierce ambition that had so wearied the old Archdeacon. Gone, or hidden. 'I spoke harshly when last we met...'

'It was forgivable. Given the circumstances.' Gerald was as eager to forget their last conversation as Gruffydd appeared to be, but he was on his guard, nonetheless. 'Er... do you bring news of your father?'

'He is well enough, and much gladdened by the finding of the holy relics.'

Gerald half turned and looked back to the reliquary where it lay upon the altar. Once again he was assailed by the doubts that had been nagging at his mind for weeks past. Not of the authenticity of the relics, for of that he was certain, but of the means by which they had been returned. Had it truly been a miracle? Or had Elidyr ab Idwal somehow taken them from Gruffydd and placed them with his own hands upon the altar of Saint Non's Chapel? Or could it be that Elidyr himself had been the very means through which the Lord had chosen to enact his miracle? Perhaps it was better that it should never be known, yet Gerald could not bear his torment of doubt.

'Gruffydd, I must have your word upon it, as you stand here within his shrine. Were the relics ever in your possession?'

'No, Archdeacon.'

Gerald closed his eyes for a moment. He could not believe that Gruffydd was lying now. 'Then Elidyr did not take them from you?'

'Elidyr? You give him more credit than he deserves! No one was more surprised than I to hear of your miracle.'

'Bishop Iorwerth's miracle, Gruffydd, or so he would have it.'

'I have heard many others say that he claims it as his own.'

'Each time he tells the story, the miracle assumes a greater glory.'

'Then long may he tell it, my lord. For the greater the glory, the more the relics can serve the cause of Wales.'

'I see you have been listening to your father. It does you credit.'

'And that is why I am here.' Gruffydd straightened as he faced the Archdeacon, his manner now formal. 'My lord Llywelyn ap Iorwerth commands that I convey to you his greetings, and his gratitude for the service you have lately rendered concerning his firstborn son. Lord Llywelyn regrets that he cannot make pilgrimage himself, but prays that this token may be put to good use in the holy name of Dewi Sant.' He took from his tunic a leather bag, heavy with Welsh gold, and handed it to the Archdeacon.

'Convey the thanks of St David's in return, Gruffydd ap Llywelyn, and I shall see that this offering is given into the Bishop's care.' Gerald paused, embarrassed. 'If you wish to see the relics, I fear you must join the other pilgrims at the squint.'

'But I would see nothing but the casket!'

'No layman is permitted beyond the rood screen.'

'Unless it be on horseback?'

The Archdeacon was not given time to reply. Cries of alarm, shouts of protest, filtered their way through the coloured glass of the windows to cloud the cool peace of the cathedral. Gruffydd followed the Archdeacon down the long aisle, quickening pace to keep up with the old man's long stride.

'How many men did you bring to St David's?' Gerald shouted over his shoulder.

'Barely a dozen, my lord. I left them with our horses by the stream. They would not have started this...'

'Never mind who cast the first stone. Wait here in the nave.'

The Archdeacon stood alone in the great arched doorway as he surveyed the scene before him.

The soldiers of the Earl Marshal were everywhere. They had herded the pilgrims, Normans, Flemings, Welshmen alike, into small groups. They had stripped a few, beaten others, and were searching every one for weapons. They confiscated every staff, every stick, the smallest blade, even the crutches of a cripple who could barely stand. It was an outrage.

Gerald de Barri sought out their leader. 'At whose bidding do these men desecrate the Sacred Hollow?'

Squire Anselm stepped forward, his thin veneer of borrowed authority crumbling before the wrath of the Archdeacon.

'I'm sorry, my lord... it is on my father's orders.'

'Your father's orders? In my cathedral?'

'I... I do nothing but remove their weapons, my lord.' Anselm took courage as he remembered his commission. His voice strengthened, but still he could not quite meet the Archdeacon's eye. 'By the authority vested in me by...'

'Within this holy place the Earl Marshal has no authority! He knows that as well as I. Come with me.'

Such was the rage upon the Archdeacon's face that many of the soldiers, for the first time in their lives, found themselves feeling sorry for William the Marshal, Earl of Pembroke.

'My lord Earl!' Gerald de Barri strode across Llech Lafar, deaf to the cheery music of the River Alun.

'William Marshal!' Gerald de Barri thrust his way through the tall gateway of the Bishop's Palace, blind to the brightly coloured pavilions and all the accoutrements that bespoke the vast extent of the Earl of Pembroke's retinue.

'*Marshal!*' Gerald de Barri stood square in the centre of the courtyard, fists tightly clenched and an uncustomary redness about his face as he looked about him for his quarry.

Heads turned, conversation stopped. A young pageboy blanched at the grim aspect of the terrible Archdeacon. The child panicked into a run towards the long rectangular building that defined the southern boundary of the courtyard.

Gerald de Barri's rage did not diminish in the short time it took for the Earl Marshal to emerge from the Bishop's chamber, followed at some distance by Bishop Iorwerth himself.

'I have come from the cathedral, my lord Earl.'

The Earl Marshal frowned at the sight of Anselm standing half hidden behind the Archdeacon. He said nothing, but waited, with the air of a man whose time is precious, for the Archdeacon to continue.

'The soldiers from Pembroke...*your* soldiers, my lord...are attacking and robbing innocent pilgrims!'

Bishop Iorwerth was shocked. He looked askance at the Earl Marshal, who made his reply without trace of remorse.

'My men are ordered only to remove from the cathedral close any weapons of war. Which, you would doubtless agree, have no business to be in this holy place. Once that is done, they will double their guard so that no more may enter.'

Bishop Iorwerth pulled himself up to his full height. 'My lord Earl, I insist that you order a halt...'

'It will be finished already, Your Grace. There were not so many

216

that a hundred of my men could not disarm in minutes. Is it not so, Anselm?'

'No armed man remains within the cathedral close, my lord.'

'None but my own, I trust. Were there many Welshmen among them?'

'The usual pilgrims, my lord, and about a dozen Northerners, well armed and with horses. They caused no trouble, but my men are holding them and if you wish to question. . .'

'Enough!' Gerald could listen no longer. 'I will not suffer such treatment of men who came here in peace and in good faith!'

The Earl Marshal spoke to his son. 'Release them immediately. Let them go free, and offer my. . . offer *your* condolence to any who have been ill used. Tell them to keep their peace, and that when their weapons are returned they will find that the Earl of Pembroke is not an ungenerous man. They may collect them at the Eastern Gate as they leave, and each shall be given half a loaf of bread to help him on his way.'

'Yes, my lord.'

'And any injured shall be given a silver penny. . . from your own purse, Anselm.'

The Earl Marshal turned back to Gerald. 'Will that satisfy you, Archdeacon? The Archbishop of Canterbury has no wish to interfere with the pilgrims. Least of all does he wish to antagonise the Welsh. . .'

'He has a curious way of showing it!'

'. . . but there must be absolute security for his visit. If he cannot be assured of that, he will not even set foot on Welsh soil.'

'Stephen Langton is no coward! Least of all when he knows there is nothing to fear.'

Gerald de Barri made his way back to the cathedral, and only now did he begin to realise the full extent of the Earl Marshal's preparations. But why had so many soldiers of the Pembroke garrison been brought to St David's? There were surely enough for a small army. Why was there a pavilion so large that it half filled the courtyard of the Bishop's Palace? Why were there so many wagons laden with provisions? And why were the Earl Marshal's own kitchen staff supervising their unloading?

Who else was coming with the Archbishop of Canterbury to the shrine of Saint David? Who could send an Earl as his courier? Who had so craven a fear of the Welsh that he would surround himself with men of war, in defence against men of God?

XLIV

It was cold on the beach below Saint Non's Chapel. The cliffs soared high on three sides to baffle the worst of the wind, but they also shielded the last slanted rays of the sinking sun. The waves rolled in with the brisk confidence of youth, only to sigh in defeat as they retreated down the golden sands, but at last their persistence was rewarded as they lapped at the very boulder upon which Gerald de Barri rested.

Bishop Iorwerth, the Earl Marshal and the soldiers of his personal bodyguard waited at a distance on a higher vantage point. They had no interest in the swirling of the waters, and their gaze searched anxiously across the calm sea of St Bride's Bay from Newgale Sands to the island of Skomer and beyond.

Gerald de Barri watched only the small fish that grasped another half day of life as the first flood of a higher wave replenished its drying pool. He yawned, and wished that someone had thought to bring some food to ease the passing of the afternoon. Nest would have thought of it. Nest and David. Angharad and William. Manorbier. Across there lay Manorbier, far from sight beyond St Bride's Bay, beyond Milford Haven and Pembroke. At Manorbier, the ocean would have been a deeper blue, the air less chill, the waiting less tedious.

Afternoon became evening, dusk became darkness. A beacon fire on the beach, another high on the cliff above, shone bright as leading lights to guide the ship safely in. Gerald abandoned his rock and walked, cold and stiff, up the sloping beach to join the Earl Marshal.

'Are you certain that the. . .the Archbishop will arrive today?'

'Nothing is certain in these times, my lord Archdeacon. But his message was clear enough.'

218

Gerald nodded. There was little to do but wait, and conversation would not be a pleasant diversion in this dour company.

When the ship revealed itself, it was not a half a league from the shore. First a tiny pinprick of light, barely distinguishable from the shifting green phosphorescence of the waves. And then, scarce fifty paces from the surf, the tall prow emerged from the darkness, framed by an idle sail.

A herald stood in the prow, searching the torchlit faces of the waiting men as the ship grounded upon the hard sand. 'Greetings to you, my lord Marshal. Is all prepared?'

'All is well.'

The cloaked figure of an old man appeared beside the herald. The light of the beacon fires glanced from his gold coronet, imparting a spark of life to his pale eyes as he steadied himself with a hand on the herald's shoulder.

The Earl Marshal bowed. 'All is ready, my Liege. And Wales rejoices to welcome its rightful King.'

John, by the Grace of God King of England, Lord of Ireland, Duke of Normandy and Aquitaine, Count of Anjou, stepped down from his sedan chair as those waiting bowed in unison. His bearers had misjudged their mark, and the advancing waves, with no respect for rank or breeding, lapped about his slippers to dampen the hem of his long purple robe. The coronet was small and finely wrought, but it weighed heavy upon the King's bowed head. His hair had all but lost the red-gold hue that marked all his kin, his face was lined with worry. He leaned heavily upon the arm of Stephen Langton, Archbishop of Canterbury.

Bishop Iorwerth was first to step forward, such was his privilege as host, and bowed deeply. The King made no acknowledgement, and indeed betrayed no sign that he knew who this man was. Nonplussed, the Bishop turned awkwardly to kneel and kiss the ruby ring on the hand of the Archbishop.

Stephen Langton might have been better placed in a knight's armour than in the robes of the Archbishop of Canterbury. He was a man in his prime, confident in his power, and with a height, a breadth and a nobly carved face that added to his innate air of authority. For a year or more he had taken the major role in the administration of England. He had mediated in the conflict between the King and the Pope, and had seen it resolved long before the barons framed their demands in the great charter of liberties.

'A. . . a pleasant journey, Your Grace?' Bishop Iorwerth faltered over his words.

'The Good Lord granted us a calm sea and a fair wind.'

'Sire,' Bishop Iorwerth bowed again. 'Saint David's is truly. . .'

The King nodded dismissively, but he was not looking at Iorwerth. 'Gerald de Barri. How fare you, my old friend?'

Bishop Iorwerth and William Marshal looked at each other and frowned. How could King John possibly be ignorant of the Archdeacon's contempt for him?

'Well enough for my years, Sire.'

'And your books?' The King abandoned the Archbishop's arm in favour of Gerald's as they walked up the cliff path. 'What of your books?'

'Progressing well, Sire, inspired by God's good grace.'

'You will read to us this evening.'

'You honour me, Sire.'

Something made Gerald look away from the King's gaunt face, up towards the western cliffs towering above the bay. Welsh horses stood motionless against the stars, their riders watching the cove below.

Prayers at the Chapel of St Non concluded, the King and his entourage began the short journey to the castle of St David's. Flanked by a heavy guard of soldiers, King John rode beside the Earl Marshal, while the Archdeacon, the Bishop and the Archbishop headed the remainder of the procession on foot.

Archbishop Langton dropped back a few paces, drawing Gerald de Barri out of the hearing of the Bishop. He spoke almost in a whisper. 'These bones, Archdeacon. . .I have heard your claims of a miracle.'

'I have claimed nothing, Your Grace. It was Bishop Iorwerth who discovered them in the Chapel of Saint Non, and his retinue witnessed it as well as I. He believes it to be a sign of Divine approval of his appointment.'

'I begin to doubt the wisdom of my choice for Bishop.'

'There were. . . there may have been others better suited than the Abbot of Talley, Your Grace.'

'Such as Giraldus Cambrensis?' The Archbishop's smile held no malice, nor did it hold a trace of regret.

'I have heard it said. You received my book, Your Grace?'

'*The Rights and Privileges of St David's?* Yes, I have read it.'

'And. . .?'

'An amusing diversion.'

'I had intended it as more than a diversion, Your Grace.'

'Quite so. It was indeed a most interesting insight into the legends of this country.'

'*Legends*, Your Grace? The events I chronicled were the history of Wales!'

Stephen Langton did not hear. He looked with distaste at the castle mound as the procession approached the gates. 'A modest enough place in which to entertain the King.'

'We have few funds left for building castles, Your Grace. Bishop de Leia's cathedral has bled the people dry.'

'A small sacrifice that the faithful should be happy to bear for the Glory of God, Archdeacon.'

Gerald de Barri remained silent. It would not do to antagonize the Archbishop of Canterbury. Not, at least, until the bones were safely pronounced to be the true relics of Saint David. But had Stephen Langton already made up his mind, regardless of what he would see in Bishop Iorwerth's bright new reliquary?

XLV

The King's entourage took their supper, by royal command, in the pavilion within the Bishop's Palace. John was in good humour. To a palate jaded with a surfeit of boar and venison, peacock and swan, the spit roasted seal and the dishes of gulls' eggs, mussels, crabs and the like were a rare delight. Bishop Iorwerth had made the supreme sacrifice of broaching his own fine wine, and was doubtful now as to whether the barrel could survive the prodigious thirst of his guests.

221

'Archdeacon, you may entertain us with your readings.'

Gerald de Barri had been expecting this, and had brought his book with him from the castle. The choice had not been an easy one. Between the King and the Earl Marshal, the English Archbishop and the Welsh-born Bishop, it was difficult indeed to tread the middle path. *The Rights and Privileges of St David's* would have been Gerald's own choice, but the Archbishop had expressly forbidden him to speak of it before the King. *A Description of Wales* eulogised the nation, but also catalogued its faults, and it would not do to air them on this occasion. *A Journey Through Wales* was a rich source of interesting anecdotes, but it would be unseemly to remind Stephen Langton of his predecessor, Archbishop Baldwin, who had met his end at the hands of the Saracens in the disastrously futile third Crusade. Little else of consequence remained, other than *On the Instruction of a Prince*. King John would be pleased to hear a commentary upon himself, Gerald knew, and a few passages could be found that might be construed as complimentary to His Royal Highness.

Amending a word here, omitting a sentence there, the Archdeacon read to the polite attention of the company. He told of King Henry the Second's campaign against the Irish, of the part played by the young Prince John, and of the glorious contribution of Gerald de Barri's own kinsmen.

The King was smiling broadly as the reading came to an end. Gerald could not have chosen a better subject, or a better time of which to tell. John looked back upon his days in Ireland with great affection. Those happy days...where his only preoccupations had been the enjoyment of swordplay and of other men's wives, when he might well have been envied, but never despised. 'We went to Ireland, you and I, Gerald, to tame those savages. And we did! We did...'

'We did indeed, Sire!'

'I never thought, then...' John stared into the ruby depths of his goblet, as if searching there for the ultimate truth. 'Never thought then that I'd be King of England.'

'Er...it was God's will, Sire, and good men in...er, Britain rejoice in your dominion.' Gerald smiled, but he was alert to the danger. King John was just as prone to sudden, unaccountable rages as any of the Plantagenets before him, and such fits were

222

always the more likely when he was in his cups. Gerald looked for support to William Marshal, but the Earl was deep in conversation with the Archbishop. He looked to Iorwerth, but the Bishop was slumped half conscious in his chair, the consequence of his determination to do justice to as much of his fine wine as he could stomach while any of it remained.

'God's will, Gerald?' The King's goblet crashed upon the table as he lurched to his feet. 'You hear that, my Lords! You hear that, Stephen? Iorwerth? And you, William the Marshal! *Look at me,* damn you! It is by God's will that I rule. I rule, not my brother Richard! *Coeur de Lion* you called him, and you spoke of him as a saint when that French arrow took him. A saint you called him! But see what the fool did to England. He brought the country to penury, the barons to open revolt. Chaos was my inheritance! You wanted to beatify him, my lords, but I put a stop to that. No Saint Richard, eh, Marshal?'

The Earl Marshal nodded stiffly. 'As you will, my Liege.'

'The Marshal bows to my will, my lords.' There was an edge of steel in the King's slurred voice. 'But why did he not bow to my will when I summoned him to Oxford?'

'My Liege, I was compelled to stay for the protection of Pembroke, and of the other castles I hold in your name. My son William has been foolish in the past, but maturity has brought him good sense. I sent him to you in the knowledge that he would be loyal to you, as loyal as I myself.'

'And loyal he was, Marshal. He was loyal, while you stayed secure in your own little kingdom! It prompts me to wonder which William is the true liegeman of the King. Perhaps the heir to your Earldom has waited long enough.'

The Earl Marshal's face remained impassive. 'If the King doubts my fealty, then he has a short memory.'

'Damn you, William!' John had wanted the Earl Marshal to beg his forgiveness, to kneel before him in supplication, but he should have known better of his liegeman.

William the Marshal was everything that the King was not. In his prime he had been both strong of limb and comely with it. In tourneys he had defeated the finest knights in Europe, and he had even bested John's elder brother, King Richard the Lionheart himself. He was chivalrous and courteous, well spoken and

223

intelligent, and it was small wonder that a man of John's ill nature should despise him. Yet John desperately needed his Marshal, and this need alone dampened his jealous rage. A king should never have to smile, John knew this well, and it was a measure of his dependence that he forced himself to do so now. 'A jest, William, nothing more.'

The Earl Marshal bowed his head to his King. God in Heaven, how he loathed this wretched little man! But he was sworn to serve the King of England, and nothing could make him betray his oath of allegiance. 'My Liege, the hour is late. You have endured a long journey, and tomorrow will be taxing for us all. Might I suggest that we retire?'

The King was not listening. His herald had appeared in the doorway, a look of confusion on his face as he made his announcement. 'My Liege, the lord Gruffydd, son of Llywelyn Lord of Gwynedd, craves audience.'

Gerald choked on his wine. For a moment he could think only that Gruffydd had come for revenge, to kill the King, or at least to challenge him to his face with his crimes. But there was more apprehension than anger on the face of Llywelyn's son as he obeyed the King's gesture and walked slowly to stand before the high table.

The King of England spoke a few quiet words to his Marshal, as if seeking confirmation that this boy really was who he claimed to be. The Earl Marshal replied behind his hand, his grey eyes never leaving Gruffydd's face, his mind struggling with the same question that perplexed the Archdeacon. Why, in God's name, had Gruffydd ap Llywelyn come here?

Llywelyn's son bowed low before the King of England.

'My father's homage to you, Sire.'

'We trust that he prospers.'

Gerald's anxious gaze shifted from one to the other. He knew that Llywelyn and his allies had been summoned to the King's court in July, and that these princes of Wales had renewed their oaths of allegiance to the Crown under the terms of the barons' charter. Llywelyn, in return, had been granted two English manors, as well as formal confirmation of the freedom of his son. What Gerald knew now was that this agreement, this acceptance

224

by Wales of the mastery of England, could only be abhorrent to Gruffydd ap Llywelyn.

'Lord Llywelyn prospers indeed, Sire. Your gifts of land were most generous.'

'A fitting token of our esteem, and of the value we place upon his allegiance to the Crown.' The King fidgeted with the jewel-encrusted hilt of his dagger as his eyes searched the face of Llywelyn's son.

Gruffydd glanced along the high table, recognising Stephen Langton and Iorwerth by their robes, passing over Gerald's anxious, questioning stare, appraising the impassive countenance of the old soldier who sat at the King's right hand. That must be William the Marshal. Gruffydd's unease deepened as he returned his gaze to the King.

'We take it, son of Llywelyn, that that is why you are here.'

'Sire?' Gruffydd's throat was dry, his voice unsteady.

'You say you bring your father's homage. Is there no token of it? And do you not also bring your own?'

Gerald de Barri bent his head, and hid his eyes behind his hand. He could not bear to watch. Gruffydd should never have come to the pavilion. It was madness to flaunt himself thus before the King. Gerald could not imagine what had persuaded him to do so, for here Gruffydd was placed in an impossible dilemma. If he knelt before the King, then he would proclaim himself the vassal of England. If he did not, then he would be seen to be at odds with his father and would, quite possibly, place his own life and liberty in danger.

'Sire...' Gruffydd cleared his throat, conscious that every eye was upon him. 'You honour me indeed. Yet I am not of an age where I may make such a pledge. A youth may not take on the garb of a squire, a squire may not don the spurs of a knight. I am overwhelmed by your generous words, yet I am bound to say that I may pay homage only to my father.'

'And your father has paid homage to us.' The King leaned forward, his eyes alight. 'Do you, then, refuse to follow your father's lead in this? You are Llywelyn's son and heir, and...'

'I am not his heir, Sire.'

'You are not Llywelyn's heir?' John raised his voice so that all should hear, and feigned surprise even though he must surely have known this already. 'You say you are no longer heir to Llywelyn?'

'It will be my half-brother who swears his allegiance to you, Sire. Your grandson Dafydd.' Gruffydd bowed and backed away from the King, seeking only escape.

'No, stay! Let us drink a toast to Dafydd, son of Llywelyn.' The King was all smiles as he set down his goblet and wiped his sleeve across his chin. 'You shall sit by the good Archdeacon. He is an old friend of your father. Eh, Gerald?'

Gerald nodded, but his attention was upon the face of Gruffydd ap Llywelyn as the boy sat by his side. Shame had coloured Gruffydd's face, choking anger made barely audible his replies to the Archdeacon's anxious questioning.

'What are you doing here? Why did you come to stand before the King?'

'I was ordered to come.'

'You must have known the danger! Why did you not leave St David's when you had the chance?'

'How was I to argue with a score of the Earl Marshal's soldiers?'

'The Earl Marshal brought you here?' Gerald could not believe it.

'Not the Earl Marshal. His son.' Gruffydd spat the words in Welsh, as he tore a piece from the saddle of mutton on the table before him.

The Archdeacon looked across the pavilion, and could just discern the figure of Anselm standing in the shadows by the entrance. 'So this is his revenge.'

XLVI

'Gerald!' The King made a sweeping gesture with his goblet, slopping the better part of its contents down the tunic of the courtier hovering behind. 'We will hear more of your readings.'

'It is late, Sire, I am not sure that . . .'

'We remember something of your *Description of Wales*. Tell us again how ignobly the Welsh fight . . . how shamefully they run away!' John dissolved into laughter at his own wit.

Gerald paled, for the King had quoted his words almost to the letter. He glanced sidelong towards Gruffydd, trying not to meet his eye.

'So these are the books you write, Gerallt Gymro.' Gruffydd spoke in quiet Welsh.

'It was but a single line, my lord, taken grievously out of context. I can scarce recall it. Perhaps I was quoting someone else's words. . .'

'And another thing you wrote. . . That we should exterminate the Welsh and use their land as a game park. You are a man of vision, Gerald, but you forget that this godless land is fit for nought but sheep!'

'A game park!' Gruffydd turned again upon the Archdeacon.

'Softly, my lord. . . I meant that the Welsh are so courageous that they can never be defeated while yet a man of them survives. Nor could they ever be enslaved.' Gerald lowered his voice to an urgent whisper. 'The King baits you, Gruffydd, can you not see that? He is in his cups, he cannot help himself. Do not allow yourself to be provoked.'

'Has Llywelyn's boy taken offence?' John leaned forward, his eyes struggling to focus. 'Has he? Are the Welsh as lacking in humour as they are in courage?'

'The courage of the Welsh could not be compared with that of the English King.' Gruffydd raised his goblet to John, who nodded at the supposed compliment.

'My daughter Joan. . . I've heard it said that she amuses herself by learning a few words of Welsh.'

'She tries to, Sire.'

'But you must concede it is an ugly language, hardly suited to a lady's sensibilities. I remember the poor child used to find even her husband's name a hurdle to her tongue.'

'The sounds are alien to the Normans, that is all. As your language is to us.'

'Yet you speak French passably well, Griffith.'

'*Diolch yn fawr, Siôn.* I had four years in England for the practice of it, by your courtesy. Would that I could offer you the same. . .'

'Gruffydd!' Gerald interrupted, knowing full well what the boy was about to say, knowing equally well how King John would respond. 'More wine, my lord?'

Gruffydd sat back and shook his head with a sigh, grateful now for the interruption. King John seemed to have noticed nothing, and returned his attention to the Bishop's wine as a courtier refilled his goblet.

Gerald sought to steer the conversation towards other matters. 'Tomorrow, Sire, will you pray with us in our cathedral?'

The King grimaced. 'After the sun's well up. And on the way you can show us this talking stone of yours.'

'Llech Lafar!' Gerald cried out the name in his surprise, regretting at once his use of Welsh in front of the King. 'Forgive me, Sire. . . but I am astonished that you know of the legend.'

'You wrote of it yourself, Archdeacon. Do you think your King illiterate?'

Gerald blanched. Dear Lord, how much of his writings had the King read? His mind stumbled as it raced through chapter upon chapter of vilification of this man. 'Sire. . . I am honoured. I. . . I find myself at a loss for words!'

'Speechless he is, my lords! You hear that? Gerald de Barri is speechless!' The King laughed, and at once the tension was gone. 'Archdeacon, when you have found your tongue, you may tell us the story of Llech Lafar once again!'

'It was Merlin Silvester, Sire, the great magician of King Arthur Pendragon's court, who first related the prophecy of the stone. Llech Lafar spans the River Alun, not a hundred paces from this very spot. One day, as a corpse was carried across for burial, the stone burst into speech.' Gerald looked apologetically at the King. 'Llech Lafar said that when a king who had conquered Ireland should set foot in Wales, then he would be slain as he walked across the stone.'

'Listen to this, my lords! Speak up, Gerald, so that all may hear.'

'It was in the reign of your illustrious father, Sire, that the legend was put to the test. King Henry the Second wished to assert his power in Wales, and he came to St David's with the avowed intent of proving the prophecy false. A great crowd gathered, and a woman was heard to cry *Avenge us this day, Llech Lafar*! King Henry laughed and stepped without fear onto the stone, and as he walked unharmed to the other side he proclaimed in a great voice *Merlin is a liar. Who will trust him now?*'

'And my father was right, my lords.' The King smiled broadly at Gerald. 'Merlin was a liar! Is that not so, Archdeacon?'

Gerald hesitated. He did not want to press the matter further, but for the sake of historical truth... 'Er, there is an interpretation that suggests, Sire, that the prophecy was not meant for King Henry, but for one of his successors. It mentions a king who has conquered Ireland. That could be taken by some to refer to yourself, Sire, as well as to your father.' He looked around the pavilion and realised that there was complete and utter silence. And every eye was upon the King.

King John slowly reached for his goblet. He eyed the contents with the distaste of a man who has already drunk too much, and drained it with long, voracious gulps. 'And that is all the more reason why we will cross the stone tomorrow and lay this foolishness to rest! I will show these Welsh savages that the King of England fears nothing!'

The company, quite spontaneously, began to applaud, and then to cheer. Gruffydd ap Llywelyn rose abruptly from the table. He looked neither right nor left as he elbowed his way from the pavilion, but King John's words were ringing in his ears as he walked in blind fury across the courtyard of the Bishop's Palace.

'The King of England fears nothing! Not the Welsh. Not their swords. Not their arrows.' King John slammed his fist onto the table as he lurched to his feet. His chair crashed backwards as he clutched at the table for support. 'The King of England fears not their legends. Not their curses. And not their talking stone!'

Archbishop Langton hastened to the King's side, and steadied the old man as he shuffled from the pavilion to his bed.

The Earl of Pembroke remained seated. He did not watch the King's departure, he did not raise his eyes from the table, lest they should betray his true feelings. Bound by his oath of allegiance to serve a man he could only despise, William Marshal suffered most of all when in King John's company. Conscious of a movement by his side, he turned to meet Gerald's curious stare. 'Your friend, Gerald. Your friend the King. What do you think of him?'

Gerald hesitated. Was William Marshal as drunk as his King, that he should speak so openly? He moved to sit in the King's chair next to the Earl Marshal, having no wish for their words to be overheard. 'I think he enjoyed the Bishop's good wine too well.'

'The drink? That is the least of his faults.'

Gerald was dismayed. He could not endorse such talk, but neither could he in all honesty disagree with it. 'My lord Earl. . . was this the only reason the King came to St David's? To brave the power of the stone, to scorn the folk tales of the Welsh as his father did?'

William Marshal shrugged his shoulders. 'At the close of the Oxford council the King merely announced that he would accompany the Archbishop to Wales. He did not explain his reasons.'

'Perhaps he believes himself safer even here in Wales than he is in England.'

'Else he thought Stephen Langton would plot behind his back if he were left to come here alone. The King has his own views upon the question of the relics, Gerald. He is not an irreligious man, nor is he a fool.'

'Perhaps he genuinely feels the call to pilgrimage. God knows he has reason enough to foster the goodwill of the Church.' Gerald frowned as a new thought occured to him. 'Has he written to the Pope for help? Could he have asked that the charter be annulled?'

'The King petitioned the Pope in May, Archdeacon, that is no secret. But, yes. . .' The Earl Marshal lowered his voice to a whisper. 'Yes, he has written again. At Oxford, even as he tried to placate the barons he acted behind their backs and sent a second message to Rome.'

'And what of the reply? Is that what you were discussing with Archbishop Langton?'

The Earl Marshal poured more wine. 'Gerald, I can tell you only that there is utter confusion. A month after the sending of the second letter, the answer to the first one arrived. It was hopelessly out of date. His Holiness the Pope had heard nothing of the charter when he drafted it.'

'But what does it say?'

'It says, Archdeacon, that all *disturbers of the King and his Kingdom* are to be made excommunicate, and their lands placed under interdict.'

Gerald crossed himself. 'Has this been done?'

'The sentence...' The Earl Marshal's voice grew louder. He was too angered, too much in despair for his country to care who heard. 'The sentence upon the barons...upon *all* of the barons, Gerald...is to be posted in every church on every Sunday and Feast Day. The tolling of bells, even the lighting of candles, are forbidden until the barons repent of the wrongs they have done the King. Any churchman who disobeys will be suspended from office.'

'But has all this been done?' The question was of great import to Gerald. If the Earl Marshal was to be among those excommunicated, then he would be placed outside the sanctity of the Church and an archdeacon had no business to be speaking to him.

'No, Gerald. Not yet. The bishops have conferred with the Pope's commissioners, and they have decided to wait...in the hope that the threat alone will bring the barons to heel.'

'It will not, of course.'

'There was talk by the barons of another council, this time at Staines, but the King refused. He will not even consider meeting them until the city of London is returned to him. I think he is in fear for his life.'

'And instead of Staines, the King comes to St David's...it is beyond belief!'

'He has always been unpredictable, but of late no one can even guess as to his motives. Always his courtiers surround him, yet always he is alone.'

Gerald scratched his head. 'Does he fear to cross Llech Lafar?'

'Has he good reason to?'

'Your men have scoured the Sacred Hollow, where is the danger?'

The Earl Marshal did not answer at once. 'Llywelyn's son, Gerald. Why is he here?'

'On pilgrimage, that is all. It can be no more than coincidence. Even I did not know the King would be coming. As to why Gruffydd came to stand before the King...I could only guess.'

The Earl Marshal glanced towards the entrance of the pavilion, but Anselm had long since returned to his post. 'Yes, Archdeacon. I might come to the same conclusion. The King could not help but to provoke Gruffydd. For all our sakes, I hope the boy does not live up to his reputation tomorrow.'

'What is his reputation, my lord Earl?'

'You know as well as I, Archdeacon.'

'And you saw him as well as I when the King vilified the Welsh! I could only marvel at his restraint. Gruffydd ap Llywelyn is not a fool, my lord Earl. He will be on his way home to Gwynedd by now, or I am no judge of the Welsh!'

'I hope so, Gerald. It would give me no pleasure to hunt down Llywelyn's son for the murder of the King of England. And yet ...if this stone of yours were to do its work tomorrow, with no living man to take the blame...'

'You must not think of it!'

'It would not just be a triumph for Wales, Gerald. All Britain would rejoice.'

The Archdeacon crossed himself.

The old soldier smiled. 'I am the King's Champion, and I will kill any man who raises his hand against the Crown. But that does not blind me to the truth. The world holds its breath as it waits for King John to die.'

XLVII

The rain of Wales sounded its drum roll upon the fabric of the King's pavilion, and made idle the gaudy banners. The path from the Bishop's Palace, flanked by the Earl Marshal's soldiers, had fast turned to mud beneath the feet of the crowd who lined its verge. Pilgrims, villagers, peasants of the see, all had come to watch the King cross Llech Lafar. Many had come to see him die.

King John was in sullen humour. He walked in silence at the head of the procession, leaning on the arm of Bishop Iorwerth, his crown slipping sideways over his thin, rain-soaked hair. Behind the King walked the Earl Marshal and the Archbishop of

Canterbury, the unspoken animosity between them clear in every step.

Archdeacon Gerald de Barri followed, deep in thought. After this day he would leave St David's. Bishop Iorwerth had become a new man, he had found a new confidence, a new fervour with the discovery of the relics of Saint David, and rarely now did he seek Gerald's counsel. As for himself, Gerald wished for nothing more than to retire to Manorbier, and yet he knew that he still had a part to play, that his own influence could still be wielded to good effect. Perhaps even in Canterbury.

As the procession neared the River Alun, the guardsmen lined both river and path, their eyes upon the King, the bridge, and the narrowing gap between the two. The soldiers formed a wall two men deep, and there could surely be no danger to King John. Not, at least, from mortal hands.

'*Llefara rŵan, Llech Lafar!*' The shout came from somewhere deep in the crowd. Gerald thought he recognised the voice, but it was quickly drowned by a dozen others, brave in their anonymity.

'Speak now, Llech Lafar!'

'Let the stone take him!'

'And the Devil take him if the stone will not!'

'Avenge us, Llech Lafar! Avenge us!'

The King of England stopped, uncertain now, his slipper poised at the very edge of Llech Lafar. He looked to the Archbishop, to the Earl Marshal, to Bishop Iorwerth, but all avoided his eye. And the crowd was growing impatient.

John dared wait no longer. 'Let no man here call the King of England coward!'

King John trod the mud of Wales into the shining wet surface of Llech Lafar. He stared at his feet as they straddled the crack across the stone, and slowly raised his eyes as a murmur of disappointment sighed from a thousand throats. His gaze met that of the Archdeacon and he smiled, and for a moment Gerald saw only the youngest son of King Henry, a child seeking his mentor's approval.

Gerald looked away towards the cathedral, towards the great Norman tower. The Earl Marshal followed his gaze, and both

233

men shared the same thought as they saw the dark figure crouched between the crenellations of the tower, the arrowhead shining in the rain. An assassin? A murderer, preparing to strike down the King, to deal the blow that would be the glory of Wales and the deliverance of England?

Gerald closed his eyes. Could murder be crime, if it rid the world of a tyrant? Who would succeed King John? The Earl Marshal as Regent? Who was this man in the tower, this martyr who would pay with his life for his great deed...for this foul murder? All these thoughts tumbled in Gerald's mind like the swollen waters of the Alun in spring. He did not move. He did not speak, and in that frozen instant, he uttered no warning. The Archdeacon and the Earl of Pembroke stood silent as gravestones as the hand of the dark angel reached out towards their King.

'My Liege!'

William Marshal flung out his arm to draw the King aside. But he was an old man, his reactions too slow, the arrow too swift.

William the Marshal stood before the King. His right hand, raised as if in benediction, was skewered by the short willow shaft to the King's left shoulder. His free hand gripped the King's tunic as the old man's knees buckled. The King's eyes rolled upwards beneath their drooping lids, his head lolled sideways, and the Crown of England fell to the Earl Marshal's feet.

And the rain of Wales mingled the blood of William Marshal with the blood of the Plantagenet Kings as it ran down the crack in Llech Lafar, to drip, drip, drip into the holy waters of the River Alun.

A shrill scream from the crowd broke the silence. In an instant, as if woken from their trance, the Bishop of St David's and the Archbishop of Canterbury hastened forward to support the King.

The Earl Marshal staggered half a pace backwards, clutched at the arrow, and tore the shaft from the King's shoulder. He turned in his rage upon the soldiers.

'Fools!' He raised his bloody arm to the tower, the hand still transfixed by the broken shaft. 'Loose your arrows, damn you! Anselm...where are you, boy? *Anselm!*'

The Earl Marshal's crossbowmen and the King's English

234

longbowmen loosed a volley of arrows towards the tower. For a moment the sky was darkened with the rush of feathers. With raucous cries the jackdaws wheeled above the cathedral, and dispersed to the refuge of the surrounding trees as the arrows fell spent to earth.

'Anselm. . .' The Earl Marshal leaned heavily on his son's shoulder. Once, half a lifetime ago, he would have jested at so trifling an injury. Greater by far than the pain of the arrow was the knowledge that his King was fallen, that he had acted too late to save him, that his own weakness now compelled him to shuffle off his responsibility onto his feckless young son. 'Anselm. . .into the cathedral with you. . .fetch me the assassin. . .'

'My lord Earl. . .you cannot!' Gerald looked across to Bishop Iorwerth. 'Your Grace, tell them they cannot bring him out if he claims sanctuary!'

Iorwerth's lip trembled. He turned away to kneel beside Llech Lafar, to aid the Archbishop in ministering to the wounded King.

Through a gently ebbing sea of pain King John heard the voices arguing over him. Gerald de Barri, speaking up against the Bishop and the Archbishop, surely defending his King, his friend, just as he had once defended a reckless and inexperienced young prince against the scorn of those Irish noblemen.

It was good to die in such company. Gerald would know what to do, he would know how to deal with those traitors. Gerald would see that the Crown of England was saved from the foul waters of this Welsh river, and Gerald would place it secure upon the head of young Henry. Pray God the child was alive and well. . . But where was he now. . .and where was the Queen? Why were they not here by the deathbed of their beloved lord? Why must the end come in this God-forsaken spot, before the eyes of those barbarians in their barbaric land? Dear God, why had he come to Wales? Why had he challenged the power of the stone? Why had he dared follow the path of his father the King? Why had he dared presume that John Softsword could ever bear the weight of the crown of Henry Plantagenet and Richard Coeur de Lion?

The sea roared over him, and jerked the King of England back to his senses as William Marshal tore the arrow from his shoulder.

Amid the finery of their retinue, the King of England, the Earl of Pembroke and the blood bespattered Archbishop of Canterbury made a sorry trio as they made their painful way back to the Bishop's Palace.

'Iorwerth!' Gerald turned to the Bishop, who stood helpless, impotent as he watched the soldiers march into the cathedral. 'You must stop them!'

Bishop Iorwerth's mouth fell open. 'Stop them? How can I?'

'The cathedral close is your dominion, Your Grace. All these lands are yours! You are not subject to the King!'

'But I am subject to the Archbishop of Canterbury.'

'To our shame and misfortune, yes. . .' Gerald muttered the words beneath his breath, then raised his voice with new resolve. 'But the Archbishop has left you to act for yourself. Your Grace, there are armed soldiers hunting a man within the sacred precincts of your cathedral. You must stop them.'

Bishop Iorwerth backed away. 'Oh. . .not now, Archdeacon. Perhaps this afternoon, when I'm feeling stronger. I am not well. . .my head. . .the shock. . .'

'Bishop Iorwerth, remember who you are!'

The Bishop of St David's waved his hand feebly as he retreated towards the palace. 'I rely upon your experience, Archdeacon. I have other, more pressing matters. . . You do it. . .'

The Bishop of St David's picked up his robes and broke into a shambling run across Llech Lafar. Gerald de Barri stood to watch him go, but turned once more towards the cathedral as the voices of the soldiers grew loud. Between them they half carried, half dragged a man from the sacred sanctuary of the cathedral. Laughing and jesting in their relief at the ease of their task, the soldiers of Pembroke pushed their prisoner out into the bright, unforgiving light.

'Help me, Gerallt Gymro.' Gruffydd ap Llywelyn reached out and clasped the Archdeacon's hand. He did not beg. He demanded Gerald's help, and he expected it without question. 'Tell them they may not break sanctuary. Tell them!'

At this moment, in the absence of the Earl Marshal and the King, and with Anselm already burdened by guilt, Gerald de Barri knew that a word from him might save the son of Llywelyn

236

Fawr. But to save Gruffydd, who had ignored every word of Gerald's wise counsel? Gruffydd, who had returned in vengeance to commit cold and bloody murder in this holy place? Gruffydd, who had dared desecrate the cathedral, who had felt secure in the belief that Gerald would protect the son of his old friend Llywelyn yet again? Save Gruffydd, and in doing so destroy the standing and influence of Gerald of Wales?

Gerald felt a warm dampness oozing between his fingers. He pushed Gruffydd's hand away, and saw the bloody gash across the boy's palm.

'My blood is on your hands, Gerallt Gymro.'

Without looking up, the Archdeacon turned his back upon the prisoner and walked away.

Gerald did not watch as the Earl Marshal's soldiers led their prisoner away. He knelt by the bank of the River Alun, bent to the chill waters and carefully washed his hands of the blood of Gruffydd ap Llywelyn.

XLVIII

The guy ropes were loosed from their pegs and the King's pavilion sighed to the ground, the tall poles drunkenly swaying their heads together like old soaks whispering the secrets of the morning's outrage.

The courtyard of the Bishop's Palace rang with preparations for the King's departure. Bishop Iorwerth strode here and there to survey in every minute particular the work of the servants, that no property of St Davids' should find its way out of his possession. His eyes avoided at all costs those of Gerald de Barri.

'Your Grace?' Gerald stood squarely in the Bishop's path. 'Your Grace!'

Bishop Iorwerth stopped before the Archdeacon, his face reddened with agitation, his eyes distraught.

'How fares the King?'

'He lives, Archdeacon. He lives to curse the Welsh and to vow their destruction. He lives to rant and rage that the relics of our Dewi Sant are accursed fakes. He calls them the Devil's work, to be denounced and cast away.'

'And the Archbishop...does he listen to such madness?'

Iorwerth nodded his head in despair. 'He sits even now with the Earl Marshal at the King's side, hanging upon his every word. The King has already made his own pronouncement, Gerald, and his Marshal will not speak out against him. I cannot believe the Archbishop will want to antagonise them further...'

'Courage, brother!' Gerald could only despise Iorwerth's weakness. 'I will speak to him.'

'You?' Iorwerth's eyes grew wide. He blessed the old Archdeacon with the sign of the Cross, backing away all the while, and did not rest until he was safe within his own secluded cell.

Slowly Gerald climbed the stair to the King's chamber. Hart's tongue ferns clung to the damp recesses of the wall, toadflax flourished in the cracks beneath his feet. How like the stairway at Manorbier, ascending to the great hall, to the savoury sweet smell of pigeon pie, to the company of his family. He could almost hear their voices, and the soft whir of wings from the dovecote above...

'Your pardon, my lord.' The soldier spoke courteously enough, even as his halberd blocked the Archdeacon's path. 'The King admits no one.'

'I am sure if you gave him my name...'

'No one, my lord. Not even Gerald of Wales.'

'Then pray ask His Grace the Archbishop if he will speak with me.'

'I...I could not do that, my lord.' Fear was plain in the soldier's eyes. It could be more than his life was worth to enter the King's presence at such a time, whatever his business.

Gerald opened his mouth to speak again, but the soldier stood to attention as the Earl Marshal emerged from the chamber and closed the door fast behind him.

'What is it, Archdeacon?'

Gerald said nothing, but gestured to the Earl Marshal to follow until they were far from the King's chamber.

'Archdeacon, where is Anselm? Does he have the assassin?'

'He has matters in hand.'

'But does he have the assassin?'

'Er...I believe so, my lord.' The Archdeacon maintained his tone of pious indifference. He had convinced himself that he must take no further part in the fate of Gruffydd ap Llywelyn. He had washed his hands of the boy, in deed and in spirit, and that was the end of the matter.

The Earl Marshal seemed surprised at his youngest son's success. 'Where is he, Archdeacon? He must be brought before the King.'

'Must the King have his revenge? Whatever the cost?'

'The King has always despised the native Welsh...well, who does not? But now his blood boils against them. He is speaking of war.'

'That would be the ruin of us all.'

'But listen...if we could make the King vent his rage upon this man and have done with it, then there might yet be hope for us.'

'Why do you assume the assassin is Welsh?'

'Archdeacon, if the little bastard isn't Welsh, then you can call me Taliesin!'

'The name would ill suit you, William Marshal.' Gerald looked about him to ensure there were no eavesdroppers. 'Anselm has taken *Gruffydd ap Llywelyn* under guard to the Bishop's castle.'

'Llywelyn's son?' The Earl Marshal half smiled, but his eyes were troubled. 'Then we must tread carefully.'

'Indeed *you* must.'

Squire Anselm waited at the gate of the castle of St David's, watching intently as the horse and rider grew ever larger on the dirt road from the Sacred Hollow. He had recognised immediately the great bay warhorse, trophy of a tournament long since forgotten, and the fine blue cloak of its rider, but the dark and fearsome countenance of his father looked quite alien. Why should the Earl Marshal frown upon him so? Had he not captured the assassin, and had he not brought him safe to the castle?

239

'My lord!' He bowed low, not daring meet his father's eyes.
'I . . . I am gladdened to see you are well, my lord. Has the wound
been attended to?'

The Earl Marshal dismounted and thrust the reins at Anselm as
if the squire were no more than a stable hand. 'You have
Llywelyn's son.'

'In the guardroom, my lord.'

The Earl Marshal allowed himself a meagre smile. 'After all
these weeks. Through trial by fire and water, at last you have
Llywelyn's son for me . . .'

Anselm patted the horse's neck as a servant came to take it from
him. 'Will you see him, my lord?'

William Marshal nodded. He would need to see Gruffydd ap
Llywelyn with his own eyes to believe that Anselm had truly taken
him prisoner this time.

A wave of laughter escaped through the thick wooden door of
the guardroom. Anselm hastened forward, his hand outstretched
for the latch, but the Earl Marshal held him back with a gesture
for silence as he strained to hear the voices from within. The idle,
easy words of the soldiers came quicker to the ear than the low,
slurred northern speech of Gruffydd ap Llywelyn.

'I expected to see your captain. . . Nevern, isn't it?'

'Oh, he's gone. Promoted up to Llawhaden. There's this
Flemish captain over us now.'

'A Fleming? Promoted over your heads?'

'That's not the worst of it, my lord. You remember those fine
horses your father gave us when we took you back up there? Well,
soon as we gets home the new captain takes them off us and puts
them in the palace stables for the Bishop's toadies to use!'

'Did you make no protest?'

'We've our families to think of. . . '

'But have you no pride?' Gruffydd's voice, low and earnest
now, was lost in the thickness of the door.

It was minutes before his voice could be heard again. Louder
now, persuasive, tugging equally at the pride and the greed of the
soldiers. '. . . and are you not weary of this place? Do you not
despise your Norman masters and their Fleming lackeys? How
can you stay to rot here in the south when you have seen my

240

Gwynedd? You have already seen the measure of Llywelyn's generosity, my friends. And that was only for bringing me safe home. Think what the rewards will be if you deliver me from the Softsword's gallows!'

Guilty and fearful, the soldiers scrambled to their feet as the Earl Marshal threw open the door. One stammered some lame excuse, others bowed to the ground, not daring to show their faces. Anselm reddened as the Earl Marshal turned upon him.

'And these are the dogs you trusted with our prisoner? The very ones who escorted him home, who had every reason to befriend him?'

Anselm had not thought of that. The notion that soldiers in a Norman castle could befriend a Welsh prisoner had entirely eluded him. 'My lord, er...their captain seems capable enough...'

'He would seem so, to you. Get this rabble back to their posts, and bring some of my own men.'

'At once my lord.'

'Anselm, *my own men*. Not the King's.'

Gruffydd ap Llywelyn remained seated on the earthen floor, his back against the wall of the hut. His insolent young eyes seemed to weigh the strain and exhaustion on the older man's face. 'How fares your wound, my lord Earl?'

William Marshal made no reply as he stood squarely in the doorway, his bound hand resting on the hilt of his broadsword. Here at last, just as he had planned before Runnymede, was the son of Llywelyn in his power. But what was to be done with him now? It had once been his aim to keep the boy as his own hostage, to make his own bargain with the Lord of Gwynedd from a position of strength. But now things were different. Too much had changed since those fearful days before the signing of the charter.

Gruffydd had become more than just a pawn in the bargaining. He could act for himself, and with little thought for the consequences. Confidence without experience, power without responsibility. Dangerous traits, as he had shown clearly enough today.

William Marshal's mind wandered down an enticing and hazardous path. What would have happened, had this Welshman's arrow done its work? With King John dead, young Henry would have become the true and undisputed heir, and he would have needed a regent to take on the burden of his troubled kingdom. What an opportunity! What a chance to ensure that the future King of England would be a wise and prudent ruler, with the fine example of his Regent, William the Marshal, to guide him! If only this clumsy fool's scheme had been successful! If only it could have been carried out by a surer hand. If only the damned arrow had passed by his own. . .

The Earl Marshal looked at his prisoner.

Gruffydd ap Llywelyn strained at the cords that bound his wrists, the blood from the gash in his hand doing nothing to loosen them. Like moths to a flame his eyes were drawn to the Earl Marshal's own right hand as it rested on the hilt of his sword.

The Earl Marshal's swollen fingers traced the full roundness of the pommel. Why should he not draw his sword and finish it here and now? He could so easily be rid of this unwelcome complication. . .but for Llywelyn.

But for Llywelyn. There was the snag. If there were no public trial, then Llywelyn would proclaim Gruffydd's death to be murder at the hands of the Normans, and he would turn the crime to his best advantage. But that was a game two could play. The Earl Marshal well remembered how gossip about the murder of Arthur of Brittany had prompted the decline in King John's fortunes, making him despised even by his own subjects. Would a fresh scandal bring about the final ruination of the King? It was said that in his rage, John had strangled Arthur with his bare hands. What if King John were to learn of the prisoner now, and command that Gruffydd be brought before him? Then indeed would the old rumours about the murder of Prince Arthur of Brittany be brought vividly back to life. . .

The Earl Marshal's fingers relaxed. It was easy to imagine the scene. Gruffydd ap Llywelyn standing before the King. . .there would have to be a weapon within the King's reach. The King goaded to lose his temper and kill the boy. . .there would have to be many witnesses. The Welsh rising in outrage. . .the rebel barons finding a ready excuse for further treachery. . .King John

242

slain by one enemy or another. . . and the glorious restoration of order by William Marshal, Earl of Pembroke, Regent to King Henry the Third.

Without a word the Earl Marshal turned on his heel and strode from the guardroom. Gruffydd ap Llywelyn's voice followed him, strident across the courtyard, like the yapping of a dog at his heels.

'You can do nothing to me, William Marshal! Nothing! Kill me, and I would become a martyr!'

'True, Son of Llywelyn. How very true!'

'My lord, I have the new guard.' Anselm stood before his father with a dozen of the Earl Marshal's soldiers beside him.

'Very well. Stay with the prisoner. Do nothing, say nothing until you hear word from me. From *me*, you understand?'

'What if the King sends guards to collect him?'

'That will not happen.'

The Earl Marshal wished for no further argument. He called for his horse, and barely looked round as his son came hurrying after him.

'My lord. . . doesn't the King know we have him?'

'Not yet.'

'But if he thinks the assassin has been allowed to escape, he will blame us. . . he will blame me.'

'I will tell him when the time is right.'

'Are you shielding Gruffydd from the King's justice? Are you protecting him, after what he's done today? After what he did to me? I was hunted across the shire, I could have been killed because of him.'

'You may yet be killed because of him.'

Anselm blanched. 'What do you mean, my lord?'

'Do not dare speak to me of the King's justice. Do not dare parade my colours and proclaim yourself more loyal than I. You have had your own share in the Welshman's evil work.'

'You do not think that I would raise my hand against the King?'

'No. You lack the courage for that. But you would trick another man into acting for you. A young hothead who had no thought for what the rewards would be. Do you imagine I did not realise why the Welshman came to the pavilion last night? And how he came by a bow...a *crossbow*, Anselm.'

'A crossbow?'

'I pulled the bolt from my own flesh! Where did a Welshman come by a Norman crossbow, Anselm? After my men, under your command, had disarmed every man in the cathedral close?'

'I...I could not say, my lord. It is strange...'

'Yes, it is strange. Strange that you be the first to betray me. Stranger still that you choose a Welshman for your ally.'

'Father...forgive me...' Anselm lowered his voice, he clutched desperately at the one straw he could see. 'I did not seek to betray you...I would have made you Regent! All the troubles of England at an end, my lord, with you the power behind the Throne! And Llywelyn's bastard would have taken the blame and died as he deserves.'

The Earl Marshal stared long at his son. He half turned, then recoiled to strike out with all the anger and frustration he had so long harboured against the King. He watched Anselm fall back, seeing mirrored in his son's face all his own treachery, all his own shame. There was no difference between them. No difference, other than that Anselm had the courage to speak the things which William Marshal kept chained fast within his loyal heart.

Anselm lay in the soft mud by the gates, a thin trickle of blood dripping slowly from his lip. He did not speak, not daring even to rise until a soldier of the Earl Marshal's guard approached. The man halted a dozen paces short, and looked uncertainly from Anselm to the Earl.

'What is it?' Anselm wiped his mouth, grateful and not a little surprised that his father had waited for him to ask the question. It seemed he was still in command of the Earl Marshal's soldiers.

'I was told to bring this to you, my lord...my lords.' The guard held out the tattered remains of a raven, a shaft from an English longbow still transfixing its breast. 'There was some fellow by the cathedral, just after the King got shot. He was waving this thing about and trying to incite the rabble to riot. He showed us his heels before we could get near, and there were too many others about to get a clear shot...but he dropped this.'

'Why bring it to me? Is there a message tied to its leg?'

'Er. . .I think they only do that with pigeons, my lord, but the old man said you'd want to see it.'

'What old man?'

'The Archdeacon, my lord.'

The Earl Marshal groaned beneath his breath. 'The fellow who dropped the raven. . .did you hear what he was saying?'

The soldier hesitated. Here was a quandary. Was he to answer truthfully, and in doing so reveal that he understood the language of his enemies? 'Er. . .the Archdeacon said he was telling everyone that the raven got in the way of the arrow that would have killed the villain on the tower. He twisted it round though, like it seemed the raven died on purpose. . .'

The Earl Marshal snorted his contempt.

'Like it sacrificed itself to save the assassin from the arrows, my lord. And the raven is. . .I mean, he was saying a raven is the spirit of King Arthur living, so the raven sacrificing itself is like a portent for. . .'

'It is true, my lord,' Anselm did not wish to appear ignorant of the enemy's weakness for superstition. 'The raven symbolises their nation, no Welshman would knowingly kill one. This fellow by the cathedral, whoever he was, must have been trying to rouse the rabble, to try to rescue the assassin in the name of King Arthur.'

'But now the raven is dead, what will that mean to the Welsh?'

'I don't know, my lord. But I'm sure the Archdeacon would be happy enough to tell us. . .'

IL

Llech Lafar spoke. Beneath the gaze of a thousand pairs of eyes Llech Lafar spoke, but it voiced only the rattle of its own death.

The polished marble trembled beneath the onslaught, the crack gaped ever wider to the wedges and mallets that executed the will of the King. The knell echoed among the graves of a hundred bishops, assailed the ears of the silent crowd, and chilled the very bones of the old Archdeacon.

245

Gerald of Wales shivered. There was no protest at the breaking of the stone. No lament. Where was Merlin now?

King John emerged from the Bishop's Palace to stand upon a makeshift podium overlooking Llech Lafar, and there he waited and watched until the crack yawned wide and the stone collapsed into the River Alun. He glared at the fearful, resentful faces of the onlookers in the Sacred Hollow, but would give them no satisfaction by crossing the Alun once again. He would not pray before the altar of their cathedral, nor would he look upon the bones in Iorwerth's casket, lest it were seen to be his acquiescence that they belonged to the Welshmen's Saint. No, he was here to talk. He was here to speak to the crowd, to show them that their King was alive and well, and to crush them with his words.

'Good people of St David's!' The King ignored the pain as he raised his arms. The half spent arrow had not penetrated deeply, though when it found its mark he had given himself up for dead. It was that shock, that infinitely long moment of terror, that made John so resolute in what he was about to say.

'Good people of St David's! See now the fragments of superstition scattered before us. Llech Lafar is no more. There will be no more talk of Merlin, nor of talking stones, nor of the murder of your King! This morning you saw the King of England brave the prophecy of the Welsh seers, and now you see him standing before you. The talking stone did not take his life, the assassin's arrow could not harm him. Look now, good people, upon your rightful King. Your true King, by right of succession, and under the protection of Almighty God!' King John's proud gaze swept the Sacred Hollow. For that moment his back was straight, his eyes clear, and he had forgotten the brooding cares and worries that awaited him in England.

The King beckoned forward the Earl Marshal. He took from his hands the body of the raven and held it aloft so that all might see. 'My friends, there is no man here among us who does not revere our forefather Arthur Pendragon. I too honour his memory, I too seek a peaceful and united Kingdom. *But King Arthur is dead.* He does not sleep, he will not return, he will never again lead his followers to victory. King Arthur is dead! He is as dead as this raven. Look you now...does it fly from our hands?'

As the bird fell to the King's feet a murmur rippled through the crowd.

'I have told you that I honour King Arthur, as do all good men of Britain. The minstrels of England sing of him just as proudly as do the bards of Wales, though I'll warrant they are not so tuneful.' King John waited for the scant laughter to subside before he spoke again. 'To honour his memory we shall carry this noble raven with us into England, there to be buried within my Tower of London. And there it will stay for ever to remind us of the events of this day!'

The murmur from the crowd swelled and burst into a cheer. King John spread wide his arms and smiled, he looked from face to face, he turned to encompass all within his benevolent embrace. These were his people, and they were happy people. His words had won them over just as Gerald had promised. They accepted him... they loved him... their true and rightful King. The sun broke through the silver-lined clouds to dance upon the Crown of England bejewelled by the rain of Wales. Cheer upon cheer echoed through the Sacred Hollow. They realised at last that King Arthur was dead and that John was his natural successor. John, King of England... King of all Britain... borne high by his loyal Welsh subjects!

And in that joyous moment, King John might almost have believed it to be true.

Gerald de Barri could not help but to smile. It had been his own wise counsel that had put the words into the King's mouth, even as it had been his own quick wits that brought the raven to his attention. But King John had not truly understood what his old tutor had been saying. He had taken the bit between his teeth, and now he had gone too far.

Gerald's thoughts ambled back to a warm afternoon at King's Quoit, when the gulls had scudded through the spray beneath the cliffs, and his nephew's children had spoken of those foolish legends so beloved of Elidyr. One tale he remembered in particular... that of King Bendigeidfran, the man they had called Bran the Blessed, *the blessed raven*. Buried beneath the White Mound, whereon now stood the Tower of London, Bran's head would guard Britain from all her enemies. It was said that the head had been removed by a jealous King Arthur because he wanted none but himself to defend the realm...yes, and when he himself was slain, his own spirit too had roamed the skies in the form of a raven. And now this bird of Wales...Bran...the very embodiment of Bendigeidfran, was on its way back to London in the unwitting hands of a Norman King. Small wonder the crowd were cheering, and not a few were laughing.

The Archdeacon turned away from the King to hide his face. Gerald liked ravens.

L

Archbishop Stephen Langton knelt at prayer in the presbytery of the Cathedral of Saint David, the gilded reliquary resting upon the altar before him. How he wished that the name of Saint David had been supplanted by that of Saint Andrew, as de Leia had intended when he built the cathedral. But the Welsh had clung stubbornly to their Patron Saint, and the finding of the bones could only secure the Son of Non more firmly in the hearts and minds of the faithful.

The Archbishop stood wearily, and smoothed his robes as Gerald de Barri approached.

'Forgive this intrusion, Your Grace.'

'You do not intrude, Archdeacon. You have as much claim upon the relics as I. A good deal more so, perhaps.'

Gerald cleared his throat. He wondered if something lay hidden behind the Archbishop's icy words. 'I thought that perhaps I might be able to assist Your Grace. My knowledge of Wales...'

'Your knowledge of Wales would avail me nothing. It is not with the Welsh that I concern myself.'

'Indeed, Your Grace?' Gerald was more surprised than he would show. Stephen Langton, he knew, had sided with the rebel barons in the drawing up of the charter of liberties. The Archbishop must surely regard Llywelyn as an ally, and one of the most loyal. Had it been his intention to pronounce the relics genuine in order to show his gratitude to the Lord of Gwynedd?

248

If that were so, then today's action by Llywelyn's son would have made him reconsider. *If he knew.* With a start, Gerald realised that the Archbishop could not yet be aware of the identity of the assassin.

Archbishop Stephen Langton, for his part, wished above all things for the King and the barons truly to put their hearts and their faith into the observance of the charter. The letter from Rome had brought him near to despair. It had brought to bear all the wrath of the Church upon the rebel barons, yet had done nothing to foster the peace. 'Are you aware of the Pope's letter, Archdeacon?'

'It came as a great shock, Your Grace.'

'A shock to us all, Archdeacon, though I'll warrant it was a pleasant surprise for the King. I must journey to Rome to put our arguments before His Holiness.'

'Then go soon, Your Grace. I don't doubt the King's own envoys will be setting the same course.'

Langton's brow darkened. 'Enemies of God's peace, Archdeacon. Traitors seeking to twist the truth for the Pope's ears, to paint a false and terrible picture of events in this remote island. They will lead His Holiness to believe that the charter was a plot against God and Rome, when in truth it defends all that is just and holy!' Stephen Langton's voice was shaking. Surely no father could have defended his child with more fervour than the Archbishop fought for his charter.

'If you would like me to write...'

'No! No, Archdeacon...' Stephen Langton sought to excuse his hasty words. 'I thank you, but it...it will take more than words. I must have some token. Something with which to impress the Pope. Something to convince him that God has not deserted this poor realm.'

'The bones of Saint David, Your Grace. Would not the miracle of their restoration serve your purpose?'

'Admirably, Brother Giraldus.'

The King and the Earl Marshal had long since returned with their guards to the Bishop's Palace, but villagers and pilgrims wandered still about the Sacred Hollow. They wept, they cursed, they stood forlorn amid the gravestones, they picked over the

249

fragments of Llech Lafar as if seeking there among the rubble for some vindication of the false prophecy of Merlin Silvester. An old woman knelt by the Alun, and washed the stones with her tears. She seemed barely human, crouched like some obscene toad, a pagan thing in this holy valley, a relic of some distant time before Dewi Sant had spread his Faith across Wales.

The Archdeacon emerged from the cathedral, and he looked at the woman and was ashamed. For he too had felt a pang of regret...of *guilt*...with the destruction of Llech Lafar. There, scrabbling in the mud, was a part of himself. A part of his own mind that believed in Merlin and Arthur, in dragons and in raven kings. He blessed the old woman with the sign of the cross and lifted the hem of his robes to wade across the Alun.

Gerald took the path to the castle, sparing not a glance for the Bishop's Palace. The Earl Marshal would be there, and the King, and he had already borne enough of their company for one day. He would retire to his cell, there to meditate upon the matter of the relics and to offer up his prayer of thanks that Stephen Langton should be so reasonable a man. But he must be sure to return in time for the Archbishop's announcement. Ah, what a sweet moment that would be! What a pleasure, what satisfaction to see the King's face when the bones were pronounced the true relics of Saint David! King John had come to crush the dreams of the Welsh, but now he would see them kindled anew!

'My lord?'

For the first time, Gerald became conscious of a light tread behind him. He recognised the voice and quickened his pace, refusing to glance behind.

'My lord Archdeacon!'

Gerald resolutely kept his eyes upon the road ahead.

'*Gerallt Gymro, please!*'

The desperate urgency in the voice brought the Archdeacon to a halt. He turned, and realised now that his stealthy companion must have followed him from the cathedral close, waiting his chance to speak unobserved by the Norman soldiers.

'What do you want now, Elidyr ab Idwal?'

The bard smiled nervously, but said nothing. Another voice came from behind the Archdeacon.

250

'We need your help, Gerallt Gymro.

The Archdeacon turned again, to find himself surrounded. There were a dozen men on the road now. They might have emerged from the bushes by the roadside, or they could have fallen from the sky itself for all the attention he had been paying. None carried weapons, but he did not like the resolute set to their faces, nor the expectation in their eyes. Gerald knew they could be none other than the escort of Gruffydd ap Llywelyn. Disarmed by the Earl Marshal's men, humiliated and disgraced by Gruffydd's capture, now they were ready to appeal for the help of Gerald of Wales. He did not know whether to be flattered or dismayed.

The fellow who had spoken stood to the fore, prominent both in stature and in bearing. His hair was a startling red, his face scarred by some past battle and yet oddly familiar. He bowed with the air of an equal. 'Iestyn ab Idwal ab Owain, my lord Archdeacon. My brother tells me you are a friend of Llywelyn Fawr.'

'Your brother?' Gerald stared foolishly, grateful for any diversion which might delay the inevitable request.

Iestyn jerked his thumb towards Elidyr. 'He says you are our friend.'

'I, er... I have no quarrel with any honest man who fears God, my son.' Gerald dared offer nothing, lest he offer too much. He knew well enough what these men wanted of him, but he could not, he would not, contrive the escape of Gruffydd ap Llywelyn. The responsibility was not his to take, and neither was the risk.

'Elidyr believes that Lord Llywelyn's son has been taken to yonder castle, my lord.'

'Indeed?' Gerald transferred his stern gaze from Iestyn to Elidyr. 'And why does Elidyr ab Idwal believe such a thing?'

The bard returned the stare bravely. 'I was by the cathedral this morning, my lord. I saw all that passed.'

'You saw all that passed? You stood to watch, did you, while Gruffydd loosed his arrow? You stood to watch as he betrayed every Welshman in Wales! I have seen no Norman treachery today. I have seen only a young Welsh hothead strike down an unarmed man on his way to pray in the Shrine of Dewi Sant! You were charged to protect Llywelyn's son, all of you, and yet you

251

allowed this to happen! Where were you all last night? Where were you this morning?'

'He sent us away, my lord.' Elidyr's fingers fidgeted with a tattered black feather as he glanced nervously towards his companions. 'I disobeyed him when I came to the cathedral this morning, but. . . well, I wanted to be there when Llech Lafar did its work, see? None of us knew what Gruffydd intended, and I'll swear he did not know himself until the Earl Marshal's son tricked him into an audience with the King. I was as surprised as anyone when the arrow came. I could not believe it. . . to think that Gruffydd could not trust in the power of the stone to do its own work. . . '

The Archdeacon jabbed his finger towards the feather. 'What were you doing with the dead raven?'

'My lord, I knew what it meant, and so did the crowd! The raven was a martyr. It flew before the arrow that would have killed Gruffydd.'

'Well, I wouldn't. . . '

'Bran the Blessed. . . don't you remember? Bendigeidfran, King Arthur, even Rhys ap Tewdwr. The raven is the very embodiment of all of them, and it died for Gruffydd, son of Llywelyn Fawr. I spoke to the crowd, I reminded them of the old tales. Think of it, my lord! A little more time and I could have stirred them to give us their help, to save Gruffydd, to give battle against the. . . ' Elidyr coloured and fell silent as a ripple of disparaging laughter swept among his companions.

Gerald took a deep breath and addressed them all. 'It is plain to see that you have failed in your task of protecting Gruffydd ap Llywelyn, and since you dare not return to Gwynedd without him, you look to me for your salvation. Look at you. . . brave warriors, valiant sons of the Eryri. You have lost your weapons, your master, your honour, and now you plead for the help of an old man!'

Iestyn only smiled. Every deed in the Archdeacon's long life, every page of his books belied those harsh words. 'We did not expect such an answer from you, Gerallt Gymro. You know you must help us.'

'Why must I help you?'

'Because if Gruffydd is put to death by the English, Llywelyn will go to war.'

'Then Llywelyn will be the loser.'

'If you believe that, my lord, then you must help us. . . if only for Llywelyn's sake.'

Gerald sighed. He might wish now that he had not always been so eager to boast of Llywelyn's friendship. 'I will do this for you, Iestyn ab Idwal, and this only. I will speak with Gruffydd ap Llywelyn, and if he has any message for you, then you shall hear it before sunrise.'

LI

'My lord! What are you doing here?'

'I live here, Anselm.' Gerald de Barri paused in his march through the castle gates and glanced to the squire's swollen mouth. 'What happened? Did Gruffydd manage to. . .'

'No. . .' Self-consciously Anselm touched his lip. 'My father.'

'What was his quarrel with you?'

Anselm did not answer at once. He could not be sure where the loyalties of Gerald of Wales lay in the matter of Gruffydd ap Llywelyn, and he had no intention of earning the Earl Marshal's further displeasure by any indiscretion. 'If it concerns you, my lord, I think you had best ask the Earl Marshal.'

'Perhaps I shall.' Gerald smiled idly and noted that Anselm, however slowly, was learning the value of prudence. 'By the by, where is Gruffydd?'

'In the guardroom, my lord.'

'Good. I shall just. . .'

'No, my lord! I cannot allow it.'

'You cannot allow it? Do you recall where you are, Squire Anselm? Does the Bishop of St David's know that you hold a prisoner in his castle? Does the Archbishop know that your soldiers run amok on Church land?'

Anselm shook his head in misery. Why did the Archdeacon have to make it seem as if everything was his fault? Why was everything so complicated? He had always thought that merely obeying orders must be easy.

Gerald left Anselm outside the guardroom and closed the door fast behind him. Slivers of watery sunlight stole through the chinks in the tightly nailed shutters to be lost in the damp straw of the floor, and it took a moment for his eyes to adjust to the darkness.

'I did not expect to see you again, Gerallt Gymro.'

'Did you not?' Gerald stared down at Llywelyn's son for a moment. The boy was sprawled against the wall, his hands tied in front of him, his eyes red in a face pale with fear. 'I talked with your friends outside the castle, Gruffydd. They were anxious for you.'

'What can they do for me now? They have no weapons, no knowledge of this place, and the Earl Marshal's men are everywhere. I tell you, Archdeacon, even your own soldiers go in fear of the Pembroke guards.'

'Oh, I don't think so. . . .'

'I have seen it! The Earl Marshal's word is the only law in this castle. Only you can help me, Gerallt Gymro. My life is in your hands.'

Gerald looked away. He wished Gruffydd had not said that. 'What shall I tell your friends? Have you a message for them to take to Llywelyn?'

'Why bother with it? My father will do nothing for me now.'

'What manner of talk is that? I'm sure he would offer a ransom, and King John would most likely accept. . . if it were enough. The King is hard pressed for all manner of things, with his army of mercenaries to provide for. Gold, cattle, sheep, good Welsh horses. . .'

'Do you really think Llywelyn would trouble himself?' Gruffydd smiled at the old man's astonishment. 'What's the matter, Gerallt? Surprising, is it? Let me tell you why Llywelyn sent me here. A pilgrimage to the shrine of Dewi Sant, it was. A penance, if you will, to clear my mind, to drive away evil thoughts, to blunt the edge of my tongue. If I die in this place he will call it the will of God and count himself well rid of me.'

'My son, did I not warn you?'

'Yes, Gerallt, you warned me. But you cannot imagine what it was like for me, returning home after four years, returning to find nothing as I remembered it. All the glories of Gwynedd were tarnished...I swear to it that even the Mountains of the Eryri were diminished. At Dinas Emrys there is no red dragon, just a new stone tower in the Norman fashion. Dinas Bran is still home to the ravens, but the king who rules now is no giant to wade the Irish sea...'

The Archdeacon held up his hands. He wished to hear no more. 'Gruffydd, it is your own memory that betrays you, not your father.'

'Do not tell me that I cannot understand my own father's words! Before a week had passed I knew exactly where I stood. I am nothing more to him than his steward or his falconer, his groom or his huntsman, no more than any of the officers of his court.'

'Most men would spend their lives dreaming of such a post!'

'I was born to expect more, I cannot help that. Think on it, Gerallt...was I to stay my hand for ever, to play the loyal son hiding in my father's shadow? Or was I to follow my own path, to lead us free of the yoke of England? I would give Wales a king the equal of the King of England! God knows I do not seek a war against my father, but only by the threat of it could I make him listen to me!'

'You are mad even to think of fighting Llywelyn! He has brought together the Welsh...well, some of them...for the first time in decades. How can you possibly believe that they would turn away from him to follow you...a youth untempered and untried! You have experienced nothing save the dungeons of Corfe. You possess nothing but what Llywelyn himself should choose to give you.'

'I did not lie in idleness for those four years, Gerallt Gymro, and I learned far more than just the language of the Normans. They despise us, Gerallt, we are nothing but savages in their eyes. And so we shall always be to them, as long as they are lords over us. Thanks to my father we are stronger now than we have ever been, and yet still we bow to the English. If he would only act now, Llywelyn could unite all the Welsh in battle and drive the English for ever from our lands. And then, God willing, Llywelyn and the King of England might rule side by side in Britain, secure in their independence, equal in the eyes of God and man.'

Gerald could not reply at once. He had once had his own dream...of standing as an equal beside the Archbishop of Canterbury. It had been so similar, and so far ever from becoming a reality.

'Do you really believe you could succeed?'

'What price failure? Think what we have now, Gerallt Gymro. Llywelyn has declared himself liegeman to King John, loyal to a man who thinks of us as no better than animals, who spits upon us, who values us only as fodder for the swords of his enemies.'

'But Gruffydd, if peace is the result...'

'Allegiance to England is a shameful peace! Llywelyn thinks as you do, Archdeacon. For him, peace is the end of it, he thinks the English will be content with what they have. *But they will not.* Allegiance to England means slavery for Wales. Men of Wales bearing arms in an English army, watching English castles rise from our mountains, seeing our very language wither and die.' Gruffydd's voice cracked. It was no longer hatred that consumed him, nor fear, nor even despair. *Hiraeth* gnawed at heart and soul, a sense of loss so deep as to become a physical pain. Homesickness, nostalgia, a longing for the old country that he scarce remembered, or perhaps had never been.

Gerald felt the weight of his years bearing heavy upon him now. He knew it to be true. He had seen it all before. He had seen English kings exploiting their Welsh allies, abusing their loyalty until the native Welshmen rose with fire and sword only to be crushed beneath the Norman heel.

Was this always to be the way? Oppression leading to rebellion, bloodshed followed by slavery, chains forged again into swords until the scant Welsh populace were all lost beneath the soil of their beloved homeland?

Were the Welsh, for all their pride, for all their courage, doomed as surely as the boy who lay pale and desolate before him now?

LII

The River Alun scattered the last glimmer of the evening sun among the waterside reeds. Here below the fishponds the river flowed unfettered, husbanded only by kingfisher and heron, and trees grew wild along its shallow banks. Few had occasion to venture through the marsh to this shaded place, and there were none to bear witness as Gerald of Wales met with the dozen men of Gwynedd.

Iestyn bowed, and more courteously than at their previous meeting. By his very presence, Gerald de Barri had risked much to help their cause.

'Please, my lord Archdeacon, be seated. Will you share our meal. . . what little we have?'

Gerald took the proffered place on the trunk of a fallen tree, and cast a curious eye about the makeshift camp.

'There's bread and cheese, my lord, and a few trout we've tickled from the river.'

Gerald nodded his approval as he blessed the food. 'Snatched from the Bishop's fishpond would be closer to the mark,' he muttered to himself, but they would taste all the better for that.

Elidyr was crouched by the fire, laboriously gutting the fish and skewering them on sticks of willow to hang above the glowing embers. He had not looked up as the Archdeacon arrived. Iestyn, for his part, could contain his anxiety no longer, and all save Elidyr crowded around as he asked the crucial question. 'Have you news of Gruffydd ap Llywelyn, my lord?'

Gerald could barely meet the eager eyes of the Welshmen. How much did they expect of him? 'Gruffydd ap Llywelyn is alive and unharmed.'

'You spoke with him?'

'I did.'

'Then how are we to free him? We are ready, he has only to give the word.'

Gerald hesitated, alarmed by Iestyn's words. He thought back upon what had been said in the guardroom. Gruffydd had spoken of many things, but had made no mention of escape. Likely as not he had thought he could win Gerald's sympathy for his cause, and that alone would be enough to gain his freedom.

'Iestyn. . . there is no need for hasty action. It might be that the safest course would be simply to inform Llywelyn as soon as you can. He will know what to do.'

'But that would take days, my lord. And many more before help could come.'

'If it came at all!'

Iestyn looked round sharply, but neither he nor Gerald could determine which man had spoken. An uneasy silence settled over the group.

It was the Archdeacon who spoke first. 'My friends, you are but twelve, and what is more you are unarmed and unaccustomed to this place. The Earl Marshal has threescore soldiers for every one of you, and he will not give up his prisoner lightly. Try to rescue Gruffydd by force and you will be killed. All of you. Where is the good in that? Be patient. Gruffydd's life is not threatened.'

'Not yet.'

'Not yet, as you say. . . but I know William Marshal. I do not doubt that he wants to keep Gruffydd alive, so be patient! I will watch what passes between the King and the Earl Marshal, and you must lie low and keep your peace so as not to put them in a worse humour.'

'But what then?'

'If God wills it, then Llywelyn may secure his release by peaceful means. Which of you will carry the news to Gwynedd?'

'I will.' Elidyr looked up from the fire for the first time. 'You are right, my lord Archdeacon. I will go and. . .'

Iestyn held up his hand. 'Wait a minute, 'ngwas i, it's not been decided.'

'Let me go, Ies. I can make a better story of it.'

'I'll not argue with that, but it might gain too much in the telling.'

Elidyr said not another word as his fellows debated the Archdeacon's suggestion, agreed upon the message, and sent two others on the long journey north.

Supper finished, the Welshmen lolled with their backs against the trees and passed the wineskin from hand to hand. Elidyr sang a ballad of the Eryri, his voice soft and melodious and true, but it seemed to Gerald that he sought his refuge in song to avoid the earnest conversation of his fellows. Soon they too lent their voices, and the songs of Gwynedd rose clear above the chatter of the River Alun, to drift with the smoke towards the pale new moon.

Gerald was content just to listen. In his books he had written of the skill of the Welsh in part-singing. It was an art he greatly admired, though not one in which he had ever ventured to express himself. What surprised him now was the discovery that Elidyr's voice was by no means the best among his fellows. Were there other bards amongst these grim faced men of Gwynedd?

The songs dissolved into heckling and laughter. Gerald was never one to withhold his own good counsel, whether he were well versed in the subject or no, and soon his companions turned upon him to insist that he provide some entertainment of his own.

'What would you suggest?' Gerald, sated with trout and wine, stretched at his ease. Here in such company he could forget all save the warmth of the evening and the friendship of his companions. Here he was more contented than. . . even than on those warm summer days in Manorbier. Could it truly have been but three months past?

'Tell us of the finding of Dewi Sant!' came an eager voice, and others were quick to take up the cry. Gerald had already mentioned, perhaps prematurely, that the Archbishop was sure to pronounce the bones the true relics, but now they were eager to hear the tale from the beginning. Only Elidyr remained silent, his eyes downcast.

Gerald began his account with the coming of Bishop Iorwerth to Llawhaden. '. . . and scarce had darkness fallen when we saw the torches massing beyond the moat. The men of Deheubarth set the castle alight with their fire arrows, they swam the moat, they breached the walls. Many good men of both sides gave their lives before the invaders fell back. But that was the mystery of it. . . there must have been hundreds waiting among the trees, yet none came in place of those who fell. You remember, Elidyr.' Gerald paused, and looked to Elidyr to take up the story.

'There is little for me to tell, my lord. I was in peril from both sides in Llawhaden, and so I fled. I was sure that even if your captain Nevern did not kill me, then the southerners would call me traitor if they captured the castle and found me within. I skirted the flames from the burning stables... worse than on the ship, it was... and thanked the saints when I found a gap in the palisade. I had not gone two paces before I lost my footing and rolled down the embankment into the moat. I nearly drowned ...I could have choked to death on the stench of the water, and scarcely had I managed to swim across when I was seized and dragged up the bank. They would have finished me then and there, had I not told them that I bore a message from Gerald of Wales.' Elidyr smiled in apology. 'I'm sorry, my lord, but I could think of nothing else to save my neck. I could not be sure what weight Llywelyn's name would carry, knowing what turncoats the southmen are.'

'Who led them? Was it the brothers Rhys and Owain?'

'I saw only Rhys...Rhys ap Gruffydd. A wiser, nobler lord by far than his uncle Rhys Gryg! He was willing to listen...even to a northman such as I. I told him that Bishop Iorwerth of St David's was in the castle, and that Gerallt Gymro himself was in danger from the arrows of his own people. I alone, it was, who persuaded him to call off the attack.'

'And then?'

'Oh...they let me go.'

There was silence as they waited for Elidyr to continue. All eyes were upon the bard, all stared in disbelief that he could reply in so few words.

'And where did you go from Llawhaden?'

'Er, northward.'

So clear was Elidyr's discomfort that the Archdeacon was reluctant to question him further. The evening had been too pleasant to mar, and there would be other opportunities to find out what Elidyr had really done next. Instead, Gerald continued his own account of the rigours of the voyage across St Bride's Bay, and of the miracle that had greeted his arrival with Bishop Iorwerth at the Chapel of Saint Non.

He was well rewarded by the wonder and delight in the faces of his audience, but he could not help but to notice that the smile upon Elidyr's face bore a bitter twist. Gerald could well understand his feelings. After all the hardships he had suffered, it must have been a great disappointment to the bard to have been denied the glory of the finding of the bones.

Iestyn too had noticed Elidyr's disquiet. He laughed as he took another draught and passed the wineskin to Gerald. 'Take no heed of him, Archdeacon. He's always like this when we talk of the finding of Dewi Sant. Envy, it is...he's jealous of your Bishop!'

Elidyr glared at Iestyn as he came to sit closer by Gerald. 'Will the Archbishop have made his pronouncement yet, my lord?'

'Perhaps. I suppose I should be there, but Stephen Langton, King John and the rest of them make for dour company.'

The Archdeacon watched Elidyr's hands as they toyed with the damp grass. Long fingers, almost too delicate, but they might yet acquire a skill upon the harp. God give him the chance. The firelight played across the old scars, deepened the dark shadows of Elidyr's downcast eyes. Something troubled him. Some ghost laid its chill hand upon Elidyr's face whenever Dewi Sant was mentioned. Gerald remembered what he had said at Llawhaden, and sought to give him solace.

'Elidyr, the bones are undoubtedly the true remains of our Saint. Tonight Archbishop Langton will make his pronouncement, and then no man will be able to call them false. It matters not from whence they came. Whether they were placed upon the altar of Saint Non by the Hand of Almighty God, or whether He gave the vision to a man to do His will, it matters not. It is a miracle all the same.'

Elidyr edged closer to the Archdeacon, his voice barely audible. 'Please, my lord...'

Gerald smiled indulgently. 'My son, what does it matter now if the truth be known? From the first I suspected that you had taken the holy relics from Gruffydd to return them to Saint Non's Chapel. There can be no shame in that! After our talk at Llawhaden I hoped you would act upon my words, and you did not disappoint me. It is a great service you have rendered...for God and His Church, for St David's and for all Wales!'

'No, my lord.' The words were torn from the bard's throat.

261

'No! Listen to me, for God's sake, before I lose my mind. Gruffydd never could have found the bones.'

'But. . . but what of the story you told in Llawhaden? The old Saxon at Corfe? The crucifix you took from him?'

'You believed that?' Elidyr laughed, a cruel rattle that shook the breath from his body. 'The cross was always mine. Do you think I would have accepted the gift of a Saxon? As for the story. . . that was mine also. Where else could the bones of Dewi Sant be, other than in the Cave of Doves on the Island of Dewi. . . Ramsey Island? It makes some manner of sense, Gerald of Wales, or it did to me at the time. The bones should have been there. . . they *should* have been, if. . . if there was a God in Heaven.'

'Elidyr!'

'A pretty story, isn't it? The best I ever made. I told it first four years ago in the dungeons of Corfe. I told it to give us the will to live, to give us a secret to hold from the Normans. Yes, and I told it to give Elidyr ab Idwal a secret to hold from his fellow prisoners. . . that he would not be left to starve in the shadows. I never told anyone exactly where the bones were to be found, see? And so I lived, and I told the story again and again, and I began to believe it myself. And I told Bishop Iorwerth, and I told Gerallt Gymro, and then the bones were found. And now, God help me, it is too late. . .'

The Archdeacon made no reply. His head was bowed, his eyes were tightly closed. He would not listen. He would pretend he was dreaming, yes, and he would forget all when the blessed light of morning came. . .

'My lord. . . I must make confession.'

Confession! Sweet Lord, what more could there be to confess! No, he would not look at the bard's haggard face, he would not see the hands that twisted one in the other to hide their shaking, he would not listen to the voice that begged to be heeded.

Elidyr sank into silence. The relics in the cathedral, so bright a beacon of hope for Wales, were for the bard a grim mockery of Dewi Sant. A fool's idol, a child's nightmare, chattering and dancing in bloody gibbet chains.

LIII

William the Marshal bowed low in the doorway of the King's chamber. He took a pace towards his liege lord, and stopped in disbelief.

The King's face matched the florid redness of the tapestries upon the walls, his eyes burned brighter than the flames of the candles upon the table. And amid all the King's retinue, closest by the King's right hand, the Earl Marshal saw Anselm, his youngest son.

'We congratulate you, Marshal.'

'My Liege?' The Earl Marshal took one more step to allow the herald to close the door behind him, but advanced no further. He recognised too well the tone of the King's voice. This was not the time to approach too close, nor to play with words.

'We congratulate you. Upon your modesty.'

'I do not understand, my Liege.'

'The assassin, Marshal. You have him in your charge yet you decline. . . doubtless through a reluctance to seek our praise. . . to bring him before us.'

Anselm's face betrayed all. Still smarting from his humiliation, he had sought his revenge by speaking to the King behind his father's back.

The Earl Marshal bowed again. 'Sire, it is true that a prisoner has been taken. But we have no means of proving his guilt. . . '

'I saw him with my own eyes!' Anselm had gone so far already, the Earl Marshal's cold gaze could not quiet him now. 'There can be no doubt.'

The King nodded, his pale eyes narrowing.

'And you knew of this, Marshal?'

'I thought it best to be sure, my Liege, before troubling you. But now I have seen the prisoner with my own eyes, and I fear that matters are not as simple. . . '

'Tell me, Marshal, what do you plan to do with this mercenary of yours? Hang him? Release him? *Or pay him his due?*'

The Earl Marshal looked from face to face in the silence. Was this what his own best loved son had been saying to the King in his absence? Could he have misjudged the boy so completely? And yet Anslem, for his part, seemed to share his own dismay. God help us and preserve us from all our progeny! The young fool had acted once again without a thought for the consequences!

'My Liege, the prisoner is no mercenary. He would take no one's gold, least of all English gold. He is . . .'

'His Grace, the Archbishop of Canterbury.'

An apologetic herald made way for Stephan Langton to enter the stifling, overcrowded chamber. The Earl Marshal fell silent at the sight of him, not wishing the fate of Llywelyn's son to be complicated yet further by the intervention of the Church.

'What do you want?' King John glared in anger at the interruption. He had long since forgotten the question of the relics.

'The. . .the bones, Sire.' Stephen Langton glanced around the room and noted with disappointment that Archdeacon Gerald de Barri was not present. He, at least, would have shown a fitting and proper respect for this most momentous pronouncement. 'I have spent long hours in vigil, I have offered up my prayers to Almighty God and all His Saints, I have. . .'

'Is that what has kept you from us since morning? The dust of the dead could have waited, Langton, the King of England can not!'

'Sire, I felt it wise to make my pronouncment as quickly as possible. It is a question of great importance to the Church and to the Nation. And through His wisdom, the Lord God has shown me. . .'

'Oh, spare us the preliminaries, Langton! Just tell us about the bones.'

The Archbishop stumbled in his speech. Much of his day before the altar had been devoted to the composition of this sermon. It would have been an oration worthy of his high office, and with *Giraldus Cambrensis* to record it, he would have. . .

'Langton, what about the bones?'

'Sire, the Good Lord in His infinite mercy has freed my mind of all doubt. The mortal remains upon the altar are in truth the holy relics of Saint David.'

The Archbishop might have expected some to fall to their knees in prayer. There might have been a hubbub of excitement, perhaps even a cheer. As it was, he was quite unprepared for the silence that pervaded the King's chamber.

The King scratched at his beard, wondering how best he could rid himself of the Archbishop. His courtiers stood uneasily, sensing his disquiet and wary to keep their distance. For them, the reaction of the King was of more immediate importance than the event itself.

The Archbishop of Canterbury looked about him. Confused by the lack of response to his momentous pronouncement, he thought back upon his words. He had perforce been brief, but surely he could not have been misunderstood?

'Yes, Sire, the true relics of Saint David are indeed restored to his Shrine. His Holiness the Pope will rejoice, and I will myself tell him of the miraculous things that have come to pass in this most holy part of Wales. . . of Britain.'

'Do you still intend to go to Rome, Langton?' The King's face remained expressionless. He had always suspected that the Archbishop's true loyalty lay with the rebel barons, despite his conspicuous efforts to display impartiality.

'I do, Sire. For such a miracle. . .'

'A miracle, yes. . . but we wonder if your audience with the Pope might happen to touch upon another matter. The matter, perhaps, of his letter concerning the barons.'

'Sire, His Holiness wrote the letter before he heard of your Charter of Liberties! He is sure to send a second letter rescinding the first, so there can be no need to. . .'

'We disagree, Archbishop. It is an excellent edict, and it will put to rest all those who would disrupt our Kingdom.' The King's cold gaze shifted to the Earl Marshal, defying him to voice an opinion.

William Marshal knew better, surely enough, yet he could not keep his silence. 'I have heard it said, my Liege, that the King himself is the greatest force in the disruption of the Kingdom, and that he should be made excommunicate along with the rest.'

'*Heard it said*, Marshal? I hear you say it now. . . a traitor's words from a traitor's lips!'

'If that is what you believe, Sire, then I beg leave to go.'

King John lurched to his feet. His eyes roamed wildly about the room, and all those present edged away, each jostling with the other so as not to be the one remaining closest to the King. 'Leave to go, Marshal? Go where? You are nothing without me!'

The Earl Marshal's jaw set firm. He turned his back upon the King, and as he did so, the King's hand fell to the hilt of his sword.

Squire Anselm, on an impulse, stepped between his father and the King, and fell to his knees amongst the flowers that bestrew the floor. Little had he thought that his spiteful words could lead to this, the very downfall of the house of William the Marshal.

'No, my Liege! The Earl Marshal has always been your Champion! He shielded you from the assassin's arrow with his own flesh. . . do not forget that, I beg of you!' Anselm bowed his head. He knew that his life had passed out of his hands. He waited for the blow that would be the ending of it.

'God's Blood, my lords, but here we have a loyal son, as well as a loyal servant of the Crown.'

Anselm looked up in astonishment at the King's soft words.

King John's grey eyes were steady now, and the squire could not look away. Such was the compelling power of the Plantagenet kings, the power that had caused thousands of good men to hurl themselves upon the Saracen spears at the call of Richard Coeur de Lion.

'A rarity indeed. A pearl beyond price in these unhappy times. What is your name again, boy?'

'Anselm, my Liege.'

'Then rise up, Anselm. . .'

Anselm hesitated. He thought, for one intoxicating moment, that he was about to be dubbed knight, that he would receive his spurs at last.

'Rise up, and fetch your prisoner to kneel before me. From his own lips we shall hear the truth of who he is and who sent him.' King John's eyes betrayed the pleasure he would take in the extracting of it.

The squire backed to the doorway, not once taking his eyes from the King's face, and William Marshal made to follow.

'Stay awhile, Marshal.' The King waved forward his minstrel, and his smile resembled the ugly gape of an adder about to strike.

'Listen to this song, a new ballad in my honour. I think it might amuse you...'

LIV

The Archdeacon stirred from an uneasy slumber, visions of fires and bones still dancing before his eyes. The camp fire had burned itself to a few smouldering embers, and only the wan moonlight could guide his weary eyes to the still forms of the Welshmen sleeping soundly about him. Whatever it was that had awoken him, there was neither sight nor sound of it now.

Gerald stretched his chilled limbs, and made his careful way through the trees to look towards the dim glow of torches that marked the castle of St David's. A cry disturbed the stillness of the night. It floated towards him, outstripping by far the dark shadow that made its ungainly way down the road from the castle mound. A monk, it was, on horseback, his cassock pulled up above his knees, his cowl billowing out behind. Gerald stepped out into the road and waved to the rider to stop, and the wonder of it was that the fellow saw him at all.

With difficulty, Brother Hugh reined in his mount and slid clumsily to the ground. He was not a well practised horseman, and the short ride from the castle had terrified him beyond measure. Even so he had kicked the horse to a gallop, for he had left a far greater terror behind.

'My lord!' Brother Hugh could barely gasp out the words. His nose oozed blood, his eyes were puffed and darkening. 'You must help...the Welsh prisoner...he said his friends were to be found along this road.'

'We are here.' Iestyn spoke softly as his fellows gathered around. 'What has happened to you, man?'

'It was the Earl Marshal's son...Anselm. He came with the King's soldiers, not his own guards from Pembroke. He said he was going to take the prisoner to the Bishop's Palace and show him to King John. I tried to reason with him...I knew what the King would do...I tried to stop them...' Brother Hugh sobbed

267

in helpless frustration. He remembered how once he had seen Squire Anselm come wretched to the castle. How ill the hospitality of St David's had been repaid!

'Brother Hugh!' Gerald shook him by the shoulder. 'Where are they now?'

'Following, I think. . .with the prisoner.'

That was enough. Without a word the Welshmen ran back through the trees to their horses.

For a moment the Archdeacon stood alone with Brother Hugh, but already he could see through the gathering gloom that the road from the castle was darkened by the plodding shapes of many men and horses.

Gerald took the reins in one hand and steered Brother Hugh with the other. It was time for them to go to the Bishop's Palace. They could have no part in what was about to take place out here on the road.

Squire Anselm was confident in his triumph, in the favour of the King and in the vengeance soon to be visited upon Gruffydd ap Llywelyn. This was a time to savour, and he was in no hurry to make it pass. From time to time he would glance behind to watch the son of Llywelyn walking amid the tight knot of the King's guards. He wished only that the moon were brighter, that he might better see the despair upon the prisoner's battered face.

It was a pity about the young monk, of course. Brother Hugh had been kind to him, months ago, when he had struggled ashore to St David's in this Welsh bastard's filthy rags. But things had changed since then, and he was soon to be a knight if he continued in the King's high esteem. He wondered if King John would perform the dubbing here in St David's, or whether he himself would be called to London. . .

Someone shouted.

The night shattered into a dozen fragments, falling upon him from every side. A fist cracked Anselm's cheekbone before his sword was half drawn, a hand sought to wrest the blade from him. He struck out blindly, but then the sword was gone and his horse was screaming as it stumbled to the ground.

Scarce daring to lift his head from the soft, muddy sanctuary of the rut in the road, Anselm saw flying hooves, running men, a battle where friend could not be distinguished from foe, where darkness itself was the greatest enemy, where scarce a single thrust could find its mark.

'*Dyma fo! Ciliwch! Ciliwch!*'

The cry rang out, repeated again and again from all about him. Had the Welshmen prevailed? Were his men all dead? Anselm twisted his body and flung his arms above his head as the horses thundered past. The Welsh had not won. They were falling back! The squire struggled to his feet and lurched like a drunkard to find refuge among the trees. Moon and stars swung wildly in their firmament, branches lashed at his bloodied face, brambles clawed at his tattered cloak. Welsh brambles, they were, dragging him down into the accursed Welsh earth.

The close, shrill whinny of a terrified horse jerked Anselm's mind back to a semblance of order. He saw soldiers...his soldiers...milling in confusion as the Welshmen on their horses broke free of the affray. He shouted at them with all his remaining strength.

'Shoot at them! Shoot, you bloody fools!'

Crossbows clicked in ragged array, a staccato counterpoint to the dull thunder of hooves as the Welsh horses galloped away into the Cambrian blackness.

Out of the final, fading beat of unshod hooves, a single cry came from the road ahead.

Squire Anselm wiped the blood from his face. He left his soldiers to nurse their wounds and limped along the road in the wake of the Welshmen. Before he had stumbled three score painful paces, he sank to his knees to utter a prayer of thanks to the Good Lord above. Before him, prone and still, lay a Welshman, the short stub of a crossbow bolt protruding from his back.

Anselm scarcely glanced at the man's face in the fading moonlight. It mattered not a jot who he was. He was Welsh, he was here, and he was dead. That was all that mattered. All that would matter to the King.

Gerald de Barri, still breathless, stood unobtrusively just within the doorway of the King's chamber. He could hear some sort of commotion behind him, but he fancied he could discern a more ominous sound. The sound, perhaps, of a sack of grain dragged across cobblestones, flattening the ferns and the toadflax that garlanded the short, steep stairway from the courtyard of the Bishop's Palace. He was thrust aside without ceremony as Anselm flung back the door.

Archbishop Stephen Langton of Canterbury, Earl William Marshal of Pembroke, Bishop Iorwerth of St David's, Gerald of Wales, courtiers, guards, servants. . . all watched in silence as the soldiers cast down their burden before King John.

The man lay face downwards, and did not move. The arrow protruded but a few inches from between his shoulder blades, and an eloquent stain oozed red into his torn tunic. Squire Anselm placed his foot in the small of the man's back, and with an effort sufficient to raise the body half clear of the floor, he drew out the quarrel with both hands. The body slumped once more, and slender fingers, better suited to harpstring than bow, clenched into a fist and then were still.

King John started from his chair. 'Why do you bring this abomination before your King?'

'The prisoner, Sire. . .'

'He was to be alive!'

'My Liege, he had friends waiting in ambush. Scores of them, and armed to the teeth. They leapt out of the shadows, we knew nothing of it until they were upon us. They fought like lions. . .'

'You had the finest soldiers in England!'

'It. . .it all happened so swiftly, my Liege. But we defeated them, and soundly! We soon had them in full flight.'

'And how many of my men did you lose in this momentous victory of yours?'

'Only five dead, my Liege. . .and another five wounded.'

'And of the enemy?'

'Er. . .he lies before you, Sire.'

'The Welshmen gave you a poor bargain!'

'My Liege, this is the very man who tried to kill you. Once I had him, I thought the others not worth the chasing.'

King John regarded Anselm with suspicion. The boy was too glib for his own good, but he would take issue with that later. 'Show us his face.'

As Anselm rolled the man onto his back, Gerald de Barri barely managed to stifle his involuntary cry. He tried to cover his confusion by making a clumsy sign of the cross over the body, but it did not escape the notice of the King.

'What troubles you, Archdeacon? Do you know this man?'

'I pity him, Sire, as I must pity all poor sinners.'

'And you, Marshal. What do you know of him?'

'Nothing, my Liege, save that he is the Welshman who tried to kill you.' The Earl Marshal almost smiled in his delight. He could scarce believe his good fortune, that he had been delivered so fitting a scapegoat.

'There was time aplenty for you to make his acquaintance, Marshal! You took him from the cathedral and kept him closeted, and now he is dead.' The King kicked at the inert form. 'Dead, and able to tell us nothing!'

'Let me explain why the assassin was not brought before you immediately, my Liege. . . I feared that you yourself might strike him down. Your valiant spirit is well known, Sire. . . and the inspiration of us all.'

'And why should I not take my due, if it so pleases me?'

Gerald de Barri saw the Earl Marshal falter, and rallied to his aid. He touched the King's sleeve and spoke quietly in his ear.

'Sire, you came to this holy place to prove yourself a true King. What then, if you had executed the assassin with your own hand? Without trial and within the very precincts of the Shrine of Saint David. . . how would that have appeared? How could you then have laid claim to be the upholder of the great Charter of Liberties to which you set the royal seal?'

The King drummed his fingers upon the table. There was a ring of truth about it all. It bore the stamp of his Marshal's customary honesty, surely enough, and of his old tutor's good sense. Perhaps, after all, they were not plotting against him. And it could not be denied that William the Marshal had put his own body between the assassin and his King. . .

The Archdeacon followed in silence as the soldiers dragged away the body of Elidyr ab Idwal. In the mortal remains of this man, the King of England had seen his justice, the Earl Marshal had found his scapegoat, and Squire Anselm had enacted his revenge.

271

LV

Manorbier

5 October, 1215

'...and they hung his body in the gibbet by the crossroads, my lords. But next morning when the King and his entourage departed from St David's, the chains were hanging empty.' Gerald de Barri paused to take the last mouthful of pigeon pie. He wiped the gravy from his chin with a piece of bread and reached for the bowl of mussels. 'Of course, they are saying in the villages that he turned into a raven and flew away.'

The Archdeacon's story held an attentive audience. William de Barri and Angharad sat by him at the head of the long table, and before them sprawled a score of friends from the neighbouring manors.

'That's just the stuff for the Welsh to weave into their legends, eh?' William grinned as he sought his wife's eye.

Angharad remained silent and morose, but a ripple of laughter swept the hall. Many had been at the Earl Marshal's banquet on the night following the tourney, and they had endured weeks of worry and uncertainty because of the lies of Elidyr ab Idwal. There were few indeed who would mourn the wretched fellow now.

Gerald did not share in the merriment. 'I should think it more likely, my lords, that the men of Gwynedd returned for him. They would want to bury him properly, and with honour.'

The castellan of Haverford laughed uproariously as he took an untidy swill from his goblet. 'They love their ravens, the Welsh...but they won't stand aside and let them have a good feed.'

Gerald de Barri winced. He knew that Angharad loathed Haverford to the very core of her Welsh soul. She resented his being there at all, but Gerald had felt compelled to return the castellan's lavish hospitality.

272

Angharad, for her part, made an effort to be polite for Gerald's sake. 'Do you really think they would have taken such a risk, my lord Haverford? Just to rescue one of their dead?'

'Aye, my lady, that they would!' The castellan paused as a servant refilled his goblet. He took the pitcher from the girl and placed it on the table before him. 'That they would! I've seen them do it before. The night after the Welsh stormed Llawhaden, it was...you'll remember that well enough, eh, Archdeacon! I'd quick-marched my men from Haverford as soon as we saw the beacon, but when the Welsh found us on their flanks they lacked the stomach for a real fight...'

'That is not quite as I remember it,' Gerald protested, despite his reluctance to interrupt Haverford lest the story be lengthened.

'Not one of them stood his ground...they just disappeared into the trees. But we'd no sooner returned to Haverford than a band of renegades attacked the town gates. Fired the palisade, killed a couple of sentries, no more than that. My captain reckons they were the same lot as attacked Llawhaden...the dogs must have followed in our tracks. They fared worse at Haverford, I'll tell you!'

Gerald frowned. 'The same men who attacked Llawhaden, you say?'

'Welshmen, anyway. But what I was going to say was...that a few months before that they'd been stealing my sheep. My men killed two or three and took one prisoner, so I had him gibbetted to show his cronies what to expect if they tried it again. Well, on that night after Llawhaden, what do you think the villains did at Haverford? After they'd set my palisade alight, they stole the gibbet from outside my very gates! They couldn't get their henchman out in one piece, rotten as he was; so they took the whole damned thing... begging your pardon, Archdeacon... cage and all!'

Gerald carefully set down the half-eaten bowl of mussels. 'Were there not two cages on the gibbet, my lord?'

'What? Oh, the other one only had some old bones in it, but they disappeared as well! I didn't use the gibbet much... preferred to give them a run and take a bit of hunting practice. The bones had been there as long as I can remember. They say he was a murderer who...'

273

The old Archdeacon rose silently from the table and walked out to the stairway overlooking the courtyard. He had to be alone. He had to think, and as he sat upon the top stair, he remembered that it was upon this thirteenth step that Elidyr ab Idwal had waited months before. Gerald buried his face in his hands to pray, and the voices in the hall grew faint as they mingled with the distant murmur of the sea beneath the cliffs of Manorbier. What were they saying? New tidings from England . . . the charter of liberties annulled by the Pope. . . Stephen Langton suspended from office . . . What did these things matter now?

Prayers gave way to the wild tumult of the Archdeacon's thoughts, swirling, swirling, like leaves in the October wind.

'*My lord, I must make confession.*' Those had been the last words of Elidyr ab Idwal, and he had let them go unheeded. But now the veil was lifted from the eyes of Gerald of Wales, and the truth was plain to see.

The Welshmen who attacked Llawhaden had gone on to Haverford, and Elidyr ab Idwal had been with them. Elidyr himself had stolen those clean-picked bones from the gibbet. Elidyr, innocent fool that he was, had taken the Archdeacon's words all too literally. What had Gerald said? '. . . *if the bones of Dewi Sant came to light by a divine revelation, then few men would question such a miracle.*' Few men indeed! Gerald of Wales himself had not thought to question it, not even when Elidyr ab Idwal had knelt before him and begged that his confession be heard.

Gerald was as much to blame as the bard himself. More so, in truth, for Gerald was a scholar and should have known better than to let his thoughts run heedless along the same craggy path as that half-crazed fool from Gwynedd.

Because of Gerald de Barri, the remains of a common criminal lay in a golden reliquary upon the High Altar of the Cathedral of Saint David.

Worst of all was Gerald's own knowledge that there the bones must stay, for the tales of the finding of Dewi Sant had grown far beyond the truth. With each telling the miracle had become more wonderful, the heavenly light more radiant, the chorus of angel voices more resplendent in its majesty.

Bishop Iorwerth had borne witness to it. The Archbishop of

Canterbury had verified the truth of it. King John himself, albeit with ill grace, had heeded Gerald's counsel and had knelt before the reliquary to offer a prayer of thanks for his deliverance from Llech Lafar.

And nothing that Gerald de Barri could do now would change one iota of it.

Epilogue

All was stillness in the Cathedral of Saint David. Tall windows showered pale moonlight upon the polished tiles of the nave, and far beyond the rood screen a barely perceptible glimmer escaped the gloom. It was the last, fitful flickering of a candle that betrayed the gilded casket upon the altar.

The Welshman paused to listen, but he dared not look around. From the painted walls mute saints accused him, mute demons urged him on. And far above the rood screen the crucified Christ stared down with infinite sadness, with infinite compassion.

Hands trembled as they prised open the reliquary. From the tower above came the rustle of feathers, the whispers of lost souls, the cries of generations yet unborn, as the most holy talisman of Wales was bundled into the mouldering folds of a piece of sackcloth.

The Welshman stumbled as an old man along the path to the high clifftop. The eastern sky blushed in shame at the sight of him, ancient trees shook their heads in despair for him, the outrage of the sea grew louder with his every faltering step. Beside the gabled silhouette of the Chapel of Saint Non, the sheep grazed without pause. They did not raise their heads to him, they did not move to make way for him, they denied his very presence in their pasture.

The Welshman walked with his burden to the edge of the cliff. He gazed down the sheer rock face, down, down to the sea-greened pools, to the beckoning, seductive fountains of phosphorescent spray.

A weathered grey skull curved in slow arc against the pale dawn sky, to be shattered asunder among the rocks far below. The sack fluttered downwards like a dark, dead bird, and its ugly mouth fell agape to spew the carrion bones into the chill embrace of the Severn Sea.

Eyes closed in prayer, the Welshman stood upon the very edge of his land, and the breeze from Gwynedd urged him gently on.

In God's hands he stood, to be cast down as a leaf in the wind. Or whatever the Judgement might be.

Historical Notes

In the Chapel of the Holy Trinity in the Cathedral of St David's there now lies a casket wherein rest the true relics of Dewi Sant.

King John died in the year following this narrative. William Marshal became Regent to the young King Henry III, and served loyally until his own death in 1219.

Gruffydd ap Llywelyn continued to oppose his father's acceptance of the English as feudal overlords, campaigning instead for complete separation. Following the death of Llywelyn Fawr in 1240, Gruffydd was imprisoned by his half-brother Dafydd and was passed into the custody of King Henry III. On the morning of 1 March, 1244, Gruffydd ap Llywelyn died in an attempt to escape from the Tower of London. It was Saint David's Day.

Giraldus Cambrensis died in the Year of Our Lord 1223. His greatest ambition, for a Church of Wales independent of Canterbury, was not realised for another six hundred and ninety seven years.

'...for his books could not pass away or perish, but the longer they lasted and the greater their antiquity, so to all future ages they would become more beloved and more precious.'

Baldwin, Archbishop of Canterbury